FREE
TRADE

JUDY W EBY

ISBN: 1477423117

ISBN 13: 9781477423110

Library of Congress Control Number:2012908620

CreateSpace, North Charleston, SC

Dedication

To the children in my life who make every day an adventure, an aventura!

Anna Tikvah Eby
Layla Eby
Jacob Eby
Morgan Eby
Benjamin Condemi
Simon Condemi
Sophie Abadilla
Isabella Peng
Dominic Moreno
Cora Suhonen

A special thank you to my wonderful friend Joanna Peng for photos used on the cover of this book.

Chapter One

EL NIÑO

Slate-gray skies shout stridently for attention over Sandra's head. Mud-brown rivers follow ruts down steep streets and pathways, scuttling inanimate debris under car wheels, around brittle weeds and cactus. A pair of scrawny dogs cling precariously to the stony edge of a gully. El Niño has been forecast to arrive for months; most people in Tijuana have seen the televised government warnings to move away from the steep, gravelly hillsides and ravines. Those with somewhere else to go have gone, calling relatives in San Diego or Mexicali or Ensenada to ask for temporary shelter.

But in the early dawn, two days before Christmas, the ferocity of the new rain has surprised the residents of Tecolote. Built in an area of canyons and ravines south of Tijuana, this unzoned region of new dwellings and stores has been rapidly improvised from used plywood, tile, cardboard, and sheet metal to serve the needs of the city's burgeoning population, and is quite literally growing out of control.

The steep, rutted road next to the small, newly stuccoed community center is now a cascade of mud and debris. As Sandra looks out from the tin-roofed porch, she sees a small child's pink-and-white canvas shoe floating in the muck. One spindly legged, prematurely old dog with long hanging teats loses her footing and is swept away downhill along with Popsicle sticks, engine oil cans, and a week's supply of paper wrappers from the tortillaria. The dog is too exhausted to yelp as it is swept under a car. Sandra, a pet owner and contributor to animal shelters in her other life, barely notices and makes no attempt to rescue it.

After a long night of helping families protect their belongings and their plywood casitas, Sandra is too tired to feel pity or concern. She feels as empty as the sodden gray pasteboard egg carton hurtling past her feet. Perhaps her husband, Dan, is right. The night before last, he told her, with something close to scorn in his voice, that she is becoming more Mexican in her thinking, less American. She tried at the time to present a logical rebuttal, but she knew that, in a way, he was right.

A year ago, she would have been fearful of a storm like this and would have stayed inside her warm, comfortable house until it passed. A year ago, when the winter rains came, she wrote a letter to her councilman to request that the potholes be filled in the streets near her San Diego neighborhood. She vaguely remembers reading about the effects of the rain on the residents of Tijuana, but it did not affect her then, physically or emotionally. She remembers discussions with her neighbors about the dilapidated shacks that were being built on Tijuana's sandy hillsides to accommodate all the newly arrived immigrants from other parts of the country.

Several of her neighbors are strong advocates of zoning laws in San Diego. They are outspoken in their criticisms about the Mexican city and the federal governments that allow people to put up stopgap shelters on vacant land—land that is vacant only because it is so obviously unsafe, land that would be classified as unbuildable on the other side of the border. Last February, when she did her monthly bills, she sent a check for one hundred dollars to the Red Cross in response to the descriptions of homeless families who needed blankets, soap, toothbrushes, rice, and beans to survive the rains and resulting mudslides that cost many people their homes and lives.

Now, at the beginning of this rainy season, predicted to be the worst in decades because of El Niño, the areas have all been rebuilt, more hurriedly than before.

And for Sandra much has changed as well. Her life has been hastily rebuilt and may also be in danger of collapse. This year, instead of making coffee and cinnamon toast for her husband, she is twenty-five miles and one ten-foot high, rusty, corrugated iron fence away from home. This year, instead of professional colleagues with advanced degrees, she works with young volunteers and unschooled community members. They are trying to establish a community center and clinic in the raw new neighborhood, named *Tecolote* after the owls that lived in the area before people displaced them.

Instead of shopping for aviation books, surfboard wax, and hiking boots for her husband and sons for Christmas, she spent yesterday accompanying Doctora Mendez as she went from one restaurant to another in Tijuana to ask for chicken necks and backs, milk, vegetables, and eggs, too old to serve to their customers. They brought these items back to the center, packed them into plastic bags, and plan to send them home with the children today for their families' Christmas dinners—if the children can get here with all this rain.

She has never stayed in Tecolote all night before. Usually, she is able to cross the border and get home by six or seven o'clock in the evening. When Dan is flying and laying over in a hotel in another city, she looks forward to relaxing and recouping her energy by making an omelet or heating up some soup for dinner. She and her black and white cat, Amigo, sit in front of the television for an hour or so, and then she goes to bed to read, a restorative habit she developed as a child, when the fights between her mother and father caused her to retreat to the magic carpet of a good book to take her away from the fears and concerns of her life.

When Dan is home, she is likely to find him in the garage, tinkering on an old Porsche he bought to restore. He often does not even realize that it is dark outside. One of the greatest strengths of their twenty-six-year marriage is that each of them has developed their own methods to replenish themselves. Dan loves to work on all types of engines, from lawnmowers to jets. In his airline job, he is more comfortable talking with the mechanics than he is making PA announcements to the passengers or flight attendants. Dan and the mechanics talk the same language. They hear the same sounds in a missing or defective piston rod. They are able to debate the needs of replacing a part, thereby delaying the flight or deferring it, with mutual respect.

Usually, when Sandra arrives home, she knocks on the garage door and sees Dan's startled expression as he looks up from his concentrated effort on a machine. He tries to show her what he is working on, how he has reworked this valve or that carburetor, and she tries to appear interested, but she finds her attention drawn to what she has in the freezer that she can heat up in the microwave for their supper. She calls him at least two times, and eventually they sit down at the small, round table in the breakfast room and eat a dinner of meatloaf or fish with potatoes and green vegetables. They tell each other about their days or talk about the latest mail or telephone call from their sons, Peter and Alex, who are both away at school.

Today, however, Peter and Alex are at home. They arrived home for Christmas yesterday while she is here in Tijuana. Sandra doesn't enjoy the thought of her husband and sons worrying about her whereabouts or her safety. She tried to call home last night, but the telephone in the center has not been working, and she didn't want to try to drive at night on the rutted and muddy roads.

Neither Dan nor the boys could imagine her present surroundings or experiences; they have never been here. Dan only visits Tijuana with visitors from out of town who insist on seeing Mexico. He first tries to convince them that Old Town San Diego, which is always filled with good Mexican food, music, and crafts for sale, will get the same effect. When they still insist on crossing the border, he reluctantly agrees; he parks on the US side, walks across the border, and escorts their visitors along the main tourist street of Tijuana, Calle Revolution. While there, his strategy for survival is to ignore the children selling Chiclets and always to stay well out of the reach of vendors selling silver necklaces, calling out, "Almost free, Señor!"

Peter, their oldest son, once told her about the time he went to Tijuana with high school classmates to drink beer and tequila before they were twenty-one. According to Peter, he was reluctant to go but was loudly outvoted by his track team, who wanted to celebrate their victory over La Jolla High School's first-place team. They piled into cars and headed south. They went to one second-floor bar after another for tequila mixed with Coke, orange juice, and rum. Peter was violently sick in the backseat of his friend's car on the drive back home and never considered going again.

Their younger son, Alex, heard for years about the notoriously wild waves on the beaches south of Tijuana. He decided to go with some friends one winter day when the surf was "extremely rad" and came back with a broken surfboard and a new respect for riptides. When she invited the boys to come with her to the Christmas party planned for today, they both protested that a trip to TJ wasn't exactly what they wanted to do on their first day home for Christmas vacation.

When Sandra left home yesterday morning, she expected to return that night—maybe not in time to fix dinner, but certainly in time to order a pizza and sit and listen to the boys talk about their year so far. It is Alex's sophomore year at Berkeley. She is eager to be with them again, to sit down next to Peter on the couch and watch his profile as he eats and tells stories about his first year of medical school. She is hungry to hear Alex's whistle again, as he sets up all the ingredients for guacamole on the counter and mashes them all together in a bowl. She wishes she had been there last night to bring them extra blankets and say goodnight. The first night home is a real opportunity to get hugs and give shoulders a light massage, brush a hand over a whiskery chin, and pretend that they still belong to her.

When she set off down Highway 5 yesterday morning, the sky was gray, and rain was in the forecast, but San Diego meteorologists have been predicting the El Niño rains for months, and each time the resulting storm delivered a quarter inch of rain that easily soaked into the dry earth. This time the forecasts were right on target. This storm is the real thing. There must be at least two inches of rain so far, and it is not easing up at all. Of course, that amount of rain in San Diego would be routed through the storm drains into the sewage system, causing little alarm. At most, there would be some runoff that would reach the ocean and cause environmental concerns and surfing advisories, but down here, the rain seeps into the cracks of roofs and walls, causing them to become water-logged and fragile. More importantly, the rain undermines the crumbly founda-tions, when there is a foundation at all, which is exceedingly rare.

As Sandra peers through the rain behind the center, she becomes aware of a movement in a small casita on the side of the hill. A blue plastic tarp is pulled aside, and a small face appears in the window of the house, built at the edge of a gully. Certainly, she must be mistaken; she thinks it must be a mask or a skeleton left over from a Dias de los Muertos fiesta at the end of October. But, no, it is a child's face, and as Sandra watches, she can see the child's mouth open and call out to her, although she cannot hear a sound in the din of the storm. Muddy water is sweeping down around both sides of the house, taking with it the dirt and stones that have reluctantly served as its foundation. It could easily be pulled down into the gully with its inhabitants inside. Who would be foolish enough to be in that house?

Sandra's first instinct is to go back into the center and tell Elvira or Petra that they should go see who is in the house. But Petra has just left the center to drive some people to the church, which sits on higher ground, and Elvira is out in search of milk and tortillas at a local bodega. A hand emerges from the window. It is a very small hand. Sandra pulls her blue cardigan sweater up to cover her head and steps off the relative safety of the concrete porch. She fights for footing and balance as she slogs uphill through the spongy earth, toward the house. With every step, she searches for courage and stamina, trying to ignore the gooey fear slithering down her spine, the panic in her brain telling her legs to stop and return to drier ground.

"I can't go into that house," she thinks, even though her legs continue to carry her forward toward the leaning dwelling. "I'll be sucked into the muck along with it," she tells herself, and a very basic part of her listens and agrees. "I've never been brave about putting myself in danger like this. What am I doing here?"

It is a question she has asked herself many times over the past few months, a question that also torments her husband and bewilders her friends and former colleagues at work. Why has she given up a good job, a well-respected position as the reading coordinator for the school district, to volunteer in Tijuana? Why does she leave her safe, comfortable neighborhood three days a week to travel through border checks and drive on rutted, narrow roads to work here until she is almost too exhausted to drive home? She spends more than an hour waiting to cross the border, with hundreds of other cars, all idling in densely packed lines.

And then there is the question Dan asks: if she is tired of her old job and wants an adventure, why doesn't she just travel with him to cities around the world? As a senior pilot, he can choose his flight assignments. He used to invite her to come with him to New York to see a play during a twenty-hour layover or to Hawaii for a day and night on the beach at Maui or Kona. When did she last take a trip with him?

A picture of their last trip together flashes into Sandra's head. She went with him to Denver. When was that? Last June? They had dinner with their friends from college. The copilot on the trip was a woman, Leslie, a slender, attractive woman who made Sandra feel a little uneasy.

It was fun, but not as much fun as their anniversary last May on Catalina Island. Dan, who belongs to a sailing club, had just passed the coastal cruising navigation course and wanted to sail a boat to the island, but Sandra objected.

"Sandra, what are you afraid of?" Dan asked her. "It isn't as if we will be at sea for weeks at a time. We will drive up to Newport Beach, rent a sailboat, and be in Catalina in ten or twelve hours. With the long daylight hours, we'll get there before nightfall."

"I know you're right. I can't explain why I feel this way. I just imagine the worst, I guess. You see bright blue skies and a nice breeze filling the sails, and I see us becalmed, with a fire starting in the engine compartment."

"That's why they have fire extinguishers on boats. Besides, we are never really going to be out of sight of land. By the time we lose sight of the mainland, we will be able to see the harbor at Avalon."

"I want to go, Dan. I just prefer to take the ferry."

"What's the difference?"

"The ferry gets there in an hour. I won't have time to worry about it."

Sandra always feels very embarrassed whenever she has to explain one of her fears. She wonders what Dan must think of her, always fearing the worst when it comes to her physical safety. She doesn't really know what he thought that time because he didn't say. The conversation ended before it turned into a fight that neither of them wanted. A few days later, Dan showed her two tickets on the fastest ferry from Long Beach to Catalina and a brochure for a hotel called Cloud Nine.

"This is great, Dan. But, why are we going from Long Beach instead of Newport?"

"Because the boat from Long Beach is the fastest one available, and the distance is shorter." There was no irony or judgment in Dan's voice. Sandra knew that he had listened to her fears and taken them seriously without trying to change her or convince her he is right. This is one of the reasons she loves him. Another reason is the kind of fun they still have when they get away by themselves.

In Catalina, they rented a golf cart and drove it through all the village streets and up to see the views from the top of the hill. Dan packed his snorkeling fins and mask and bought Sandra some new ones at a shop near the harbor. They walked hand in hand down the pebbly beaches to the shore and swam hand in hand on the surface of the cold, clear water. Below them swam red-gold garibaldi and long, narrow fish with inquisitive eyes.

"Look, Dan. That fish is wearing sequins!" Sandra remembers sputtering, as they took their faces out of the water to clear their masks. Dan showed her how to spit in her mask and rub it around to clear away the fog. Sandra remembers that she felt more buoyant and curious on that expedition than she had for many years.

"I don't think I'm forty-something today," she said. "I'm ten…maybe eleven."

"I hope not," Dan said, with a grin on his face. "When I see your breasts underwater, I want to do things with you that are not legal with a ten year old." The cast was perfect. She was hooked. Within a few minutes, they were picking up their clothes from the shore and walking back up the hill to the Cloud Nine Inn.

Their third-floor, corner room was positioned so that the whole village and the sea lay spread out below them. They left all the windows open, so they could pretend that they were still on the beach. There were no other hotels nearby as tall as the Cloud Nine. The one across the street was only two stories tall. Their privacy was assured. A quick shower to get the salt off and they were wrapped up together in the king-size bed, oblivious to anything but each other.

"Making love is what we do best," thinks Sandra, as she laughs to herself, remembering the noises that finally penetrated their consciousness. First, they heard street noises, a truck engine nearby. But that didn't alarm them. The street was three floors below. Then, they heard men's voices very close to their windows. First Dan and then Sandra looked out the window in disbelief.

"I've got them!" A man perched in a cherry picker was no more than three feet away from them. No, it wasn't a photographer mistaking them for a couple of celebrities. It was a PG & E man removing some balloons from the electric wires going into their hotel.

Perhaps they hadn't been seen. Perhaps they had. The truck drove uphill, and they collapsed into laughter. Their lovemaking afterward was just a little more delicious than usual. Dan called it their X-rated anniversary and would never explain what he meant to the boys. As Sandra remembers this happy time, she thinks to herself that she is a fool not to take Dan up on his invitations to travel with him more than she does. Although, come to think about it, he hasn't invited her recently. In fact, it seems that Dan's invitations to fly with him have sputtered to a stop this fall, like an engine running low on fuel. Is it because she has said no once too often? Is it because he could not understand her explanations of why she preferred to stay home so that she wouldn't miss her visits to the center? Did he interpret her refusals as insults, even though she has tried to describe the satisfaction she is receiving by taking books to the center and watching the children carefully choose which book they want to read aloud to her?

Thoughts of Dan and books dissolve as Sandra approaches the sodden house and calls out, "Hola! Quién está?" Her sweater and her gray-brown hair are thoroughly wet by now, as are her khaki pants and shoes. In her pants pockets are her car keys, driver's license, and a small amount of cash in both dollars and pesos—all she brought with her to the center except for the boxes of books, pens, markers, and art supplies, which is what she spends her money on these days.

From inside the little home, the blue plastic tarp is lifted, and the face of a small child appears again in what suffices for a window but is, in reality, a space between a sheet of plywood and a stack of adobe bricks. The plastic tarp is lowered again, and Sandra hears movement and talking inside. After several months of working with families in Tijuana, she still understands only about half of what they say, and that is in the best conditions, facing the person talking and discussing topics with which she is familiar, such as books and food.

But she understands the anxiety in the voices of a woman and a child inside the house. She thinks she catches the word "tormenta" (a fierce storm), and seguridad (safety). Hearing these words, she knows that the family inside is aware of their plight, but the tone of their voices tells her they don't know what to do about it.

The door opens a crack, and Sandra recognizes one of her students, Lupe, a second grader who loves to read the Clifford books Sandra has brought to the center. The child stands silently, looking up at Sandra.

"Hola, Lupe. Es como Clifford y la tormenta?" Sandra says to the child.

"Si," the child responds quietly.

Sandra wishes that she brought a big, red dog named Clifford, one who could prop up the house or pluck it and its occupants to safety. But she didn't, and she sees no one else nearby who can help. All other occupants of the neighborhood, or colonia, are inside whatever shelter they could find.

"Ven!" Sandra says to the child. "Dondé está tu mama? Ven al centro conmigo ahorita!" If she can get them to leave their home and come to the shelter, she knows they will be much safer. Where is the child's mother?

"Mi mama está enferma," whispers the child.

Sick? Even more reason to come away from this leaky house. The intensity of the rain increases as she stands there. It is coming horizontally now from the west, hitting the house broadside; the storm is sweeping up moisture from the Pacific Ocean and combining it with El Niño's unexplained anger. Sandra motions that she wants to come inside, and Lupe, raised to be polite and deferential to adults, stands aside to allow her to enter.

Inside, there is little light except what leaks through the one window and the gaps between building materials in the walls. Lupe's mother is lying down in the only bed in the house, a thin double mattress, probably a cast off carted down here from San Diego. She is partially covered with cotton blankets, not nearly warm enough to keep off the chill of this storm. That the woman is hugely pregnant is immediately evident. A grimace on her face tells Sandra that the "illness" is more than likely imminent childbirth. No wonder she did not leave her home last night when most of the other residents went to the church or the center. The walls of the small home shudder, and a new gust of wind and rain knocks one wall farther askew, leaning inward right over the mother's bed.

"Ayudame," pleads the woman. "Ayuda m'ija, por favor." Her eyes are locked onto Sandra's, causing her to feel a strong emotional connection with the woman and her family.

Instinctively, welcome feelings of warmth and resolve overlay Sandra's fear. It is this deepening of feeling that is the real reason Sandra keeps coming to Tecolote. There is no way to explain this to a husband who understands satisfaction in terms of a smooth-running engine. Sandra craves being useful, important, valuable to another human being. It makes her feel alive, like when her children were small and needed her every minute. She felt something similar during her first years teaching first grade, when she would see the children's eyes light up as they learned they could decipher the words on the page and read their own stories. She also has this intensity of feeling making love with Dan when he returns from a trip, and they have missed each other for several days. That hasn't really changed, at least not until very recently, when he began to seem pre-occupied with other thoughts and projects from the moment he steps into their house.

"Yo voy llevar Lupe al centro conmigo," Sandra tells the woman in the bed, explaining that she will take Lupe with her to the center. "Entonces, yo voy llamar la doctora y Padre Jaime para usted." The only plan she can think of is to call the doctor who comes to the clinic three days a week or the priest who looks after everyone in the neighborhood with a type of selfless love that Sandra hasn't seen in any religious person since she was a child. Father Jaime, a transplanted Jesuit from Cincinnati who has worked with the people in this neighborhood for sixteen years, will know what to do—if she can find him.

But, there is no time to put her plan into action, no time left to call la doctora or the priest. The concrete blocks that are the foundation of the small house begin, at this moment, to shift and merge with the muddy torrent that surrounds them all. The mud begins to slide down the hillside, taking the plywood and tin, the cotton blankets and the mattress, the women and the child with them. Mud pours in past the blue tarp, ripping it away like a used Kleenex. The child cries with fear and holds onto Sandra as the home begins to move like a log in a flume ride at a water park, bumping and twisting down the hillside, gaining momentum and speed as tons of mud and wet rock carry them all into the gully below.

Chapter Two

BARE ROOTS

"Damn it to hell, where is she?" Dan Seaquist asks his two grown sons again. He stares at the telephone wishing for the power to make it ring.

"Dad, if you don't know, how do you expect us to?" answers Alex helplessly.

"Let's call the highway patrol," suggests Peter. The older son—he believes people in his family expect him to take on responsibilities that he isn't ready to assume.

"She has never stayed away all night before. This crazy project of hers has gotten her so enthralled; she can't think about anything else. Why can't she just find something to do closer to home? There are a lot of kids that could use her skills right here in San Diego." Dan's voice has a bitter edge to it that his sons are not accustomed to hearing. He is usually in such complete control—the perfect pilot. Sometimes, they tell each other privately that he is the perfect autopilot, especially when he makes a predictable response to some of their youthful suggestions.

"I'm kind of proud of her for going down there, if you want my opinion." Alex gets up from the breakfast table to let in the cat. "Amigo, where is our mom?" he says aloud, as he pours dry food into the cat's bowl. Amigo eats hungrily, unaware of the tension in the room.

"Hello, is this the highway patrol?" says Peter into the telephone. "Have there been any accidents reported on Highway 5 between Tijuana and San Diego involving a blue Volvo sedan with a woman driving?" He listens and then reports that there have been no car accidents on the US side of the border in the past twelve hours. This causes a long silence as each of the men thinks about what to do next.

"Do you know the telephone number down there, Dad?" asks Alex.

"Yes, it is in her address book, and I tried it, but it doesn't answer," replies Dan. The boys have noted that he looks older today than the last time they saw him, which was only a month before on Thanksgiving. His skin is puffier than usual, and there is a lot of gray in his twenty-four-hour beard.

"Well, let's just go down there and find her," says Peter.

"Where? I don't know where this place is, and I have no idea how to find it, especially in this rain," responds Dan.

"Who else can we call then, Dad? Who would know where it is and how to get there?" Peter is glad that his logical, deductive reasoning hasn't shut down just because he is on break.

"I don't know who to call," Dan answers. "She goes down there some days with a Mexican woman doctor, but I have no idea what her name is or where she lives."

"Maybe Hanna knows where it is," suggests Alex. Hanna has been their mother's best friend for many years. The two women know each other's schedules and talk about their plans and decisions regularly.

"That's a great idea. I'll call her—even if it is early. What time is it?"

"About seven thirty, Dad. Try her right now," Alex prompts.

Dan uses the speed dial on the phone to call Hanna, but her daughter, Kate, answers the phone sleepily and tells him that Hanna has gone up to Seattle to visit another friend for Christmas. As Kate goes to look for the number in Seattle, Dan waits impatiently, gripping the phone as if it were a monkey wrench.

A light truck pulls up in front of the house. The three men rush outside to see if it could possibly contain Sandra, but it is just the gardener, Miguel. They are about to go back inside, when he hails them.

"Good morning, sir," calls Miguel. "I know I am supposed to work here today, but I don't think I can put in those bare root roses in all this rain, much less mow the grass. Is that okay with you?"

"What? Oh sure," responds Dan, without really hearing the question. Then he thinks that Sandra may have talked with Miguel about her new project. Maybe he would know where in hell this place called Tecolote is.

"Miguel," Dan says as he approaches the workman, "do you know how to find Tecolote? I think that's what it's called. In Tijuana?"

"Tecolote, señor? Si. I know it. That is where Mrs. Sandra has been going to work, verdad?"

"Yes," Dan shouts, with new hope in his voice. "Can you take us down there? I'll be glad to pay you. Mrs. Seaquist went down there yesterday and still hasn't returned."

"I'll take you, of course. But there is no need to pay me. I cannot work today anyway, and I want to help you find your wife. She has always been very kind to me."

The boys change into warmer clothes, and Dan grabs some bread and fruit from the refrigerator. Dan thinks about offering to drive, but he isn't able to picture himself driving in Tijuana, taking directions from the hired man. It will be better all the way around to let Miguel drive. He knows the roads and the conditions far better than any of them does. It is a very tight fit for all four men in Miguel's small Toyota truck cab—the two men in the front seats while Peter and Alex crowd their long legs into the space behind the cab. Nobody complains. It feels good to be doing something, going somewhere.

As they head on the surface streets toward Highway 5, Miguel's radio is playing Mexican music. On the highway itself, they find that they have to open the windows to prevent them from fogging up entirely, with four of them breathing hard on the wet, gray morning. The music on the radio stops, and an announcer begins to speak in Spanish. Dan wishes that Miguel would turn it off and is about to ask him to do so, when Miguel raises his hand and says, "Listen."

They all listen, but Miguel is the only one who understands what he hears. His face looks very grave as he translates. "There are many deaths reported in Tijuana this morning. The rain has caused some hillsides to collapse, many canyons to fill up with water. There are people reported missing in many areas of the city."

"Does he mention Tecolote?" asks Alex. It is the first time that he has really considered this situation to be a serious threat to his mother's safety.

"No, he doesn't mention that colonia," answers Miguel. "But I am not surprised that he doesn't. Tecolote is not close to el centro. The news from Tecolote will not be reported yet, I don't think."

"What type of terrain is this Tecolote?" asks Peter, hoping to be reassured that it is relatively flat and near a major highway.

"I'm afraid it is one of the most remote and hilly colonias in the city," responds Miguel honestly. "It always has problems during the rain, but especially now since the Sony plant is built on a mesa above it, and the land that was cleared to

13

build the factory dumps into the canyons. When the rain hits that loose rubble, it takes it all downhill. It is something like seeing an avalanche of mud."

The three Seaquists do not like the pictures in their minds. All three are skiers and have seen snowslides. Alex went off the groomed trail last year at Mammoth on his snowboard and caused a minor snowslide. The power of that white mass bearing down on trees and everything else in its path convinced him never to go off-trail again. Now, in his mind, he sees the same effect but in a yellow mud color. Why has his mother gone this far off-trail? How could she have done this to all of them? It isn't fair, he thinks to himself.

The men are quiet for a while, until they reach the border between Mexico and the United States. It is early, and very few cars are going south. Still, when they pass through the checkpoint, a red sign lights up the word *revision*, indicating that they must turn in for an inspection by Mexican border agents. Miguel pulls into the inspection area and waits politely for the agent. One agent peers inside the cab of the truck and asks them what they are bringing into Mexico. Another agent looks under the tarp on the truck bed.

"I am bringing nothing, señor. These tools in the back are what I use for work. Today I am coming only to help this gentleman find his wife."

"These tools are worth hundreds of dollars. You must pay duty on them if you bring them into the country," answers the border guard.

Miguel is very frustrated and concerned at this turn of events. In his haste to be helpful, he hasn't considered that his power mower, rakes, saws, shovels, pickaxe, and wheelbarrow, along with some plastic garbage cans and boxes of leaf bags, are all in the bed of the truck.

Dan pulls out his wallet and takes out a fifty dollar bill. He thrusts it at the border agent. "Here," he says, with all the authority he can muster from his cramped position in the small truck. "Tell them we must go because my wife may be in danger."

Miguel explains the situation again and either the money or the explanation works, because the border agent calmly waves them ahead and says, "Pasé."

Now they are careening down wet roads, through crowded city streets that are completely unfamiliar to the three Norté-Americano men. They pass through streets lined with upholstery shops, furniture manufacturing businesses, and taco stands and begin grinding up a long hill with steep gravelly hillsides on the right side of the road. The heavy rain is causing mud and gravel to pour off the hillside and onto the road. Frequently Miguel has to steer around large rocks that clutter the street. Other older, more heavily laden vehicles are struggling to make the ascent. Miguel deftly steers around the slower trucks and cabs filled with workers going to the maquiladoras for the day shift.

As they reach the crest of the hill, they are looking south, at the ragged edges of one of the fastest growing cities in the world. Sleek, modern factories have been hastily constructed on the tops of the mesas. Sad, disheveled casitas line every canyon and cling to every hillside.

Turning on his left-turn signal, Miguel says, "We turn left here at La Gloria. There is a police station on this road. I will stop and find out if they know anything."

At the police station there are a large variety of police cars out front, many of them appear to be secondhand cars bought from police forces north of the border. Miguel goes inside, while Dan and his sons wait impatiently.

When Miguel reappears, he says, "They don't have any reports of your wife, señor. They suggest I go to the iglesia and talk with Padre Jaime. He knows the people who work at the community center."

Dan is surprised at how efficiently Miguel is handling this emergency. He is getting them where they need to be, slowly but surely, asking the right questions and getting answers. Dan is not used to being the confused and unknowledgeable passenger, and he doesn't like not being in control, but he is slowly gaining confidence in his pilot this morning and with this confidence comes a growing respect.

Perhaps Dan conveys some of this to Miguel in the way he answers. "Thank you. I feel like we're getting somewhere now. Let's go find the padre."

The roads here are much more rugged than any of the city streets or highways they have passed so far. They are in a semirural area at the south end of the city. Raw, half-finished buildings appear to have been pressed onto the knobby, weedy land that has been used as grazing pastures until recently. There are no more paved roads. The twisted streets curl up hills, past small makeshift businesses that sell tortillas, Fanta soda, and Bimbo bread. At a curve in the road are a pile of old lumber and a sign advertising tri-ply for sale, which Miguel explains is the Spanish word for plywood. Much of it has been used once, at least. Scavenged from other projects, it is available for resale to aspiring homeowners in this upstart community.

"Señor," says Miguel, "I think that is the church of Padre Jaime." He points to a small, cream-colored, stucco-and-brick building located on a rise above the road. A sign above the front door reads "Iglesia del Salvador."

As the truck comes to a stop near the building, the men observe many people coming in and out of the building with pots, bottles of soda, and eating utensils. Cardboard boxes filled with clothing and the contents of kitchens are being unloaded by several men and claimed by their owners, who are carrying them inside the building. Two of the men unloading the truck are dark-skinned men in faded t-shirts, one reading "San Diego Padres," and the other, "Dr. Seuss Race for Literacy, 1994." The third man is a very tall, freckled man with stooped shoulders and a thin, almost emaciated frame, who is standing in the truck and handing down boxes to the others. He is wearing jeans and a carpenter's apron over an old, stained winter jacket with stuffing coming out of it in several places.

"Do you want me to talk to them?" asks Miguel.

"Please." Dan Seaquist is relieved to find his voice again. "Ask them where we can find the priest and the center where Sandra works."

"Let me out of here," Alex says, pushing on the seat back after Miguel gets out of the car. Peter is right behind his brother as they escape from the crowded space in the back of the truck cab. Dan gets out of his side of the truck more reluctantly. He steps down into wet clay mud and feels the treads of his running shoes take on a thick layer of muck. He stands by the side of the truck, watching Miguel and his sons walk purposefully toward the men unloading the truck.

"Con permiso, señor," begins Miguel, as he approaches the workmen. The tall, slender man is standing in a stooped position at the back of the truck, handing down boxes to the other helpers. He looks down at Miguel and notices Alex and Peter following close behind him.

"Are you here to help?" he asks in English, handing a box of clothing down toward Miguel. "Good, come take over here while I go back to the center and bring back some more people who have no way to get here."

"Bueno, señor." Miguel automatically takes the box and holds onto it. "But we are here to look for an American woman named Sandra Seaquist. Do you know where we can find Father Jaime?"

"I am Father Jaime," responds the man, as he jumps down from the truck bed. He speaks to the men who are helping him and tells them that they should finish the job without him. Then he wipes his hands on his apron and asks Miguel to bring the others and follow him. Dan pulls himself away from the truck and trails along behind the others as they go into the small church.

Inside, the dark church is lit by a few low-wattage light bulbs and a rack of candles on the right side of the room. There are no church pews; instead thirty or more unmatched kitchen chairs are set up in rows facing the altar. Many chairs are occupied by Mexican women and children, who appear to be waiting for something to occur. Padre Jaime leads them to a corner of the room and turns to face them.

"You say you are looking for Sandra?" he prompts.

"Si, Padre," responds Miguel. "This is her family: Señor Seaquist and her two sons." Padre Jaime extends a long arm toward Dan, and the two men shake hands.

"We appreciate the work your wife is doing at our center. These are your sons?" he asks, as he extends his hand to Peter and Alex.

"Buenos dias," Alex says heartily. "I'm Alex and this is my brother, Peter."

"Habla Espanol? Muy bueno," the priest says with a warm smile.

"Only un poco," answers Alex.

"Have you seen her this morning?" asks Peter. "We've been worried about her because she didn't come home last night, and she hasn't even called."

"The phones are not very reliable in this weather. The phone at the center went out yesterday about noon. But I did see her this morning, very early. She was there at the center to help the people who have been evacuated from their homes. Guadalupe!" he calls out to a woman sitting in a chair nearby. "Has vista la Señora Sandra esta manana?"

The conversation between the priest and the woman generates the welcome knowledge that Sandra has been seen a few hours before at the center and that she was heard to say that she planned to try to drive her car home as soon as it was light enough to see the obstacles in the roads. Buoyed by this knowledge, Miguel and the Seaquists say thank you to the priest and hurry back to Miguel's truck armed with directions on how to reach the center about a mile and a half from the church.

The roads near the church are lined with small businesses and houses. They pass an adobe brick factory behind a tall chain-link fence. Then the road pitches up again, and they travel over several short hills. Miguel points to a hand-painted sign on a piece of old, weathered wood that reads TECO. He tells them this is the sign he is looking for; it indicates the way to the area known as Tecolote.

Alex clutches the front seat ahead of him as the truck strains its gears going up a rutted track on the face of the hill. At the crest, the vehicle tips crazily forward and then pitches down toward a patchwork village. On the other side of the valley, a gleaming white factory looms high above the scene on a flat mesa. The blue lettering on the building spells out the very familiar name from the Japanese electronics industry.

Miguel's passengers look with disbelief at the scene below. Shacks cling to the sides of bluffs while others are crowded together into gullies. They all seem to have been built right next to rivers and creeks. As the truck descends, they pass an arroyo coming down from a mesa. It is filled with fast-moving water, rocks, weeds, and other debris. A faded, old recreational vehicle is lying on its side in the midst of the torrent. Water pours in one window and carries small domestic objects out another, as they creep past. Perhaps it was the proud home of a small family a few days before. Miguel is driving about five miles per hour to safely maneuver down the hill.

"Why do people build their houses right next to these rivers?" Alex asks.

"They don't, dogface," answers his brother. "This land is dry most of the year. The only water around here is the kind delivered on water trucks like those." He points to a truck loaded with ten-gallon water bottles, sitting on the side of the road, its back wheels up to the rims in mud.

"Well, then tell me this, smartass. What is Mom doing down here, anyway? Dad, did you know she was coming to a place like this?"

Dan cannot think of a way to answer this question. He remains silent. Peter adds to the tension felt by all four men by commenting, "There could be all kinds of disease carried by this water. When it stops raining, the dead animals and sewage in the water will turn into little pockets of decay and bacteria. Cholera, for sure, and maybe even—"

"Shut up, idiot!" yells Alex. "Dad, tell the doctor to practice medicine somewhere else today, will you? Dad, can't you say something? What is going on here?"

The truck swerves to avoid a chicken in the road and staggers to a stop. The voices in the cab cease as Miguel points to a modest building at the intersection of the road they are traveling and a steep, mud-laden road perpendicular to it on one plane and tilted at a steep angle on another. The only sound they can hear for a moment is the hard, relentless rain beating on the metal roof over their heads. Then, Miguel points to the right and says, "I think this is the center, señor, the place where Mrs. Sandra has been coming to work."

Dan and his sons wipe the condensation off the windows, so they can look out the side of the truck. They see a small building made of stucco and cement blocks. In front of the building is a cement sidewalk with a bench, empty now except for the rain. Climbing out of the truck, they find that the only entrance to the building is at the corner and down a set of five steep stairs on the side of the building facing the steep hill. Each step is outsized in comparison to US

18

standards for stairs, and there is no railing. Dan pictures his short-legged wife going up and down these stairs, carrying the boxes of books she is always bringing down here. Funny, she has never mentioned this to him. If she had, he could have come down and at least built a railing for people to hang on to. At the base of the stairs, they find a wrought iron gate, standing slightly open.

"Hola!" calls Miguel, as he pushes open the gate and enters the enclosed patio. They are now protected from the rain by a corrugated plastic roof. Ahead are two doorways. Two small boys are peering at them from one doorway, so they head in that direction. Miguel speaks to them in Spanish, and they disappear inside. A few moments later, a small, dark-haired Mexican woman comes to the door.

"Bueno," she says, with a tired but welcoming expression on her face.

"Bueno, Señora." responds Miguel. "Buscamos para Señora Sandra. Sabe donde está ella?"

"No, señor. La busco tambien. Ella estaba aqui hasta una hora, y entonces…."

Miguel translates. "The señora doesn't know where Sandra is. She seems— how you say it—puzzled about this. She says that Mrs. Sandra was here until about an hour ago."

"Where is her car?" asks Dan. "Maybe she has gone home."

"I'll ask her." Miguel asks his question and is told to look down the hill. Visitors to the center usually park on the street below because the space in front of the center is used as a taxi and bus stop for the community.

"Gracias, señora."

The men pass back through the enclosed patio, and at the wrought iron gate, they turn right and start walking downhill, immediately filling their shoes and coating their pants legs with mud. As they hurry downhill, they hear a voice call after them.

A young woman with blond hair comes out of the center and runs toward them. She speaks to them in strongly accented English, although the accent she uses does not seem to be Spanish.

"Allo," she calls. "You are looking for Sandra? I will help you."

The men stop to wait for her to catch up with them. In the rain, their introductions are brief, but they learn that her name is Petra and that she is a volunteer in the center also.

"I will show you where the cars park." She leads them at an angle across the muddy street. There sits Sandra's red Mazda, its wheels awash in mud. Dan uses his key to unlock the door and look inside. There is no sign that Sandra has been in the car recently. It is clean inside. If she had gotten in during this rain, the floors would be muddy.

Panic begins to rise up in Dan's throat. He has let himself believe that if they could just find the center where Sandra works, they would be at the end of their search, but now he suspects that they are just at the beginning.

"Where could she have gone?" he asks Petra.

"Where was she the last time you saw her?" asks Peter.

Alex and Miguel are looking around, trying to get clues from their surroundings. Alex sees signs of frantic activity on a hillside behind the center. Several people are working on the hillside, throwing aside pieces of wood and concrete blocks. "Look!" Alex points out this scene to the others.

Petra evaluates the scene quickly and says with conviction, "That is a…it was the home of one of the children we see at the center." She runs across the road and goes up the hill toward the activity, with Sandra's family following close behind.

"I will meet you there," calls Miguel. "I will get my truck, my tools." He veers back up the street they descended a few minutes ago.

Dan and Alex run behind Petra, but Peter quickly overtakes her and sprints ahead. Until this moment, he has found this whole trip to be an annoying way to begin his vacation. Now, he welcomes the thought that his mother is doing work down here with a serious purpose. She is probably up there helping dig out some poor family that has become trapped in their house when the earth above them turned into a mudslide. He imagines how surprised she will be when she sees him coming to help her. This picture gives him the extra energy he needs to vault up the hill. He wants to be the first one she sees. She might even think that it was his idea to come down and help her.

Alex moves ahead but stays abreast of his father. The scene is surreal to him. The whole morning has seemed like a very bad dream. "Okay, time to wake up now," he tells himself. Then he muses on what he means by "wake up." Wake up to what? Reality? Tragedy? What is his father thinking? The grim and fearful look on Dan's face is completely unfamiliar to Alex, who is used to seeing his father in control of his actions, his words, and his feelings, at least the ones he expresses out loud.

The noise of the digging and the shouting among the people at work is louder now. They can see that there are four men and two school-age boys helping unearth what can now be seen more clearly as a mud-covered pile of wood, tin, and bricks.

"Where is she?" asks Peter, as he comes to a standstill and sees no sign of his mother digging or pulling off debris.

Petra yells ahead, "Que pasó? Quien está?"

One man pauses to look at them but keeps his hold on the large piece of timber he is propping up. Dan takes in the scene and recognizes it immediately. It is a very familiar scene after all. What he is looking at is the same type of scene he has observed in the one aircraft accident he witnessed. The area of the home has been compressed by a sudden impact. The space inside it has been reduced greatly, and there are people inside—people trapped by rubble and possibly badly hurt by fallen objects or building materials. He feels some of his strength returning. He knows what to do now. He approaches the man holding the timber and puts his weight under it as well. His sons follow his lead and begin to assist the men as they try to pull away the tin roof, but it is stuck, still connected to other timbers and beams.

Instead of pulling it, they begin to work together to lift it up, and with the added manpower, they are able to do so. Petra picks up a book that is lying face-down in the mud. It is a child's book, its vivid pictures of a large, red dog splattered with mud and badly torn.

"Sandra!" she calls out. "Are you inside?"

Muffled voices are heard from inside the dwelling as the roof is raised. They hear soft cries and voices in Spanish, "Ayudanos."

Petra responds to the voices in Spanish, asking how they are doing and who is in the house. Then she turns to Dan.

"Your wife is in there with them," she says. "She came to help them this morning. But now, they say, she is not moving or making any noise."

"We're here, Sandra!" yells Dan. "Can you hear me?"

"Mom!" Alex starts pulling debris away from the hole to widen it and allow more air to enter the space where he heard the voices.

"Mom?" says Peter, questioning the veracity of his own ears.

They begin working again to dismantle the house and release those trapped inside. Miguel's truck becomes audible, and he comes on the scene bringing shovels and rakes. He sends Alex back for an ax and some rope. Petra talks reassuringly to the child she heard inside the hovel, while they all work together. No one could say who is in charge, who leads, and who follows. Brown, weathered hands and pale hands adept at working with surfboard wax and climbing ropes and the throttles of a jumbo jet all look alike in the mud, and all work together to accomplish the task.

As he strains to lift the timber higher and allow Petra to get underneath and climb inside the remains of the shack, Dan's thoughts crash in on top of him with an impact similar to the one he is certain his wife has just experienced. Why does she come down here and expose herself to this danger? Dan can't stop this angry thought. He asked her if she knew what she was doing down here, and she told him she didn't feel any danger. As if mirroring his own thoughts, Peter asks angrily, "Dad, why did you let her come?"

Dan doesn't answer his son, but the question loads an additional sense of responsibility on top of his feelings of dread. Doesn't she know her family comes first? Dan's resentment tumbles around in his head. She took a risk, an unnecessary risk. He thinks of the risks he takes in his job, but they are controlled risks. And besides, he is well paid for what he does. Nobody pays her to do this.

"Dad, it will be all right," Alex says, to reassure himself, as well as his father. "She's got to be all right. We'll get her out of here, just like we got her out of that whirlpool the time we went rafting."

"I think I hear her voice," says Petra. "Does that sound like her?"

Dan strains to listen, but all he can hear are the Mexican men talking among themselves in a language he doesn't understand.

"Shut up!" he yells at them. They stop speaking in midsentence.

He listens again carefully, hoping to hear the voice he knows he would recognize in any imaginable situation. Not that this is an imaginable situation. This is Sandra here—the same woman who wouldn't travel with him to Mexico City last year because she was afraid of being caught in a high-rise during an earthquake.

Outwardly, Dan's physical body is completely involved in the rescue efforts, assisting Miguel and the other men with the shovels. His long years of training as a military and then a commercial pilot allow him to continue to function. But, inwardly, Dan can't contain his feelings of outrage. He wonders if he is to blame, if he was such a lousy husband that she came down here to pay me back. He thinks of the good life they have had, especially when the boys were young. She has always been such a good mother. He knows it's hard on women to have their children leave home and wonders if he should have paid more attention to her. The worry flashes through his mind that she might think that he has been fooling around on her. Is that it? Did she get herself in this situation to pay him back for being attracted to Leslie? Is that why she insisted on coming down here so close to Christmas?

"We're getting there." Miguel's voice interrupts Dan's thoughts. "Here, Petra, squeeze through and see if you can reach someone in there."

Petra gets down on her belly and pushes herself on the slippery mud into the hole they have wedged out. She reaches in with her arm and feels a small hand grab hold.

"I've got you," Petra exclaims triumphantly. "Vamanos!" She holds on to the child's hand while others dig a space for her to climb through. Dan watches his sons put all their effort into saving this unknown child.

"Sandra," he says, "you've got to be okay. You would be so proud of your sons if you could see them now."

Chapter Three

PACIFIC RIM NEW YEAR'S DAY ONE YEAR EARLIER

There must be more to this story. Why Mexico? Is it just an accident of geography? Tecolote is less than an hour from Horton's Plaza, the shopping center in downtown San Diego with a Nordstrom and a Disney Store.

Bullshit, any San Diegan will tell you. Tijuana is not on the map. The Thomas's guide that lists every lane and cul-de-sac in San Diego County shows Tijuana as a blank pink space with a river running through it. To go down to Tijuana for the day, you have to stop before you cross the border and buy special insurance for your car.

Consider this story: A principal of a middle school in San Diego drove some friends from out of town to Tijuana one day to see the sights. A Tijuana taxi turned left from the right-hand lane in front of him, and both cars had dented fenders. The principal was kept at the police station on Calle Ocho until his wife came down with the cash to buy his freedom. He was told he was guilty until proven innocent. Now, that's another country, right?

Of course, the woman who cleans his house has another story. She lives in Tijuana and frequently comes across the border to take her children shopping for clothes and school supplies at the Target in San Ysidro. Once, when they were coming out of the store, her daughter put a soda on the hood of a Lexus, and it spilled. The owner came out and called the police. Next thing she knew, she and her kids were being searched for drugs—by a San Diego cop with the last name of Juarez!

Now, the real story here is not whether Sandra is being middle-aged crazy. If that was it, she could certainly see a doctor and get a hormone patch. That would fix her up; then she might just sign up for a quilting class and get on with her life. And the story is not—as Dan's guilty conscience hinted—that she is bent on revenge because she is suspicious that her husband is having an affair with his female copilot. It isn't even as simple as empty nest syndrome, watching her children leave home and needing another target for her maternal instinct, other than her cat, Amigo.

But, wait, the name of her cat does sort of give away one of the themes of this story. Sandra is a person for whom friendship is very important, and for whom borders are like backyard fences that are meant to protect the neighbor's plum trees.

When Sandra was growing up in Reno, Nevada, if she wanted one of those plums, she simply climbed over and got it—got several, in fact. But, the thing is, she shared the ones she didn't eat herself. Does that make her Johnny Appleseed? Maybe that's how she sees herself still—a slightly overweight, middle-aged, female Johnny Appleseed with more gray than brown in her hair. Only, for her, what she sows is the love of words that have been planted between the covers of books.

Dan, on the other hand, is a person for whom tradition and respect for authority are very important. One day, when Dan was seven, he found a policeman's hat in the street near his home in Lancaster, Pennsylvania. He put it on and went walking up and down the sidewalk until his mother saw him and called him in. "What do you think you are doing?" she said, with real alarm in her voice. "Do you want to be arrested for impersonating an officer?" This is a true story. So, Dan joined the navy and risked his life for five years in order to be able to wear his own blue hat with a gold braid. Afterward, he signed on with a major airline, the one you fly to Hawaii or Washington, DC, on your honeymoons and business trips. He's very proud of the hat he wears now and of the four gold stripes on his sleeves.

No, the real story here is about people like you and me, people who live in a changing world and are trying to adapt as best they can—people who have hopes and dreams and the means to realize some, but not all, of them. There it is, you see. They have to choose. They are each individuals who have made many choices in their lives up to this point, and, by and large, their choices have turned out to be the best ones for them. They're still married, aren't they? After twenty-six years? That says something for them. Don't discount them yet.

"You'd be so proud of your sons" is something Sandra frequently says to Dan when he calls home from a trip to hear how things are going at home. For twenty-two of the twenty-six years they have been married, they have been parents. The previous fall, both boys went away to school, leaving them alone to discover what else they might have in common.

Sandra's position as a school district reading coordinator has little in common with her husband's career as an airline pilot. The only books he reads these days are his flight manuals. For leisure, Dan enjoys skiing, sailing, watching sports on television, and working on his 1968 Porsche. Sandra prefers walking, pottery classes, and cooking. When they go to the bookstore or library together, Dan never leaves the aviation and mechanics shelves, while Sandra quickly claims her weekly quota of new fiction and mystery books.

Last night, at a New Year's Eve party in their neighborhood, Sandra overheard Dan tell a neighbor that the one thing he has in common with his wife is that she likes to cook and he likes to eat. With that comment fresh in her mind, on New Year's Day, almost a full year before her Christmas Eve experience in Tijuana, Sandra only knows that she needs to reconsider her priorities. She has made some tentative new decisions about her life and is driving along Torrey Pines Road to meet a friend who she can count on to understand, or at least listen to, what she is experiencing.

"Great day for a walk," Sandra says, as she gets out of her car. "I left Dan home with the football games on television, and each of us is sure the other one is nuts. Think we'll need a jacket?"

"I'd bring it," says Hanna, peering through the cedar trees to assess the seriousness of the come hither fog playing hide-and-seek at the edge of the bluffs. "We'll probably take them off and put them on a half dozen times, though. This fog can't seem to make up its mind."

Hanna gets her worn, blue backpack out of her faded blue Volvo sedan and tosses it up on the rooftop bike rack. She reaches inside for two large navel oranges and a Diet Pepsi. Sandra stuffs a package of dried bananas and a couple of napkins in her jacket pocket. Then the two women start walking down the blacktop road toward the bluff trails.

They walk along the Torrey Pines Golf Club for a few hundred yards, still empty this early on New Year's Day, and then turn seaward on a sandy path lined with manzanita and several varieties of sage. Sandra breathes in the spicy smells of these plants and begins to feel a familiar and very welcome stretch of the muscles in the back of her legs. It makes her want to gallop as she did when she was eight years old, practicing to be a palomino in her back yard. But she knows she ought to pace herself. She isn't eight years old anymore, and this is a long path down to the sea, with a fairly rigorous climb back to the top. Besides, she hasn't seen Hanna for a long time, and they want to walk at a pace that allows them to talk.

"Do you ever feel…oh, I don't know…kind of vulnerable on New Year's Day?" Sandra asks, as she ties her jacket sleeves around her waist.

"Vulnerable?" repeats Hanna, as she stops to examine a lemonade berry shrub. "That question sounds like an offer to help fix things, as usual. Are you aware that whenever I indicate any sign of low energy or uncertainty about my life, you are right there with a quick fix?" Even as she says this aloud, Hanna has to admit that she appreciates the way Sandra cares enough to ask.

As if to make amends for her sharp tone of voice, Hanna pinches the buds of the plant and inhales the sharp sweet scent deeply then holds the sprig of lemonade berry out toward Sandra's nose, who also delights in the small, tart aroma.

"That wasn't a very diplomatic question, was it?" concedes Sandra.

"I guess I don't feel any more vulnerable today than I have been feeling for the past several months." Hanna shrugs her shoulders then proceeds off ahead of Sandra down the path toward the sea.

Walking behind her friend, Sandra interprets Hanna's body language as a sign of wanting to shrug off responsibility. Since last summer, when her job as a systems analyst for a defense contractor was replaced by a twenty-something kid with a laptop computer, Hanna has been on unemployment. Sandra is worried about what will happen when the unemployment checks stop coming.

"Maybe I feel vulnerable too. I feel like I am stepping into the unknown by taking this leave from my job." Sandra wrinkles her brow and clenches her teeth briefly, as she thinks with some regret of her familiar desk and file cabinets at the board of education administration building. Recent public scrutiny has generated many newspaper editorials, which assert that too much of the school district's budget is being spent on central office administrators when it is needed to hire more teachers and reduce class size. In response, the board offered selected administrators time off without pay for a semester, while they reorganized.

"It seemed like such a good opportunity when the associate superintendent announced it, and Dan encouraged me to try something new," she continues. What she doesn't say is that she suspects that Dan's real motivation is to have her home and available when he is home. When she was working, his days off rarely coincided with hers. When he wanted to go sailing on a Thursday, he had to make his own sandwiches and find someone else to crew for him. Besides, he has always wanted her to go with him on his trips. But Sandra doesn't travel so easily. Two years ago, Sandra took Dan up on his invitation to fly to New York City with him for a twenty-eight-hour layover. When Dan's plane took off from La Guardia Airport the next morning, Sandra was left holding her overnight bag. A strike by another carrier meant that there were no seats to San Diego or even Los Angeles for another forty-two hours. Sandra had to stay in an airport hotel by herself for two more nights. For her, this took courage.

Of the two women, Hanna has always been known as the brave one. She goes camping alone in the desert and takes dirt roads in her eight-year-old Volvo, without a AAA card. One time Sandra went along for a ride to Mount Laguna, but when Hanna turned up a dirt road to see if she could find a great view of the sea, Sandra clenched her teeth and kept her attention on the US Geological Survey map to reassure herself that she knew where they were and how to get back to where they came from.

On the crest of a hill, catching their first view of the sea, Sandra widens her eyes and smiles broadly in her determined way. "Of course it's a wonderful opportunity—having time off to do what I want to do—so why do I suddenly feel so tense about it? Why do I feel as if I really have to prove myself even harder now?"

"Sandra, you've been trying to prove yourself for as long as I've known you," responds Hanna emphatically, as she waits for Sandra with some impatience. "Who are you trying to impress now? Your mother? She's gone. You don't have to live up to her expectations anymore."

"I never did anyway," says Sandra quietly. Stinging tears instantly brim in Sandra's eyes as she recalls standing beside her mother's slender body in the hospice bed a year ago. A hard worker herself, Lizbeth's responses to Sandra's accomplishments in school or helping with housework were always variations on the theme of "Well, you could have done better."

"Oh, let's change the subject. I'm sorry I even brought it up in the first place. Let's just enjoy the day, this view," Sandra says. Walking faster than is comfortable for her on the uneven path, Sandra stumbles on a root exposed in the ground beneath her feet. She catches her balance just in time, and sweeping both of her hands through her hair as if to comb out the cobwebs of fear, she starts walking carefully down the path again, choosing each step deliberately to avoid the ruts.

29

Hanna, who likes to walk fast and does so with confidence, bounds down the path, ignoring the ruts and stones in her way. She has dressed for a cool day in loose-fitting, comfortable clothes and added a bright, teal blue-and-orange scarf on her way out the door. She has a collection of bright scarves that she wears with otherwise plain clothing. The effect is at once elegant and comfortable. Her warm, usually slightly bemused smile and the frequent smile lines near her hazel eyes dress up her face in much the same way.

On Sandra's sturdy thighs, her jeans are stretched to reveal individual stitches in the seams. They will just have to fit; there is no way she will ever buy a larger size. She has tucked in her pumpkin-colored jersey shirt and tied her green windbreaker around her waist. Her fashion strategy is to hope that these bright colors will detract from, or at least make up for, her extra weight. Her short, brown hair is cut to accommodate its natural waves and is just beginning to show the gray roots that her hairdresser colors every month.

Sandra uses a little makeup, relying on products she buys at the supermarket when she shops for groceries. Her warm, brown eyes are highlighted with mascara. She hopes that people notice her eyes and overlook her crooked front teeth when they meet her. Sandra considers her teeth the badge of her working-class background. In her own mind, they set her apart, somehow, from people with straight, even teeth. When she is introduced to someone else with irregular teeth, she feels more at ease than she does when she meets people with orthodontically correct smiles.

Sandra has to run to catch up with Hanna as they trudge uphill through an area burned last year in a destructive brushfire. The skeletons of small oak trees and manzanita bushes are blackened but still standing, like tin soldiers on a dirt play lot.

"How's Kate?" Sandra asks, thinking of Hanna's irrepressible daughter, who dropped out of college almost two years ago as a protest, when a favorite woman professor did not receive tenure. "Is she going to Mesa again this semester?"

"No," answers Hanna. "She just got a letter of acceptance from San Francisco State. She starts January twenty-fifth."

"That's great!" exclaims Sandra. "That's a perfect place for her." She pictures Kate with her long hair, unshaven legs, and her interest in the environment and women's issues fitting in very well up in San Francisco, especially at the state university.

"Now you can have your house back to yourself," adds Sandra.

"Yes, I'll enjoy having more space, and I can move my computer out of the dining room and back to the extra bedroom again. But, I have to say that I'll miss Kate's energy. I enjoy having her friends come over. Maybe it makes me feel younger to be surrounded by, and sometimes even included in, Kate's activities."

"You can make the extra bedroom into an office," says Sandra. "You can think again about starting your own business."

"I don't know," muses Hanna. "I'd have to take courses on computer graphics and the Internet. Everything about computers has changed since I was laid off."

"Well, anyway, it will be great to visit you again and have a quiet dinner in your dining room, like we used to when Kate was at college."

The path they are on now opens out onto a full view of the Pacific Ocean a hundred feet below. In this winter light, the sea is mauve and gray, against a sky the color of pewter with white clouds like soapsuds. The two women stand silently, appreciating the scene, scanning the waves down below to catch a glimpse of the dolphins who sometimes surf these shores.

A blue-and-gray bird darts across the path at eye level. Hanna spots the bird's mate on top of a red-limbed manzanita. She identifies it as a scrub jay, common to the coastal area. The trait that both women have in common is an unlimited capacity for appreciating, truly celebrating, the beauty of their natural surroundings. They stay still for some moments to take in huge, deep, and delicious breaths of the salty air. Then, as if to reward their attention, a bottle-green humming bird approaches and shows an interest in Hanna's bright scarf.

"I wish I'd worn my red, wool scarf," Hanna says, with a joyful expression on her face. "I've had hummingbirds actually take bits of fluff off of it for their nests." The small bird flies away at the sound of Hanna's voice, and the friends walk on as the path begins to curve downward now, toward the beach, hidden by sandy bluffs so fragile that they literally crumble underfoot.

Their talk turns again, quite naturally, to their children, who are trying to gain their independence and, in the process, causing their parents to become independent again as well, ready or not.

"So, how does Alex like Berkeley?" Hanna asks Sandra. "Did he have a good first semester?"

"Yes, he loves it. It's definitely the right school for him. He thinks San Diego is boring now." As Sandra answers, they reach the top of the rise and begin to head directly down toward the sea.

"And how is Peter? Any word on his medical school applications yet?"

"No, none at all. It's maddening. I'm beginning to worry that he didn't apply to enough schools." Sandra's voice is full of the consternation of a parent who has always been able to protect her child, but no longer has any influence. In the past, as a respected school administrator, a reading specialist for the school district, she had some useful influence with his teachers as well. When he missed the gifted program cut-off score by only a few percentiles, she arranged for him to take the test again, and of course he passed. But now, his future is out of her hands and in the hands of ten highly respected medical school admission committees.

"I'm sure he'll hear soon," reassured Hanna. "He's bound to get in with his grades and his test scores. Plus, he's a great guy. He'll make a great doctor. Anyone could see that."

"Yes, my sister Karen thinks he is a natural healer, ever since the day she and Peter and I hiked to that waterfall in the Cascades. But how will the admissions departments know that if they don't even give him a chance to interview?" Sandra hates her voice when it whines like this.

Hanna turns the conversation to a safer topic. "Then Alex isn't bothered by the size of the school or the large classes at Berkeley?" she asks. She leads the way down the dirt path, noticing that it has become deeply rutted in the past few months even though the rains have been relatively sparse this year.

"Not so far," answers Sandra. "He came home for Christmas break, but he spent most of his time with friends, some of them from Berkeley. They've formed this group called the Explorers Club, and they go hiking and traveling together. They hiked in the Cuyamacas last week, and then yesterday they left for the Grand Canyon."

Sandra walks behind her friend on the rocky and rutted path, picking her footing more slowly than Hanna does. In her mind, though, she lets her imagination take her to the rim of the Grand Canyon. She can vividly picture herself as a member of a group of good friends heading down the Bright Star trail to the floor of the Grand Canyon. The path is probably no more treacherous than this one except for the height and the sheer drop on one side of the trail.

Sandra is very adventurous in her imagination and enjoys planning such trips, even talking about going on them with friends and her husband and children. In reality, though, her fears, phobias perhaps, have prevented her from actually following through on most of the adventures she talks about. In her mind, she ridicules herself as the worst type of armchair traveler. She knows that, on many occasions, she has discussed sailing trips and soaring as if she truly intended to go on them, while, all the time, inside, she suspects that she will back out at the last minute and cancel the trip because of her fears.

"And your ski trip, did it turn out well last week?" Sandra inquires of Hanna.

"Well, Lake Tahoe was great, but that is my last trip with a singles group," answers Hanna quite forcibly.

"Did you ski North Star?"

"Yes, have you skied North Star?"

"Well, I've been there. I've gone cross-country skiing there, but you know how I feel about downhill skiing." One of Sandra's strongest, most intractable phobias is of the chairlifts at ski resorts. She tried to go on a few of them many years ago but each time wrestled with disabling fantasies of being trapped, dangling on a ski lift that has stopped in midair, without any way to get down to earth. She can't explain to herself, let alone others, why she fears this experience so profoundly. She only knows that unless she can literally learn to turn off her own imagination, she will never be comfortable on a ski lift or gondola.

Hanna, for her part, considers what she wants to tell about her trip to Lake Tahoe. It was conceived in hope, what was for her outright enthusiasm, a rarity these days. She heard about the trip from an instructor at a school of holistic health where she is taking a course on massage techniques. Usually, she avoids singles clubs and singles trips. But, she allowed herself to hope that this one would be special, that it would enrich her life and help heal her spirit, reverse her diminishing vision of life as an adventure. It didn't. The trip to Lake Tahoe was a great disappointment, except for the skiing.

"The skiing was great," she volunteers in an even voice. "The views are as spectacular as this one."

The two women have reached a sandy knoll just a few yards above the ocean. The fog is sparser now, and the sun's light behind the thinning clouds appears like a large pearl hidden behind a gauze curtain. They stop for a minute and gaze out at the sea without speaking. Suddenly the silence is ripped open by the sound of two jet fighters streaking overhead and then heading out to sea. They watch as the planes disappear, and they begin walking again.

"Did you meet anyone?" insists Sandra. Hanna has been single for years. She was married, briefly, to a man who wanted to avoid the draft during the Vietnam War. They lived in Philadelphia, but after three years Hanna returned to San Diego with Kate. The only explanation she has ever given about the breakup of her marriage is that there wasn't enough reason to stay together.

Sandra has never felt that way about her own marriage. There have always been plenty of reasons for her and Dan to stay together, especially after the two boys were born. In addition to the enjoyment they have always had playing and talking with their children, they share a strong sexual attraction that has not diminished over the years. Dan still cannot take his eyes off of Sandra when she wears her short silk robes or nothing at all. He seems to find her as attractive as ever, despite her fears about her extra weight. Sandra loves Dan's wiry strength and his smells, and is still turned on by how handsome he looks in his uniform. After he returns from one of his trips, they are both anxious to see each other and hold each other, with their bodies pressed together, as if to say, "Yes, I'm still here for you. I still choose you. Now let's get these clothes off and make love."

Not that they escape the resentments, hurt feelings, and disagreements of any long-lasting relationship. It is just that they have always had at least five good experiences for each negative one, and when a problem occurs, they've always found a way to apologize and to forgive each other. At this point in time, Sandra cannot picture any crisis or situation that would cause a damaging break in their marriage.

"How many more women than men were there?" asks Sandra, who is always hoping that her friend will meet someone like Dan, someone she can rely on and love.

"There were only four men out of twenty of us, and two of those men were attached to women in the group." Hanna's voice registers the chagrin and dismay she felt when the group assembled at the social center in the condominium complex at North Star. Her hopes for an exciting holiday burst, and her positive expectations leaked away when she looked at the fourteen other unattached women in the group and saw the same disappointment in their eyes.

"I spent most of my time skiing alone," Hanna admits. "What really bummed me out is that on Christmas Eve, I tried to get people together for some kind of a celebration, but people just weren't willing to even sit down together for a meal. I was putting some food out on a table, and one man just sat down and began eating before the rest even came to the table." Hanna's voice registers a shocked puzzlement as she remembers this event.

"I guess many people don't even know how to celebrate together anymore," suggests Sandra warily.

"Well, we do!" states Hanna with renewed energy. "We take these wonderful walks instead of sitting home moping."

"Yes, or watching men crack skulls for sport on TV," says Sandra.

They both tacitly agree to stop talking about the past and celebrate and fully appreciate the present. The path that has been leading them down to the sea in switchbacks, punctuated with occasional steps carved out of rock, now flattens out, and with a few more steps, they reach the seashore. Nearby, a number of people are walking barefoot on the beach. Two small children are digging in the wet sand near the shore, and another is exploring a large flat rock that is accessible only during low tide.

The fog has disappeared, and the sunlight warms their shoulders and brightens their faces. They spread out their windbreakers next to an eroded mound of sand and are able to sit and lean their backs comfortably against the sun-heated sand spilling out of the hillside.

For a few minutes, they are quiet as they contemplate the physical beauty of this breeze-swept beach. The colors are enough to satisfy one's senses. The dark green manzanita and ice plant on the hillsides contrast with the bright ochers and siennas of the sandy bluffs in a stunning and completely gratifying visual reward for their long walk. But, in this particular setting, at the westernmost edge of the continent, the vegetation and landforms are only the side shows. The main event is the vibrant dance of white foamy waves curling over translucent aquamarine water in a rhythmic march toward the shore. As one foam-clad wave sweeps up and bows to the beach-walkers, another forms tall and aloof behind it, just as a troupe of ballerinas in white tutus does on the stage.

Accompanying the visual imagery of the sea and shore is the music made by the natural orchestra. The breeze is the string section, elicited by the groves of pine trees that are seen on the bluffs both stage left and right. The tympani of crashing waves and the snare drum of the sand being jostled by the sea are stage center, and in front of them are the flutes and oboes in the voices of children and their parents calling to each other as they create their castles and ooh and ah over their treasures of shells, smooth stones, and sand dollars.

There are smells, as well, of white sage and pine, hot sand and salt air, and of seaweed and dying shellfish that have lain too long in the sand. To these smells, Hanna adds the citrus of navel oranges that she picked this morning from a tree in her yard. She peels one open and hands sticky sections to her good friend, and they both devour them with greedy delight, tasting the sweet, tart juiciness that is probably the very essence of what they live for, of what each one of them truly wants out of life.

Chapter Four

BURIAL GROUND

"It's hard to believe this is January, isn't it?" Lou Piechowski stands in front of a small crowd of men and women dressed for walking in jeans, T-shirts, sweaters, sweatpants, and canvas walking shoes. Sandra Seaquist is among them. She has enjoyed the walk to Torrey Pines and is determined to walk every day in order to lose some weight and build up her stamina.

"The sunlight is warm enough to raise the dead. That's a joke, folks. But seriously, I know that many of you are transplanted from other climates, where the chief mode of transportation at this time of year is a snowplow." He pauses for laughter and then continues, "While here, January is the month when our best oranges grow." As he speaks, Lou unzips his windbreaker. Glancing at Sandra, who is once again wearing her jacket tied around her waist, he says, "I'd wear my jacket like that too, if the arms were just long enough."

Sandra doesn't know whether to smile or not, so she just raises her eyebrows in an expression that shows her discomfort at being singled out in the group.

"Okay, we're going to get started with our walking tour of Mt. Hope Cemetery. How many are new to Walk and Talk?" Eight or ten hands are raised among the group of thirty or so adults who are gathered for the tour.

"Did you read about it in the paper?"

"It is in 'The Reader,'" answers Josette, the current president of the group known as Walk and Talk, International. "For those of you who don't know about our group, we publish a newsletter once a month that lists all the walking tours we sponsor. You can get on the mailing list for just fifteen dollars a year if you fill out one of these cards."

Several people reach for the cards and then begin to search their pockets and belly bags for pens or pencils as Diane, a founding member of the group, explains, "We run about one hundred eighty different walks every month, in every neighborhood and at every time of day. Some start as early as five thirty in the morning, but there are others offered throughout the day and evening."

"Well, let's get started with this one," Lou joins in. "What we've planned today, folks, is to meet some of the characters who made San Diego what it is today. We'll see where the great, the not so great, the fathers, and the mothers of our city are laid to rest. Let's begin with a ghost story."

Lou begins to stride toward a nearby hillside studded with headstones of granite and cement. His heart is beating too loudly again, causing a thudding in his ears that he tries to ignore. He shouldn't have had that second burrito for lunch. He can feel the heartburn beginning to sear his gut.

Sandra tries to stay near the front of the group, so she can hear and see everything. She doesn't know anyone in the group. But, she'd like to. New faces, new places, new everything—that's been her mantra for the past couple of weeks. New possibilities, new options—"Whoops, better watch where I'm going," she thinks.

"We're looking for a marker for Wu Tso, pronounced 'chow,'" Lou calls out to the group trailing him up the hill. "Here it is." He pauses in front of a plain granite stone with the inscription: Wu Tso Lee, 1837–1889, and Mandy, his wife, 1844–1908. Gradually, the group of walkers assembles and becomes quiet, as Lou begins describing the lives of the Chinese man and his American-born wife who settled in San Diego shortly after the Civil War.

"Wu Tso came to San Francisco from China right after the gold rush. He worked on a railroad gang in the Sierras for many years, but he was lucky to be a good cook, so he escaped the hard work of laying track by becoming a cook for the crew. He came down to San Diego when the Santa Fe started its operations here and opened a restaurant on Fifth Street. His wife, Mandy, was said to have run another type of establishment that served different appetites on the second floor of the building. The building is gone now. It's a parking lot. Any questions?"

"Does anyone know how Wu Tso and Mandy met?" asks a sturdy, gray-haired woman wearing walking shorts and a sun visor. The sun visor advertises a popular brand of Mexican beer that immediately causes Lou's mouth to water. He can taste the bitter cold bite of that beer right now. He'll pick some up on his way home. Cold, he likes it very cold, so he usually buys it at a deli near his home where the refrigerators keep things much colder than his old icebox does.

"Not that I know of," he answers. "They came to San Diego together from Northern California. But it is unusual for the time for a Chinese man and a white woman to be married. Not that anyone ever saw the marriage license either, but they are known as man and wife. Now, let's go to another part of the cemetery, which used to be known as the colored section."

Lou walks down toward the graves that are located in a gully near the trolley tracks. When it rains, this area is flooded and muddy. Of course, it doesn't rain very often in San Diego, but even so, this low-lying area collects debris blown from the train or elsewhere. He stops in front of a concrete stone marked, simply, Robinson.

"The Robinsons were also merchants in early San Diego. Curtis Robinson opened one of the first dry goods stores in the boom time right after the Civil War. His sons and grandchildren ran it until 1929 when it went bust in the depression. San Diego really grew during and right after the Civil War. Many people came here when their own lives were messed up by the war. A lot of them came from the South. That's probably why the cemetery is segregated. A lot of John Crow laws were established here by the settlers from other southern states."

"Next, we'll see one of the grand ladies of San Diego, Kate Sessions," Lou says, with the pride in his voice that all San Diegans feel about Kate Sessions. He starts walking purposefully toward a stand of twisted juniper trees on a pretty knoll. As he walks, he overhears a nearby conversation.

"John Crow?" says a bearded man quizzically.

"Yeah, must have been a Southern California brother of Jim Crow," responds a companion in a San Diego Padres ball cap.

But Lou doesn't mind. He knew that as a historian, he lacks a few facts and is satisfied if he gets within a decade of the correct dates, but he is confident in his ability to tell a good story and help people see what he does in this city. He likes San Diego better than any place else he's ever lived. It is so accessible. The stories of the past that he loves to read about are so vividly etched in his mind that it is as if he can see the characters from these cemetery plots walking and talking right next to the living people.

And there is never any question in his mind about which characters he prefers. No living, breathing human being attracts his interest as much as Wu Tso, Curt Robinson, and others like them. He lives alone in small apartment in a Victorian building near downtown San Diego, furnished with stuff he bought at a Salvation Army store fifteen years ago. Today, as he opened the blinds, one relic came apart, and the yellowed slats fell to the floor in a heap. They are still there; he'll have to do something to replace the blind today or tomorrow. He would hate to have to resort to covering the window with a sheet or towel. That would be a bit too tacky, even for Lou.

Most days, Lou wakes at seven or eight o'clock and makes a pot of coffee in the old percolator that is one of the few possessions he has left from the days of a very brief marriage more than twenty years ago. It was a wedding present from his aunt Ida, so he'd made sure he kept it when everything else was going out the door and into the rented van his wife Myra hired. She left without too much warning, on a morning like this one. A bright, sunny day early in the new year of—was it 1967 or '68? She met a navy guy, a goddamn officer type, at the bank where she worked. He walked in to open a new account and left with Myra.

"She never thought I'd get my act together," thinks Lou, as he strides up the hill, keeping some distance between himself and the hangers-on. Maybe she is right. I always hoped to be a…a what? Even now, it is very difficult for Lou to put into words his fuzzy dream of becoming an important teacher or civic leader or community organizer. His formal education ended when he joined the navy right after graduating from high school in Omaha, Nebraska, in June of 1958. Boot camp in San Diego and then a desk job ordering supplies for VAW-11, a squadron of propeller-driven planes with over-sized radar domes mounted on their backs.

The squadron was located on North Island, in the middle of San Diego Bay. Lou met his wife Myra at a local hangout called the Mexican Village in 1964, and after they were married, they lived in a sunny apartment near the Italian bakeries on India Street. Every morning except Sunday, they would wake up to the smell of fresh bread baking. One or the other of them, usually Lou, would get dressed and go buy a loaf of bread still warm to the touch. Myra would make strong Yuban coffee in the pot Lou's aunt Ida had given them, and they'd eat the bread with eggs cooked sunny-side up.

"God, those days I thought I could do anything, be anything," thinks Lou as he walks. Some people, other people, seem to be able to construct something real out of their dreams, but mine just crumbled. Not Kate's, though. She made something happen with her life. Lou arrives at the gravesite of Kate Sessions, almost hidden beneath a huge, twisted juniper tree. When the walkers gather around the grave, he begins to talk quietly, almost reverently about her life and work.

"Kate Sessions is known as the mother of San Diego. There may be a lot of fathers, but only one real mother. Kate had a vision of a series of parks that would make San Diego a beautiful place to live, and she is credited with planning the horticulture in and around Balboa Park. Of course, this tree is planted here for a reason. Do you know what it is?"

Sandra's attention is focused on Lou's words. Someone in the group knows that Kate Sessions introduced the first twisted juniper to the city and that she used the tree frequently in her landscape planning for the city. Hearing the respect for Kate Sessions in Lou's voice causes Sandra to imagine herself being discussed as one of the mothers of San Diego fifty years from now. But what would people remember about her? For many years, she was a very good first grade teacher; she also taught Head Start for several summers when Dan was laid off from his airline job, and they needed the extra money. She has a natural empathy for children, which her students enthusiastically returned after they tested her enough to discover that her regard for them was authentic and not just a veneer learned in classroom management courses.

After spending a few hours observing and talking to a child, she seemed to know, intuitively, what each needed most; she was usually capable of creating lessons that sparked interest in even the slowest learner and hooked them with exhilarating feelings of success. She designed lessons that turned learning math facts into intriguing problem-solving games and geography lessons into treasure hunts. Long before the whole language approach to teaching reading made it fashionable, Sandra allowed her students to choose what they wanted to read and grouped children according to their interests rather than according to their scores on standardized tests of basic skills.

But Sandra knew that, as good a teacher as she was, her restless personality made it difficult to stay in the same job year after year. So, ten years ago, she had gone back to school for a master's degree as a reading specialist, and her efforts led to a promotion, to an administrative job in her school district. But, although her new job has a better salary and more prestige, Sandra finds that curriculum planning and selecting books for other teachers to use is not nearly as satisfying as working with the children directly. Also, budget cuts and reductions in the property taxes that support education have made her job less secure every year. Luckily, she has tenure. She knows that if things really get bad, she can always go back to the classroom. With her seniority, she will never be laid off.

Still, she has not been a classroom teacher for ten years. She wonders if she can still manage a classroom of twenty or more children, if she still has the energy and creativity to plan new, exciting lessons every day. Would she still want to spend each evening patiently correcting papers to diagnose the learning problems and create new lesson plans for her students? Does she still want to do these things? It really comes down to the question of "Who am I?" Twenty-five years ago, she knew the answer to that question. She was a wife and a teacher. Then, a few years later, she was a mother. After that, she was a busy administrator trying to learn on the job and teach others as well. She thinks that she still is all of those things—or at least she could be if she wanted to be. But does she? What does she want now? Who is she now?

Her temporary answer to all these questions was to take a semester off when it was offered. She hopes that with time and new explorations, she'll be able to answer those questions again. Dan encouraged her to do it. He has always wanted her to have more time to travel with him, and even though they are still paying their sons' tuition, Dan is now flying as a captain of an Airbus 320, and they can afford to live on his salary alone if they choose. Sandra is alternately elated and apprehensive about her sabbatical, as she likes to call it.

It has the potential to be a wonderful year. Although she has loved living in San Diego ever since she moved here with Dan when he was in the navy, there is still a lot more she would like to know about the area. This Walk and Talk outing is a first step in her search. She is eager to get the exercise she needs and, at the same time, learn about the history of the area and experience all the natural beauty of the place without feeling like she should be doing something else.

When she told Peter and Alex about all the exciting things she is planning to do this year, they were delighted for her. She has signed up for watercolor lessons at a small art studio near her home; they begin next week. She has sent away for a brochure for a volunteer group called Rolling Readers. They assign people to a school or library to read aloud the wonderful children's books that she used to like to read to her children or her students. It is an opportunity to get back to working with children again and to try to recapture, at least in a small way, the satisfactions she felt as a classroom teacher.

Sandra is happy to begin a new year. Last year, Dan went through a period of self-doubt, but he seems much happier now. Always aware of his responsibilities to provide well for his family, and thinking of the double college tuitions ahead, he decided last year to fly as a first officer on 747s to Australia and the Orient. The bigger the plane, the bigger the paycheck—this is one of the facts of life for commercial pilots. But, the long trips wore him out, physically and mentally. Fourteen to sixteen hours of bored attentiveness had threatened to destroy his love of flying. So, this fall he took a bid as a captain on the smaller Airbus, which is used for destinations no more than five hours away. Now, he gets to make three or four takeoffs and landings a day, instead of one. For Dan, landings and takeoffs are the best part of flying—always interesting—and he prides himself on his smooth, gentle touchdowns even in tricky winds.

During this inner assessment of her life and marriage, Sandra has walked with the tour group to several more gravesites and listened to Lou tell about the ghost of a young woman who supposedly haunted the Hotel Del Coronado. Her grave has fresh flowers on it. Lou tells them that he suspects that they are put there by the hotel manager, in appreciation for the extra business her notoriety brings. They have kept her hotel suite unchanged for a hundred years, and reservations for it are booked a year in advance at a premium rate.

Finally, the group gathers at the obelisk of Alonzo Horton, thought to be the first man of European ancestry to come to San Diego. Lou describes how Horton made a great deal of money in land speculation and encouraged the development of many commercial enterprises. In tribute, his name has been given to Horton Plaza, a multistory complex of shops and restaurants in the center of San Diego that has revitalized the downtown area. While most US cities are suffering what can be called "ring around the collar," an outward flight of businesses and shopping centers to a ring on the outskirts of the urban areas, San Diego's focal point for business, shopping, entertainment, and bay-front tourist attractions is in or very near the center of the city. This includes Balboa Park, with its museums and zoo, less than two miles from downtown.

"There is so much to do and see here in San Diego," thinks Sandra with renewed delight in her decision to take a semester off. But then, her active and often self-critical mind reminds her that San Diego's wealth of opportunities for fun—especially outdoor activities—is a great benefit and a serious flaw at the same time. It is too easy, even for her, to spend her days playing outdoors, instead of accomplishing something remarkable and using her intelligence and creativity for a noble purpose.

Already, Sandra is beginning to question whether she will choose to go back to work full time next fall. How can she give up this freedom? Will she be willing to give up the time she has for reading or the early morning walks along the beach to go to work every morning at eight o'clock? For years, she has done it because her family needed the money she earned and because she believed she was making an important contribution to the school children and the community. But lately, she is not so sure. Is that the only thing she can do? Is there something else she can do that will matter even more? Has her work really made a difference? What can she still do with my life? What does she still have to learn so that she can do something important with her life?

For Sandra, who is bombarded by inner thoughts and questions like this frequently these days, her fun-loving, childlike musings are often followed by conscientious, well-meaning reflections, which are then replaced again by a more cynical voice, as they are now. Is it really possible for one person to do anything of lasting value? The social issues and problems are so enormous. There are more homeless people in San Diego now than ever before, and some of them are families. She can't do anything to protect the children of Bosnia. Migrants seem to illegally cross the Tijuana-San Diego border in an endless stress. What can she do about that? Every day there are stories in the paper about violent deaths caused by people with too many guns and too little hope. What can one person do?

As with other periods of inner turmoil, she aborts these questions by turning her attention back to the mundane details of her own relatively secure, safe middle-class life. She begins to search in her belly bag for the keys to her car as she realizes that Lou is finishing up his remarks about Alonzo Horton. Then, she begins to feel happy again. Out here in the sunshine with the enormous trees overhead and the well-cared-for lawn underfoot, who can feel despondent? Sandra can't, not for long anyway. She listens as Lou describes still another interesting opportunity, another event to mark on her calendar of things to do.

"How many of you would be interested in a walking tour of Tijuana?" asks Lou. Tentatively, Sandra raises her arm and looks around. About a third of the crowd seems to be interested. Sandra has lived in San Diego for many years but seldom goes to Tijuana. Dan sometimes jokes that he lives in North Tijuana when he is traveling in Oregon or Washington, where California residents are anathema, but he never wants to visit Tijuana himself.

When out of town guests come to visit, Sandra sometimes suggests Tijuana as an option for a day trip, but most times other tourist attractions are given priority. For the visitors who express an interest in heading south of the border, Dan cajoles them out of it by suggesting that they go to Old Town instead, which has all the color and flavors of Mexico, with clean water. But Sandra has a curiosity about Tijuana that has nothing to do with tourist attractions or cheap liquor. The caring part of Sandra that is genuinely empathetic toward other human beings wants to understand what it is like to live in Mexico, to be a Mexican woman, raising children, working for a living, planning for the future. Do Mexican women have the same hopes for their children that Sandra does? Do they crave time for themselves to paint or walk on the beach like she does? How do they cope with the low wages, the contaminated water supply?

Sandra shudders at the vision of having to put up with the conditions of poverty that are common for so many people in so many parts of the world. She thinks that maybe she should not go on the walking tour to Tijuana at all. It would be much easier not to see the details of their lives down there. In fact, seeing that reality might just make Sandra's life more difficult. Already, she is plagued by these issues and questions, especially this year when she can't count on using her ordinary excuse; she can hear her own words, spoken a number of times in the past, "Well, of course I would do more, but I'm working full time and have two children at home still."

Disconsolately, Sandra trudges away toward her car. Those reasons are no longer valid. She isn't working, and her children are away at school now. But she still doesn't have the slightest idea what she can do to change the world.

Chapter Five

THE CARETAKERS

A battered, grayish green Toyota pickup truck loaded with lawn and gardening equipment moves ponderously up the hill in a neighborhood of comfortable single-family homes built in the 1930s and 1940s. The planners of this neighborhood named each street after a poet and aligned them in alphabetical order. It is one of the prettiest neighborhoods in the city of San Diego and is inhabited by residents who spend as much time and money on their gardens as many people do on food and clothing.

There is no dominant style or architectural trend evident in the houses. Many houses are Spanish-style, made of pale cream or sandstone stucco and red tile roofs, but there are almost as many wood-frame ranch houses in pastel blues and yellows. The truck passes by a gray clapboard Cape Cod–style house and an English Tudor with leaded glass windows. Miguel Ramirez, the driver, breaks at a stop sign near the top of the hill and turns right onto Cummings Street. He stops in front of a Spanish-style house with teal blue shutters and a pair of twisted juniper trees guarding the front door.

Miguel and his assistant, Sergio, get out of the truck and unload the lawn-mower onto the sidewalk. From where they stand, the two men can see an expansive view of the entire city of San Diego and most of North Island, the naval air station separated from the city by a mile of water. Sightseeing boats and navy cruisers share the bay with the occasional sailboat. Miguel takes a moment to appreciate the view, especially the two aircraft carriers at North Island. One, the USS *Constellation*, has just returned from an eight-month tour of the Middle East. Miguel briefly imagines himself arriving home on such a ship and his wife and two children waiting eagerly and proudly to welcome him home. Then, he comes out of his reverie and tells Sergio to trim the boxwood hedges that enclose two sides of the corner lot.

Both men have the deeply tanned skin and dark brown hair of their Latin American heritage and are dressed in dark work pants and T-shirts. Miguel also wears a navy blue ball cap with USS *Kitty Hawk* inscribed on it in faded gold letters, which he bought on a ship tour several years ago. He is about thirty-five years old, although even he does not know his age for certain, since no records were kept of his birth in Honduras. He has the compact, agile body of a man who has worked hard all his life. His eyes and the rest of his facial features are handsome and appealing, especially to women. He has the engaging manner often developed by a man who has grown up confident that he is the favorite son of a strong-willed and affectionate mother.

Sergio, originally from Oaxaca, Mexico, moves at a slower pace and carries some extra weight in his belly. He is probably older than Miguel but seems content to have Miguel assign tasks for both of them. There is little need for discussion, as they come here every week and are both familiar with the lawn and gardens and what their boss, Jeff, wants them to do each week.

"Late January," Miguel thinks as he takes a rake, pruning shears, and a large empty carton around to the back of the house. The roses need cutting back. He can put off pruning the fruit trees for another week or so. He'll rake up the dead leaves today. Mrs. Seaquist—she likes to weed the vegetable garden herself. He decides that he will have time to retie some of the climbing plants and regrade the side garden, so the water flows better.

The back patio is a sunny brick area enclosed by a stucco wall covered with purple wisteria and white jasmine plants tied up to trellises. Along the back of the house, under the windows of the living and dining room, is a shallow garden of rose bushes. Miguel puts on his gloves, picks up the pruning shears, and begins to cut the woody stems of the first rose bush. A quiet man in his outward demeanor, Miguel has a restless spirit that sometimes talks to him while he works, reflecting on the plants, the work itself, his family, and his own aspirations—past, present, and future.

"Hoy, I need to cut the roses back for their own good, just as I myself was cut back when I left my home in San Pedro Sula," Miguel thinks. He is not, in his soul, the simple workman that most Norte-Americanos believe him to be. Had he, as a young boy, been encouraged to nurture his own intellect the way he does other people's roses, Miguel might have become a poet and have a street named after him.

"These dark roses remind me of the ones that grew on the plaza near my mother's house," muses Miguel, as he prunes the tough, woody branches of a mature rose bush with blooms the color of cinnamon. "It is her hopes for me that I smell, her dreams that I would somehow grow up to be a man she could count on. The hot, spicy aroma fills my whole head with hope and despair. I have become a man, but how can my mother count on me when I am living so far away?"

Turning his attention to a small, tidy bush, Miguel cups the blossom of a soft, open rose with widely spread petals blending pale shades of pink and orange together. "This rose reminds me of my wife, Rosa, and her scent enters my senses like a mist. It is gentle and warmly sweet, like honey and peach juice, as it tickles my nose and palate. She gives her scent freely and joyfully."

Moving on to a third rose plant, Miguel kneels down to tend to this knobby-kneed and gangly plant with its one bright yellow rose. "It reminds me of my own small son, my baby. It has the same magnetic odor of juicy mangos, sweet bananas, and...is it...yes, a faint hint of urine seeping out. I receive that same sensation when my son leaps into my arms at the end of my work day. I know that I should trim this plant back quite vigorously, but I also know that I will not. How can I inhibit the growth of this energetic little rose bush? It needs water and sunlight. There is no time for sleep in its busy little life."

At the sight of the next bush, Miguel catches his breath in a rush of recognition. "The full sweet scent of this glowing flesh-pink blossom causes my heart to beat with alarm. It is my daughter's almost-grown-up smell, intimate and dear to me but at the same time alarmingly unfamiliar. She is growing just like this bush, toward the sun, away from me—her father, who loves her. Doesn't she know the dangers of growing too fast? How can I protect her? How can I warn her? She laughs at my words. She thinks I'm an uneducated campesino. What can I tell her that she doesn't already know, that she hasn't already learned in that expensive private school on the hill?"

Neither Miguel's anguish nor his perceptiveness are evident at all on his round face with his bright, clear eyes and quiet smile. When Sandra Seaquist opens the door to the patio and sees Miguel trimming her roses, she notices nothing unusual. She smiles and calls out, "Hello," as she comes out the back-door, hugging her sweater to her chest.

"I was hoping you wouldn't have to do that yet," she says. "It's always a shame to see the roses cut back. Don't you agree?" She reaches down to the carton of discarded leaves and stems to take up a small bud that would never have its season.

"I saved the best blooms for you, Mrs. Seaquist," says Miguel. "They are on the table."

"Thank you, Miguel. I appreciate that. Would you like to take some home also?"

"Yes, I would. Gracias," answers Miguel. He pictures giving the flowers to Rosa. She will like them. He would also like to be able to give one of the dark red roses to his mother, but she is in Honduras, still. One of her neighbors recently telephoned to tell Miguel that his mother is ailing, with an illness that no one can name. Miguel experienced new urgency in his wish to visit his mother, or better yet, go get her and bring her north to live with his family. He left Honduras when he was only fifteen years old. His mother, Salina, had many other children to support at the time. She worked very hard. But now, her other children are grown and gone too. She is alone, being looked after from time to time by the neighbor.

Miguel and Sandra talk about the wisteria for a moment. One of the plants is also ailing, and Miguel has no idea why. It gets as much water and sun as the others, but the leaves are dry and brittle, and there are few purple blooms compared to the other vines.

"This may sound strange, but a friend told me that one of her wisteria vines seemed to pull its own roots up out of the ground this year. Have you ever seen anything like that?" asks Sandra.

"Never before," answers Miguel. "A plant committing suicide? Now that is something I have never seen or heard before."

They look with regret at the wisteria as Miguel uses his hoe to break up the soil around it and reform a depression of earth designed to capture the little rain that falls in this climate. Then, as Sandra starts to go back inside her house, he adds, somewhat shyly, "Oh, I want to tell you…my children—they like the paint sets you gave me for their Christmas."

"Oh, good." Sandra's pleasure at hearing this is very evident in her quick smile. "I remembered that you told me that they both enjoy art. Have they painted any pictures for you yet?"

"Yes, many good ones. I will bring one for you next week."

"Wonderful. Tell them I'll put it on my refrigerator." She waves good-bye and steps inside, closing the patio door behind her.

Miguel waters the wisteria, giving an extra amount to the dry, brittle plant, and then begins to tie up the new shoots, so they will continue to cover the wall with their color and perfume.

A half hour later, as Miguel and Sergio are loading the lawnmower back into the truck bed, the front door of the house opens, and Mr. Seaquist comes out carrying a suitcase in one hand and a heavy, black flight bag in the other. He is about the same size as Miguel but appears to be larger. Perhaps it is the navy blue uniform he wears with four bright gold stripes on the sleeves and a pair of gold wings on the front pocket. On his head is the hat of an officer, with gold braid on the brim. Miguel stands up straighter but keeps his eyes cast down at the sight of this commanding uniform. The first time he saw Mr. Seaquist wearing it, he thought it was for the US Navy, but now, seeing it so close, Miguel can see that it isn't a navy uniform; there are differences in the jacket and the crest on the hat.

"Still, it is a uniform of much importance," thinks Miguel. He is probably a pilot for an airline company. Miguel's spirit suddenly feels intensely shy and ill at ease; meanwhile, Sergio seems not to have noticed the man at all. He slams shut the truck's tailgate, picks up the carton of grass and stems, and takes them to the back gate to put them in the garbage can. Miguel busies himself at the truck, loading the rake and hoe, but keeps watching out of the corners of his eyes as Mr. Seaquist walks toward the driveway, turns away from the gardener without a word or glance, and methodically loads his luggage into his car, a dark green sedan.

He is going to the airport, no doubt, thinks Miguel, as Mr. Seaquist starts up his car and drives away. From there he can fly anywhere in the world, perhaps even to Honduras. Miguel shakes his head in disbelief. How can it be that this man can wear this uniform and fly his airplane to my own country, when I cannot go myself? I cannot go to see my mother, and I cannot bring her here.

Miguel has completed the job of loading the truck and reorganized the way the mower is situated in the bed. Sergio gets into the passenger seat, and Miguel finds the truck keys in the pocket of his work pants and climbs into the driver's seat. He starts the truck and drives away from the house. He takes the truck back to Jeff and gets his own car, an aging, rust-red Pinto with no front headlight on the left side. Then he drives north through Mission Bay to pick up his wife from the house where she works as a housekeeper.

Up a winding street near the top of Mount Soledad, he drives into a cul-de-sac with two houses. One of them, a long, low, gray wood house trimmed with white painted shutters is set on a large level lot. Behind the house, in the distance, Miguel can see the Pacific Ocean gleaming, a sapphire blue today, although each day it is different. The driveway is made of red brick and curves around to the front of the house.

Inside the house, Rosa is rearranging a collection of shells and knickknacks on a bookshelf in the enclosed porch. She has her sweater on and is ready to go home for the day. When she sees Miguel's car, Rosa calls good-bye to Mrs. Blumenthal, who is sitting in the living room on the couch, doing needlepoint. Despite her ninety-four years, her eyesight is excellent. She can do jigsaw puzzles, read, and do needlework, although she usually asks Rosa to thread her needles for her.

"I wish you would take that painting with you," calls Mrs. Blumenthal.

"I cannot do that, Mrs. B," answers Rosa, as she walks outside toward Miguel's car. "It is too big for my house. It belongs in a museum."

Rosa came to work for the Blumenthals ten years ago, when she first came to San Diego. At that time Mr. Blumenthal was alive, and Rosa only came once a week; but after he died five years ago, Mrs. B asked Rosa to come every day to keep her company as much as to clean her house. It is an easy house to keep clean, but there are many things that need dusting and polishing and rearranging. The living room has vaulted ceilings and a view of the ocean from the long western wall. On the fireplace mantle stand two matching Sevres vases and an imposing Seth Thomas clock. A credenza in the dining room is filled with crystal so thin that Rosa thinks it looks like cellophane paper and china that has fleurs-de-lis hand-painted with fourteen-karat gold.

Lillie Blumenthal has outlived all of her family and most of her friends. She lives alone in the house she shared with her husband since the 1950s, when they moved to San Diego from Aurora, Illinois. With no children of her own, and no living relatives, Lillie has to make all decisions on her own and take the steps necessary to look after her welfare, even to the point of anticipating the time when she can no longer take care of herself.

She remembers the day that Rosa first came to work for her. She was a very young woman, but Lillie felt from the very beginning that she could depend on Rosa. There is strength in Rosa's thin arms, and Lillie, who trusts her own instincts completely, feels certain that the kindness in Rosa's eyes is genuine, not something that can be applied with a makeup brush. Rosa's wavy black hair, held back with a large barrette, shows off her clear skin and clear wide-set eyes.

In contrast, Lillie has short white hair with a permanent wave. Her skin has grown very pale over the years, and she attempts to brighten it with a touch of rouge. Rosa has tried to show her how to use a brush to apply the color to her cheeks, to spread out the color and make it appear more natural, but Lillie prefers the cream products she learned to use as a young woman. She has remained very slender and stands straight and tall, except for a mild stoop in her shoulders.

Rosa shows a natural understanding of how Lillie's old muscles and ligaments get stiff from sitting too long in one place. Rosa often invents reasons for Lillie to stand up and walk from one place to another, to see a crack in a plate or to examine a new flower on a plant outdoors. Rosa also seems to know what her employer has an appetite for, even when Lillie doesn't think she is hungry at all. On days when Lillie seems a bit overtired or achy, Rosa makes flan. The cool, slippery sweet custard is as comforting to Lillie as her mother's tapioca and rice puddings were when she was a small child in the large brick house in Illinois.

Over the years, Lillie's trust in Rosa has grown to the point that she now has her own key to the house. Rosa shows respect for Mrs. B's art objects and jewelry but seems to have no personal interest in them. They are honest with each other about their likes and dislikes, and tell each other their opinions about news events. Lillie thinks that NAFTA, for example, is a timely and expedient way to create a large unified market that can compete with the Japanese. But Rosa isn't so sure. She tells Mrs. B about her friends from Tijuana who work in the factories known as *maquiladoras* and their fears that NAFTA will simply mean longer hours for them at very low pay.

Oprah is Lillie's favorite program, while Rosa prefers the daytime serials. If Mrs. B falls asleep during the afternoon, she is likely to wake up to soap operas in Spanish on channel 12, the television station from Tijuana. Lillie peels potatoes or polishes the silver while she watches the romantic melodramas unfold. Lillie thinks that the Mexican soap operas are beginning to look more and more like those in the United States. In just the past year or so, the sets of the Mexican dramas have become more opulent, and the clothes and hairstyles of the Mexican actors and actresses are identical to those worn in the programs from New York City. Lillie has seen many social and political changes in her lifetime, and she says that she would not be at all surprised to see a blending of the Mexican and American cultures and economies in the next century.

For many years, Lillie and Rosa had a relationship that was perhaps more typical of an employer and her employee. But, gradually, Lillie began to depend on seeing Rosa's smile as much as she did on the clean, ironed clothes or shiny bathroom tile and faucets. When Rosa once asked if she could bring her daughter, Maria, with her the next day, because the neighbor who cared for the little girl was ill, Lillie had misgivings. She wasn't used to children. Would the little girl take the books off the shelves or rearrange her collection of antique snuff boxes? Would she make noise and mischief? But Lillie's natural curiosity outweighed these concerns. "Bring her for a day, Rosa," she said. "We'll see how it goes."

Maria was only three or four years old at the time. She surprised Lillie most of all with her shyness and her grace. She was used to seeing her mother work and did not attempt to distract her. Instead, she sat on the floor, as close to her mother as she could get, and quietly played with a frayed stuffed donkey or a string of clay beads. Mrs. B worried that the beads might be coated with a lead based paint and wanted to take them away, but she thought she had no right to interfere. Who was she to tell a mother how to take care of her child? She who waited in vain for twenty years to produce a child.

Looking through a jewelry box on her dresser, Lillie found a string of pearls on a sturdy string and offered them to the child in exchange for the clay beads. Rosa would not hear of it. "No, Mrs. B, we cannot take these valuable objects. Please put them away."

"But Rosa," Lillie tried to insist, "these are not valuable to me. I thought perhaps the beads she has might have lead in the paint. Perhaps you are right, though. These pearls are not a good thing for her to have either. If the string breaks, she can swallow one."

"I don't know about lead in the paint. What is it? It is not good for children to eat?"

"Yes, that's right, Rosa. Lead can harm children. It can damage their brains."

Rosa snatched the beads away from her child and threw them into the garbage bin beneath the sink. The child looked at both women with wide eyes but did not question their right to take away her plaything. Lillie put the pearls in her pocket and opened a cupboard to get a box of cookies. She offered one to the child, who reached out her small, chubby, brown hand to take it from Lillie. When their fingers met, a current passed between them as well. Rosa and Miguel might call it the spirit of God, but Lillie experienced it as an electric shock that roused her dormant maternal feelings. It was over in a brief second, but for the rest of the day, the child watched Lillie with great interest, and Lillie found herself watching back.

When Rosa and Maria got ready to leave that day, ten years ago, Rosa told Lillie that she would not have to bring Maria the next week because she had located another neighbor who would take her. But Maria let go of her mother's hand and reached for Lillie. Without thought or analysis, Lillie leaned down and hugged the small girl to her chest, smelling the unfamiliar but exceedingly pleasant oil from her hair, and did not want to let her go.

"Please bring her whenever you need to, Rosa," she said, as she stood up again and watched them depart. "She is no trouble. In fact, Rosa, would you understand this, if I say, please do bring her with you? I prefer it." In this way, Lillie Blumenthal, a woman who had been childless for eighty-four years, took an opportunity that she knew would never come again.

The days of Maria's daytime visits are over now, and have been for a number of years. When she reached the age of six, she began school and now comes to visit Mrs. B only during school holidays. Still, the strong bond between the woman and the child has persisted. They are always happy to see each other and enjoy spending time together sitting on the couch reading picture books or gardening in the back yard.

Last year, Rosa confided in Mrs. B her concerns about sending Maria to the school in their East San Diego neighborhood, where the tough, street-wise kids from the neighborhood frightened Maria, and sometimes threatened their teachers as well. Rosa and Miguel worried about Maria when she had to walk home alone. Lillie suggested that Rosa call Roycemore, the private school down the hill from her house, to find out whether there were scholarships available for Latinas. At first, Rosa was reluctant to do so. She didn't know what to say on the telephone. But Mrs. B helped her to practice the questions and stood near the phone as she talked. Application papers were sent to Maria Ramirez, in care of the Blumenthal residence. As the Blumenthal family had endowed the school with a considerable amount of money over the years, it was no surprise to Mrs. B when Rosa told her that Maria had been accepted to the school on a full scholarship, but, this one time, she withheld the whole truth and just displayed her delight that Maria would have this opportunity.

The opportunity, however, is not without its price. On this January evening, as Miguel and Rosa go to pick up their daughter at school, they pull their battered Pinto into the parking lot and park it between a Jaguar and a BMW. Maria hurries toward them in haste, opens the back door of the car, climbs in, and slams the door shut.

"Let's get out of here," she says, dropping her books and papers on the floor with a thud.

"Qué pasa, Maria?" asks her mother. Miguel starts the car and backs out of the parking space, watching the carefully dressed woman in the Jaguar watch him.

"Speak English, Mama," answers Maria. Her voice is quiet but grim. She looks away from her mother as she speaks.

"You seem upset. It upsets me to see you this way. What is it that happened for you?"

"Oh, Mama, you cannot understand."

"Try to tell us, Maria," Miguel says, as he turns right out of the parking lot and heads toward Highway 5, the major freeway that bisects San Diego and then continues to the border between the United States and Baja California, Mexico.

"I was invited to a party," says Maria, in a barely audible voice.

"Invited to a party? That is good news, no?"

"No, Papa, that is not good news. How can I go to one of their parties? I won't do it."

"Never mind, Maria, there is no need for you to go if you don't want to," says her mother.

"Who invited you, Maria?" asks Miguel, suddenly concerned about something other than Maria's pride. "Is it a boy?"

"No, Papa, it is a girl, but boys are also invited."

"Well, then, you are right not to go. I do not want you to go if boys are going."

"What do you mean? You are saying I can't go?" Maria curls her body up into a tight ball on the back seat of the car and begins to sob. For a few minutes, there is no other sound. No one knows what to say.

Chapter Six

EARTH MOVEMENTS

Sandra wakes up, startled. Downstairs the tall case clock in the living room chimes four times. Is that what woke her? Then she thinks that Amigo jumped on her bed. Was he trying to warn her about something—a fire or an intruder? But, no, the cat is a heavy, dormant weight near her feet. Where is Dan? Is he in the bathroom or getting his uniform on to go to work? No, Dan isn't here; he left yesterday, to fly a four-day trip.

Sandra gets up, looks out the window at the patio below, and seeing nothing alarming outside, heads for the bathroom, where she takes an aspirin, drinks a glass of water, and goes back to bed. The aspirin has the effect it usually does for her; it calms down her jumpy muscles and jittery nerves enough so that she can fall asleep again. She sleeps deeply and dreams about walking through an apartment building filled with people who are visiting from other places and are, for no explainable reason, delayed. They have journeys they want to continue, but, instead, they are inexplicably detained in this place for an indefinite amount of time. In the dream, Sandra sees herself as the manager or caretaker of this place. She is somehow responsible for the well-being of the visitors but is not sure what she can do for them.

As the dream continues, Sandra visits several different apartments and encounters people who are variously sad, angry, elated, and indifferent to her. She attempts to find out what it is that they want and where they are going, but she is unable to get any information that makes sense to her. An angry man shouts invectives at her with a face so red and angry that it is distorted in size and shape. The mouth is huge in comparison to the rest of his face, and as he speaks, spittle sprays on her and hangs in strings from his lower lip and jaw. Sandra runs away from this frightening apparition with her heart pounding and her breath ragged.

Down the hall, in another unit, a sad, very old woman with long white hair, wearing a very thin nightdress, lies on a cot with her back to the door. She has curled into a fetal position and will not or cannot turn to look at Sandra. Nothing Sandra can say, even in the softest and warmest voice, rouses the old woman. In fact, she seems to diminish and become smaller and slighter as Sandra stands looking down at her. With a heaviness in her limbs, Sandra makes herself walk away and close the door.

She next encounters a young boy who is standing in the hallway by himself, laughing with such force that he seems unable to stop at all. As Sandra approaches him, he doubles over with laughter and holds his stomach with an expression on his face that seems more like pain than joy. Sandra does not feel that she has the power to interrupt him, and she passes by him without being noticed.

As she walks away, her own power seems to be leaking out of her body like helium out of a balloon. She feels weak in a profound way, unable to drag her legs another step, unable to call for help herself, unable to lift a hand to call attention to her plight.

Then, with enormous relief, she feels the bristly tongue of her cat, Amigo, and sees that it is morning and that she is in her own bed in her sunny, east-facing bedroom. The sunlight pours through the glass and bathes her dream-sodden limbs with its healing heat. She is able to stretch, unclench her jaw, and open it in a nourishing yawn. She rolls her shoulders around and shrugs them up and down, releasing some of the tension that has gathered like a heap of gravel in her upper back and neck.

The cat stretches too and leaps off the bed to the windowsill, where he begins to clean her front paws. Sandra gets out of bed and smooths out the worn, but still lovely, patchwork cotton quilt that was hand-stitched by her grand-mother. She mentally assesses the messages that are being asserted by her body, and creates some priorities out of the jumbled transmissions: go to the bath-room, brush her teeth, wash her face, comb her hair, find her slippers, change her nightgown for a fleece jumpsuit, go downstairs, start the water for tea, feed Amigo, open the blinds, cut a banana on some granola, get the newspaper off the front lawn, pour milk on her cereal, and turn on the radio.

The headlines on the front page of the newspaper describe a raise in fees planned for the state university system, the mayor's state of the city message describing the progress on the new downtown central library, and a story about a bitter cold wave gripping the northeastern states, breaking records for cold temperatures, of twenty to forty degrees below zero. Sandra looks up from this story and looks again out her doorway, past the twisted juniper trees that grow on either side of the walk, and appreciates anew the soft, warm dew that has formed in the night and the slight chill in the area shaded by the house. By all appearances, it will be another wonderful day, with a promise of sunlight and sweet smells from the flowers and herbs that grow year-round in her yard.

When Sandra returns to the kitchen, the water is boiling. She selects two Earl Grey tea bags from a painted tin and pours the steamy water over them into her favorite white-and-blue teapot. It begins to release its bergamot scent almost immediately, and Sandra purposely allows herself the luxury of inhaling that aroma before she adds a generous dollop of honey to the pot and replaces the lid. After all these details of her comfortable morning ritual have been completed, she reaches up to turn on the portable radio that stands on the tiled shelf above her sink.

"The death toll stands at two hundred but is feared to go much higher. Rescuers are finding the roads impassable because of bridges and overpasses that collapsed on the roadways. At this time, the damage appears to be greatest in the mountain villages west of Mexico City itself. The earthquake is thought to be the same type of subduction quake that occurred in 1985, but not quite as severe. This one measured 6.6 on the Richter scale and struck at 4:01 this morning."

Sandra's first feeling is one of relief that the earthquake struck so far away—that again, as in other recent catastrophes, she and her home have been spared. Then, she has a chilling thought. Where was Dan sleeping when the earthquake struck? He left Saturday for a four-day trip with three nighttime layovers: one each in San Francisco, Mexico City, and Denver. Where was he sleeping last night?

With a thudding heart, Sandra looks for the UNICEF desk calendar on the telephone table, where both Dan and she record their appointments and plans. Wednesday, February 23, shows "Denver," written in Dan's handwriting. Sandra relaxes her chest muscles and exhales the breath she has been holding, with an audible sigh. But then, she realizes with renewed alarm that today is Wednesday and that it is tonight that Dan is scheduled to spend in Denver. Her eyes travel back to the calendar with resistance. She turns the page back to Tuesday, February 22, where Dan has written "Mex. C."

Her eyes travel to the telephone. Can she call him? He usually stays at a Hilton or Marriott near the airport. But in some locales, she has heard him say, they go into the city for their layovers. She looks up the number for his flight operations crew desk. They would know where he is. Maybe they will even know if he is safe. She dials the crew desk number but gets only a recorded message that says, "Due to an irregular condition, this number is busy. Please try your call again later." After several repeated attempts, Sandra realizes that the flight operations system is already too overloaded to accept her call.

Taking her teacup into the living room, Sandra turns on the television set. The first scene she sees is a stucco apartment building collapsed like a set of children's blocks onto the flattened first floor. Suddenly, a brief memory of her dream recurs in her head. The details of the dream are already evaporating, but some images remain: the apartment building, people needing her, an angry man, her limbs feeling like jelly, her inability to help. She suddenly sees the old woman curled up on the cot with her back to the door. Was it her own mother, who died last January? Sandra feels sudden tears spew up, starting from deep inside her body and erupting from her eyes with a force of grief that she has not felt for some time, that she thought had passed several months ago.

Sandra's mother, Lizbeth, died of breast cancer at the San Diego Hospice almost exactly a year ago. During Lizbeth's last few weeks of life, Sandra tried to care for her mother at home, but she was unable to do anything to stop the progress of the disease and had to watch helplessly as the cancer literally surfaced like small volcanoes on the skin of Lizbeth's wasted and scarred chest. Pus and blood had to be cleansed from these wounds twice a day, and Sandra learned from the hospice home-care nurses how to change the bandages. She tried to support her mother emotionally as well as physically, just as she had tried to do during all of her growing-up years.

Sandra was the oldest of four children, the only one who understood why Lizbeth divorced her husband and took her children across the country to start again. Sandra watched helplessly, for the most part, as Lizbeth worked two jobs to support their family. She worked as a secretary at the city hall during the daytime, but as expenses mounted, she took on a night job as a waitress in a restaurant that served "broasted" chicken. The happiest times Sandra can remember were late at night, helping her mother count her tips. But even with the tips, there was always tension about which of the overdue bills to pay and which to leave for another month.

As Sandra sobs silently, burning tears coursing down her cheeks, she surrenders herself to her feelings of grief for her mother, fear for Dan's safety, and her own sense of isolation from reality. Meanwhile, the television network ends its brief report on the earthquake and turns to a series of commercials for toothpaste, coffee, and an allergy remedy. When the morning news continues, the reporters have turned to other stories of more interest to its viewers: the top grossing movie of the week, the surf report, and a possible injury to a hockey player that might keep him sidelined from tonight's game in Toronto.

Frustrated, Sandra punches the remote until she again sees scenes of destruction from the earthquake. The pictures are grainy and unprofessional looking. The reporter is speaking in Spanish as he describes the scene. Sandra looks at the channel number she has selected. It is channel 12, broadcasting from Tijuana. Although she cannot understand many words, Sandra watches with her full attention as residents of Mexico City appear to be telling stories of awaking in the night to the sudden convulsive movement of the earth, causing the plaster walls to disintegrate and floors to buckle beneath their beds. A young father, holding the hand of his son, makes gestures that Sandra interprets to mean that he tried to open the door, but it was jammed shut. He had literally punched a hole with his fist through door to get to his child.

Sandra can vividly imagine the fear felt by the young father. Ever since her own first child was born more than twenty years ago, she is aware of having a heightened sensitivity to any story or event involving young children or parents in any sort of danger. It is as if she feels their pain and fear herself. As she watches stories of this latest disaster, her sudden tears end, replaced by shivers of concern and by curiosity to learn all the details of how people in the quake zone feel—what they experienced and how it has changed their lives.

Sometimes this very same combination of empathy and curiosity causes Sandra to doubt her own goodness as a person. Is she just a thrill seeker? Is she no different from the people who actually buy the tabloid newspapers at the supermarket? She herself only reads the headlines—and those surreptitiously—as she unloads groceries onto the checkout counter. She knows that if an earthquake struck a city in the United States, like the one in LA a few years ago, she and most of her compatriots would be glued to the television set for several days and evenings and would read voraciously the newspaper accounts of the earthquake, especially stories that described people's fear and outrage and accounts of people reaching out to their neighbors in acts of unusual courage or friendship. The fact that this disaster has struck another country probably means that the coverage will be brief ten-second summaries of death counts on the evening news.

She is glad she has discovered this foreign channel on her television set. It is the first time she has ever paused at this channel, which is located between her public television channel and an LA channel. She watches the faces of people, not very much different from her, who happen to live a few hundred miles south, whose lives have been changed by this disaster. They tell about losing family members, their homes, and possessions, while she sits here watching them from her own secure house, drinking her favorite tea in her favorite mug. She identifies strongly with the fear on people's faces and wonders if they are now afraid to go back into their houses. She would be. If she lived through an earthquake as severe as this one, she would probably spend the rest of the night outdoors, in her yard or in her car. Sandra has a sudden vision of returning to her home and seeing it filled with debris and fragments of her family's belongings.

The telephone interrupts her voyeurism, if that is what it is; she still isn't sure about that, but she takes the precaution of muting the television before answering the phone so that whoever is on the other line will not picture her here, glued to the television set.

"Sandra, are you all right?" It is Dan. He is fine. The quake jolted him awake, but the hotel where he is staying is not damaged, and he has just eaten his breakfast in the cafe, before calling her.

"Of course I'm all right. What about you?"

"I have to say, it was not pleasant to feel this building shake like it did. It was kind of a bucking movement, maybe what riding a camel must feel like."

Dan's answers reassure her. The hotel where he and the other US flight crews stay is in excellent shape. It is one of the newest buildings in the city, with the latest building codes, built after the last major earthquake, and selected for that reason by the hotel committee of his union. From his window, he cannot see any signs of massive destruction. Sandra begins to relax and believes that everything is going to be okay.

"When do you leave for home, or do you still have to go to Denver tonight?"

"I don't know when we'll get out of here. They've closed the airport for now. I think they're assessing the damage, although most of the worst of it seems to be west of here. I have to stand by until the company tells me what they want me to do next. Meanwhile, I just have to wait here or at the airport."

"I'm sure glad you're not hurt," says Sandra. She can feel her bones and muscles lighten as the tension and fear in them leaves her body in waves. "But what about aftershocks?"

"They're severe, that's for sure, but nothing I can't handle," answers Dan, in the voice he uses when he wants to reassure passengers that a departure delay was caused by a malfunction in a cockpit instrument, but that it is nothing to worry about, nothing he and the mechanics cannot handle with ease. "Sit back and relax, and we'll be on our way to our destination in a very short time," Sandra can almost hear him say.

"Dan, you know the funniest thing happened. I woke up this morning at four o'clock. It was as if I knew something happened to you...or one of the kids."

"Four o'clock? Interesting, but you know what, Sandy? We're an hour ahead here. So your four o'clock would have been an hour after the earthquake here. It would have been five o'clock here."

"Oh, I guess you're right. I thought for a minute that we just had some kind of ESP thing between us. But I guess not." Sandra pauses. "Well, what were you doing at five o'clock?"

"I was probably back to sleep by that time. Listen, Sandy, I've got to run. My copilot is knocking on the door. We're going to the airport to talk to dispatch. I'll call you again when I find out what the plan is."

"Okay." Sandra is reluctant to let him hang up the phone. The connection is good, and she wants to keep hearing the sound of his voice. "I hope you don't have to stay a few more days."

"I don't suppose you want to fly down here and keep me company?" They both laugh at this ridiculous idea; that Sandra would even think of putting herself in the path of a major earthquake is absurd to both of them. Their laughter dissipates even more of their tension, and they end their conversation, each reassured that the other is still there for the other, unhurt, and that their lives are essentially undamaged and unchanged by this arbitrary calamity.

When she hangs up the phone, Sandra looks around her high-ceilinged living room with its six multipaned windows and carefully chosen furniture, all pristine and unmoved. She thinks about the valuable, antique cherry tall case clock that she and Dan recently brought back from Pennsylvania. They went to Lancaster to visit Dan's parents before Christmas and brought the clock back with them. The clock has been in the Seaquist family for many generations and was given to Dan by his father, Simon, when he and Dan's mother, Josephine, finally made the decision to sell their family home and move into a retirement center.

Sandra knows that Simon Seaquist probably found it very difficult to part with the clock, having owned and cared for its internal workings for more than forty years. He was more than a little fearful about having it transported all the way to California. But the Seaquists are not people who discuss their feelings; in fact they are people who make a very special point of not discussing or even hinting at their feelings. So much so, in fact, that the transfer of ownership of the clock was neither given nor received in any real sense, as it occurred with no hint of emotion. Simon simply announced at dinner the first evening of their visit, "You'll take the clock with you this trip, Dan." And Sandra watched as her husband calmly accepted this statement without even saying thank you. The two men talked instead of moving companies and how to pack the works of the clock with down pillows and Styrofoam into a carryon bag. At the end of the visit, Dan carried the clock mechanism, face, and the brass key with them on the airplane from Philadelphia. The weights, case, and pendulum were shipped on a truck and arrived a week later.

In the predominantly Mennonite community where he grew up, Dan developed his capacity for stoicism and providing for others early in his life. As a young boy, he had a paper route before school and a lawn-mowing or snow-shoveling business after school. He saved most of his money because there were few things that he wanted to buy. He used his money, instead, to help with his own school expenses and wanted, at first, to buy things for his mother. But his mother had her own things. She has a collection of rare, antique cut-glass vases, pitchers, and stemware that she keeps in a cherry cabinet. The silver tea and coffee services she displays, but rarely uses, have been in her family for many years.

Despite her attachment to the silver, crystal, and china, Josephine showed little interest in cooking and rarely entertained. Frequently she served her family the same meal over and over again and did not seem to think that this was unusual. Dan remembered one winter when they had oatmeal at every breakfast for several months. On most Sunday afternoons, after a long worship service at the Mennonite church, Josephine prepared well-done roast beef, green beans with ham, mashed potatoes, soft white rolls, butter, corn relish, and watermelon pickles. Then she would set the dining table with her best linen tablecloth and napkins, silverware with an S on each handle, the good china, and her cut-glass stemware and serving pieces.

At the table, Simon cut and served the meat, and Josephine spooned carefully measured portions of vegetables onto each plate. Everyone at the table received exactly the same amount of every food, and no one began eating until everyone was served and a prayer was said. Dinner conversations were some-what difficult, as many topics were tacitly forbidden by longstanding custom. Political observations, questioning or comparing religions, difficulties at work, struggles with a relationship, worries about money, social problems, and per-sonal hopes and ambitions were simply never mentioned at the table. If asked why these kinds of conversations were disallowed, Josephine was quick to point out that it would not aid digestion to talk about such unpleasant matters at the dinner table.

Descriptions of the weather—current, past, or forecast—were encouraged, as were compliments about the tenderness of the meat or the piping hotness of the dinner rolls. Stories about the condition of the paint on the house, the health of the grass or tomatoes in the summer, and good buys at grocery or depart-ment stores were also allowed. Sandra gradually learned, as she was inducted into the family more than twenty years before, that conversations at her in-laws' house must be polite, unstrained by differences of opinions, and designed to sup-port the Seaquists' illusion that their own particular lives were forever protected from danger, disease, and change. When Sandra occasionally tested the family's resolve on this issue by trying to talk about a troubled child in her classroom or a concern about the inequalities she observed in the educational system, her comments were invariably met by Josephine's downcast eyes and a small, patient shrug of Simon's shoulders.

After a brief silence, which was how the family dealt with this type of social error, or during any other awkward pause in the conversation at the table, Josephine would make a valiant attempt to smooth out the ruffled surface of their lives by enthusiastically lecturing on the family history of each piece of cut glass on the table, noting the quality and value of each object in detail. If encour-aged, she would go into the living room and bring back a book on American glassware to show pictures of the pieces she owned, and identify which items were registered patterns.

Yes, his mother had her own things. The dime store vases that Dan had cho-sen for her birthday, or pottery cups he made for her on Mother's Day, were received with such politeness that he understood quite early in life that gifts are prickly things. Potentially, they were a source of embarrassment more than any-thing else; they brought the threat of discomfort to both the giver and receiver. He saved even more money after that. He decided, as a very young man, that it was safer to use his money to provide the basics and avoid generous and sponta-neous actions.

FREE TRADE

When Dan married Sandra, they had difficulty reconciling their very different expectations about birthdays and holidays. In the same years that Dan had learned to withhold his offerings in order to avoid controversy, Sandra babysat and worked in a catalogue store to earn money for her expenses. With her extra cash, she learned to seek out unusual presents and plan special events in an effort to take care of her mother and her sister and brothers by surprising them with gifts and celebrations that took their minds off their worries, at least temporarily. She bought trick ice cubes and magic cards for her brothers, horse statues for her sister, and beautiful scarves and earrings for her mother. When her mother had to work, Sandra made birthday cakes for each member of the family, trying each year to create a coconut cake for her mother that would earn a warm smile and special hug.

As young adults, in their own home, Dan had wanted to make as little fuss as possible about their birthdays and anniversaries, but Sandra insisted on celebrating each event with cakes and balloons and a happy heap of presents wrapped in a variety of papers and ribbons. Dan acquiesced to her greater need, or more accurately, to her ferocious and eloquent pleadings, in this matter. Over the years, he began to enjoy the hoopla of birthday parties, Sandra-style. He now admits freely that he enjoys being the one surprised or feted on his birthday, and he lets himself get caught up in Sandra's extravagant shopping and party planning for Christmas and New Year.

Sandra recalls the first time she and Dan flew to Pennsylvania with their son, Peter, who was then only a few months old, to show him off to his grandparents. Simon and Josephine approved of their new grandson and noticed his resemblance to ancestors and relatives on both sides of the family. Josephine declined to hold him because her hands were wet from doing the dishes or because he was sleeping so soundly that it would be a shame to disturb him, but she did smile and give him several nice pats on his well-covered bottom. Simon was more effusive than Dan could ever remember him being. His eyes got moist when he saw Peter for the first time, and he told Dan and Sandra with obvious sincerity, "Now, your real life will begin."

In most marriages, a time comes when the couple realizes that they are free to choose their own values and make their own traditions, that they are no longer bound by the expectations of their birth families. That moment arrived for Sandra and Dan, with sudden insight and lasting consequences, when they were flying back to San Diego from this tense and unsatisfying visit. An hour or so after they were airborne, Sandra leaned against Dan's arm and held their son close to both of their faces, so that they could both feel his silky skin and smell his damp, milky, pear-like scent.

"Dan," she asked with a hopeful rush of energy, "what do you really want for Peter when he grows up? I mean, what do you hope for, when you think about him grown up? Do you want him to fly planes like you do or be an artist or become president or what?"

For Dan, who normally takes time to think about questions like this, because he first searches for hidden meanings and tries to decide if there is a right answer he is supposed to come up with, the pause between her question and his response was unusually brief. It was almost as if he had been thinking about the question before she asked it.

"I want him to want to come home for Christmas!" Dan said with an assured urgency that was rare for him. The words needed no further explanation or interpretation. Sandra knew exactly what Dan meant. She could picture herself, Dan, and their children, in the Christmases of their future, in comfortable rooms that would be filled with happy, loud exchanges of things and ideas and expressions of love and fear and pain and delight. As he stroked Peter's small head in his large hand, Sandra could tell that Dan was imagining a very similar picture, and the moment changed the course of their lives.

Together, they worked to create a family atmosphere that encouraged celebrations of each person's accomplishments, including great landings, swim team victories, or Sandra's recent success at persuading other committee members to select a literature-based curriculum for the school district. The next big celebration will hopefully be for Peter's acceptance to medical school. In addition, discussions of politics and philosophical dilemmas are occasionally heard at their dinner table, and Sandra is secretly delighted when their sons articulate their opinions with such force that they make her change her own mind.

Coming out of her reverie about her own life, Sandra confronts the scene of the earthquake on the television screen again. She sees the tear-stained face of a dark-haired woman weeping as she carries a quilt and a bag of her belongings away from her damaged apartment building. Sandra switches off the television, rinses out her teacup, and gets out the telephone book to find the number of the Red Cross, intent on sending a check to the Mexico earthquake relief fund immediately.

Chapter Seven

HIGHER EDUCATION

Hillcrest, just north of downtown San Diego, is the part of town that most freely encourages self-expression and rewards risk taking. Architecturally, the area is an attractive jumble of neon, glittered storefronts and quiet, musty "shoppes" on the long, east-west thoroughfares of University, Washington, and Robinson Avenues. Craftsman-style bungalows and aging Victorian houses are juxtaposed next to trendy restaurants, gay bars, hot dog stands, flower stands, coffeehouses, and family-owned stationery stores.

Everyone in Chicago and Boston knows that Southern Californians don't work much. They are all out surfing or jogging or flying kites. When they are indoors, however, there is much evidence that one thing San Diegans are doing is reading. Bookstores abound in San Diego. In one block in the Midway district, a few blocks from the "All Nude! All Bare!" bars that sprang up years ago to entice the new recruits at the nearby naval training center and remain today because of civic inertia, there are three enormous chain bookstores. Open from nine in the morning to eleven at night every day, all three are apparently thriving, as their filled parking lots and Help Wanted signs attest.

In Hillcrest, and its upscale neighbor, Mission Hills, there are no chain stores, but dozens of book stores thrive, apparently because they have discovered that specialization is as lucrative in the book trade as it is in medicine. Within a few blocks of each other are Grounds for Murder, The Cook's Bookshop, The Controversial Bookstore, and The Blue Door (specializing in women's issues).

Most of the coffeehouses provide customers with cases of books and foreign magazines to encourage long, leisurely stays over several cups of coffee. Tables and espresso machines at The Study, take second place to cases filled with well-thumbed copies of Ellery Queen and Zane Grey and frayed paperbacks by Langston Hughes and T. S. Eliot. Hillcrest patrons have come to expect nothing less. In fact, they expect quite a bit more. If a prospective coffeehouse proprietor expects to make a success with just an open mike, fresh roasted coffee beans, and a selection of desserts imported from La Jolla's French Pastry Shop or Sam's Home Made Cheese Cakes, he or she is likely to be out of business within months. There is fierce competition in Hillcrest within the coffeehouse trade.

On a sparkling evening in late March, just after a rare rainfall has cleaned away all particles of smog and pollen from the air, Hanna Lenhart and Sandra Seaquist come out of the Hillcrest Cinema and walk down the curved stucco stairway to ground level.

"Look up," Hanna says, and points. The two women stop on the stairway, blocking the passage of other moviegoers behind them without even noticing. The clouds are parting like stage curtains, revealing Orion, with Betelgeuse on his right shoulder, against a cobalt sky.

"Let's walk somewhere."

"Great, forget the car. We'll come back for it later."

"How 'bout Better Worlde Galleria?" suggests Hanna, who lives in this neighborhood, in a small, gray, two-bedroom craftsman-style house only a half block from University Avenue.

"Perfect," responds Sandra, bounding down the rest of the steps with a burst of happy excitement. As much as she enjoys family life, she also requires periodic evenings out with women friends to brighten up a week. Dan is out of town, flying to Orlando and then south to Mexico and Guatemala this week, leaving her free to take long baths at four o'clock in the afternoon, have a dinner of salad and bread, and meet her good friend for an evening out.

The two women drink in the fresh, still, damp night air with as much gusto as they would a good glass of Napa merlot, as they walk west on Washington for the eight or ten blocks to Mission Hills. Turning right on Goldfinch Street, they arrive at the Better Worlde, a gray frame two-story house converted into a commercial establishment. A half dozen wrought iron tables and chairs are set about in front of the shop, surrounded by an iron railing. Inside, the women are greeted by a pleasantly bewildering array of choices. Straight ahead is a tall, glass case filled with pastries and topped with large jars of biscotti. Espresso machines clink and hiss behind the counter, releasing their steaming Italian roasted smells.

A large room on the left has been turned into a boutique filled with cotton madras garments from India, beaded belts and scarves from Morocco, one-of-a-kind earrings collaged from shellacked paper, and homemade soaps with no animal fat. To the right are magazine racks filled with newspapers and glossy tabloids from France, Germany, and Italy. Behind all three front rooms is the area set aside for performances by local talent, an eclectic series of events including pantomime, blues, and, on Monday nights, grand opera, among others.

Tonight a woman guitarist is playing soulful tunes that seem to focus on a recent depression she has survived, but just barely. "I feels the blues blow through the town; my world is spinning upside down."

The bitter words and melancholy music make Sandra reflect on the dichotomy she often observes among many Californians. They are either on top of the world or in the dumps, rarely in between. Sandra has noticed over the years that long-time residents of California seem to believe that they are entitled to joy. If joy eludes them for any length of time; if, for example, they remain single beyond a few months, contract an illness, or lose a job, their shocked resentment often turns into a form of malaise that is very difficult to escape. Many baby boomers' high expectations include a perfect life to go with the perfect weather.

The children of the baby boomers don't seem to share their parents' expectations. They can often be heard telling each other and their parents that if it doesn't happen, it probably isn't meant to be. That is how Hanna's daughter, Kate, explains her frequent job changes and course drops, and Hanna tends to accept that explanation. In Sandra's view, Hanna herself seems to be precariously hovering on the edge of a full-blown depression because of the shame she feels over losing her job and being unable to replace it. A year ago, Hanna earned a salary that allowed her to buy her own house, take frequent trips to Europe and New England, go out to dinner whenever she chose, and buy new shoes at Nordstrom. Now she shops at resale stores, goes out for coffee instead of dinner, camps in the mountains and deserts nearby when she needs to get away, and is "renting" out two bedrooms of her house to Kate and her friends to supplement her income.

Steering Hanna away from the music, Sandra suggests they take their coffee outside. As they would both rather talk to each other than listen to music, and they both look for excuses to be outdoors at night, Hanna is in ready agreement.

They have light jackets, and there is no wind. It is delicious to be sitting outside, drinking raspberry-flavored cafe mocha, and sharing a crumbly blond brownie.

"You got your hair cut, didn't you?" asks Hanna, with narrowed eyes and a sideways shake of her head. "I think it's longer on the left than it is on the right."

"Shaved is more like it, isn't it?" Sandra says, as she reaches self-consciously to fluff up the top of her very short haircut, to give it more body.

"Well, it's not too bad. It's just a lot shorter than I'm used to seeing on you. Is it part of your new look to go with your year off?"

"So, tell me about the film you saw last night," says Sandra.

"*Turtles Can Fly*. Very sad," says Hanna. "It takes place in Iraq just after Saddam is removed from power. A young boy in Iraq clears his village of land mines."

"Oh, I would have a very difficult time seeing that. Imagine the lives of people caught up in war like that."

"Yes. Movies are as close as we get to these tragedies." Hanna offers Sandra a bite of her brownie.

"I don't know," responds Sandra, ignoring the brownie. "I think that movies like those are the conscience of America. I think we go to see them for the same reason our parents went to church every Sunday, to get our fix of duty and responsibility and brotherhood. The trouble is we do the same thing after seeing the movie that they did after church. We go out for dinner or home to our safe, secure homes in our safe, secure neighborhoods and forget that there are needy people out there who don't have what we take for granted."

Hanna looks away from Sandra, casts her eyes at an upward angle, and presses her lips together in a puzzled grimace. She pauses for a few ticks of silence before replying in a slow, patient voice. "I don't think that we can be responsible for the rest of the world. What gives us that right, much less that responsibility?"

"I'm not saying that we are responsible for the entire world," Sandra says, sitting forward on her chair and hunching her shoulders as if in response to a chilly breeze.

"Well, that's what I hear. What are we supposed to do—give away one-tenth of our financial resources to the poor? We already do that. It's called taxes. We're already overtaxed as it is. Or do you want us to each take in one homeless or immigrant family and let them live in our family room?"

"I don't know, Hanna. I don't know what I want us to do. But I do know that it is a struggle for me to enjoy my own comfort when I am so aware that others don't have the same advantages I do."

"Well, then you support them. I'll take care of the people in my family. That's what I believe in. If people just take responsibility for their own families, we wouldn't have so many out on the streets."

Sandra is dismayed at the degree of discomfort she is feeling during this conversation with her friend. Normally they talk about their children, travel plans, or careers. When they do, each feels supported and encouraged by the other. At least that is how Sandra generally feels.

Now, in the face of Hanna's blast at the idea of supporting the poor and paying too many taxes, Sandra can feel a heat in her belly like bile or heartburn. She knows that if she doesn't change the subject, she will say something in anger that might hurt her friend's feelings. She stuffs down her ire but resolves to examine it later. For now, she chooses to lead them both out of this prickly mess.

"Hey, okay, I agree with you that families are the best resource we have. And I know that your family does look after each other, more than most. Like your aunt Charlotte. How is she anyway?"

Hanna nods her head and drinks the last dregs of her coffee. "She's about the same, according to my sister Gloria. She can talk fine about what is happening this minute but can't remember where the bathroom is. Gloria called the other day. I think she's wishing I would come visit again and give her a break."

"Has your aunt had a definitive diagnosis for Alzheimer's? Do they know for sure?" asks Sandra, folding her napkin into smaller and smaller squares.

"Well, I guess they can't really do that. You can't tell for sure that it is Alzheimer's disease until the patient dies and they look at the brain itself; but she has all the classic symptoms. It is relatively slow moving for her, though. She has been like this for several years."

"How old is she?"

"About seventy-five, I think. She is a couple of years younger than my mother. Yes, about seventy-five."

"Do your other sisters help take care of her sometimes?"

"No, not really. She lives with Gloria because they are both in Albuquerque. Now that Gloria has gone back to school, it's hard for her to spend as much time with her as she should."

"You went to help out last year, right after you got laid off, didn't you?"

"Yes, and I'm thinking about going again. There's really nothing to keep me here."

"Want to walk back to the car?" suggests Sandra. They clean off the table and head east toward the theater parking lot, where their two cars are parked.

"So, is Kate going to stay up at San Francisco State for summer school?" asks Sandra.

"Yes, she's been here this weekend to pick up more of her stuff. She thinks she has a line on an apartment near Twin Peaks, with a couple of other people."

"Great, how did she find it?"

"One of her new housemates used to go to school with her in Oregon. Now she's in graduate school."

"And what year will Kate be?"

"I don't know. It depends on whether she changes majors. She has at least two years to go."

"So she's driving up this weekend," repeats Sandra. "Alex has to get back up to Berkeley after his spring break. Do you suppose she'd mind giving him a ride?"

"Probably not, but I don't speak for her. Have Alex call her is my suggestion."

"I will. He can take his guitar easier in a car than he can on a crowded plane."

The two friends walk back to the parking lot, where they retrieve their cars. Hanna drives home and lets herself into her downstairs bedroom without disturbing her daughter and her friends, who are upstairs making bathroom noises and getting ready for bed. She has missed this noise while Kate's been gone. She doesn't really mind sharing her home at all. Why does Sandra think she has all the answers? Really, she doesn't even have a clue about how hard it is to live alone and support yourself. If Sandra didn't have her husband's steady income, she would probably be a lot less interested in saving the rest of humanity.

On Sunday morning, Kate packs up her clothes, books, stereo, and CDs into the Volkswagen Jetta her father gave her for high school graduation. Hanna wakes up early to help her daughter pack, but Kate is all done and ready to go. They stand outside, on the front porch of the house. Hanna gets a small, flat, tissue-wrapped package out of her car and gives it to her daughter.

"What's this? A going-away present?" Kate takes it almost grudgingly. She wants as little fanfare as possible. She is just going to the Bay Area. What is the big deal, anyway? Tearing away the tape and opening the package, she finds that it contains one of her mother's favorite scarves, a large square of soft wool in golds, tans, and coral red. Kate throws it carelessly around her shoulders. It isn't exactly her style, but it is a nice gesture. Hanna tries to tie the ends into a graceful knot, but Kate has reached the limit of her desire to be mothered. She moves away from her mother and takes the ends of the scarves into her own hands. She reaches up and behind her head, using the scarf to tie back her long, straight, dark blond hair. With her straight, sleeveless denim dress over a man's red, long-sleeved winter underwear top, Kate has again achieved the slightly comical and highly individual fashion statement that she prefers. Her gray, deep-set eyes and wide mouth over straight, strong teeth give her face a sense of power that Kate has learned to use to her advantage. She lets her mother hug her briefly, and then she gets in the car and drives away, waving out the window.

Kate finds stopping and picking up Alex to be a bit of an inconvenience. He is only a freshman and will probably have tons of stuff he wants to take back to school. But it will be nice to have company on the long, boring drive after they get through LA Getting through LA, however, is usually anything but boring.

At the Seaquist house, Sandra is anxiously trying to help Alex find his things and put them in the car. She tries to rearrange some of Kate's things in the trunk to fit in a couple of Alex's boxes. They put Alex's guitar in the back seat, on top of everything else. At last Alex is ready, and Sandra runs back into the house and returns with a large brown bag and a six-pack of pop. "Here are some sandwiches and cookies for your trip," she says, thrusting the bag through the open window. She kisses and hugs her son one more time. Alex moves the lunch bag off his seat, climbs into the car, and gestures to Kate with his left hand to get the car in gear and move on.

Alex fits his long legs under the dashboard and puts on his seat belt. He looks too preppie for Berkeley, thinks Kate, but she then realizes that even Berkeley might have changed in the last few years. He wears a pale blue Oxford shirt with an emblem of a horse and rider on the pocket that Kate knows has doubled the cost of the shirt, even though she doesn't know what brand it represents. His tan chino pants are freshly creased, and his socks match exactly. His penny loafers look brand new. Kate has to admit he is a great-looking kid, with deep brown eyes and a ready smile. He is also sporting an amazing amount of facial hair for a freshman.

"How old are you, now?" she inquires, reaching out to tweak his beard.

Alex pulls away, reflexively, but with a grin on his face. "I'm nineteen," he answers. "This runs in my family. My father was shaving every day when he was sixteen."

Kate and Alex know each other from the family gatherings their two moms occasionally arrange, but they have never really had a chance to talk for any length of time. Now they have ten hours to fill up. Of course, there is always music.

Alex brings out his tapes and asks Kate if she likes Queen and Phish, two of his current favorites. They are all right with her, so they listen for a while, filling in with small talk, until they near the immigration checkpoint north of San Diego County, on land that belongs to the Camp Pendleton Marine Base. They observe the ten-foot-high fence that extends for seven miles along Highway 5. It is designed to prevent illegal immigrants from crossing the highway so that they can be more easily captured by border agents if they try to get out of a car or van.

"I don't understand this whole idea," Alex says, as they slow down for the border guards to look in their car and wave them on.

"The way they figure it is that the illegals have to come through this way to get to LA. This highway is the only access through Camp Pendleton, so if they want to get north of San Diego, they have to come on this highway," explains Kate.

"You mean that the Mexicans who cross the border illegally at Tijuana are just going to drive themselves up here?"

"Well, they probably don't drive themselves. Most of them get help from coyotes—"

"Coyotes?"

"No, not that kind, dupe. *Coyotes* is the name for smugglers who get people across the border for a price. Many of the people who cross want to get to LA because they have family there, or because they think they'll get a better job in a bigger city, or just to put a few more miles between them and the border. So some coyotes will smuggle an illegal through this checkpoint, too, for more money."

"Well, then why didn't they stop us and look under these piles in the back seats?"

"Because of our obvious honesty, of course," jokes Kate. "No, really, they probably would have if either of us were dark-skinned or looked Mexican. I'm kind of surprised they didn't stop us with that beard of yours," Kate laughs.

"What do you mean—my beard?" rejoins Alex. "If they had seen your baggie of 'oregano,' they would have hauled you in for questioning."

"You don't want to walk the rest of the way, do you? Seems to me that those shoes of yours would get pretty ratty by the time you get to school."

Kate is enjoying this. She would have probably enjoyed having a younger brother to tease. She thinks boys are okay, as long as she doesn't try to get serious about anything. That is the message most of the young men she knows have given her at least. They seem to enjoy being around her and giving her a hard time, but so far, romantic attachments with men have never materialized. Most of the men she knows use her as a sounding board for their problems with other women.

Is it something she expects from men, so they live up to her expectations? To hear her father on the subject, that is probably close to the truth. He lives in Philadelphia with his second wife, and whenever Kate visits them, she feels they are assessing her appearance, her speech patterns, and her ideas from the moment she steps off the plane. Neal, her father, wanted her to be an achiever like him and his new wife, Connie—that is for sure. Neal is a vice president for Citicorp, and his wife is a realtor in a multimillion dollar sales club, or something like that. They don't understand that their careers don't impress or interest her very much. She appreciates that her father can afford to buy her this car for her high school graduation, and he has paid every tuition bill she ever presented to him, without complaint, but that doesn't mean he owns her mind, does it? Not likely.

The immigration checkpoint behind them, they face the next hurdle of getting around Los Angeles. Kate drives by instinct most of the time, although at the intersection of Highway 5 and I-405, she asks Alex to consult a map. Together they decide on the 405 because it is a newer highway, and by early afternoon, they are north of Los Angeles, heading up Highway 5 toward the Bay Area.

They stop at a rest area to stretch their legs and eat the lunch Sandra made for them. It is pretty good: turkey, lettuce, and tomato sandwiches and chocolate chip cookies. Being a vegetarian, Kate takes the turkey out of her sandwich, and Alex piles it on his.

"So, is your brother serious about going to medical school?" asks Kate, between bites. She has taken out a chunk of cheese from her own stash and cuts slices of it to put on her sandwich.

"Serious? He'd better be," Alex asserts, as he swipes one of the slices of cheese from Kate's knife and adds it to his already generous sandwich. "Do you know what it costs to apply to medical school? I think my parents wrote a check for three hundred dollars, just for the application."

"Yeah, but that is for a multiple application form. That's not for just one school."

"Right. He applied to twelve schools."

"Which ones?"

"Oh, he doesn't discriminate. He applied to all the UC schools, Stanford, Harvard, Northwestern, and the University of Washington. Maybe there are a few more."

"Good schools. UCSF Medical School is right near where my new apartment is. Maybe we'll all be up in the Bay Area next fall."

"Well…" Alex hesitates then plunges on, "I don't think so. You see, he got turned down at UCSF and Stanford."

"He did? My mother didn't tell me that. It seems like she would have, if your mother told her about it."

"That's just it—my mother doesn't know. Peter hasn't told either of my parents about this. I called him up at school last week, and he had just received several letters that day. They were all rejections. I just found out because I was calling him to ask if he wants to go skiing with me in April. I don't think he would have called me with the news."

Kate certainly understands this logic. She has omitted telling her father about being on probation at her last school, and about several rejections she received over the past few years when she applied to reenter four-year schools but was not accepted because of the incompletes on her transcripts. Her mother knows about most of them. She is less judgmental, more laid back. "Well, he'll probably get into the University of Washington, where he goes."

"Not necessarily. What he found out is that they mainly accept only residents of Washington, Idaho, Alaska, and a couple of other states in the Northwest. But he claimed residency in California on his application."

"Wow, what a bummer. I thought he has good grades."

"Good?—they're amazing. He has a 3.89, and he's in the honors program. He'll graduate magna cum laude for sure and probably get Phi Beta Kappa, too."

"Well, how did he do on the MCAT?" Kate asks.

"He says his scores are good but not great. Two tens and an eleven. I don't really know what that means."

"They are good. I have a friend who was admitted to UCSD medical school last year with three tens."

"Well, hopefully, he'll get in there. It's one of the schools he still hasn't heard from."

"Yeah, I hope so, too." Kate stands up and brushes the crumbs from her sandwich off her dress. "I'm heading for the restroom. Be back in a sec."

Back on the road, Alex drives for a while.

"So, what are you majoring in?" Alex asks, as he checks over his shoulder and then smoothly swings over to the left lane to pass a slow truck.

"Women's studies," Kate answers, squirming a bit, trying to get comfortable in the passenger seat of her own car. She likes to drive, especially her own car. She prefers not to loan it out or even share driving, but it has been a long and difficult trek through Los Angeles, and Alex seems like a competent enough guy.

She begins to relax as she sees that he is at ease behind the wheel and drives with effortless enjoyment.

"What exactly is that?" asks Alex. "I mean, I don't want to sound like a dork, but I have no clue what you would study about women for four years."

"You are a freshman, aren't you?" says Kate. "Really, I'm shocked that you don't know, going to Berkeley." She emphasizes the last word in a way that indicates scorn mixed with respect.

"Hey, listen, I am just lucky to know my way to the bathroom at Berkeley. That's a big place, and every program seems like it is unique in the nation, if not the world."

"Right," says Kate. "Well, time to enlighten a poor, downtrodden, male freshman, I guess. Women's studies is a program about the contributions woman have made to the world."

"Like what?"

"Like literature, music, art, political leadership, scientific achievements…"

"Okay, I get it. But what do you do with it?"

"With what?"

"With the major? What do you do when you graduate with a major in women's studies?"

"Is that why we go to college? To get a job?"

"Yeah! That's why I'm going."

"Well, then you ought to just go to a vocational school instead of taking up space at one of the country's best universities." Kate pulls away from Alex and puts her back up against the car door.

"No way. I want the kind of job you can only get by going to one of the world's best universities."

"Well, at least you're honest," concedes Kate. "And here I thought you were going to get laid."

Alex is quiet. Beneath that beard, Kate thinks she even notices some reddening.

"Sorry, I didn't mean that," says Kate. "It just came out. Really. I guess sometimes I'm as guilty of stereotyping men as they are of us."

Alex glances over at Kate to read her face. Her expression seems to be in congruence with her words. She is genuinely sorry.

"Hey, don't sweat it. I guess I do sound a little mercenary myself."

"Yeah, no more than Bill Gates." They both laugh and recover their poise. "So, do you have a girlfriend?"

"Well, I think so." Alex wipes his hand off on his chinos and then puts his hand back on the steering wheel. "I'll know more when I get back to school."

"What does that mean? Your girlfriend has been thinking about whether she likes you or not?"

"No, at least not exactly. You see, she is Korean, and her parents have this big thing about her marrying a Korean."

"Well, you're not marrying her. You just want to date her, right?"

"Absolutely, but she believed she had to talk to them about it over the Easter break. I mean 'spring' break. They don't even celebrate Easter or Christmas or anything."

"So, she went home to her parents to ask if she can date a Caucasian man. Now that is exactly why we have a program called *women's studies*. For centuries, women have put up with that kind of crap because they don't know any better. They believed their fathers and their husbands would take care of them and tell them who to marry and when to have babies. I hope your girlfriend is enrolled in a course in women's studies."

"Well, she may have to before she graduates. We already have to take three courses, in Asian American Experiences, African American History, and Native Cultures. I wouldn't be a bit surprised if the women on campus have spent spring break persuading the chancellor to require every man on campus to take a course on women's issues."

"Hey, thanks. That's a great idea. Now I know what I'll push for at San Francisco State."

"Yeah, well, I'm going to get my Explorers Club together when I get back to the dorm tonight and warn them."

"Explorers Club? Sounds interesting."

"It is. Some guys I met this fall and I formed this club. I mean, every other ethnic group has their own organization, and we felt left out. So we decided to have our own club, based on what we have in common."

"Which is what? Some kind of exploring, obviously."

"Right. We all like to hike and ski and go…well, you know, exploring."

"So where have you explored so far?"

"We went to Yosemite, first. That was last fall. Then, some of us who live in Southern California, we went up to the Cuyamacas in December, right after finals. Then, after Christmas, we went to the Grand Canyon."

"Really? I'm impressed. That's audacious." Kate is too self-conscious to use the trite phrase "that's awesome," but she has grown up using it. Now, she has trained herself to replace it with this adjective.

"Yeah. I know. I'm pretty proud of it myself."

That evening, in San Diego, Sandra waits for the telephone to ring, hoping that Alex will remember to call her and tell her he has arrived safely at Foothill Dorm on Hearst Street in Berkeley. While she waits, she rereads the Sunday paper, especially the want ads. She imagines herself out in the job market again.

It could be true, after all. If she decides not to return to the school district, she can start fresh in a whole new career. She looks at listings under "Social Services," thinking that maybe she can find a job working with children some way.

There are plenty of listings. The section on social services is longer than any except sales positions. Help is wanted in hospitals, mental health agencies, the Salvation Army, St. Vincent De Paul, shelters for battered women, abused children, community service agencies, church service agencies, and drug and alcohol treatment centers. What does this long list say about our society? It is dizzying to think about. Then, she also notices the salaries offered for these positions. From seven dollars an hour to an ear-popping thirty thousand a year, tops—for full-time positions. Even teachers earn more than that.

Sandra turns to listings for computer programmers, thinking about her friend Hanna. There are a fair number of jobs there, too. Why isn't Hanna out looking for one? Is it fair to be critical of Hanna for not taking a more active role in looking for a new job? Sandra is not working either right now, but she is not taking unemployment. But what if she didn't have Dan's paycheck to fall back on? Wouldn't she be tempted to take the full amount of unemployment too? It is hard to imagine and even harder to answer.

Sandra spots a listing that seems perfect for Hanna: a computer programmer needed to work for a government agency, good benefits, opportunity for advancement, even comp time, allowing the employee to work extra hours and save up time for extended vacations. That is sure to appeal to Hanna. Sandra reaches for the phone to call her friend. No answer. She leaves a message on Hanna's machine, reading the ad aloud and telling the page number in the paper where it is listed.

Chapter Eight

THE AMERICAN DREAM

Sandra wakes up before it is light. Is she dreaming of another earthquake? The room is quiet; the windows are not rattling. Dan is sleeping peacefully a few inches from her. Between them, she feels the small warmth of Amigo, who has nestled himself between their thighs. Sandra reaches down and touches Amigo's soft fur. She lays her hand on Amigo's back, which causes the cat to stretch and turn over in response to Sandra's attention.

As she quietly strokes the cat, Sandra feels Dan's large, warm hand reach down and touch her own. With no other movement or sound, they both caress the cat and one another's fingers. A sudden movement of Dan's knee causes Amigo to leap away from his place between them. As he pads softly off the bed and jumps down to the floor, Dan and Sandra continue to touch and stroke one another's hands. The familiarity of Dan's hand is at once arousing and comforting to Sandra, and she feels, again, waves of gratitude for the many wonderful aspects of her life, of their life together.

After a few moments, Dan's feet creep closer to hers under the covers. He explores her ankles, feet, and legs with the smooth sole of his foot, and she makes attempts to tickle his foot with her toes. To look at their two heads above the covers, it would appear that both of them are sleeping soundly, but beneath the covers and within their bodies, both are quite pleasantly awake and are beginning to feel a stirring of sensual power in their toes and fingers, arms and legs, diffusing inward.

Sandra nudges her body closer to Dan's, and he wraps an arm around her, pulling her head to his chest. Her nose tickles as it encounters the curly hair on his chest, and as much as she enjoys being held close, she pushes away just enough to breathe freely and then wraps her arm around him. In the same way that they have explored fingers and toes, they each begin to touch and massage the other's back with their hands. Sandra presses her palm and fingers on Dan's upper back and pulls his body close to hers. Dan strokes her spine with his hand, which then comes to rest on the rise of her buttocks. He pulls her hips toward his.

"I think I'd like to brush my teeth," interrupts Sandra, which might have been interpreted as a brush off by a couple who are less secure with each other's habits and preferences. For Dan, rather than feeling rejected, Sandra's quiet statement is just more of a turn-on. He knows from their many years of lovemaking that 'brushing her teeth' is a euphemism for washing all the parts of her body that he likes to explore, a definite signal that Sandra is feeling just the way he is this morning.

He kisses her eyes and cheeks and then rolls away to allow her to get out of the bed. She walks sleepily toward the bathroom in the short, cream, silk nightgown he gave her for Christmas. He listens with sleepy amusement at the gurgles and splashes she makes at the sink. When she returns, he gets up and brushes his own teeth and then washes his partially erect cock with warm water and a soft cotton cloth.

Back in bed, Sandra and Dan press the fronts of their bodies together and use the strength in their arms and legs to reach over and around each other, connecting themselves into a lover's knot. Dan presses his face close to Sandra's, and they begin to kiss each other's lips and explore teeth and mouths with their tongues. Dan loves to kiss Sandra's warm lips and soft face. Sandra usually tires of it far too soon for him, but only because she gets interested in other, more intimate inspections of his body. How can he object? He lies on his back and extends his now erect penis to Sandra like a gift, which she accepts hungrily. Soon, like children playing in a tent, they are lost to the world, inhabiting a world of their own creation under their covers, the nurturing and stimulating world of their sexual life, which no one else knows or shares or, they believe, can possibly ever imagine.

Sandra and Dan are both willing and active sexual explorers, getting as much pleasure out of discovering and satisfying each other's needs and desires as they do out of having their own needs met. They became lovers for the first time in their early twenties, when Sandra was in college and Dan in flight training for the navy. The first time they made love, they both felt that a strong, almost invincible bond had developed between them, made of an alloy of trust and lust that they had never experienced before in their lives. It was quite a new and very welcome feeling for both of them, and they didn't want to take a chance on losing it. A few months later, they got married and moved to San Diego together.

Over the years, they have come to believe that their sexual love is the glue that keeps them connected, very synergistically attached to each other. Because of Dan's career, their marriage has been a continual series of partings and meetings, and the pattern that developed early in their marriage still holds true in the present day. When Dan comes home from a trip lasting several days, they are both drawn like magnets toward each other's bodies, with an electric awareness of the other's presence that blocks out all other stimuli. They touch hands, bump into each other, or otherwise make physical contact until they can get off alone together and gratify their sensual needs.

Afterward, the warm sexual glow they create is diluted, but just as gratifying, a link between them that lasts a few hours or, even, after particularly spectacular lovemaking, a day or so. They can then give their full attention elsewhere, well assured that their connection is intact, has, in fact, been renewed. It is also very likely that when they know Dan is leaving, as he is today, they will feel their sexual batteries blink on in the morning as if to say, "Reenergize me before you leave." In their private language, either Dan or Sandra can make a quiet, public comment about batteries that need to be recharged and know, without a doubt, that they have just passed an important message to each other.

Quiet and still together after making love on this morning in early April, Dan and Sandra fall asleep again and wake later to pangs of intense hunger for eggs, toast, orange juice, and coffee (for Dan) and tea (for Sandra). Both are ravenous for something to replenish their bodies with nutrients and fluids. It is past nine o'clock, and although Sandra is free today, Dan has to go to work. He begins mentally preparing himself to pack his bag and get his uniform together. He knows that he has to be in LA shortly after noon for a three-day trip, but he can't remember where it goes. He gets up to look for his April schedule. More and more lately, he has been enjoying her new freedom from schedules and responsibilities, and imagining the trips the two of them can take now that she isn't working.

Sandra gets dressed and heads downstairs to make coffee. Dan is not far behind her. He gets the newspaper off the front walk and brings it to the breakfast table. As they eat and read the paper, they glance up from time to time to see neighbors walking by on the sidewalk in front of their house. Dan likes to read aloud every story he finds interesting, from accusations about police brutality to accounts of scientific breakthroughs in cancer research. Any story related to aviation is certain to capture his interest, and he will read the first few lines aloud to see if he can attract Sandra's interest as well.

Sandra prefers news stories about government and social issues these days. She nods and says "mmm" or "uh-huh" to Dan's readings, while ignoring his words completely. She becomes immersed in descriptions of charter schools or articles about neighborhood groups in the barrio getting together to paint over graffiti or picket a crack house in order to drive out drug dealers. She often wonders if she would be welcome to go assist these endeavors. Would they want to have people like her involved in their projects, or would they see her as an intrusive busybody? How does one begin to show an interest in being involved or helping mend the social fabric of the community?

Dan brings her attention back to their own neighborhood by stealing the last half piece of toast off her plate, just when she has it perfectly buttered and spread with apple butter they bought in Julian at the apple festival last fall.

"Hey, give me that!" She reaches for the toast, but it is gone in two bites.

"Sorry, I didn't think you wanted it. It was just sitting there getting cold. I'll make you another one just like it." Dan gets up and rummages in the breadbox. He finds a piece and puts it into the toaster.

"No, don't bother. I don't really need it." Sandra rubs her belly with disbelief. It just doesn't seem fair. Dan eats twice what she does and doesn't gain weight. She has cut out all snack foods, buys fat-free yogurt instead of ice cream, and rarely has seconds, but still her body seems to have settled into this round shape and will not give up an inch.

As Dan waits for the toaster, he notices Sandra's dismayed look. He wishes she wouldn't be so hard on herself. He thinks she is a very attractive woman, with full breasts and a straight, healthy body. She can wrap her legs around him with an athletic grace that he appreciates and admires. He doubts whether his legs can do that anymore, probably never could. So what if she has a belly. It was a lot bigger during her pregnancies, and she seemed attractive even then.

"I'll eat it then. I need my strength, after that..." He rolls his eyes upward toward their bedroom.

Sandra smiles. "Yes, well, if it is too difficult for you, we can always get separate bedrooms."

"Right. We do have separate bedrooms half of the time. All I want different is for you to…"

The front doorbell chimes, startling both of them. Are they fully dressed yet? Ready for visitors or strangers? Sandra has on the white cotton dress with appliquéd flowers that she wears on the mornings when Dan is home for breakfast.

"I'll go," she says.

Walking to the front door, Sandra can see the gardener's truck out the window. It is probably just Miguel, wanting to ask her about a hedge or shrub that needs trimming. She opens the door to find Jeff Greene, the owner of the Good Neighbor Landscape Company that employs Miguel.

"Hello, Mrs. Seaquist," Jeff says. "Sorry to bother you, but I'll be doing the work myself today, and I won't be able to get to the hedge for a few weeks. It's too big a job for me to do alone."

"Why, Mr. Greene? Where are Miguel and Sergio? Not sick, I hope?" Behind her, Dan bounds up the stairs to shower and get dressed for work. He doesn't take a close interest in the gardening, unless the twisted junipers become overgrown and threaten to close out the light or act like a barricade at the front door.

"No, not sick. Things have been kind of slow for my business lately, and I had to let Sergio go. Then, Miguel didn't show up for work this week, so I'm kind of on my own."

"Didn't show? That doesn't seem like Miguel, does it? He seems to love this work." Sandra's interest in Miguel's welfare surprises Jeff. When he told his other customers that he was working by himself, their only concern was whether he could do as good a job as two men.

"If it's a problem, I can charge you less than usual, but I will try to do all the lawn mowing and the weeding and trimming, just like usual," he says, trying to reassure his customer.

"No, that's not what I'm concerned about. I'm just wondering what happened to Miguel. Did he get another job?" Sandra steps outside on the front walk with Jeff.

"No, he didn't get another job. I didn't lay him off. I am hoping to be able to keep him on because he is such a good worker. Heck, sometimes I think he knows more about plants than I do, and I went to school for it."

"Then what happened?" Sandra insists. Even as she continues to ask questions, she wonders why she is so concerned about a gardener. What difference does it make to her why Miguel has quit, or even whether he has been fired, or "let go," as Jeff put it? She just knows that she is concerned. Miguel is a steady and careful worker. She can trust him to do a good job, and he has made many excellent suggestions about trimming shrubs to let in the light or moving a plant from one area of the yard to another where it would grow better. Besides, he just seems like a very nice human being, someone she enjoys seeing every week. Is that so odd? To care about the well-being of a Mexican gardener?

Some of her neighbors would probably think so. They hire the cheapest labor they can get. Occasionally, at gatherings, Sandra has heard her neighbors discuss with pride how little they can pay to get help for housecleaning, babysitting, or gardening. When Sandra first moved to San Diego, women were transported from Tijuana to do housecleaning for five dollars a day. Now, although the rate is higher, in relative terms it hasn't changed all that much. Mexican men still gather at certain street corners in the city to be hired for the day. The going rate is under minimum wage, and no one complains.

Jeff, encouraged by Sandra's interest, talks more freely than he has been able to in weeks. "I feel awful about this, Mrs. Seaquist. I try to pay the men a living wage, but then I have to charge my customers accordingly. Meanwhile, there's a lot of competition in this business."

"I know," agrees Sandra. "The other day I got a flyer stuck in my mail slot advertising gardening at half the rate I pay you. I have to tell you that I was tempted to call them."

"Well, a lot of my customers have called them or others like them. Those men are working for a few dollars a day, and there are a lot of them who will do it. There are a lot of Vietnamese gardeners now who cut lawns and do basic maintenance. It's interesting to see how times change. The Japanese used to do the gardening jobs in this area, then it was mostly Mexicans, and now the Vietnamese are coming on strong."

"I have to leave in ten minutes, Sandra," Dan calls down the stairs. Sandra needs to change her clothes before she can drive Dan to the airport.

"Well, I'll stay with you, Mr. Green, but I hope Miguel will be back on the job soon."

"We both do. It depends on what happens when he gets back from Honduras."

"From Honduras?"

"Yes, what I've heard is that he left for Tegucigalpa on a bus. At least I think that's where he goes. He heard that his mother is sick, and he wanted to go get her and bring her here."

"Can he do that? Can he bring her into the US?"

"Well, probably not. Legally, he can only bring her as far as Tijuana."

"Oh, well at least they would be closer to each other."

"Well…" Jeff hesitated. "He might end up living with his mother because his wife is so upset with him right now that she isn't sure she wants him back."

"She told you that?"

"Yes, she stopped by last night on her way home from her job in La Jolla. At first she wanted to find out if he is staying with me. When I told her that I don't know where he is, she told me that he must have gone to Honduras to see his mother."

"Sandra, I'm all packed and ready to go. Are you driving me to the airport or not?" Dan comes down the stairs in his uniform, picks up his flight bag, which has been in the front closet since his last trip, and carries it to the front porch.

"Of course I'm driving you," Sandra says to her husband. To Jeff, she adds, "Well, I wish you would keep me informed. If there's anything I can do…"

Dan sweeps past Sandra and walks quickly to the driveway, getting in the passenger seat of Sandra's red Mazda, nodding to Jeff as he goes past. Sandra has a moment of sheer exasperation with her husband. He is a kind and considerate husband and father, but he seems completely unaware of how aloof he appears to people outside the family. Of course, she reminds herself, he doesn't act that way on his airplane. There he is friendly and helpful, introducing himself to the flight crew and making sure he gets their names correct. He often greets passengers at the door after landings, to smile and thank them for choosing his airline.

But Sandra cannot understand why he simply ignores working people as if they aren't even there. Housecleaners, gardeners, waitresses, and parking attendants he treats as if they are invisible. There is still some of his parents' upbringing left in him, even after all these years. Josephine always treated people who worked for her very condescendingly, referring to them as the "help." Dan grew up believing that the friends and relatives of his parents deserve respect and courtesy, but that the people who work for them are simply—what, support systems?

Sandra hurries back inside to find her purse then closes the front door and goes to the driver's seat of her car. Starting the engine, she thinks of reprimanding Dan for his lack of courtesy, but then reconsiders this action. She tries very hard to keep things smooth and easy between them just before he goes to work. As a captain, Dan has a lot of responsibility and a long day's and usually night's work ahead of him. She chooses, instead, to bring up a subject they both enjoy talking about.

"Where are you flying this trip?" she asks.

"Let's see," Dan answers. He takes a computer-generated data sheet out of his inside coat pocket and reads it. "Tonight, I'll be in Seattle."

"Great! Will you have time to see Peter?"

Dan looks at the flight schedule again. "Yes, I should have plenty of time to meet him tomorrow for breakfast if he's free. We don't leave until noon. Then, we go back to San Francisco, through Mexico City, and on to Guatemala. Not my favorite trip."

"Well, I suggest that you call Peter from the airport and give him some warning. We could have called him this morning from home."

"I'll call him as soon as you drop me off. Want to come with me?"

"Well, I would, but I'm not exactly dressed for travel. Next time, okay? Besides, I've got plans for the next few days myself."

After dropping Dan off at the airport, Sandra returns home and gets dressed for her day. It is a day she has been looking forward to for some time. This morning, she will take her first watercolor lesson, and this afternoon she has an interview with a volunteer organization called Rolling Readers. She heard about it on a local radio talk show recently, and it seemed like just the kind of activity she would enjoy. Volunteers in the organization read aloud to children. What could be more fun than these two new experiences she has planned for herself today? She is really very delighted with the way that this semester off is unfolding. She is carefully choosing activities and people that renew her creative spirit and enthusiasm for life. Really, her life can't be much better than it is right now.

It is hard to choose what to wear for an art class. Will it be messy? She pulls out some washable taupe cotton pants and a top that has taupe mixed with teal and burnt orange. But what about her interview later? She doesn't really have time to change in between. The class is from one to three, and the interview is at three thirty.

Well, these clothes should be acceptable for an interview with a volunteer program that focuses on children. She will probably dress very informally when she reads aloud to the children, so why should she have to dress any different for the interview? Thinking of Hanna's flair with scarves, Sandra rummages through her top dresser drawer and finds a silk scarf of her own. It has the teal and taupe colors too. She ties it around her neck. Her shoulders are larger than Hanna's. Her scarf doesn't lay the same graceful way, but it is a nice touch. She'll leave it.

At the art studio, a small storefront near Point Loma High School, Sandra meets the teacher, Martha, a tall blond woman about her age, with a big grin and friendly gray eyes. There are several other women standing or sitting around the long wooden tables with sawhorse legs. From their conversation, Sandra can tell that they are all pretty much beginners, as she is. She feels more at ease than she expected. It is the first time she has tried something brand new in quite a while. In fact, as a child, she became convinced that art wasn't her thing, that she had no talent for drawing or painting. In elementary school, her drawings always seemed just like geometric shapes lying flat on the paper. They never seemed to have any substance or life. Her teachers seemed to agree. They always walked past her desk and chose another student's work to hold up and display for the rest of the class to emulate. As soon as she was in junior high and able to choose elective courses, she never took art again.

"So why am I here today?" she wonders. Perhaps because of those memories. All through college, she registered only for the types of courses she knew she could ace: literature, writing, educational methods and theories. It wasn't just for the grade point average, it was more because she wanted to succeed at what she did so that she could earn esteem from her teachers and thus for herself. But, now, for some reason, she seems to have more permission to attempt something that doesn't come easy. Why? Because she has already succeeded at many things over the years: her career, her marriage, raising her children? Is that why? Has she finally convinced herself that she is a competent person, that she has achieved something with her life? Perhaps she feels that she can afford to fail again. In fact, it feels great to be a beginner at something again. It feels youthful and exhilarating.

Sandra and the other four students, all women between the ages of thirty-five and sixty, sit expectantly around the outside of the tables facing their teacher. "God, it feels good to be on this side of the desk again," thinks Sandra. She has been a teacher for over twenty years. Yes, it is certainly time to be the student again. On the wall of the studio are framed watercolor paintings. One is of subtly drawn, pale mauve flowers set against an azure sky; another shows a bright, sun-drenched adobe village in ochers and violets with splashes of bougainvillea pink. Sandra wonders if she will I ever be able to paint like that. It seems unlikely, but she is still very happy to be there.

The women around the table introduce themselves in positive, hopeful, middle-aged images. Devon is a former social worker who now owns her own business, a flower stall in La Jolla. She wants to learn how to paint flowers, of course. Susan is a practicing marriage and family counselor who wants something in her life that is colorful and exotic and just for her, to replenish the energy she gives her clients day after day. Rhonda is coming back up from a broken marriage. She has that gray, empty look of a recently divorced woman. She needs some color. Sandra admires her for choosing to come here, to replenish her self-respect with a new pursuit.

As Sandra introduces herself, she tells about her semester off and her hopes to discover some talents hidden away. The group responds warmly. Martha, their teacher, introduces herself last. She has taught art in the school system, but art programs have all been cut in the past few years. Martha started teaching art to children in her home. The response was so great that she rented this studio and advertised in a neighborhood publication. Her eyes are still full of the delight she feels for her burgeoning new business. She made a profit from the very first month, and you can tell by looking at her that she is thoroughly enjoying what she is doing.

Sandra looks around her. The other women are watching and listening to Martha intently. It seems as if they have already gotten something immensely valuable from her before they even pick up a brush. They have heard a success story from a woman their own age, who has turned a career loss around and created a happy, fulfilling business of her own.

Introductions over, Martha distributes long, clear-handled paintbrushes; white plastic palettes; stiff, creamy watercolor paper; and tubes of paint in alizarin crimson, raw sienna, ultramarine blue, hookers green, and cadmium yellow. The students squeeze out globs of paint onto their palettes and begin to mix colors, to form new hues and apply them to the paper in free-flowing shapes. It is deeply satisfying work, or play, or perhaps a combination of work and play, the best combination there is for children or adults of any age.

The two hours are over in a flash. Sandra pays for her supplies and takes them to her car with almost the same pride she felt taking home her first child from the hospital when he was born. "Well, perhaps," thinks Sandra, "that is a bit of an overstatement." But still, there is this new, unmistakable pride in her heart. She has a new baby to nurture inside herself, at least. And this time, she intends to encourage her artistic talents or skills and see where they lead.

But now she has to hurry to her next appointment. The Rolling Readers program has an office in University Town Center, a sprawling shopping center east of Interstate 5, near La Jolla. She drives north and locates a parking place near the building. She checks her image in the car mirror, straightens her scarf, fluffs up her hair, and reapplies her lipstick.

The volunteer organization has an office in a health education outreach center sponsored by Scripps Hospital. Inside, the receptionist directs her to a small office filled with stacks of children's books on tables and open boxes of books on the floor. Sandra looks for titles she recognizes and sees several, although many others are unfamiliar. There seem to be a great many books with dark-skinned children on the covers, and some of the books are written in Spanish. The director of the program, or so she assumes, is typing at a computer keyboard. He finishes a sentence, presses the Save key, and stands up.

"Hi, I'm Robert Condon," he says, extending his hand toward her. She takes it, and they both smile. It is the second time she has felt such a warm welcome in one day. Robert beams as he tells her how happy he is to have her come for the interview, how much it would mean to the kids of San Diego to have a professional educator, a reading specialist, join their efforts.

Sandra feels strangely shy about this respect for her career accomplishments. It is strange, but even after only a few weeks away from work, she already feels that it is behind her, that it no longer defines her. Sandra thinks that she really no longer knows who she is. She has for so many years defined herself as a wife, mother, and teacher, but now her children are grown and gone, and her career is in question. Who is she? The only answer that surfaces is that she is a person in search of…But the sentence and the concept are both unfinished in her mind.

She brings the conversation back to the present. "It is great to see all these books here. This one is a favorite of mine." She picks up a book entitled *Alexander and the Terrible, Horrible, No Good, Very Bad Day*. "I used to read this to my son, Alexander, when he was little, and I know that the children in schools always want to hear it. They never get tired of it."

"Yes, it's a great book," agrees Robert. "We have lots of great books. We give them away to the children we read to." Robert goes on to describe the program he initiated a few years ago. "When my own children were born, I found myself wanting to do something for children who didn't have all the advantages my kids do."

"Yes," Sandra says, and nods. "I remember having those same feelings when my children were little. But I never knew what to do except to be the best teacher I could be."

"Well, that is perfect. Being a teacher, you can make a contribution that I couldn't make. I was a car salesman." Robert's voice is full of energy and excitement. Sandra finds herself becoming very involved in his story.

"You were a car salesman, and now you are head of a reading program? How did that happen? Why did you want to do this?"

"Well, the reason I think this thing happened was because of where I came from," responded Robert. "I grew up in LA, in an area called Boyle Heights, and later we moved to Huntington Park, which is about seventy-five percent Hispanic or African American. My mom is part of the equation. She grew up in the south and saw the hurts the black people there experienced. I remember that when I was growing up, in the sixties, she wouldn't allow us to say the word 'nigger.' She was pretty passionate about that. I got from her this feeling that I have to do something with my life, something to make the world a better place. Of course, I also bought the whole American Dream thing. I mean, I really believed all that stuff about America, that everyone should have a chance and everything.

"But what I saw in the LA schools was discouraging. A halfway decent student like me got honors classes, and they were okay. But the rest of the students could hardly read. I was in sports programs. A lot of my friends were black and Hispanic. They couldn't read. I remember one time in my senior year, we were taking a required health course, and we were all asked to read a paragraph aloud. Some of my best friends were in that class, sports friends. They sounded like third graders when they tried to read their paragraphs out loud. I remember feeling so bad for them. What choices did they have? Not as many as I did. Not as many as my kids would have. I wanted every kid in America to have all the confidence that comes from being a good reader."

Sandra remembers having very similar feelings about America; she remembers getting goose bumps saying the Pledge of Allegiance when she was a little girl. Where have those feelings all gone? Can she get some of them back? It seems almost possible, listening to this man.

Robert is going on with his story. "When I became a parent myself, I loved reading to my kids. It is such a positive thing. They responded so well and seemed so happy while I was reading. That's what really got this started. I'd never volunteered for anything in my life, but one day I called the mayor's office and told the person that answered the phone that I wanted to read aloud to children once a week. This staffer told me she'd get back to me, and she did. She called me back a few days later and gave me three possible places to begin: the Forty-First Street Head Start Program, the Harbor Summit School for homeless children, and the Linda Vista Boys and Girls Club. I couldn't decide which one to go to, so I decided to go to all three.

"First, I called the directors of these programs and told them what I wanted to do. None of them turned me down. I gathered up some of my favorite books and went to read. The kids loved it. I was someone new in their lives, and I brought all these books. Every week, the crowds kept growing. The teachers loved it, and, of course, I got all sorts of rewards from the kids. They'd give me hugs and cheer when I arrived to read. The feeling grew—that this is such an important thing to be doing. I told everybody how excited I was about it. The first volunteer I ever recruited was the woman who worked in the deli near my car dealership. Every afternoon, I'd go over there to buy ice cream, and I told her about reading at the Head Start. She said, 'I could do that. I'd like to do that.' So I told her she could read at the Head Start from now on, and then I started recruiting other volunteers, and now we have three thousand volunteers in San Diego County alone reading to about eighty thousand children."

Robert is breathless, and Sandra can understand why.

"I'm very interested in becoming part of this program," she tells Robert. "Sign me up. Where do I read?"

"Well, we have a site open at a housing project in East San Diego. If you are interested, I'll call Jackie Harris at the San Diego Housing Commission, and she'll arrange for you to visit the site."

"Go ahead; call her." Sandra sits back in the chair and waits while Robert makes the call. She imagines herself going to the library and choosing several children's books and then taking them to the housing project to read. Probably, many of the children who live there speak Spanish, but that doesn't alarm her. She knows she can choose books that have lively, interesting illustrations and that she can translate a few words here and there from English to Spanish so that they can follow along.

Robert gets off the phone and hands her an address. She is to report to the site next Monday, May 1, at four o'clock in the afternoon. The children will just be getting home from school at that time, and she can read aloud outside at a covered patio or inside an extra garage. Robert answers her other questions and then allows her to choose thirty books to take with her to give away to the children at the end of her first reading program. Walking out of the office and going back to her car, Sandra feels as happy and as proud as she was in first grade, walking home with her first primer, to read aloud to her parents.

Chapter Nine

TRAVEL PLANS

The bus grinds its gears as it struggles over the winding, rutted road in the mountains of Chiapas. Miguel looks out the window and sees a faded portrait of Mexican revolutionary hero Emilio Zapata, on a rusting water tank. "Viva la Revolucion" is painted underneath in large red letters. How does it happen that Miguel is transported from the calm climate of San Diego to the bristling and recently violent climate of southern Mexico?

Three days before, Miguel went to the international bus station in Tijuana when his wife's anger drove him away. He didn't want to leave his family. They are his whole life. Rosa, usually patient and loving with him and their two children, surprised all of them with her anger that night. Why? What had he done but try to please their daughter?

He remembers the day that Maria told them about being invited to a party. She said that she didn't want to go, but later it seemed that she did want to go. Miguel is sure of his feelings. He doesn't want her to go to unchaperoned parties with Norte-Americano boys. He believes that they do not value his daughter for who she is, but only see her as an easy target for their sexual fantasies. A Latina girl is not safe among such boys.

How could he ever have allowed his daughter to go to that school? It seemed to Miguel that he was not even consulted. His wife and the woman she works for seemed to have it all worked out between them. That was his first mistake, to have allowed that decision to stand, unchallenged. His daughter does deserve the best. He agrees with that. She is as smart as any Norte-Americana girl, and she does excel in school subjects, but still, she is placed in an impossible situation at that school. How can she ever succeed when she is suddenly surrounded by the flagrant wealth and excesses of the other students?

Miguel is keenly aware of the differences among people in San Diego. He works for people whose children drive off to high school in their sports cars and jeeps. He has spent many afternoons working in their yards, when the young people come home. They turn on their CD players, their music bellowing insistent demands and demeaning insults. Is he the only one who thinks that American music sounds like whining? The sons and daughters of many of his employers seem to have nothing to do after two fifteen in the afternoon. They eat; they watch television; they talk on the telephone; and they leave in their cars for a while and return with plastic sacks from Game Stop or Target or Burger King, full of all the loot they buy with their extra cash.

In contrast, Miguel remembers his own growing up. The only thing he ever went to buy was a bottle of Tequila for his father. His only means of transportation were his feet or a second-class bus like the one he is riding right now.

The bus slows down on a particularly rutted road. Outside, Miguel sees a young boy walking along the side of the road. He is a dark-skinned boy, probably an Indian or Mestizo. He is barefooted and wears only a thin shirt, and on his back, he is carrying a load of firewood that he has cut from the mountains. He has no car, no CD player, probably no land that belongs to him or his family.

Miguel remembers his childhood in Honduras. His father worked as a car mechanic at a small neighborhood shop; he usually gave his money to the liquor store. His parents were always fighting, and his father often came home drunk and hit them and shouted at them and then fell asleep. When Miguel was seven years old, his mother got the courage to leave and take the younger children with her. But she didn't take Miguel. He and his two older brothers were expected to stay with their father. The two older brothers left to take care of themselves. They sold newspapers and got jobs at a stockyard, cleaning up the blood from the freshly killed cattle.

Miguel's stomach rumbles with hunger. He wishes the bus would stop, so he can buy a taco from a roadside vendor. A mangy dog lopes along the road and then veers off into the brush, looking for a meal. Miguel feels a sudden sympathy for the dog's lonely and desperate life. It is a kinship that he remembers feeling often as a young boy. Has he been foolish to believe that it is over for him, that solitary search for survival?

When he was fifteen, believing that he had no future in Honduras, Miguel decided to join the army. He went to the army headquarters, but they turned him away because he was too young. Miguel talked to his father and got him to come back to the headquarters with him and sign a paper saying he was old enough to join. For two years, he served as a soldier in the Honduran army, patrolling streets of the villages and searching in the forests for Nicaraguan communists.

After two years in the army, he looked for a job for about six months but was not able to find one. He had no skills and had spent only three years in school. At the age of seventeen, Miguel and his nineteen-year-old brother, Luis, decided to leave Honduras. They traveled on this same route, perhaps on this same bus, through Chiapas, Mexico City, and then to Nuevo Laredo, a border town across the Rio Grande from the state of Texas. There they attempted to cross the border into the United States but were unsuccessful. The coyotes in Nuevo Laredo charged too much money to lead them across the river. The going rate was four hundred dollars, and the two brothers had only a few pesos.

So they spent their pesos on another bus to Tijuana. Luis had a girlfriend from Honduras who had gone to Los Angeles. It was one of the reasons he wanted to go to the United States. He thought he could get her to help them cross the border or at least pay for the coyote. When they got to Tijuana, there were many coyotes meeting the bus and offering their services. Luis called his girlfriend in Los Angeles. She gave him the name and telephone number of her uncle in San Diego. Luis called the man collect, and when he identified himself as a fellow Honduran, the uncle agreed to help. He talked with the coyotes on the phone and promised to pay them when they delivered his countryman to a safe house in San Diego County.

That night, at eleven o'clock, as the US Border Patrol helicopters churned up the sand along the border, trying to herd the humans back to where they came from, the two brothers and their guides crept across the border in the area of Tijuana known as the Zona Norte. While others were less fortunate that night, or had hired less talented coyotes, and were tracked down by dogs or border guards in green-and-white trucks with flashing lights, Miguel and Luis walked, crawled, and ran through the maze of canyons for five hours. On the US side, they walked along Otay Mesa and eventually located the apartment in San Ysidro, the designated meeting place. The uncle was there as promised but only with enough money to pay for one of them. He hadn't understood that there were two brothers and was willing to pay only for his niece's friend.

The coyotes threatened to take Miguel back across the border with them, but the uncle agreed to return the next day with the money to pay for his passage. Miguel stayed all night in the crowded apartment, sleeping fitfully on a blanket spread out on the floor. He knew that it was unlikely that his brother or the uncle could raise the extra three hundred dollars. The next day, he simply walked out the door of the apartment; the clothes he was wearing were his only possession.

He walked to the center of San Diego, asking Spanish-speaking people along the way where he could get a job. One person told him to try the fields in Rancho Penasquitos and gave him a dollar for bus fare. He rode north on the bus with hunger gnawing at him. He hadn't eaten for two days. When he got off the bus, he saw fields of tomatoes that needed picking, but there were enough field hands working that day. No one would hire him. He started walking again. When he saw some bushes at the side of the road, he crawled into them and went to sleep. He was lonely, hungry, and scared. All night he prayed to God to help him.

The next day, when he woke up, he ate tomatoes from the fields. He saw some houses being built, and he approached an American construction worker and asked for a job. The man knew enough Spanish to understand and hired him for four dollars an hour. At the end of the day, Miguel had money but didn't know where to spend it. He asked his boss if he would take him to the store, so he could buy food. The man took him to a convenience store, where Miguel bought bread, bologna, and milk.

On Saturday he had only half a day's work. He took a bus back to San Diego that evening and found a cheap hotel for the night. On Sunday morning he started walking and saw people going into a small Christian church on Market Street near downtown San Diego. He followed them inside and stayed for the church service and Bible school. He talked with the minister and told him that he had nowhere to go. The minister invited him to his house for lunch and arranged for him to meet a Cuban American who allowed him to stay with him in his small apartment. Miguel ate his meals at a mission for several weeks, while he looked for work.

When he met a man from Honduras who had a woodworking shop a couple of miles east on Market Street, he was grateful to accept a job, even though the man paid him only one dollar an hour. Miguel worked for the carpenter as a sander and learned how to paint and stain the cabinets before long.

One Sunday morning at the church, Miguel saw a beautiful young woman attending the service. He approached her and asked her if she would go out for breakfast with him. Her name was Rosa; she came from Durango, a moderate-sized city in the interior of Mexico. She was working as a maid in a motel. They were attracted to each other, but neither of them had a good model for how to conduct a courtship or a successful relationship. Miguel was swept along by Rosa's romantic ideas of marriage, which she had learned from movies and magazines. For several months, they spent their time together at church or in a park, and Rosa convinced Miguel to save their money to buy an engagement ring, a wedding dress, and a security deposit on their own apartment.

Miguel got a second job, sweeping out a business at night, but he was very worried about how he could support a wife. A week before they were to be married, he became extremely nervous about the big step he was about to take. He took his half of the savings out of the bank, crossed back to Tijuana, and got on a bus bound for Honduras. For three weeks he didn't call Rosa; she had no idea where he had gone. In Honduras, he found that his mother had remarried. Her new husband was very hostile to Miguel. He wanted nothing to do with any of her children by her first husband. Miguel's father had not changed. He was still drinking and cared for no one but himself.

Miguel called Rosa. He was afraid to tell her of his confusion about their marriage, so he told her, instead, that the border guards had caught him without papers and deported him to Honduras. Rosa cried with relief to hear from him again and insisted on sending him the money for his return trip. Miguel was happy to hear that she still cared for him, that he didn't have to be alone, that, if he could just ignore his fears, he could return to the United States and create a family of his own. He got back on the bus and retraced his journey to Tijuana. Because he was familiar with the geography at the border, he did not need to hire a coyote. Instead, he joined a group of road runners who sat watchfully at the border in Tijuana every day, waiting for the right moment to race down the hills onto Interstate 5, where they made a dash for freedom by running north on the southbound lanes of the highway. They ran alongside the highway, weaving in and out of lanes of traffic going in the opposite direction, secure in the knowledge that the border patrol trucks could not chase them against traffic.

After a mile or so on the highway, Miguel dropped off the road into a ditch and then onto a street in San Ysidro where he was able to blend in among other Latino men who lived there. From a compatriot on the street, he asked for change to take the red trolley into San Diego and was soon reunited with Rosa.

His confusion and indecision had vanished. He knew for certain now that there was nothing he wanted more than to become a good husband to Rosa and have a steady job so that he could provide a decent home for his family.

They got married in the church on Market Street where they met and moved into a small room together in the back of a tan, stucco house on Twenty-Second Street in East San Diego. They had no kitchen, car, or telephone, but they did have shelter and privacy to learn to understand each other's desires, moods, and habits. They relied on the bus and trolley service, which was slow but adequate. They bought prepared food and used the pay phone across the street at the Square Deal Market, a Latino food and liquor store, which was painted bright blue on the outside and was covered with murals depicting proud aspects of Latino culture.

Rosa worked as a maid at the motel for several months until a friend told her about the possibility of a job in a private home in La Jolla. At first, she was skeptical. Being a motel housekeeper seemed more independent than becoming a servant for a rich family, but, out of curiosity, one day she took the bus to La Jolla to meet Mrs. Blumenthal. She decided to work for one day per week for the Blumenthals and keep her motel job, too. A year later, when Mr. Blumenthal died, Rosa was easily persuaded to take the full-time position Mrs. B offered her.

Meanwhile, in the first few months of their marriage, the carpentry shop that employed Miguel closed down. Afraid to tell Rosa that he had no work, he hid his feelings of shame and anxiety about not being able to provide for her; each morning at five thirty or six, he went to a parking lot of a large liquor store on Market Street, where immigrants congregated in the mornings to get day-labor jobs. For many weeks, he got only short-term jobs loading heavy materials on and off trucks or picking avocados or oranges. He didn't mind the work, but he did mind not knowing from day to day whether he would have work and not being able to tell Rosa where he was working and when to expect him home.

One day, Jeff Greene drove by, looking for another man for his fledgling landscaping company. He selected Miguel because of his direct, honest gaze and straight back. The two men worked well together. They were about the same age; both had new wives and became expectant fathers about the same time. Despite the language barrier, Jeff found it easy to communicate with Miguel, and he only had to teach him or show him something once. In fact, Miguel was quick to agree to do a job that he had never done before and was very able, very competent at all phases of the gardening business within a few months.

When their first child, Maria, was born, the landlady at their rooming house told them they couldn't stay any longer. With their steady jobs, Rosa and Miguel were able to afford a small, one-bedroom apartment on the second floor of a nearby house that had a small yard with a few citrus trees. Miguel asked the landlord about setting out his own plants and got his permission. With his growing knowledge about soil conditions and plant foods, Miguel was able to turn his small plot into a very productive garden, growing lettuce, squash, tomatoes, cilantro, onions, and three types of peppers—everything Rosa needed to make salsa, salads, and seasoning for meats, beans, and rice.

As their children were born and grew up, Miguel and Rosa moved downstairs into the largest apartment in the house. Anna, an older Mexican American widow living on her husband's social security, moved into the upstairs apartment and became their friend and the babysitter for their children. She cared for Maria for several years and now lavishes her attention on Miguel and Rosa's young son, Carlos, who is almost ready for kindergarten.

"So why am I leaving them?" Miguel asks his spirit, as he sits shivering and hungry on the drafty bus in the mountains of Chiapas. "What can make me so angry that I will put this much distance between me and the three people I love?"

Miguel's spirit is often restless and readily seeks adventure on any occasion, so perhaps Miguel's inner conversation does not resolve any of the difficult issues he is facing. What he knows in his heart is that he wants to be with his family, that he wants to be shown the respect he deserves as the man and therefore the head of his family, that he wants to be able to provide what his family needs and a few of their wants as well. His daughter, Maria, is receiving a very different upbringing than he received. For this, he is very proud.

Perhaps, Miguel thinks, I was hasty in my invitation to Maria and her friends. I wanted Maria to feel proud of herself, her family, and her Latin American heritage. I wanted to see the other young students at her school up close, to determine if they are good enough for my daughter or if they are a danger to her, especially the young men.

Last Friday afternoon, Miguel went alone to pick up his daughter from school because Rosa was staying late at Mrs. B's to help with a party. As Maria said good-bye to her friends and got into their car, Miguel impulsively suggested that she invite them all to go to Old Town for a taco. At first, Maria rejected the idea as impossible, but Miguel reassured her. He had just been paid; he had plenty of money, and he wanted to meet her friends. How could she deny him that? Reluctantly, she agreed and went to talk to her friends in a nearby car. They agreed to meet at El Bandino, a popular Mexican restaurant in an old, two-story hacienda in the historic section of town, where San Diego's earliest citizens, both Latinos and Europeans, first settled.

When Maria and her father arrived at El Bandino, a dozen of Maria's classmates were there to greet them. They had driven their fast cars on a shortcut and were already seated at a large table, drinking pitchers of soda and eating chips and salsa. Miguel had expected only three or four friends, but the word had quickly been passed from car to car that Maria's father was popping for Mexican food at Old Town, and it seemed like as good a place as any to spend Friday evening. Shortly after Maria and her father were seated at the table, another carload of kids arrived. Miguel began to fear that even his week's pay would not cover the bill.

It came out about even. He had earned extra that week by trimming some trees and bushes next to the Seaquists' garage, and Jeff had added the additional thirty dollars to his pay. The tip he left was pitifully small for such a large crowd, but he was able to cover the food and drink. Meanwhile, he observed the young people as they ate and talked and came to the conclusion that there was no way he could generalize about them. Some seemed genuinely interested in Maria as a friend, and others were indifferent to her. Some were polite to the waitresses and asked quietly for others to pass the pitcher of soda, while others were rude and demanding. One young man jealously guarded a bowl of guacamole for his own until he was no longer hungry. He then put out his lighted cigarette by plunging it into the remaining avocado dip. Miguel was happy to observe that this behavior sent a ripple of disgust across Maria's face too. In fact, she did not seem to be enjoying any of the meal. Instead, she sat quietly, her eyes darting from her classmates to her father's face and back again. When they left the restaurant, she stuck close to her father and said good-bye to her classmates with relief.

"Mama's going to kill us," she said in the car on the way home.

Miguel believed that death would be an easy answer to the inner turmoil he was experiencing. The money he just spent was owed to the landlord for the month's rent. Why had he acted so impulsively? How could he explain it to Rosa?

At home, Miguel played trucks on the floor with Carlos, while Maria barricaded herself in her bedroom with a book. When Rosa came home, she was tired after serving and cleaning up for a rare evening gathering Mrs. Blumenthal had organized for an arts council she supported. Miguel waited a full hour before reporting his blunder. It was not long enough. She grabbed Carlos up off the floor and cried loud angry sobs while she held him and rocked him. She said many angry words, some disparaging Miguel's behavior ("living a fantasy, acting like a rich man, ridiculo"), others about his general character ("imbecile, boastful, thoughtless").

Miguel listened to her anger with his head down, agreeing with her completely, until, her anger still not assuaged, she began to demean his manhood. "You think you are some super stud, don't you? Ha!" Even when Maria came out of her bedroom, Rosa continued to harangue him in front of his daughter. It was more than he could stand. The indecision he felt at the time of his marriage returned. Again, he allowed himself to believe that perhaps he should have stayed in Honduras, that he would be better off in his own native land. Thoughts of his ill mother in San Pedro Sula emerged in the thick stew of shamed feelings. He left the house and drove his car to a used car dealer, who offered him a couple of hundred dollars for it. He took the red trolley to the border at Tijuana and walked to the international bus station, where he bought the cheapest ticket he could find to Mexico City, and transferred there to the bus he is on now, going home to help his mother. It is the only thing he can think of that will allow his spirit to revive itself and throw off his shame and self-doubt.

****

While Miguel Ortiz is traveling south, Dan Seaquist is traveling north from San Diego. His trip is different in many, but not all, respects from Miguel's journey. Each man is traveling to provide for and support his family; each has a strong need for respect from the woman and children in his life; and each wishes he could protect his children from threats brought about by outside influences.

Dan's trip begins at San Diego Airport, where he boards a commuter plane for Los Angeles. At Los Angeles International Airport, Dan goes to his airline dispatch office and prepares the paperwork for his four-day trip. His first day is an easy one: Los Angeles to San Francisco and then on to Seattle, where he is scheduled to lay over at the Marriott Hotel. The next day there will be time to see his son, Peter, who lives near the university in northeast Seattle. Then he will head back through San Francisco to Mexico City and Guatemala City before returning to LAX and then home to San Diego.

In dispatch, Dan is happy to see that the name of his first officer ends in a *z*. Sanchez, Martinez, and other Latin American names are becoming more common among flight crews, although they are still relatively rare. Dan, who speaks very little Spanish himself, is always glad to see that his first officer is possibly a "talker," airline slang for a crewmember who can speak the language of the trip's destination. Many times, however, Dan has found that the crewmember with a Spanish surname is not bilingual. Many are second- or third-generation citizens of the United States, who have grown up speaking only English.

When the first officer, David Gomez, arrives and introduces himself to Dan, he admits that he does understand Spanish reasonably well but uses it only on his flights to Latin American countries. At home, in Laguna Beach, he and his Anglo wife and children speak only English. David goes to walk around the airplane while Dan finishes calculating the fuel needed for the trip, and then the two meet again in the cockpit of the airplane. They conduct their pretakeoff checklists and agree that Dan will fly the first leg of the trip, David the second, and that they will alternate in that way for the entire four-day sequence.

Even after twenty-five years of flying, it is still a thrill for Dan to taxi the airplane out to the runway and set the jet engines to maximum for an efficient and safe takeoff. Out over the Pacific Ocean, the pilots begin to swap flying stories as they study each other's flying techniques and get to know each other. Crewmembers are expected to be able to fly and communicate effectively with new partners just as well as they do with partners who know each other well.

As captain of the airplane, Dan is responsible for every aspect of the flight, except when to serve the coffee. It is a responsibility that Dan takes very seriously, but he knows that it is also important to have a light, easy interaction with other members of the crew. Crew training emphasizes routine, standardized performance expectations so that any pilot can fly with any copilot, and both will have the same understandings of procedures. Performances are monitored by yearly retraining and testing and occasionally by FAA or company check pilots, who ride along in the cockpit to observe a crew's performance.

Dan and David get along well right away. They both learned to fly in the US Navy, and both pilots have an easy, relaxed control of the airplane and fly with confidence. Their landings are excellent, each of them working especially hard to impress the other pilot with his skill at gliding down toward the airport and setting the plane smoothly on the first twelve hundred feet of the runway.

At Seattle, they are met by a hotel van and are taken to the Marriott, where they have a brief dinner and then go upstairs to their rooms. The next morning, Dan wakes up early and rents a car to drive to the U District to spend the morning with his son before he heads out on the one o'clock plane to San Francisco. Peter is awake when Dan arrives at the small frame house on Eighth Avenue that he shares with three other students. The promise of a free breakfast at the IHOP is enough to get him moving quickly at getting dressed and shaved. They walk through the chilly, frosty morning to the restaurant and order the biggest breakfasts on the menu.

Peter seems quiet to Dan, but he attributes it to early-morning sleepiness. When he does talk, it is to ask about Dan's flight, about his mother's activities, and his brother, Alex.

"So, Dad, do you know Alex has a new girlfriend?"

"Mm...let's see. New since when?" answers Dan, reluctantly giving the menu back to the waitress. "New since last week. I guess that Korean girl he liked didn't get the okay from her parents, and they never went out again."

"That's strange, isn't it?" responds Dan, but he doesn't sound like he has heard what Peter says. "So, tell me, what are you hearing from the medical schools?"

"It's not good news, Dad."

"No? What about UCSD? Did you hear from them yet?"

"I've heard from every school except Washington and UCSD, and they all turned me down. I can't believe it, Dad."

"Wow! What do they want? You've got the grades, the honors research, good test scores..."

"I don't know, Dad. My profs say that there are more medical school applicants this year than ever before. Washington has to accept students from four other states besides this one, and California residents aren't at the top of their list. Stanford has five thousand applicants for one hundred twenty places, so I guess I understand it; but I really counted on getting accepted to several places. I kept thinking about which one I would choose."

"Well, you still have two possibilities. I'm sure one of them will come through."

"Yeah, I hope so."

They eat and talk about other events at the university and in Peter's life. Two of his roommates graduated the year before but continue to live in the house while they look for jobs. This kind of talk scares Dan. Peter is only six months from graduation himself. What if he doesn't get into medical school? He'll be out there in this fickle job market with a degree in physical anthropology. What will happen to his son then? Dan doesn't share any of these foreboding thoughts with Peter. He stuffs them down to wherever he learned to stuff uncomfortable feelings as a child.

After breakfast they walk around the campus until it is time for Dan to drive back to Sea-Tac. Dan hugs Peter good-bye and reminds him that his parents love him and are proud of him no matter what happens to medical school. Peter hugs back, and, for a moment, he almost believes that it doesn't matter, that it will all turn out just fine, that he will continue to be the bright, rule-following oldest son who achieves well in school. But what will happen if there is no more school to go to? What will he do then?

Peter leaves his dad at the restaurant and goes to his biology lab to put in some extra time on his honors thesis research. He is studying the muscles of the legs of frogs to determine whether daily electrical stimulation of the long muscles causes them to grow stronger or weaker. If a certain level of stimulation results in an improvement of muscle tone and strength, it can have implications for assisting people whose muscles are weakened by disease or injury.

Dan returns his rented car at Sea-Tac Airport and continues on his flight plan. Their route goes to San Francisco, where Dan makes a great landing in the fog. Before they take off for Mexico City, the duty flight manager motions for Dan to come into his office.

"You're taking flight 1033 to Guatemala City today, correct?"

"That's right, through Mexico City."

"Well, I don't want to alarm you, but the State Department has just issued a travel advisory for Guatemala. Something about the possibility of a general strike."

"Interesting," says Dan, putting on his cool, we-can-handle-anything voice and face. "Do you know what the problem is?"

"I have no idea what the reason is," the flight manager replies, "but I advise you to refuel as soon as you get into Guatemala, in case something happens and we want you to get the plane out of there as soon as possible."

"Yeah, that sounds like an excellent plan. I'll do it."

Dan goes to find David to tell him of the complication. Again, he is glad that David can speak Spanish. Their trip down is uneventful, although it is never boring to fly into Mexico or Guatemala. Both airports have very complex landing procedures, designed to circumvent mountains and high buildings near the airports.

In Guatemala City, late at night, the pilots and flight attendants are transported by a limo with darkened windows to their hotel in the center of the city. It is an especially beautiful hotel, filled with carved-wood pillars and doors of richly polished wood. Upscale shops near the hotel display expensive handmade clothing, jewelry, and silver. Dan and David are too exhausted to notice. They have only a short layover; by eight thirty the next morning, they will be on their way back to Mexico and then home to Los Angeles. No one at the hotel seems concerned about the State Department's warning, so they go to their rooms. Dan props up the pillows on the very comfortable bed, orders a sandwich from room service, watches the news from WGN-Chicago on the cable TV, and then goes to sleep.

****

On the same day, Miguel's bus crosses the border from Mexico to Guatemala. He notices that there is extra attention paid to people's papers by the border agents and soldiers who board the bus and peer closely at the travelers. They travel without incident, arriving in Guatemala City late at night, where Miguel has an eight- or ten-hour wait for the next bus to San Pedro Sula. He curls up on a wooden bench in the bus station, ignoring the excited discussions between workers who want wage increases and intractable government officials who refuse to hear their demands, just as they have for over thirty years.

Chapter Ten

NEIGHBORHOOD WATCH

On the first day of May, Sandra Seaquist feels a sense of excitement that has been missing in her life for quite a long time. In the morning, she walks to the branch library near her home and goes to the children's section. It has been a while since she visited this part of the library. She used to come here with her children when they were small and kneel down on the floor to help them find wonderful picture books to take home. Her position as reading coordinator at the school district meant that she kept current with children's literature in order to recommend selections for the reading curriculum, but she missed choosing books and paging through them with children on either side of her, sharing their eagerness to read and hear the story unfold.

Some of her favorite books leap off the shelf and into her lap as she searches for reading material for her new venture. In the afternoon, after the children come home from school, she will be taking these books to the site selected for her by the Rolling Readers program, where she will meet the children and read aloud to them for the first time.

Corduroy by Don Freeman—perfect. She pages through the story of a dark-skinned girl who visits the toy department of a big store with her mother but doesn't have enough money to buy the very bear she always wanted. Of course she gets the bear at the end and takes him home to her small apartment. The story seems like a good match for children living in a housing project. They are likely to have experienced just such a shopping trip. *Abuela* by Arthur Dorros and Elisa

Kleven—this is a new one for Sandra, but it seems right on target. The wonderful pictures of a girl named Rosalba and her abuela, who loves adventure—the book has many Spanish words woven into the story. Sandra reaches with delight for *Amazing Grace* by Mary Hoffman and Caroline Binch. The grinning face of an African American girl on the cover warms Sandra's heart. She hopes there will be just such a girl at the reading time today. The story tells about Grace's frustration with a school play when she wants to play Peter Pan but is told that she can't be Peter because he is a boy, and besides he isn't black. Of course, she does play Peter in the end—such a hopeful story, and the pictures are stunning.

But all three of these books have girls as protagonists, heroines really. Sandra searches for some with boys at the center of the action and comes up with *Alexander and the Terrible, Horrible, No Good, Very Bad Day* by Judith Viorst. This book never fails to delight children, who have all felt just as rejected and discouraged as Alexander and love to laugh about it. Four books will be plenty for one day, but Sandra decides to search for one more, just in case she has time for it. She finds *You're the Scaredy Cat* by Mercer Mayer. It is a hilarious story of two brothers who decide to camp out for the night and are scared inside by a great, green garbage can monster.

Taking the books to the checkout desk at the library, she feels as excited about the books as she did when she was a child going to the library. She remembers walking home with her stack of books each week, thinking with relish about which one she would read first. As she gets out her library card to hand it to the librarian, her neighbor, Jan Froelich, is just coming in to return books.

"Hi, Sandra. I'm glad to see you today. You remember the neighborhood watch meeting tonight at my house?" Jan says, as she drops her books on the counter.

"Oh, is that tonight?" Sandra hedges. She saw the flyer sitting on her breakfast table that morning but didn't want to call and commit herself to it. It doesn't seem like a very romantic way to spend May Day. Dan will be coming home about dinnertime, and she would much rather have the evening alone with him.

"Yes, it's tonight, and we need you to be there. Is Dan home tonight?"

"Well, he may get in, but sometimes he's delayed." The librarian hands Sandra her five books and returns her card. Sandra slips it back into her wallet and picks up her books.

"Say, those books look interesting," says Jan. "Your children are a little old for them though. Do you have company? Or are you reading them for school?"

"I'm reading aloud to some children today. It's a volunteer program I just heard about, called Rolling Readers." Sandra starts walking to the door. Jan walks along beside her.

"Sounds interesting. So try to make it tonight, okay?" Jan heads for her car, a luxury sedan with vanity plates DOCS CAR. "Oh, do you need a ride home?"

"No," answers Sandra. "I want to walk. It's such a nice day."

They wave good-bye to each other, and Sandra heads up the hill to her house.

Later in the afternoon, she leaves a note for Dan in case he gets home before she does, drives around downtown San Diego, and then heads east on Market Street. The houses and apartment buildings in this part of town are older than those in her neighborhood. This area was settled early in the history of the city. There are a few large, old Victorian houses mixed in with the craftsman-style bungalows and stucco homes. Small businesses line Market Street for many blocks, followed by the large cemeteries. Sandra recalls her walk through Mount Hope Cemetery in early January. At the time, she wanted to find a way to do more, contribute something to the community, and here she is on the way to doing just that kind of thing. She feels proud of her decision to try out this program.

As she stops for a red light, she notices that there are a number of dark-skinned young men standing around on the corner of the street. Are they gang members? Should she lock her door? They don't seem to notice her. A car pulls up next to her, a very old, dark blue Cadillac with a muffler missing or something. Anyway, it makes a lot of noise. She looks into the car. Three black men look back at her, laugh at something, and the driver guns the engine, making it louder still. With relief, she notices that the light has turned green. She starts across the intersection but drives slowly. She thinks she would prefer to drive behind the Cadillac rather than in front of it.

She looks for the street numbers on the buildings as she passes them—a taco shop, a boarded up gas station, a liquor store, and a video store; none of them has an address clear enough to read. Another stop light and then she sees the 805 intersection. Her destination is just on the other side. There it is. She pulls into a parking lot that serves ten four-flat apartment buildings. There are at least a dozen children in the parking lot, tossing a football, riding a skate board, pushing a small child in a stroller. Where should she park?

An eager young girl, about eight years old, approaches her car. "Are you the reading lady?" she asks.

Sandra rolls down her car window. "Yes, I am. Do you know where I can park?"

"Just a minute. I'll find out." The girl dashes off to the front door of a downstairs apartment. When she returns, she is accompanied by a man wearing a blue shirt with *San Diego Housing Commission* above the pocket.

"Hi, I'm Manuel Ortega, the building manager," he says, thrusting his hand through the window of the car. "You can park in this spot," he says. "The family assigned to that spot doesn't have a car."

"Great. Can you watch the children for me, so I don't hit them?" Sandra steers carefully through the parking lot, scattering the children in front of her. Many approach the car as soon as she turns off the engine and gets out with her books.

"What are you going to read? Can I see?" say two of the children, while others are shyer, watching quietly and making way as Sandra follows Mr. Ortega to a concrete patio with a wooden trellis overhead.

"You can read here, if you don't mind being outside, or you can read in the living room of my house," he tells Sandra.

"Oh, I like it right here," says Sandra.

"Jesse, go get Mrs.—what is your name?"

"Mrs. Seaquist. Sandra Seaquist."

"Go get Mrs. Seaquist a chair."

A young boy runs inside a ground floor apartment and returns with a wooden chair. His mother follows him outside. She seems interested but reticent about coming forward. Sandra approaches her and introduces herself. She hopes that she will remember the names of the people she is meeting today. Mrs. Flores—think of flowers, she reminds herself.

"Do you want blankets for the children?" asks Mrs. Flores.

"That's a great idea," agrees Sandra.

Mrs. Flores brings out several Mexican blankets, and the children spread them on the concrete. There are about ten children from about three to twelve years of age, sitting waiting expectantly as Sandra settles herself on the chair and introduces herself.

"Hello, boys and girls. My name is Mrs. Seaquist. I came to read some of my favorite stories to you today. But first I think we'll play a little guessing game. Do you like guessing games?"

The children agree that guessing games are okay by them, and Sandra tells them the rules for Twenty Questions, reminding the children to ask questions that can be answered yes or no. "Now, here is the puzzle you have to solve. I brought my most valuable possession with me today. I have it right here. Can you guess what it is?"

"Easy!" says an eager girl with a dozen braids in her hair. "You brought a book."

"You are right that I like books, but that is not my most valuable possession," Sandra answers. She can tell that this young lady is perceptive about what adults want to hear. "What is your name?"

"Felicia," answers the girl.

"Good guess, Felicia. Who has another guess?"

"Is it your ring?" proposes a younger girl with almond-shaped eyes and long, straight black hair.

"This ring is very important to me," answers Sandra, with a smile. "But it is not my most valuable possession. Tell us your name."

"Cassandra," says the girl, squirming with pleasure at being asked.

"Your name and my first name are very similar," responds Sandra, and tells the children her first name.

"Is it your car?" asks a boy with curly black hair.

"No, it isn't my car. That's in the parking lot. My most valuable possession is right here."

The children examine her more closely. The only jewelry she wears is the wedding ring on her left hand. She is carrying five books and wearing a small, leather belly bag around her waist.

"I know! I know!" shouts a rambunctious boy about six years old. "It's your money, right?" He is full of excitement, sure of his correct response.

"Tell me your name," Sandra responds.

The boy gets suddenly shy. "He's Georgie," calls out another child.

"Well, Georgie, I'm sorry, but it isn't my money. Remember, you can ask other types of questions to find out what the possession is like. You might want to ask about its size or shape."

"What size is it?" responds Georgie, in a rush.

"No, you can't do that. You have to ask yes or no questions," admonishes an older boy.

"Is it big?" asks a girl with a sticky fruit juice mustache.

"Will it fit in your purse?" asks Felicia, pointing to Sandra's waist.

"Yes," says Sandra. "It does fit in my purse."

"I know. I know."

Several hands go up, but the guesses of a pen, a wallet, a picture, and a lipstick are all incorrect. Then, Sandra adds to the mystery. "Here's another clue. I bet many of you have the exact same possession, and if you don't have one, you can get one, easy." She unzips her belly bag, takes out her wallet, and searches among her credit cards and driver's license.

"I've got one. I've got one," exclaims a tall, slender dark-skinned boy. He reaches into his pocket and pulls out a plastic wallet. Opening it, he and Sandra both pull out the same thing: a tan plastic card that says "San Diego Public Library."

"Exactly right," says Sandra, with delight in her voice. "What is your name? Here, let me see your card." She reads, "Eric Rodriguez, Jr. Is that right?"

"Well, everyone just calls me Junior," the boy responds.

"How long have you had your library card?" asks Sandra.

"About a year," the boy answers.

"Is it one of your favorite possessions?" asks Sandra.

"I dunno. I guess so," the boy agrees.

"Well, I call it my most valuable possession because it means I own all the books in the whole city. I can take any book that I like home with me for three whole weeks. That's where I got all of these books that I'm going to read today."

"Can we go with you to the library next time?" asks Felicia.

"Well, I don't think you'd all fit in my car, but I will bring books to read to you every Monday after school. Now, how about if I read one? How many of you know this book?" Sandra holds up *Amazing Grace*. Just as she has hoped, Felicia's lovely face resembles the girl on the cover, and Sandra can hardly wait to get on with reading the story.

She reads well, with lively animation and good variety of volume and expression, causing the children to experience the different points of view of the characters in the story. When she finishes the book, the children clap and beg for another one. Felicia asks if she can look at the book about Grace, and Sandra hands it to her, as she plunges into Alexander's terrible, horrible, no good, very bad day.

As she reads, she notices that some parents are observing from their front porches, and one Asian mother brings her shy children downstairs and encourages them to join the group. Sandra nods and smiles at each child who joins the group, and pretty soon the children are jostling each other in order to sit closer and closer to her.

At the end of the hour, as she is gathering up her books, a child asks shyly, "Who pays you to do this?"

"No one," answers Sandra. "I'm doing it because I want to."

Walking back to her car, several parents smile at her. One approaches to say, "Thank you. I don't speak English very well, but I want my children to learn."

"My pleasure," says Sandra, and it has, indeed, been a very great pleasure. She feels a warm, glowing satisfaction that she has missed since her own children grew up and went away.

Driving home, she is already imagining the kinds of books she wants to find for next week: some sports books to capture the interest of some boys who continued their basketball game and didn't join the reading session today, some more scary monster stories, maybe, and definitely more books that have Spanish words. The children loved correcting her pronunciation when she read *Abuela*. She can probably even learn to speak better Spanish from the children.

When she pulls into her driveway, Dan is home, washing his car in the driveway. She goes over to him and regales him with stories about her new adventure. Afterward, they put together a simple dinner of soup, bagels, and tuna salad. Dan is glad to be home. He tells Sandra about his meeting with Peter, and they discuss their concerns about whether he will be admitted to medical school, and if not, what he will do next. He also describes his four-day trip, highlighting the best and worst landings he made. Sandra is alarmed when Dan describes the State Department advisory about travel to Guatemala, but Dan minimizes it, saying that it is just about worker's wages and that he didn't see any sign of trouble while he was there.

When the phone rings, they decide not to answer it, but just sit happily at the table and let the answering machine pick it up. Of course, they can hear the message. It is Jan Froelich, their neighbor in the Tudor house diagonally across the street. "Hello, Sandra, when you come tonight, can you bring a couple of folding chairs? Bye."

"What's that about?" asks Dan.

"Oh, you know, that neighborhood watch meeting. We don't have to go."

"That's all right. I don't mind going. I haven't seen Tom or Grant for quite a while."

They clean up the dishes together and watch the tail end of the news before walking across the street with their folding chairs. At the Froehlich's house, several neighbors are already there. Tom Froehlich, a cardiologist at Sharp's Hospital, has been called away for an emergency, but his wife Jan is the organizer of the group and hands Dan and Sandra a newsletter as they come in. Grant Prescott greets Dan warmly and draws him into a conversation about a recent trip he has taken on Dan's airline. Sandra sits on the couch and chats with Jean Prescott, who is wearing a warm up suit over her tennis clothes. She plays at least once a day and is rarely seen in any other costume. They discuss her tennis game, and she encourages Sandra to consider taking up the sport now that she has so much free time.

Jan waits for a few more neighbors to come in and then begins the meeting. "I've given you a newsletter that describes all of the recent break-ins and car thefts in the area. Is it my imagination, or does this list get longer every year?"

"It's awful," says Jean, leaning forward on the couch next to Sandra. "One of my tennis partners just had her garage burgled. Is that a word? Anyway, she was even home at the time, at least she thinks she was, and the door of the garage was open because she had just taken out the garbage a while before; when she looked again, her son's bike was gone. She thinks she saw some Mexican riding it away." Jean speaks without pause, as if it is important to keep the conversation in the air.

"I agree. This neighborhood used to be such a nice place to live, and now we have to lock the door of our car even when it's in our own driveway," says Jan.

"It's the graffiti that I can't stand," says Grant Prescott. "The walls around the high school are covered with it, and even that street sign by your house is covered with some type of symbols, Dan."

"I know. I'll call the city tomorrow and have them repaint it or replace it," answers Dan.

"The worst time of day is when school gets out. With these open enrollment policies, we get all kinds of kids walking through our neighborhood," Fran Stennett offers helpfully. "Our hedge is ruined. These big black kids walk by on their way to the bus, and they throw each other around and knock big holes in my hedge."

"Yes," agrees Jan, "one of the times we need to be most vigilant is after school, until the kids from those neighborhoods get on their buses or drive away."

The front door opens, and Dr. Froehlich walks in, looking tired and hungry and startled to see so many people in his living room. He recovers quickly and turns on his genial host face. "Hello, folks. Nice to see you."

"It's the neighborhood watch night, Tom. You remember, I told you this morning," his wife says.

"Oh, sure. Well, we could have used more of a neighborhood watch today. Someone held up the service station on Rosecrans and shot the cashier in the chest. I've just spent the last four hours trying to sew him back up." The group takes this news very hard. Rosecrans Street is just down the hill from their homes. Many conversations start at once, with Grant Prescott saying that this kind of thing didn't used to happen in this neighborhood and that it is probably some migrant worker or Mexican drug dealer high on his own product.

Sandra is alarmed to hear her husband, Dan, support this conjecture. "No, he probably wasn't high. When they're most dangerous is when they come down and want more drugs. He was probably strung out."

"When they used to come over the border and work during the day and then go back at night, these people were okay. They appreciated what we gave them. Now, they all think they have a right to move right in and take anything they see," says Jean, crossing her arms in front of her body as if to ward off a blow. "Don't you agree?" she says, turning to Sandra.

"I don't know" is all that Sandra can think of to say. And she doesn't know what she thinks about any of these issues. Her safety is important to her, and she doesn't like the way the kids from the high school act on their way to and from school, but she can't tell much difference between the behavior of the neighborhood kids and the commuters. Many of the neighborhood boys are loud and push at each other. She remembers her two boys doing the same kinds of things when they were in high school.

"I think we've got to take a stand. Write to the mayor or go to the city council and demand that we have better police protection right here," urges Grant Prescott. "All the extra cops we pay for aren't just needed in the barrio. Do you know how long you'd have to wait for a police car to respond to 911 here?"

"Yes, we're the ones who pay most of the taxes," Dan puts in. "We pay for the welfare and the cops and the public defenders who try to get these people back out on the streets as soon as possible."

"Exactly, Dan," agrees Tom Froehlich. "I heard on Rush Limbaugh today that half the medical services at the hospitals these days are going to illegal immigrants who come up here and act like they're having an emergency, and we have to provide services to them whether they can pay or have insurance or not."

"Right," Dan continues. "What are we? They just see us as marks that they can take advantage of. They've learned how to manipulate our laws and systems better than we have ourselves."

Sandra is looking at her husband as if he were a stranger she just met that evening. Is this what he really thinks, or is he just trying to fit in with his neighbors? Either way, Sandra is alarmed to hear him generalize about "these people." What is this meeting really about, anyway? Is it a community effort to improve their lives and look out for each other, or is it a vigilante group in the making, firing each other up and justifying each other's prejudices?

"Wait a minute," Sandra ventures. "What are we afraid of? We live in one of the safest, most comfortable neighborhoods in this city. What about people who live in the poorer neighborhoods and face the danger of gangs every day?"

"What's the point of that comment, Sandra?" asks Tom. "Isn't that exactly why we're meeting, so that our neighborhood doesn't turn into one of those war zones?"

"Yes," chimes in Jean, turning to face Sandra on the couch. "We have a right to protect ourselves, don't we? That's all we're talking about—protecting our lives and property. We can't count on—"

"You scare me, Sandra," interrupts Grant. "Those people in the barrio are there because they want to stick together with their kind. Besides, most of them are waiting for handouts. Do you know how much this city spends on free housing for all the immigrants from Mexico? And now they're pouring in from Laos and Ethiopia and who knows where else."

Dan looks puzzled to see his wife take the brunt of resentment pouring forth like gasoline spilling out of a full tank. He tries to placate his neighbors and calm down the situation. "Wait a minute, Grant. Sandra didn't mean anything by her comment. We both love this neighborhood and want to see it remain just as it is. You've got to remember that Sandra has worked in the school system for years, and she has been a little bit influenced by the policies of this liberal school board. They think bussing kids from one part of the city to another will solve all the social ills of our city, but of course, it just provokes more."

Sandra stands up. "Dan, that's not what I think at all. I don't know if bussing kids from a housing project to Point Loma High School is the best thing for them or for our kids, but I do know that every kid in this city deserves our concern and our love. I think what we should be doing is to form some kind of neighborhood organization that builds bridges between neighborhoods. I won't belong to a neighborhood association that wants to erect barriers to protect themselves." Everyone in the room is very quiet. Sandra knows she should just stop talking right now, before she alienates every person in the room. She should just say something "nice," something "neighborly" to placate the feelings of the people who are all looking at her with apprehension, as if she were about to dive off a ledge into a tiny swimming pool. But she can't stop. Her neighbors remind her very much of Dan's mother, who refused to discuss any controversial topic unless she was sure that everyone in the room had the same opinion as she did, and then she'd hold forth on the subject as if she was a lecturer in front of a very sympathetic audience.

"Look at the barriers we are building in Tijuana," Sandra goes on. "Steel fences ten feet high all along the border and floodlights like at a football stadium. Is that what you want to do to our neighborhood? Do you want to build a fence around it and only let in people with white skin who make over a hundred thousand dollars a year?"

Grant has recovered from his surprised silence. "Maybe we do. What's wrong with that? Don't people have a right to protect what we've earned?"

"I'm sure Sandra doesn't mean any harm," says their hostess, Jan. "I've got some coffee brewing. Let's just table this whole discussion and have a cup of coffee and some cookies."

"Thank you, Jan," says Dan, gesturing to Sandra with his eyes and a faintly perceptible nod of his head. "I've had a long day today. It started in Guatemala. I think we had better head for home."

Sandra agrees to this plan and follows Dan to the door. When they cross the street to their own home, Dan goes upstairs and Sandra goes to the kitchen. Amigo comes up to her and rubs his body along Sandra's leg, looking for an extra meal. Sandra picks him up and rubs her face in the cat's warm fur, looking for comfort perhaps, acceptance without question maybe. But cats aren't very good at that, and Amigo struggles to get down and look once more in her bowl. Sandra washes a few untidy dishes and stands looking out the kitchen window at the lemon tree growing just a few feet away.

Dan comes downstairs and finds her in the kitchen. "Here," he says, handing her a pink card and a small box. "It's May Day, remember?"

Sandra tries to smile. She takes the card and opens the box. Inside is a pair of silver and turquoise earrings, in the shape of flowers. They are very pretty. A big part of Sandra wants to just enjoy them and wrap her arms around her husband and then go upstairs with him and make love. But another part of her is rigid and aloof, angry with Dan for his remarks supporting the bigotry and self-centered protectiveness expressed by their neighbors.

"Where did these come from?" she asks, holding the earrings out to Dan. "Mexico? What did you pay for them? Five dollars? Aren't you afraid that the

Mexican artist who made them is just ripping you off? Taking advantage of you?" The rage Sandra still feels amazes her. What is the source of her anger? This is Dan she is haranguing. Sure, he can be a bit myopic at times, but he has usually been fair. At least that's how she has always seen him. Is it Dan who has changed, or is it her?

Dan takes the earrings and puts them back in the box. He has that blank look on his face that he used to get with his mother, when gave her a present she obviously didn't appreciate or when he didn't know the right answer and was afraid to say something that was not correct. He blinks his eyes, without speaking.

"What's the matter? Can't you talk?" asks Sandra, working herself into a real temper. "You sure had lots to say across the street," she spits out, like a cat that is cornered and wants to scare off an attacker.

This image of herself scares her more than anything else. She walks around Dan and goes upstairs to the bathroom, where she changes into a nightgown and brushes her teeth. When she returns to their bedroom, Dan is in bed with the lights out. She gets in beside him, careful not to touch him, and curls up, facing away from him. He falls asleep quickly; she lies awake for several hours, thinking about her life, her job, her visit to the housing project today, and the great pleasure she got out of reading to the children there, all minority children, most of them immigrants from other countries.

Dan never seems to question their comfortable life. He grew up with comfort and security. It is his birthright. But Sandra grew up in a home that was never secure, where there was never enough money to go around. Which is a better environment for growing human beings? As adults, with her good job and Dan's generous salary, they have easily been able to afford everything they've needed for many, many years. They have this wonderful house, two nice cars; both of their boys have had everything they needed and are now in good colleges. Isn't that what they worked for?

"So why am I so unsettled now?" Her thoughts go on in great turmoil inside her head. And why is Dan so comfortable and smug with our life, expecting it to always remain just as it is today. Or is that just my interpretation? Is it Dan who has changed?

No, Sandra thinks, Dan isn't changing. He is living the life we planned for ourselves, what we worked for the past twenty years. It's me that is changing, and that feels very, very scary. I guess I used to focus on different responsibilities than I do now. I talked with the neighbors about child rearing and gardening, and we seemed to have a lot in common. It's only now, when my interests seem to be changing and theirs have stayed the same, that I feel so at odds with them. And Dan, he seems to be satisfied with the way things are. He doesn't want to rock the boat—at least his neighborhood boat. But he sure rocked ours tonight by saying that my ideas don't mean anything. What if we drift apart? What if I want to do things with my life that Dan won't approve of? But what do I want to do with my life? I don't really know. I just know that I can't go backward. I can't repeat the things I've already done over and over again.

I've had a great life, better than I ever imagined as a child, but I can't just coast now. The kids are grown; they don't need me very much anymore. I've probably achieved everything I can at work, unless I want to be a superintendent, which I don't. The higher up you go in administration, the further and further you get away from the children themselves. I guess I want to find something that I can do where I am still needed. Dan won't disagree with that.

Sandra wants to turn over and hold Dan in her arms and rub her face along his bare back. But she doesn't. Something, some resentment over his easy agreement with the neighbors' conservative, self-serving views has awakened a new fear in her.

****

Sleep finally reaches out for Sandra, and exhausted from her day, she lets herself move toward it. Dan traveled all the way from Guatemala today, but in some ways he never left home at all; while she stayed in San Diego and traveled to another world. All she knows for sure, as she succumbs to the welcome darkness, is that she wants her neighborhood to include those wonderful smiling children that she read to today.

Chapter Eleven

TOURIST TRADE

One afternoon in early May, Hanna and Sandra set out to meet the elements, hoping that the storm that is forecast for the area will truly materialize. Often, rainstorms are predicted but then swing north, missing the San Diego area. Barriers of high pressure are as omnipresent off the coast of San Diego as are the steel walls along the Mexican border. In a climate with such consistent weather, a windy, rain-filled storm is not something they want to miss. They put their rain ponchos into Hanna's car and drive to Ocean Beach, where even the edge of a storm causes giant waves to swell, to the delight of surfers and looky-loos alike.

Gray, heavy clouds sweep toward them as they drive west the short distance to the beach. Tendrils of cloud reach down toward the Ocean Beach pier as if to catch one of the fishing boats and haul it up into its mesh. The tide is in. This is truly a cause for celebration. The storm's power combines with the high tide and causes huge waves to rise up to the bottom of the half-mile-long pier at the end of Niagara Street. On days such as these, the street is aptly named, as the thunderous surf is a close match to the sounds of falling water at Niagara Falls.

When they park their car at Dog Beach, there is still no rain falling, but it appears to be imminent. Only a few dogs and their keepers are chasing sticks or Frisbees on the beach. The usual coterie of homeless men are huddled near the lifeguard station and public restroom, looking for shelter. Their shopping carts are piled high and covered with black plastic or olive drab tarps. Sandra and Hanna pass them without a glance. A few years ago, the first homeless men were rare enough to warrant gawking at or at least surveying with surreptitious glances.

Now, the sight is accepted as commonplace by most Americans. A home-less woman merits at least a second glance, but even they are becoming more commonplace every day. Panhandlers and beggars used to be a phenomenon that American tourists had to put up with when they traveled to Asia, Africa, and South America. Now, they are part of the landscape in any large city in the United States, freed from prisons, mental hospitals, and the armed forces to roam, unattended, unprotected, and uncared for by the rest of the population, who continue to think that homeless people called "them" are fundamentally different from people like "us," and that "we" will never descend to the same depths as "they" have.

Is that bearded old man, who is sitting dispiritedly on the low concrete bench, a schizophrenic who refuses to take his medicine? Or a Vietnam veteran who bought Nixon's preaching about no peace without honor and shot his quota of gooks before being sent home to rot? Is that young, barefooted man with long hair, leaning against the wall of the women's restroom, a drug addict who shot up his last paycheck? Or a clinically depressed graduate of UCLA, who worked in the defense industry, until the company was sold to maximize shareholders' gains for a quick, short-term profit?

"So, where is Dan flying these days?" asks Hanna, as the two women approach the stairway leading up from the beach to the concrete pier that juts out into the ocean in the shape of a capital *T*.

"He's flying domestic this month. I think he goes to Albuquerque and Pittsburgh for his layovers. For once, he has weekends off."

Sandra bounds up the steps ahead of Hanna. Her walking regimen is paying off. She hasn't lost any weight, but she does feel lighter, or at least she has more energy and is able to carry her own weight more easily.

"Carry her own weight," her thoughts echo. Good description. That's what she is working on, in more ways than one.

"That's a coincidence," calls Hanna to Sandra, who is leaning over the edge of the pier, looking out at the porcelain-gray sky studded with high piles of lighter-colored clouds that look like very generous dollops of whipped cream.

"What is?" asks Sandra. "Let's go all the way to the end."

"Of course, but we're apt to get wet before we get back."

"Who cares? We can take it." They walk out on the concrete pier, passing a small, wizened Asian man sitting on a campstool, his fishing pole wedged between his knees. Ahead are two very small children playing with a tackle box. "Probably his grandchildren," thinks Sandra.

Below the pier on the north side, six or seven surfers in black propylene wet suits with purple, aqua, and hot pink accents are sitting on their surfboards, waiting for the best waves. In this location, the best waves seem to be right next to the pier—or is it that the surfers choose this spot because they like an audience? It is fun to watch them, as they lie prone on their stomachs, paddling into position and then quickly rising to their feet as the wave beneath them cradles their weight and propels them forward in graceful diagonals. It is a lot like flying, thinks Sandra. They swoop and bank their bodies to take advantage of the lift, just as a pilot does.

The women pass the little cafe and bait stand out near the end of the pier. The smells of stale coffee and herring are never appetizing. Neither Hanna nor Sandra has ever been tempted to stop for a cup of coffee or a snack. They continue to the junction of the *T* and turn left, to the south, toward the wind, toward the clouds and the vision of the rain meeting the surface of the ocean about a half mile away.

"It looks like a gray-blue shower curtain," says Hanna.

"Well, that's what it is," agrees Sandra, and they laugh together at their unintentional wordplay.

"Shall we stay and see what's behind it?" asks Hanna.

"I don't mind. It just feels great to be out here, doesn't it?"

"Yes, it's the right place for today."

They gaze back at the shore. Cliffs of eroded sandstone march south from the pier, topped with fragile boxes of wood and stucco that look like they can easily be pitched over the brink in a serious storm or earthquake. Beneath them, homeowners have tried various means to shore up the earth and protect their property. Retaining walls made of concrete blocks, metal, deeply rooted ice plant, and boulders have all been brought in to defend the works of man from the forces of nature. "But nature is relentless," thinks Sandra. Especially if they are right about their forecasts for El Niño, which is being predicted to bring unusual amounts of rain to California this winter. Those houses won't be there a few years from now. She points toward one house, where the corner of a fence built around the lot a few years ago is now partially suspended in midair.

"People are always trying to erect fences to protect themselves from every type of assault, aren't we?" muses Sandra out loud.

"Yes, remember that Bible story about building your house on sand or rock? That's what it reminds me of," says Hanna.

"Yes, that's very appropriate. What it says to me, at this point in my life, is how nothing ever stays the same and that we're kind of foolish if we expect it to," suggests Sandra.

"What it says to me is that we shouldn't rely on our possessions or our property so much. There's got to be something inside us to keep us safe," says Hanna, pushing back and motioning to Sandra to walk back toward the main part of the pier.

Reluctantly, Sandra follows. The rain is closing in on them, and they will probably be very wet before they get back to the car.

"So, you were saying that Dan is flying to Albuquerque this month. I might take one of his flights myself," Hanna says, as the two women turn right at the pier's end and walk briskly back toward the beach.

"Really? Where are you going?" asks Sandra.

"I think I'll go back to Albuquerque and give my sister some help with my aunt Charlotte."

"How long will you stay?"

"I'm not really sure. I'll have to see how things are when I get there. If they want me to stay, I might be there a few months."

"Wow. I'll really miss you. Now that we both have time off, I've really enjoyed the times we have together to go walking and other stuff."

"Yeah, but I'm restless. I got my last unemployment check this week, and I guess it's time for me to figure out what comes next."

"But how can you do that in Albuquerque? Don't you need to be here to see what opportunities there are for you here?"

"Who says I'm going to stay here? I'm not so sure. Maybe I'll sell my house and get a motor home and just keep traveling. Maybe I'll move to Albuquerque."

Sandra feels that the breath has just gone out of her lungs, as in an unexpected blow. "Not stay here? I didn't know you were thinking about moving away?"

"What is there for me here?" answers Hanna, in a challenging tone of voice.

"What do you mean? You have your house, your sister, good friends," Sandra says, pointing to herself. "You had a good job here, and you can get another one if you'd just get out there and look for one, now that you know you have to support yourself again."

"Well, I don't think I want to work full time any more. It isn't worth it."

They reach the end of the pier and start down the stairs. In the parking lot below, cars are parked, with people sitting inside sheltered from the rain that is now beginning to hit the ground in large plops. The two friends make a dash down the sidewalk toward the parking lot at Dog Beach, where they parked Hanna's car. When they arrive, they are both winded. They sit in the front seat of the car and watch as the windows steam up from their heavy breathing.

Hanna recovers first. "You know, Sandra, I used to take my lunch to work, and then during my lunch hour, I'd drive to a marina or a park and sit for half an hour feeling like I'd just escaped from prison. Now that I haven't been working for a year, I feel like I just can't go back to it. It will be just like admitting myself to a prison voluntarily."

Sandra nods, trying to analyze this image of work as a prison against her own experience. True, she is certainly enjoying her respite from work just as much as Hanna is. Also, she can remember days in her little cubicle at the administration building typing a report on her word processor and looking up to find that the day had disappeared. She isn't sure she wants to go back to that either. But, what is it about Hanna's situation that disturbs her? Is it the unemployment checks?

"I'm sorry, Hanna. I don't mean to imply that you were on the dole," Sandra says.

As if reading her friend's mind, Hanna asserts, "The trouble is, Sandra, that you judge everyone by your own values. Just because you have a career that you enjoy, you think everyone else should be enjoying theirs. Just because you get involved in some volunteer project, you think everyone else should too."

"I do?" Sandra considers this and decides that her friend may be right. "I think I should go back to work myself," she says. "It seems like whenever I take time off of work, I just get myself into trouble by thinking about everything too much. When I was working full time, I didn't have time to think about so many issues. I thought about my job, my house, my family. That pretty much took all my energy. But now, I have given myself permission to take time to think about my life, and it's like I can't turn it off. My questions and the dilemmas I pose for myself are becoming overwhelming in a way."

"I think I know what you mean," says Hanna, as she drives into Sandra's driveway and puts the engine of her car in neutral. "Remember how we were looking at the house back there on Sunset Cliffs and the ground was giving way under its yard? Sometimes, I think that's the way I feel about my life right now. I mean, we're not really mothers anymore. The jobs we liked for a long time are boring. You've got a husband at least. I don't even have that stability in my life. It feels like I built my house on sand."

Sandra reaches for her friend to give her a hug. The seat belt stops her. "Another barrier in my life," she thinks, stabbing the orange button at the base of the straps and extricating herself from its grasp. "What I do know, Hanna, is that I care for you very much, and I want you to be happy and safe, and I want us to go on being friends—close friends—just as we are today."

"Me, too," responds Hanna, accepting her friend's nurturing hug with real gratitude. There isn't much of that in her life right now, either. "I do appreciate your ideas and your honesty. I just need time to think about everything, with a little distance. I'll call you when I get home from New Mexico. Okay?"

"Well, I guess so. But I'll miss you. Call me from Albuquerque. I'll come with Dan on one of his trips to see you and meet your sister and aunt."

Sandra gets out of the car, feeling such a sense of loss. She goes to the house and takes the mail out of the box on the way in the front door. "Everything keeps changing, Amigo," she says, as her cat meets her at the door. "But at least here at home, I can keep things the way I like them."

Taking in the mail, Sandra notices the May newsletter from Walk and Talk. On the front page is the announcement of a special bus and walking tour of Tijuana. Sandra remembers Walkabout Lou talking about this trip, and she raised her hand, saying she'd go. Does that mean she is obligated to go? Of course not, but it does sound interesting—a bit scary, but very interesting. The write-up describes the trip as "a thorough exploration of our neighboring city." The bus will take people to various neighborhoods, where the group will walk around for a mile or so at each stop. It is coming up fast, at the end of this week. Should I go? Maybe Hanna will go, that will make it more…what…safe? No, I don't need Hanna to go with me. Talk about independence. Of course I want to go. Sandra reaches for the phone and calls Walk and Talk to register for the trip before she can change her mind.

When Friday arrives, the clouds and rain have swept away the dust and grime from the area. The new spring leaves on the trees seem buoyant with energy. Flowers are brighter; the horizon is free of haze. It is a great morning for a walk. Sandra dresses in a cotton jumpsuit and ties a bright belt around her waist. She goes through her wallet and takes out her credit cards and library card and puts them in her dresser drawer. She considers leaving her driver's license as well but decides to take it as identification, just in case she should need it.

She is taking sixty dollars, which should cover lunch and the small purchases she will likely make in the marketplace. Before leaving the house, she eats some yogurt with melon and granola for breakfast and gives Amigo an extra helping of Friskies Salmon Buffet.

Driving to the Walk and Talk meeting place at the trolley station in downtown San Diego, Sandra feels ready for an adventure. After all, Mexico is another country. As close as it is geographically, the trip to Tijuana has the promise of discovery that fits Sandra's whole sense of finding out about herself and her life at this point in time. Dan showed little reaction when she told him she was going to take the trip. He rarely discourages her from going anywhere, even when he has no interest in going himself.

A crowd of people are gathered near Walkabout Lou at the trolley station. He hands Sandra a sign-up sheet when she joins the group, and she writes her name. She sees Diane and Ellen, two women she sometimes walks with, and joins them as they wait for the trolley. Lou explains their itinerary. They will take the trolley to the border, walk across, and then board a blue bus, which will take them to the bullring at Las Playas and drop them there for a walk along the beach. At the southern edge of the beach, the bus will meet them and take them back to the crowded thoroughfare known as Calle Revolucion, where there are many restaurants and shops selling goods and services of all types. After lunch and a walk on Revolucion, the bus will take them on a tour of the Universidad de Autonomica de Baja California, the Zona Rio business district, the airport high on the mesa, and then to a neighborhood of middle-class homes high on a hill. Of course that is the schedule, but Walkabout Lou can also be counted on for a few surprises thrown in.

The trolley ride through the south bay is pleasant and quickly over. From the windows of her trolley car, Sandra can see the hills of Tijuana rising in the near distance. She imagines herself exploring every hill in the city, learning what it is like to live in another country. At the last station, the group straggles off the bus and walks on sidewalks near Interstate 5 to the pedestrian walkway across the border. The heavy, iron rotating gate groans and creaks as Sandra pushes through the fully enclosed stile encased in its metal bars. Only one person can go through at a time. The mechanism seems to say, "No turning back now."

On the other side stand several people waiting quietly for reasons Sandra cannot imagine. Perhaps they are waiting for friends or family to come through the stile. A man with a black shirt and white religious collar faces the stream of tourists, holding a can and a sign asking for donations for a Christian orphanage. Sandra wonders if the money in that can will go to benefit children; she has read that some collectors are genuine, while others are fraudulent. How can one tell the difference?

Propelled along by the people behind her, Sandra walks up a winding ramp to a footbridge across the new concrete drainage system, as wide as a river, which it turns into a few times a year. A sour, sooty smell rises from the river, which is littered with a few old tires and some cardboard. For the most part, though, it is clean and efficient looking.

On the footbridge sit tired mothers with dark skin and Indian features, holding a baby or two and extending a plastic or Styrofoam cup. Sandra has dollars but little change, and no pesos. What is a reasonable amount to put in the women's cups? A dime? A peso? The two amounts are fairly close in value these days—ten pesos to a dollar.

Near the seated mothers are other small children, boys and girls, three to eight years old, extending boxes of Chiclets to the passersby. Sandra digs in her belly bag and finds three quarters. She offers one to a young girl and is about to take a cellophane-wrapped package of four Chiclets when the other children nearby notice this transaction. Suddenly, she is surrounded by six or seven children, all thrusting their boxes at her, asking, entreating—a few pushy children demanding that she buy from them too. She zips up her belly bag and gives her other two quarters to the youngest children in the group then holds up both hands to show that she has no more change. The band of children follow her briefly then give their attention to another walker who has brought a handful of coins along, just for this purpose.

When they descend from the footbridge, they are greeted by the smells of cooking meat from taco and carne asada stands directly in their path. Limonada, slices of melon, avocados, and tomatoes are available nearby. Taxi drivers approach them and offer to drive them to town, to jai alai, to the Zona Rio, but Walkabout Lou gathers his flock around him and points them toward a sturdy blue bus a hundred feet down the road.

As Sandra walks in that direction, she notices new signs of prosperity since the last time she visited Tijuana. Neon signs blaze the names of cafes and offer margaritas y cervesa on a multistoried plaza that she doesn't remember from the last time she and Dan visited. Vendors call softly from storefronts, "Amiga, amiga. Come inside. Look. I can save you money." Tidy piles of multicolored blankets are stacked in front of several stores. Piñatas in the shape of burros, rainbows, and even Teenage Ninja Turtles hang overhead. Sandra is sorry to get into the bus so quickly. She would enjoy poking around here, looking for treasures. As if reading her mind, a man approaches her, holding a dozen metal chains on his arm. "Amiga, try one on. I give you a good price." Another man comes up behind him and extends a silver chain to Sandra. "Here, amiga. Free for you today."

"Free?" Sandra blurts out.

"Sure, try it on, señora."

But they have reached the steps of the bus, and Sandra thinks it's better to just get on the bus, although she is intrigued with the man's marketing strategy. She sits down next to Diane.

"I wonder what he means by 'free'?" she muses aloud.

"Oh, he probably just wants you to try it on; then he will tell you it is free to try on, but ten dollars to keep," suggests Diane, as the bus begins to move out of the crowded border crossing area and on to a four-lane highway, Mexico 1, heading west toward the Pacific Ocean.

Sandra, who is sitting on the right side of the bus, is suddenly confronted with the sight of the ten-foot-high corrugated steel wall a few feet away from her face. It stretches west along the highway for as far as she can see. The wall was constructed in the early 1990s to prevent illegal immigrants from simply walking across the border. It is a rusty color, with graffiti painted on it in many bright colors. Soon the level land gives way to hills, allowing Sandra to peer over the steel barrier onto lower land below. She sees hilly, desert terrain, similar to the land all around San Diego, but quite barren. Only a few hardy cacti dot the hills. A dirt track has been created parallel to the highway but on the US side of the border. On the road, green-and-white border patrol vehicles are parked, with idling engines, ready to give chase to the next hapless immigrant foolish enough to try to cross in broad daylight.

Lou stands up and begins to describe the microculture that exists at the border. As the highway begins to curve south, the terrain becomes even more rough and hilly. He points out groups of people that have gathered near the wall in areas that allow a clear vista across the border. Most of them are men, although there are a few women as well. They sit on hills, watching the border guards watch them. Taco stands and ice cream wagons are parked near the wall. Vendors offer their wares to the captive audience of border crossers.

The bus swoops down a long, curving rise with a sign that warns "Curva Peligro" on the side of the road. On the left side of the bus, Sandra sees that every canyon is filled with small shacks and houses. Lou points out the new concrete drainage ditch carved in the middle of a crevice. It was built this year, he tells the tour group, after heavy rains the year before had swept down the canyon. The flood destroyed many small houses, and mud buried and killed several inhabitants. Soon, the bus turns off the main highway onto a two-lane road, toward Las Playas, the beach area just south of Tijuana. Newer stucco homes and shops line the road. Sandra can see the ocean ahead of the bus. The bus stops in the parking lot of a large bull ring.

Lou leads the group on a moderately paced walk down the roads near the beach. He points out schools and new shopping areas. This area is inhabited by middle-class Mexicanos and many gringos who rent or lease homes in the area. Most have come to Tijuana to save money. They can live in a large, oceanfront home here for what it costs for a small condominium in San Diego. Also, many people feel safer in Mexico, where personal ownership of handguns is illegal. Lou quotes statistics that say there are at least one million handguns registered in San Diego County. Sandra is startled to think about that, the new concept that this relatively undeveloped country is considered safer than her own, at least in terms of personal safety from crime.

Soon they return to the bus, which drives them back into the tourist area, the busy marketplace lining Calle Revolucion. They are released for an hour of shopping and lunch. Sandra, Diane, and three other walkers eat at Caesar's Grill, where they all try the Caesar salad, which originated there. Its garlicky dressing and crunchy croutons are very satisfying. Sandra vows to try again to make her own Caesar dressing when she gets home. It is one of the most highly prized imports from Mexico that she can imagine.

After lunch, the tour group gathers at Mexitlan, a museum filled with hundreds of examples of Mexican ancient treasures and architectural accomplishments. For an hour, Sandra walks up and down the pathways, gazing with wonder and appreciation at scale models of the Aztec pyramids, Spanish cathedrals, the giant soccer stadium and modern skyscrapers from Mexico City. Maybe Dan has seen many of these wonders on his trips, but she hasn't heard him talk about them. Usually, he just reports on what the food is like at the hotel he stays in. She went with him once to Acapulco for a week and to Cabo San Lucas, at the end of Baja California, but they stayed at resort hotels and spent most of their time sunning themselves on the beach. Now she knows that she wants to plan an extended trip to Mexico and search out some of these national treasures.

The bus takes them on one more extended tour of other parts of the city east of the tourist areas. Sandra sees the newly prosperous financial district, with several glass-and-steel high-rises. Men and women in business suits, carrying briefcases made of leather, walk purposefully in these streets. Then, the driver puts the bus into its lowest gears to climb up a long, curving road to the top of Otay Mesa, where the Tijuana airport is located. The runway extends east and west along the border of the two countries. The omnipresent, rusting corrugated steel barrier has been erected here too, paralleling the runway and the road on which the bus is traveling. Across the border is empty grassland, which has been kept vacant by the San Diego city council for several years while negotiators attempt to create a plan for a bi-city, bi-national airport. Discussed for more than a decade, it is no longer even in the news.

Sandra feels a sense of revulsion that her own city and the country she has been loyal to her entire life have had the audacity to erect this iron curtain only a few years after cheering when the Berlin Wall was torn down. She remembers her comments to her neighbors a few weeks ago, accusing them of wanting to erect just such a barrier around their neighborhood. But isn't she just as guilty as they are of discrimination and self-protectionism? She helped Dan select their house for its beauty and, most of all, for the sense of safety and security she feels when she walks the quiet streets. Everybody who lives there appears to be comfortable with what they have. They are not likely to come looking for more by climbing in her bedroom windows.

Who is she kidding with her self-righteous judgments about her neighbors? They are just upfront about their desire for security, while she has been denying her own concerns lately in favor of some far-fetched notion she has begun to develop of being a member of a culturally diverse community. But doesn't a sense of community begin at home? How can she expect the larger community to communicate and interact when she is unable to communicate or accept the ideas of her closest family and neighbors?

All of these questions—they seem to flood her mind these days. None of them are even remotely answerable. What are the sources of the anxiety everyone seems to be feeling these days? Is it economic scarcity? Cultural blinders? Distrust of politicians and government? Confusion between what people need and what they want out of life? A sense of entitlement that her generation seems to have developed for the good life—the easy, comfortable life? Certainly that seems evident among her neighbors and many of her friends. It seems that middle-class Americans have an expectation that their professional careers, comfortable homes, safe neighborhoods, and material possessions are sacrosanct, the baseline or rock upon which their lives are built. But what if these expectations are shaken, jarred off their foundations? Then, Sandra wonders, would we get off our leather couches and pick up a shovel and hammer to rebuild, or would we just whine and complain, standing at our doors, pointing fingers at everyone else, blame, blame, blame?

"Imagine what Dan or our neighbors would feel if they were suddenly transported to an area on the outside of the barriers, if the barriers were erected to protect people from them," thinks Sandra, as the bus arrives at the Otay Mesa border crossing. A US customs official comes on board and asks perfunctorily, "All US citizens?"

There is a chorus of yeses, and the border agent steps off the bus, waving it through the semipermeable barrier between two nations.

She looks back at the boundary between her own country and its neighbor, and imagines what it would feel like if it had been erected by the Mexican government to prevent her from entering Mexico. She would be insulted and angered by such an affront. Her good friend, Hanna, might feel very intimidated by it and withdraw even more into herself; someone like her neighbor Grant might be incited to rebel against it, seeing it as a challenge to his masculinity.

Her son, Alex, might be a lot more confused about his own self-worth if he had grown up with a wall between himself and what he perceived to be very attractive people and activities on the other side. And Dan, how would Dan react if he were suddenly stopped at the border and prevented from crossing it as he is so used to doing? With a shudder, Sandra sees Dan's easygoing "I can handle any emergency" expression change to self-doubt and confusion, causing him to question his own competence and act in a bumptious or subservient way to placate the authorities who prevent his access. And she wonders if she herself would just pose endless questions about why she thinks she deserves access or freedom anyway, just as she seems to be questioning everything else in her life right now.

After their uneventful border crossing back into the United States, Sandra turns her thoughts to the anniversary celebration Dan has planned for them next week. She tries to recall her last visit to Catalina. Dan seems excited about the prospects of snorkeling, although he is obviously disappointed that she won't sail over there. Is her fear of sailing another of her self-imposed borders? Ironic, really, to live on the edge of a continent and be unable to cross the ocean because of her fears. Maybe she should tell him to go ahead and plan the trip the way he had wanted it. Maybe she can take something to calm her nerves and enjoy the experience of sailing, free from any restraints. But when she tested this idea in her imagination, she knew she wasn't ready for that much freedom.

At home, she hears the phone ringing as she is turning the key in the door. She hurries inside, stumbling over the cat, and picks up the phone in the kitchen on its fourth ring.

"Hello."

"Hello, Mom."

It is Peter. A strange time of day for him to call. Just hearing two words, she knows that something is bothering him. She sits down at the kitchen table.

"How are you?" she asks, giving him the space he needs to reveal what is on his mind.

"Okay, I guess."

"Okay? What's happening? No class this morning?"

"Yeah, I'm on my way to anthropology, but I just got the mail, and it looks like I'm on the waiting list here at Washington."

"The waiting list? That's a tough one, isn't it? That means you have to be in suspense for another few weeks. What about UCSD? I know you'd prefer to go to school somewhere else, but it's a very good school."

"No, I got turned down there, too. I got that letter a few days ago, but I decided not to call until I heard from my last chance."

"So..." Sandra pauses, trying to think of what words to use. First, do no harm—isn't that a medical philosophy? Well, it is appropriate here, too, talking with your child who has just been wounded by the system. "I'm sorry, Peter. What do you know about waiting lists?"

"I've been offered the opportunity to talk to the dean of the medical school here at Washington. It came with my letter. I guess I'll take him up on it. It can't hurt."

"Yes, it could be a very good thing to do. You might learn a lot."

"Yeah, that's the idea. If I go for the interview, I think he will mainly review my application and tell me how to make myself more competitive for next year."

"Next year—that seems like a long way off, doesn't it?"

"It seems like forever, but if I don't get in, that's what I'm going to do. Apply again."

"You're more sure than ever that medical school is what you want?"

"I am. I don't see myself doing anything else. Or at least I don't see myself being happy doing anything else."

"When is your interview with the dean?"

"Next week, Wednesday."

"Do you want me to tell Dad, or do you want to call him yourself?

"When will he be home?"

"Tomorrow; try around dinnertime. Or I can have him call you."

"No, I'll call him. But, Mom, I think you better let him know before then. He's not going to take it too well, and I'd rather have him used to the idea before I talk to him."

"Peter, your dad is not going to be ashamed of you just because you didn't get into medical school."

"No, I don't mean that. He's going to be upset about the selection process. He's going to tell me that someone else less qualified than me got my place just because he's black or tan or Mexican. You know what I mean. Right now, I just have to live with the system as it is, and I don't want to hear Dad get all righteous about it, okay?"

"I'll talk to him. Call your brother, why don't you?"

"I have. We had a good talk last night. I never really appreciated his ability to listen and ask the right questions before. Anyway, I've got to go."

"Me, too. Bye, Peter."

"Bye, Mom."

Chapter Twelve

TRIVIAL PURSUITS

On a warm June morning, a few days after Sandra's tour of Tijuana and her and Dan's anniversary trip to Catalina, they are sitting on their patio having coffee and muffins and reading the paper. It is Saturday, Dan's favorite day to reorganize things. Lately, he has reorganized his tools and other implements of construction and has begun to reorganize the drawer full of family photos. Today, he plans to buy several new photo albums and spend the morning, at least, arranging pictures into several different categories. He describes his plans to Sandra as they finish up their breakfast.

"I want to put all of our family pictures in one album and all of my flying pictures in another," he tells her. "I've been taking a lot of pictures of the different airports I fly into. Some of these places I may never get to fly into again."

"Why do you say that? You're not that close to retirement. You've got eleven more years to fly."

"I know, but it can happen. Either our airline will pull out of a city for economic reasons or the political climate can make it impossible to fly in and out of. I'd like to have a record of all the airports I've ever landed in, but I won't quite make that goal."

"Okay, great. Go for it," Sandra says, as she gathers up the newspaper and stacks it next to the back door, to be taken out later to the recycling bin. She knows that Dan's flying career is very important to him and that someday he'll enjoy looking back at a photo album of all the places he's flown, but to her his pictures of runways and airport buildings look remarkably similar.

"I'm planning to call Peter and find out about his interview with the dean. Do you want to talk to him about it?" asks Sandra.

"No, not right now. You find out what you can and tell me." Dan doesn't look up from his picture albums.

"Why don't you call him?"

"You're better at those conversations than I am, Sandra. I don't know what to say to him."

"Well, you'd know what to say to him if he got accepted."

"Yeah! That's easy. I'll tell you what I'd like to say. I'd like to call my state representative and ask him why my son didn't get into any of the California medical schools. They were supposed to get rid of that affirmative action quota system this year, but now I'm not so sure."

"You mean you think Peter didn't get into the UC system because he's white?"

"What am I supposed to think? He has the grades, the test scores, the recommendations. If his last name was Wong or Chavez, he'd be admitted in a minute."

"I don't know what to say to that, Dan. If it's true, it's a terrible thing. Our son deserves the same access to the schools in this state as anyone else does."

"Well, we'll never know. Colleges have their academic games and loopholes just the same as any other industry. Just like at my airline. We didn't hire minorities for years and years. Now, if your last name is Hispanic or Asian you can be hired with about half the required flying hours as the rest of us guys."

"Or if you are a woman pilot. They are hired more easily these days too, isn't that right?"

"Yes, so I guess if you want to be a doctor or a pilot these days, you'd better be a black woman with a Spanish surname."

Dan gathers up his photos and puts them away.

Sandra rubs the back of her neck to relieve the ache that has just developed. She feels that her hair is getting shaggy again and decides to call and see if she can get in for a quick haircut today. She cleans up the breakfast dishes and takes a quick look through her cabinets and refrigerator to see what she needs from the store. As she is making her grocery list, Dan walks by and ruffles her hair.

"You're actually making a list, huh?" he says teasingly. "Where will you leave it this time, on the counter or in the car?"

"I'll pin it to my shirt," retorts Sandra, who is aware of her reputation for making careful lists and then mislaying them before she gets to the store. "Is there anything you want from the store?"

"A Mac Pro laptop," says Dan with a gleam in his eye. He is thinking of getting one, and this is a good way to send up a trial balloon.

"Those aren't the kind of apples I can buy at the supermarket. But you gave me a good idea. I think I'll make pork chops with stewed apples for dinner tonight. Do you want to invite anyone over?"

"Well, we can try to invite the Froelichs or the Prescotts, but I'm not sure how they'd react after your outburst last month."

"My outburst? Is that how you still think about it? I thought we had talked that through. I thought you understood how I was feeling that night." Sandra stands up to face Dan, who immediately starts backing out the kitchen door.

"I guess I understand how you are feeling. What I don't understand is why you think you have to share all of your feelings with everyone who comes in contact with you. Can't you just hold in some of your emotion for the sake of neighborly courtesy?" Dan raises his voice more than is usual for him.

Sandra can tell that this issue is far from clear to him and is not settled between them as she hoped, even though they discussed it for several days immediately after the neighborhood watch meeting. When Dan left for his trip after that, she thought that she had convinced him that her questions about prejudice and discrimination in their own neighborhood were justified. But now she can tell that he had just agreed with her to quiet her down or placate her, and that his own real feelings are still divided between his loyalty to her and his sense of duty to his neighbors.

"Oh, you want me to stuff my feelings like you do, is that it?" she challenges. "Or do you want me to act like your mother and pretend I don't have any ideas of my own?"

"How did my mother get into this?" asks Dan, standing with his hand on the doorknob. "I think you need to appreciate what this neighborhood means to us and take some responsibility for lowering the barriers that you've created between us and our friends."

This statement catches Sandra unprepared. She can think of no reply to make. It is true that in standing up for more distant members of society, she has created a rift between herself and her, or their, own neighbors.

"Okay, I hear you," she offers quietly. "I'll call and invite them over and see what I can do to patch up what I've done."

"Fine. I'm going to the camera store to drop off some negatives. I'll see you later."

Dan goes out the backdoor and gets into his car. Sandra picks up the phone to call the Froelichs. Even as she dials their number, she hopes fervently that they are out or at least that they are already busy that evening. But Jan answers and seems glad to hear from Sandra. She readily accepts the invitation to dinner and promises to bring some fresh strawberries for dessert. Another call to the Prescott house nets similar results. Jean has just won her tennis match and is in good spirits. Sandra invites them to come for dinner. Jean checks with Tom, who can be heard saying in the background, "Sure, no problem, it's about time they called."

Now, Sandra has to rework her grocery list in earnest, adding several additional items she'll need for dinner: Bibb lettuce, French bread, butter, and a couple bottles of Chardonnay. As she writes, she dials Peter's number in Seattle.

He is awake but hungry. He doesn't want to talk very long because he wants to go make some breakfast. He sounds cranky. Sandra wants to ask if he has heard anything more about the waiting list yet, but she hates to bring it up. When he hears something, he will tell her—she is sure.

Her call to Alex at Berkeley is more rewarding. He wants to talk. His class in world geography is very exciting to him. He wonders aloud what he can do if he studies geography as a major. He loves to hike and go on the adventures with his Explorers Club. They are planning another weekend trip to Yosemite. Sandra sits down and jots down ideas on a notepad as they talk. She has rarely heard him so enthusiastic about anything. What can he do for a career that will allow him to be an explorer? She suggests mapmaking, working for the US Geological Survey, or Rand McNally. Neither of them knows whether this is a reasonable goal or how to get into such a career, but it feels exhilarating to discuss it. He talks about being a ranger at one of the national parks, but that sounds a bit too isolated, too remote.

"Maybe not," suggests Sandra. "Some of the parks are close enough to towns and cities to allow you to have the best of both worlds."

"Maybe while I'm at Yosemite next week, I'll get an application for a summer job there."

"That's a great idea," Sandra agrees enthusiastically. She feels so proud of her sons, each formulating ideas of how they can use their own special talents and interests in their careers. Of course, the downside is that they have both chosen careers that will be very difficult to break into these days. There are so many candidates for medical school, and there will probably be just as many competitors for a summer job at Yosemite. Still, it feels wonderful to hear her sons discuss their ideas and plans with hope and confidence. She and Alex say good-bye somewhat reluctantly. He promises to come home for at least a couple of weeks of his summer vacation even if he does get a job at Yosemite.

Sandra goes to the store, gets her groceries, and brings them back home. Dan is busy spreading photos out all over the dining room table. She goes back out to the library to select books to read on Monday when she goes back to the Market Street housing project. Later, she prepares the pork chops and sautéed apples with raisins and cinnamon to serve with them. She has to ask Dan three times to remove the last photos from the table so that she can set it for dinner.

That evening, the table is set, with fresh flowers from their garden in the center. Sandra is rinsing out the lettuce when the Prescotts arrive. She calls to greet them from the kitchen. The Froelichs comes shortly afterward, and Jan brings her fresh strawberries into the kitchen. Sandra talks with animation about the fresh fruit and vegetables they are able to get these days at the farmers' market. Soon they are talking as comfortably together as they always have.

In the living room, Dan pours wine for everyone, and they discuss Grant's recent business trip to Beijing. He tells about seeing the Olympic Stadium there, and they discuss the amazing changes taking place in Asia.

Of course, travel talk always reminds Dan of the airports he has flown into. He gets out his picture album of airport photos to show his neighbors the unusually difficult terrain and landing patterns at Hong Kong, Guatemala City, and Caracas, Venezuela, while Sandra goes into the kitchen to heat the rolls and dress the salad. Dan gets more wine. Tom Froehlich makes a comment about pork chops and cholesterol, but it is a good-natured remark. He isn't really criticizing her menu. In fact, he happily takes a large chop when the platter comes around and spoons on lots of apples next to it. Everyone exclaims over the good food.

"Is this one of the Pennsylvania Dutch recipes you grew up with?" Jean asks Dan.

"No. At least, I don't think so," replies Dan. "I don't remember my mother making this."

"I just cut it out of a magazine," volunteers Sandra. "But it turned out pretty good, didn't it?" It is a relief to go on to ordinary conversation. Sandra hopes so much that the evening will go smoothly and that the tension between her and

Dan will be reduced as a result. Their guests seem to have the same hopes. No one mentions the neighborhood watch meeting, and everyone seems to have a store of anecdotes about food, vacations, sports, and landscaping that gets them all safely through the long dinner hour.

After dinner, Sandra suggests that they play a game. Tom says he won't stay if he is forced to play charades. Grant suggests poker, but Jan says she can never remember which hands win over other hands. Dan brings out Monopoly, but they all agree that it is too late to start such a long game. Then Jean asks Sandra if they have a Trivial Pursuit game. Sandra reviews the contents of her upstairs closet in her mind and thinks that she can see the large, blue box back in a corner. She goes up to look and finds it, just where she has pictured it.

Clearing off the dining room table, they form themselves into teams and set up the game. For the rest of the evening, they concentrate all their intelligence and energy on such questions as "What kind of pipe does General Douglas MacArthur smoke?" and "Who did Ringo Starr marry in 1981?" The only time there is even the hint of tension in the evening is when Grant asks Sandra's team the question "Who shot Martin Luther King, Jr.?" Sandra has the feeling that there might be considerable differences of opinion about King's life and career if they ventured to discuss it, but they all tacitly avoid any comments and go quickly on to the next question, "What letter is on the left end of the middle row of letters on a typewriter keyboard?"

When the game plays itself out, and Grant and Jan are declared the winners, they all agree that it has been a great evening and that they really ought to do this more often. Jean says she has to be on the tennis court early the next morning, and the others trail after her as they walk across the street to their own homes.

Dan and Sandra agree that it has been a nice evening. Dan puts his arms around Sandra as she is rinsing out dishes at the sink and putting them into the dishwasher. She turns around and presses her body close to his. They stand still for several moments, neither wanting to break away. Dan holds her head with his large, strong hands, and she can hear his heart beat steadily, consistently in his chest. One of the things she loves best about being married to Dan is his steadiness, his reliable, constant support and his predictable behavior. He keeps her grounded, gives her the sense of stability she wanted so badly when she was growing up. She is glad that she has been able to contribute to their stability tonight by smoothing things over with their neighbors.

"Come on, you can do those dishes in the morning," he says, breaking away at last.

"I can do them?" she counters in a light tone.

"Okay, okay, we'll do them. Let's go upstairs."

Sandra dries her hands and follows Dan upstairs. At the top of the stairs, Dan asks, "Do you want to use the bathroom first?"

"No," she answers, "you go ahead."

When Dan returns from the bathroom, wearing a short silk paisley robe she gave him for some birthday, Sandra gives in to his teasing seductiveness and begins to enjoy herself. When he begins to kiss her belly, she pulls away, ashamed of her soft, round stomach, but he just pulls her back and burrows his face into her warmth, murmuring that she is so soft, so smooth, so loving.

"Soft in the belly," she says aloud, and thinks about the Paul Simon song about being soft in the middle. It is a song about being middle aged, she guesses. Middle aged, middle class, in the midst of a comfortable life. What is wrong with that? Nothing. So why does she feel so guilty about it all of a sudden? Well, maybe "guilty" is too strong a word, but she certainly feels defensive and confused about it.

Well, Dan certainly isn't soft, not anymore, and Sandra soon forgets about her concerns about her belly and her neighbors and gives Dan's loving body her full attention.

Afterward, she watches the moon travel across the double hung windows in their room and listens to Dan's untroubled breathing. Sandra tosses around on her side of the bed, looking in vain for a comfortable position. But comfort is something she has walked away from this year. Her assumptions that she has raised her own children successfully and can now devote more time to her own pleasures seem like an empty goal now. Her comfortable and secure relationship with Dan even seems in flux.

But what is she supposed to do to satisfy her conscience or whatever it is gnawing at her these days? Is it as simple as that? Her conscience is bothering her? But what is a "conscience"? Is it that she is becoming conscious of things that she has neglected because she has been so busy having a career and raising a family and taking care of her house? Conscience and consciousness—are they as close in meaning as they are in sound?

And does that mean that before, when she was so busy, it was all right not to be conscious of any further responsibilities outside her own immediate family, but now that she has more time, it is not all right? Does it mean that she doesn't need to worry about having a guilty conscience about what she has not been

FREE TRADE

aware of in the past, but now that she is becoming aware of these issues, she has to face them or feel guilty?

But face them how? In response, she sees Jean's face brightly suggesting that she take up tennis now that she has so much time. Dan's face appears, wanting to kiss her and make love. Grant's face hovers nearby with a snarl on it, suggesting that she is somehow a traitor to her neighbors for speaking about political and social issues she can't possibly understand, and Dan's face nods, agreeing complacently with the neighbor, denying her with his words, "Sandra doesn't mean anything...doesn't mean anything."

Sandra gets out of bed, taking her pillow with her, and goes to the guest room across the hall. The moon has followed her into this west-facing room. She curls up on the sofa bed but feels very cold. She gets up and finds a quilt that was hand-crocheted by her mother. She grabs it thankfully, like a child taking a blankie to bed with her. Covering herself with it, she smells a scent that reminds her of her mother, now dead for over a year. The tears come hot and scalding. It would be so wonderful to be taken care of again. Or it would be almost as good to have a baby or young child of her own to care for. She can do that so well, so easily. She knows what to give, how to make the world a happy and secure place for an infant, but it seems like so much more is expected of her now. She is now supposed to take responsibility for the entire world, or at least her own community, to gain approval from her own conscience.

But expected by whom? No one is telling her what to do, no one at all—not Dan, not her neighbors, not Hanna. Her mother never expected her to contribute to the world in any way. In fact, the only expectations she isn't living up to are her own. Somehow, she has come to believe that she should become a mother to the children she reads to on Mondays, and to all children who need more than they are getting. Who does she think she is? Robin Hood? What is she supposed to do? Take from her neighbors and give to the poor? Is there anyone else in the world who feels like she does? Sandra longs more than anything to be able to pick up the phone and call her mother, to spill out all these late-night thoughts and questions. But all she can do is hug the quilt closer and try to answer them on her own.

146

Chapter Thirteen

AIR TRAFFIC CONTROL

Sandra stuffs the paperback into the zippered compartment of her suitcase and hurries to the bathroom to finish putting her cosmetics into the small plastic case she has received as a promotion from Estee Lauder. It is the perfect size for traveling and already contains a miniature mascara and a lipstick that she likes. She hesitates about whether to take the purse-sized cologne or not. She rarely wears cologne at home, but maybe she will on this trip. She puts it in and takes a quick look in the mirror. Her hair looks slept in, which it has been. She brushes down a few stray ends with water.

Dan calls her from downstairs, "We need to go if we want to catch the eight-thirty plane."

Sandra takes one last look in the mirror, raises her eyebrows to smooth out the lines between her eyes, and takes her suitcase downstairs. It is still a great pleasure to anticipate a trip with Dan, even after all these years. His usual schedule consists of several cities in one day, but today he only has to fly to Denver with a long layover at a downtown hotel. Sandra is not looking forward to the brief flight up to Los Angeles on a commuter plane, but after that she will be on Dan's plane.

"Just a minute," she says, going into the kitchen to look for her address book. "I have to find Mary's phone number. When we get there this evening, I'm going to call and see if she and Pat can meet us for dinner. Is that okay with you?"

"Sure," Dan answers. "Maybe she'll know some interesting place to go for dinner. I always stay right near the hotel when I'm alone, but I'm sure there are more exciting places to go."

Sandra puts out cans of cat food and calls her neighbor, Jan, to remind her to feed Amigo that night and the next morning. Driving to the airport, Sandra is almost sorry to leave town. It is a beautiful day at the beginning of May. Clouds billow at the end of Point Loma, and the air seems fresh and nourishing, as if it is loaded with vitamins.

In Los Angeles, Dan goes to his flight office to prepare the paperwork for his trip. Sandra goes directly to the gate and waits for the departure with the other passengers. It is almost a full flight. As a standby passenger, traveling on a reduced fair ticket, she has to wait until the last moment before the gate agents will assign her a seat. When she boards, she looks into the cockpit and gives Dan a big smile. He looks happy to have her come along. He introduces her to his copilot, a young woman named Leslie, who is slim and athletic looking. She wears a uniform similar to Dan's, and it doesn't bulge anywhere. Sandra briefly imagines her own rounded shape trying to squeeze into those clothes. The sleeves of the jacket would probably feel tight, and her stomach would poke out.

Sandra takes her seat and puts on her seatbelt. She leafs through a magazine, waiting to take off. She finds an interesting article describing the work of court appointed special advocates, or CASAs, volunteers who are appointed by the court to represent the needs of children who have been removed from their parents' custody and placed in foster homes. Sandra finds a list of such programs at the end of the article. One of the programs is in San Diego County. Sandra takes down the address and phone number of the office, thinking that she might call and investigate it when she gets home.

When they take off, Sandra forgets about the magazines and refuses the coffee offered by the flight attendant. She listens to Dan's smooth, confident voice over the intercom describing their route and the altitude they will be flying to Denver. The plane passes through the sparsely scattered clouds. Below, the landscape seems to rise to meet the plane as they fly over the snow-clogged San Gorgornio Mountains with glistening lakes collecting the runoff.

Then the desert spreads out as far as Sandra can see. Sandra enjoys looking for landmarks. There is Joshua Tree, where they camped with the boys a few years ago. She remembers Peter finding a lizard and trying to keep it in a cookie box for an afternoon. On the left side of the airplane is Death Valley, a place that Sandra has never ventured. Is it the name of the place that has kept her away?

The flight attendant comes by and offers fruit and muffins. Sandra decides she is hungry after all and gladly accepts them. What a luxury to be served hot coffee and fresh fruit while watching the natural beauty of the West slide by underneath.

"My name is Nance," says the flight attendant. "Is Captain Seaquist your husband?"

"Yes," answers Sandra.

"I enjoy flying with him," Nance tells Sandra. "He is always polite, always takes the time to get the names of the flight attendants, and treats us all like important members of the team.

"Yes, that sounds like Dan," Sandra says happily.

"It isn't always that way," continues Nance. "Some captains seem to think that a flight attendant is an interchangeable part with about as much value as a windshield wiper."

"Is it different when you are flying with the women pilots?" Sandra asks.

"Oh, I don't want to generalize," responds Nance quietly, so that they are not overheard by other passengers. "I'll just say that Captain Seaquist is definitely one of the 'good ones.' By the way, can I show you a photo?" asks Nance, changing the subject with a grin.

"Of course," answers Sandra. She especially enjoys the camaraderie with flight crew when she flies with her husband.

Nance shows Sandra a photo of a young Asian child. "This is my new daughter, Sophie," says Nance.

"How wonderful!" Sandra says, as she looks at a small, round face with large, dark eyes. She looks up questioningly.

"My husband Nick and I adopted her from China three months ago."

"She is lovely. I'd like to see her in person. Where do you and your husband live?"

"We live in San Diego. Nick is a photographer, with a studio in Little Italy."

"Oh, we live in San Diego too," says Sandra. "I would love to meet your daughter. Sophie? A beautiful name. My sons are grown up. I would really enjoy getting to know your daughter."

The two women exchange phone numbers, and Nance hurries off to assist another passenger.

Sandra thinks about the encounter. She would really like to have a little girl in her life. She also thinks about the way Nance described Dan. She isn't surprised. Dan is always courteous and polite to all their friends and even some of the more difficult relatives on her side of the family. She sits back and enjoys the feeling, close to gratitude, of being the wife of a man who can carry her up into the skies, support her while she looks with awe at the world, and bring her back down again safely, and does it with grace and unquestioning self-confidence.

Grinning to herself, Sandra carries out the metaphor in her imagination. In contrast to this image she has just spun of her husband's powers, who is she? Looking down on the desert landscape, Sandra spots a tiny motor vehicle on a two-lane highway. That is her. She is the driver of a fat, tired jeep going along a highway—to where? Sandra sees herself driving off the asphalt and onto a bumpy corduroy road leading away from the main road.

What a scary thought! Why does she see herself like that? Here she is blessed with a life that anyone would envy. "If I had never taken this year off," Sandra thinks with self-reproach, "I would never have even questioned all these things. I would have been contentedly field testing a new reading series or arranging for an in-service for teachers on the new California state achievement tests that stressed problem solving and writing skills instead of rote memory. The worthiness of that goal would have kept me satisfied, and I would not be wrestling with these personal issues of what I want to do with the rest of the time I have on this earth."

Sandra takes her eyes away from the dry hills and deserts below and picks up the airline magazine. An article on the Olympics in Beijing catches her attention. Maybe someday, she and Dan can go there. In a few years, Sandra thinks, he will be senior enough to bid the 747, and then his routes will include China, Japan, and Australia. So much to look forward to.

In Denver that afternoon, Sandra calls Mary and her husband, Pat, from the airport hotel where she and Dan are staying. They are very happy to hear from her and arrange to pick them up at the hotel and take them to a restaurant in Golden, west of Denver, near the Coors Brewery.

When Mary arrives at the hotel, she looks fit and tan as usual. Her hair is a little longer and has some lighter streaks in it than Sandra remembers.

At the restaurant, they are seated in a roomy booth of makes of blond wood. The menus are large and interesting. Sandra is very glad she has made the trip with Dan this time.

"So, how are the kids? Has Peter heard about medical school yet?" asks Pat.

"He's on the waiting list at Washington. It's the school he most wanted, but for us it's no bargain, being out-of-state residents," answers Dan cautiously, not wanting to reveal any more than that.

"I'm surprised, if I were on the admissions team, I'd certainly select him," responds Pat.

"Well, I wish you were." Dan shuts the menu with a clap.

"Dan, I talked with Peter yesterday," says Sandra. "He had that interview with the medical school dean, and what he found out is that his application is excellent except for one thing."

"What is that?" Dan is interested. Maybe there is a way to make this turn out right after all.

"The dean told Peter that if he wanted to strengthen his application he needed to have some evidence of service to the community."

"Service to the community! What does that mean?"

"I guess it means some type of volunteer work," answers Sandra.

"Yes, that is very important these days," offers Mary. "Our daughter wrote her essay for Duke on her summer work cooking and delivering meals to AIDS patients, and I think it really helped."

"Does the dean have any suggestions?" asks Dan. Sandra knows they are having this conversation in the wrong place at the wrong time. She should never have brought up this subject with friends around. But now that she has started, she can't really change the subject.

"Actually, yes. Peter says the dean was very willing to listen to his ideas, and when he talked about being on the track team, the dean told him about a program for disabled teenagers that the university is offering this summer. Peter told him about the time he organized the wheelchair derby in high school, and the dean offered him a chance to do it again for this program."

"Okay, that's progress," Dan says slowly. The tension in his face lessens. He picks up the wine list. "What do you think? Merlot? Cabernet?"

"What are you two planning for your anniversary this year," Sandra asks after they have ordered.. "Can you believe its twenty-six years ago for all of us?"

"We're going to Hawaii," answers Mary. "It is the first time we have both had time off from work for a long time, too long." Mary and Pat smile almost shyly at each other.

"How about you? What did you do? Yours was last week, wasn't it?"

"We went to Catalina Island," answers Dan. "I wanted to sail over there, but Sandra wasn't up for it."

"I thought you liked sailing." Mary looks questioningly at Sandra.

"Well, I do. In the harbor, or right outside."

"Yeah, it would be great if we lived on a lake, so she can swim to shore. But we happen to live near the Pacific Ocean," Dan says, as he reaches for the salt and upsets a slender vase in the center of the table. There is a moment of silence as the two women right the vase and dab at the spilled water with their napkins.

"Hey, those Padres are looking pretty good this year, Dan." The two men trade jabs about the Rockies and the Padres as a way to retreat from the possible tension the previous subject has raised.

"Sandra, I thought you loved sailing," Mary goes on. "The last time we were there, we had a great time on the boat. Didn't you take the sailing lessons along with Dan?"

"Well, I started them, but I was so busy with work and all…"

"Do you think that if you take the rest of the lessons, you'd feel more comfortable on the boat?"

Roommates still, thinks Sandra. She doesn't know how to answer the questions. Or she doesn't want to answer them. Sandra hates her fears becoming known to others. More than anything, she hates talking about them out loud. If she could change them, she would, and she wished people would realize that they just can't talk her out of them.

Dan banters with Pat, defending the Padres over the Rockies, while inside he feels like a wildcat is trapped in his gut. His childhood has trained him to be polite and respectful of women, especially his mother and now his wife, but he deserves respect as well. Why couldn't Sandra have trusted him and gone along with his idea to sail the fifty or so miles from San Diego to Catalina. He had planned a route that took them up the coast to Newport and then across the channel…Damn it, it isn't even the ocean at all, just a channel. Then he gets control of himself. Feelings aren't all they're cracked up to be, he thinks to himself. Better to just stuff them down and forget it, again.

In their hotel room that night, there is something missing. Dan turns on the television to CNN and watches the late news, while Sandra takes a very long bath. When she comes out, he is asleep, with his two alarm clocks set and ready to spring him from this place at "zero dark thirty" the next morning.

When she hears the alarms, Sandra snoozes. Dan shaves, showers, puts on his uniform, and kisses her lightly on the cheek as he leaves.

"Don't wake up. I'll see you at home in a few days."

Walking out the door of the hotel room, Dan feels like he's been let out of school. Sandra is always trying to improve things, teach people things they should know, change the goddamn world, but she can't seem to change the things in herself that limit their good times. He has decided to be a good sport about the sailing trip to Catalina. He bought tickets for the ferry; they went and had a very good time; but Dan resents the fact that she wouldn't sail over there with him. Why doesn't she trust him?

He imagines the conversation last night at dinner if he had had his way. "Yes, we had a great time. We sailed this thirty-four-foot boat over there and stayed aboard her in the harbor at Avalon. When we got tired of Avalon, we just put to sea and went down to Tween Harbors for a day."

Not that he has anything to prove, but he wants to try some new things now that the boys have left home. He misses them more than he expected to. The house seems so still when he comes home now, like the air has been vacuumed out along with their rock music. The telephone rings a lot less, and when it does, Dan finds himself hoping that it will be Peter with good news about getting into med school or Alex calling to talk about taking flying lessons when he comes home for summer vacation.

"I should call them more often," Dan thinks, as he punches the button on the elevator to take him down to the lobby of the hotel. He always waits for Sandra to call them or for them to call—just like his dad. He never calls Dan on his own. His mother calls, and then she puts his father on for a few minutes. They talk about his clocks or Dan's flying, and then he says he'll put Mother back on. Dan wonders if he is going to do that with his kids too, repeat that pattern.

"Maybe one or both of the boys will be interested in sailing with me," he thinks. Not to Catalina, but there's a race to Ensenada that sounds very interesting. Maybe they'd be Dan's crew, and they could spend the day together out on the sea, just the three of us. Of course, you have to spend the night in Ensenada, but that wouldn't be so bad if they stay aboard the boat. They could go in and have a few beers at—what's the name of that place that everyone goes down there? Husongs or something like that. "We can go in, have a few beers, and then go back to the boat; take our own sandwiches, so we don't get sick on that Mexican food."

The elevator door opens onto the lobby, where Leslie, the copilot, is waiting for him, drinking a cup of coffee from a paper cup. Even this early in the morning, she looks rested, alert. Her shoulder-length blond hair is held back with a large barrette below the cap she wears. Women pilots are allowed to choose between the traditional brimmed hat the men wear or a slightly softer style similar to the caps the WAVES wore in World War II. Dan notices that Leslie is wearing the traditional cap like his own. His has gold "scrambled eggs" on the brim, signifying that he is a captain, while her hat brim is plain glossy black. The limo driver starts to grab Dan's bag, but Dan indicates that he can handle his own. The driver reaches for Leslie's bag, but she, too, waves him off and swings her bag up into the van. They climb in and start off on the short drive to Denver International Airport, where their plane is being fueled and loaded with water and food for their flight to Chicago.

"So, how did you spend the evening?" Dan asks, to make conversation and get his mind off the situation at home.

"I was studying for my PC," answers Leslie. "I come back here next week for my annual check ride. Do you ever get used to these things?"

"Never," Dan answers, happy to have a subject he can talk about, and vent a little tension at the same time. "I had mine in April, and I almost thought we would have to come back a third day for our simulation ride. My copilot was brand new, and his already low confidence took a hit that day."

On board their aircraft, Dan and Leslie swing into a comfortable rhythm setting up the cockpit for the first leg of the trip.

"It's your leg to Chicago. Weather is not the best for this early in the morning. May can be a dicey month for flying in the Midwest."

"I know it. I lived there for the first twenty years of my life."

"You did? Where?"

"Evanston, the suburb north of Chicago."

"I know it. Northwestern, right? Did you go to school there?"

"Almost. I got this idea in my head when I was in high school that I wanted to be an astronaut, so I planned to go to the Air Force Academy. It seemed like a logical first step. But I didn't know that when I graduated from high school, the air force was not yet ready for me."

"You mean you applied and didn't get in?"

"No, I mean that I wrote for an application, and they sent me one, but when they found out I was a girl, they wrote me a letter saying that they didn't take female applicants."

"What year was this?" Dan has finished setting up the computer on his side of the panel to take off when they get the go-ahead from air traffic control. He listens for a moment to the radio in his ear. "We're ready when you are," he says into the microphone that relays his message to the flight attendant in the rear of the plane.

"Back in the 'zero dark nineties,'" laughs Leslie, as she adjusts her seat for departure, pulling it up and using the electric motor to raise it so that she can see out of the cockpit window without straining. "They don't build these seats for people my size. I should bring a pillow to sit on."

As they taxi out to the runway, Leslie tells Dan the rest of the story—about the disappointment she felt that summer as she prepared to go to Northwestern, her second choice. Then, in June, her congressman called her to ask if she was serious about wanting to go to the Air Force Academy. She and one other woman were admitted that fall, after all.

Dan watches Leslie as she handles the throttle and instruments with confidence and grace. They make a smooth climb-out from the airport, entering some low clouds at eight thousand feet and leaving them behind at ten thousand. Dan looks out the window as the clouds seem to settle down below them like cotton mattresses. He loves this part of each flight.

As they level off at thirty-two thousand feet, Dan pushes the call button. When the flight attendant responds, he asks Leslie, "Do you want to eat first or shall I?"

"Go ahead," she says, and smiles. "I can wait. I'll just have a coffee with two creams."

"So, tell me more about the Air Force Academy. Don't worry about me. I was navy. You can name names, and they won't mean anything to me."

"Annapolis?" she asks.

"No, USC. I joined the navy in 1985; only stayed in for five years."

"Well, academy life was not exactly what I expected."

Dan feels a lot of admiration for the courage Leslie has shown. She is a hell of a good pilot. He wishes he had her on his last check ride instead of the guy they'd paired him with. Check rides are bad enough, but, when he is paired with a pilot that doesn't study or doesn't have the right stuff, he looks bad too. If Leslie had been there last month, he is sure the two of them would have sailed through with flying colors.

Sailed through. Yeah, that too.

Dan watches with approval as Leslie gently guides the plane to the right in response to an air traffic control order to change their heading. There are thunderstorm cumulus cloud formations directly in front of the nose. The air, which has been smooth up to this point, begins to unravel in a series of ripples.

"This feels like my father's Morgan going over the wake of a powerboat at forty-five degrees." Leslie is holding the yolk of the plane at arm's length, looking out over the instrument panel at the clouds with a sparkle in her eyes.

Dan is puzzled. Has he said the word "sailing" out loud or is Leslie a mind reader? "A Morgan—that is a boat I'd like to sail sometime. Are you a sailor like your dad?"

"Sailing is my other passion," answers Leslie. "I grew up sailing on Lake Michigan. My Dad taught me to do celestial navigation on a race to Mackinaw one night. That's when I decided to be an astronaut. Do you sail?"

"Yes, but I'm more of a beginner. I just completed the course on coastal navigation."

"San Diego is a great place to sail. Isn't that where you and your wife live?"

"Yes, I enjoy it. My wife isn't so keen on it, but…" Dan interrupts himself. "Let's call ATC and ask for ride reports," he suggests.

"Good idea. We've probably got our work cut out for us for the remainder of this trip. Do you want to put on the seat belt sign?"

The two pilots concentrate their efforts on communications between the ground controllers at Chicago and reprogramming their computers to match the new vectors. They talk to the flight attendants, and Dan makes an announcement to the passengers that mild to moderate turbulence is expected until they reach their destination. Leslie listens to him talking to the passengers, and she is reminded of the confident tone of voice that her father used with her when they were sailing in a thunderstorm on Lake Michigan. Her father is the person she admires more than anyone in the world. Someday, perhaps, she will find a man who matches his characteristics, but up to now, she hasn't. Not even with all the men in the air force. Maybe that is because she has had to work so hard to prove herself at every stage of her aviation career.

Airline flying seems to be an easier fit for her. She hopes that someday she'll find a man who shares her love of flying and sailing, and then she might have something approximating a private life as well as a career.

****

Sandra hails a taxi when she arrives back in San Diego and sits in the back of the cab trying to ignore the smells of cigarette smoke and mildew. It will be very good to get home. Even such a short trip as this makes her appreciate coming home to her comfortable house with its comfortable smells. She decides she will put on a good CD when she gets home—maybe the Satie piano pieces. They are always a comfort. She pictures herself curling up on the couch with a library book. First she will open the windows to let in a nice breeze, and then she'll get herself a cup of tea—that new herbal tea with the strong cinnamon flavor.

But her hopes for quiet and solitude are dashed when the cab stops at the front door, and she sees the gardener, Miguel, using a power mower on the lawn. A woman who appears to be helping him today is using a leaf blower on the sidewalk. She can't even hear the taxi driver as he turns around to tell her the fare. She can read it on the dashboard and gives him a two-dollar tip. She always feels badly for the cab driver who gets her as a fare. The trip is so short from the airport to her house that they must feel disappointed or even resentful to get her after the long wait for passengers at the airport.

Sandra gets out and carries her small overnight bag toward the front door. Miguel sees her and stops the motor on the mower.

"Hello," he says to her with a smile. "This is my wife working with me today." Miguel waves his arm at the woman, who also stops the engine on the machine she is operating.

"Oh, hello. Nice to meet you," Sandra says to the woman, who responds with a shy smile. "And how are you, Miguel? Busy these days?"

"Yes, very busy. I have more customers than I can do on my own."

"So, you've asked your wife to help?"

"Well, yes, but she is not helping me for that reason. The reason is she worked for a very nice woman, Mrs. Blumenthal. Do you know her?"

"No, that name isn't familiar," answers Sandra.

"Mrs. Blumenthal has gone to the hospital and doesn't need Rosa to work for her now."

"I'm sorry to hear that," says Sandra. She smiles again at the small, pretty Mexican woman holding the leaf blower. "What work did you do for Mrs. Blumenthal?"

"I do everything she needs. She is a very nice lady, but very old. I think she has ninety years or maybe more."

"Did you work for her every day?" asks Sandra.

"Five days. She lives in La Jolla. She has a big house, many pictures and things that need dusting. Many windows that need washing." Rosa looks at Sandra's windows, which are streaked with moisture and the fine black particles that descend from the airplanes that are always passing overhead.

Sandra realizes that Rosa and Miguel are waiting expectantly. They probably hope that Sandra will hire Rosa to do housework for her. The family probably counted on the money Rosa earned. Sandra considers making an offer of one day a week to help them out, but then thinks again and decides to go inside, have her cup of coffee, and think about this for a few minutes, at least. "Let me know when you are finished, Miguel. Nice to meet you, Rosa."

She unlocks the door and goes inside. Amigo appears from under the dining room table. He mews for food and company, and Sandra responds eagerly. She puts.....and watches the cat gobble down his kibble in a few gulps. Then he sits and cleans his whiskers with his paws while Sandra makes her tea and rummages through the cupboard for the package of cookies she remembered hiding from herself a few days ago.

Her plan to listen to music and read is put on hold until the gardening noises subside. She longs for silence and to have her house completely to herself. She needs to think about Dan and the messages she got from him last night in Denver. She does not need to think about someone else's problems right now. Besides, she doesn't want someone to clean her house. She doesn't want someone else coming in and going through the papers strewn on her desk, even if the person doesn't speak or read English very well. She tried having a housecleaning service one time, when she was working, and she found it a pain. On the morning the service was to come, she had to clean up all the messes in the boys' rooms, tidy up the kitchen, stack up her unfinished business, and straighten up Dan's charts and ALPA magazines before she went to work.

Now it would be even worse. She isn't working, and if a cleaning person were to come, she would feel very awkward deciding how much to help or not help in her own house. She would probably want to go out while the person cleaned just to not feel in the way. But what if she doesn't want to go out that day? And what about trusting the person while she is away? Though Rosa certainly looked like a pleasant and probably very trustworthy person.

That's not the real point, thinks Sandra, as she nibbles a cookie and sips her cinnamon tea in the sunny breakfast room. The real point is that I wasn't looking for a person to clean my house, but now I feel like I ought to hire Rosa because she lost her other client and her family needs the money. I wonder if I can just give her the fifty dollars or so a week and pay her not to come. But that will be an insult to her, or at least an act of charity when what she wants is respect and a job of her own. Well, then, let her find a job somewhere else, with someone who needs her work. That's the only reasonable solution.

Maybe I can ask Janet Froelich if she wants a cleaning person, thinks Sandra, as the telephone rings and interrupts her thoughts. With a sense of relief, Sandra picks up the receiver, hoping it is Dan calling from O'Hare Airport.

"Hi, Mom. Qué paso?" It is the especially lively voice of Alex, the voice he uses when he wants to ask for something that he knows is a stretch. Sandra relaxes into her chair again and breathes a welcome smile into the phone. Mother and son talk easily together.

"Are your finals this week?" she asks.

"Yes, two this week and one next Monday. Then I'll be home…for a while."

"For a while? What does that mean? Aren't you going to get a job around here for the summer."

"Well, I know that was my plan originally, but here's the deal."

"The deal?"

"Yes, it's a great deal. It's going to save you and Dad all kinds of money. You know how expensive the dorm is here?"

"I don't remember exactly, but…"

"Well, it's more than tuition, and we're paying for meals, and the thing is—I hardly ever make it to the meals. So, these guys I know started think-ing, and what we're going to do is go in together and get an apartment together."

"Which guys?"

"This one guy, Luke, is from my econ class. He's an A student. No worry about partying all the time. We'll study all right."

"Yes, and the other guys?"

"Well, they're not exactly guys. Luke knows these two girls who are already looking for a place, and the thing is they found one, but it's too big and too expensive for them alone, so they've asked us to go in with them."

"Two guys and two girls? Alex, is that realistic?"

"What do you mean, Mom? We're not going to sleep with them. We'll each have our own room. And you know, Mom, how you always tell me that you wish I had a sister so I'd understand women better, so when I do get married…"

"Wow, Alex, this is a lot to think about. Can we wait until your dad gets home to make a decision?"

"No, Mom. Do you know how hard it is to find a good apartment near the university? If I don't say yes, they'll ask someone else."

"We're talking about a September lease, right?" asks Sandra.

There is a pause that answers her question. "If we wait till September, Mom, there'll be no chance at all to find a good place. This one is available now because the people who lived in it are all graduating next week. We have to sign a year's lease from June to June."

Sandra can see the consequences of any response she might make. If she says no, she is standing in the way of Alex's transition from childhood to adulthood. He has had a year in the dorm and is probably ready now to have a place of his own. The sharing isn't a bad thing, even with the girls. They'd probably keep the place neater than if it were four men living together. The sex issue isn't one she wants to get into at all with Alex. From what she can see, he is careful and discriminating in his relationships.

"What does your girlfriend think about this?" Sandra asks.

"She's out of the picture, Mom. Didn't I tell you that? You know, with her parents and all. They really have brainwashed her to believe that she should only be serious about a Korean man. I really don't have a chance. She won't even tell them about me, and when I suggested that I go to her house to meet them, she kept putting it off. Finally, I asked her when I was going to meet them, and she said she is afraid to even tell them she is dating me. That is it for me. That's not what I believe in. It's not how I was raised."

Is this just sweet talk, designed to break down her defenses on the apartment decision? No, Alex doesn't play those games. He is telling her that he has enough self-respect to make a grown-up decision and take responsibility for it. He will probably not spend much time at home this summer anyway. He will either be working or out with friends most of the time.

"Okay, Alex, I'll tell you what. You can sign the lease. Just come home next week, and we'll all sit down together to work out the details of who pays what, okay?"

"What do you mean, 'who pays what'? You would be paying for the dorm, so can't you just pay for the rent instead and give me a couple of hundred a month for food?"

"I don't know right now. Dad will have some ideas about that, too. But I'm telling you that we can work this out if we all sit down and talk about it together. We might want you to pay a share of the expenses with your summer job."

The doorbell rings. Sandra looks out the window and sees Miguel standing on the front porch. Rosa is sitting in the car.

"I've got to go now, Alex," Sandra says. "We'll see you next week and make it work. I love you."

"I love you, too, Mom. Bye."

Sandra goes to the front door and opens it. She writes a check for Miguel's work for the month and gives it to him with a smile.

"Please tell Rosa that I just don't need anyone right now for housework. But I'll ask my neighbors if they do, okay?"

"Thank you, Mrs. Sandra. I'll tell her. See you next week."

Miguel gives her the same warm, pleasant smile as always as he turns and walks out of the house toward his truck. Immediately, Sandra is filled with feelings of guilt. They aren't asking for very much, just the opportunity to work for a living. If Rosa doesn't work for her, then who will she work for? Obviously, she is using her husband's contacts to look for work. So, he can probably introduce her to other people that he does gardening for. But she will need several clients to make up for the one who hired her five days a week. Why not us? What am I really giving up? We can afford fifty dollars for a clean house, if that's what she charges. I pay that to have my hair cut. We pay that for a dinner out or a couple of tickets to a play.

"Miguel, wait a moment." Sandra walks toward the truck and reaches it as Miguel is climbing into the driver's seat. Rosa opens the window on her side.

"Rosa, I think it will be very nice to have someone help once a week. Why don't you come next Wednesday with Miguel, and you can work inside while he works out. Is that all right?"

"It's great, Mrs. Seaquist. That way I won't have to take the bus. You are a very nice lady to think of that. I will do a good job for you. First thing, we'll start on those windows. Okay?"

"Okay," agrees Sandra, and extends her hand to shake Rosa's smaller one. "It will be great to start seeing clearly around here for once."

Chapter Fourteen

TURN, TURN, TURN

Sandra tries on her best pair of navy blue pumps, discards them, and puts on a more comfortable pair of black low-heel shoes. Her feet aren't used to grown-up shoes anymore. She hasn't worn heels since before last Christmas at work. Her navy blue and white striped suit will do. She dusts off the purse that goes with it. Just getting dressed to go into her old office is surprisingly difficult to do. What will she feel when she gets there and sees someone sitting at her old desk? Well, that's partly what she is going in for, to see how it feels to be back.

She is glad Dan isn't home from his trip yet to see how disorganized she is. He would be asking her what her decision is about her job, and she would hate to tell him that she doesn't know yet what she will decide. Her boss, Dr. James Goodenow, has asked her to come in today, and she knows that she will have to tell him yes or no.

A quick breakfast of sliced banana on toast spread with peanut butter and a cup of herbal tea and Sandra is looking for her car keys. Amigo comes up to her and rubs against her legs as if to say, "Stay home with me." As Sandra bends over to pick up the cat and give it a quick hug, the telephone rings. She knows that she should let the machine pick it up because she just has time to get across town to the administration building and find a parking place, but she can't resist a ringing phone.

"Hello."

"Hello. Is Captain Seaquist available?" asks a woman with a crisp, professional voice.

"No. Is this the crew desk?" answers Sandra. "He's on his way up to LA for his trip."

"No, this isn't the crew desk. I'm his copilot this month. I'll talk to him in dispatch. Thank you."

"He should be there soon. He took the seven-thirty shuttle. Is there any message?"

"No, no message. Thank you."

Sandra holds on to the phone for a moment before hanging up the receiver. This woman and her husband will be spending the next few days together. Strange. But, okay. She trusts Dan. For more than twenty-four years he has had the same type of temptations with flight attendants, and he has never shown any interest in straying. Why would it be any different with a copilot? Besides, the woman is probably happily married herself.

Sandra's eyes are tearing up. She dabs at them with a napkin and sees the black mascara smudge the cloth. That means it is smudged on her face as well. She goes into the bathroom to look in the mirror and repair the damage. Her face is familiar, but at the same time, unfamiliar. It looks more like her mother's face than her own. The lines etching themselves along the side of her nose and down to her mouth make her seem to be frowning or scowling. She crinkles up her mouth into a grin, but that just looks ludicrous, like a clown face, happy-sad or sad-happy.

Is this the face of a school administrator? Yes, it could be. Most of the other people who work in her office are her age or older. Age forty-five, fifty, even sixty is exactly the age of a proper school administrator. There are many happy-sad or sad-happy faces in her office. Is that where she belongs? Back behind her desk, deciding how to increase the reading test scores for the city of San Diego? It isn't a trivial goal. It is an important one. These five months off have given her, if anything, a much greater respect for reading and books. She has had time to read a lot more herself, and she has read dozens of wonderful children's books as a Rolling Reader volunteer.

Would she have to give up the volunteering if she went back to work? Wouldn't that be ironic? To be a reading specialist and give up reading to children because her job wouldn't allow it.

As she leaves the bright June sunshine and enters the dusk of the administration building corridor, she is assaulted by the odor of dust and cleaning fluid.

She passes by the superintendent's office and continues down the hall toward the office of the director of curriculum. Dr. Goodenow's secretary greets her warmly and offers a cup of coffee. Sandra refuses, remembering the metallic taste of the coffee brewed in the lounge next door. She puts on her best face, asks the secretary how her children are doing, and waits for Jim to get off the phone. When he hangs up, he motions her to come in, and she enters his office with a strange reluctance that reminds her of being called to the principal's office as a child.

"Good to see you, Sandra. You're looking well. I think I need a six-month leave, too." Jim Goodenow is few years younger than Sandra, but today he looks older. His skin has a gold tinge that Sandra doesn't remember. She decides not to ask about his health.

"Busy as ever, I see," she says instead.

"Oh, yes. The budget cuts, at war with the mandate to cut class size in the primary grades, have been...But you know how it is. We're having a lot of trouble satisfying the teachers' union, and you know how we're scrambling for classroom space."

Jim Goodenow goes on to describe the efforts they are making to influence the state board of education on issues relating to teacher credentialing and the choice of a statewide reading assessment plan. Sandra sits in her chair, pretending to give these matters her complete attention. She nods when it seems appropriate and shakes her head in dismay as Jim talks about all the good work that will likely be undone by the use of a standardized test that measures word recognition and decoding skills rather than reading for meaning.

Internally, Sandra watches herself and is shocked at how little these matters seem to mean to her. It isn't that they aren't important issues. They are almost too important, and the prospects for a positive resolution to them seem fleeting at best. She recalls that many of these same arguments were being debated twenty-some years ago when she was doing her master's degree in education and when she took her first teaching job at Glorietta School. Since then, the pendulum has swung back and forth a half dozen times. Sandra has realized that it won't end during her career and that her lifelong commitment to working within the system has resulted in few, if any, real improvements in the life of children.

Many, probably the same number as twenty years ago, don't learn how to read, and many of those who learn to read, don't enjoy it. The emphasis on reading skills and test scores has produced a population that reads what they have to read to get by. In contrast to this, Sandra has an image of the children she has been reading aloud to at the housing project. Last week, as she drove into the parking lot, they surrounded her car. She got out and had four or five children all holding on to her arm to see the books she brought to read. Other children were yelling up to the apartments of friends to come down "because the reading lady is here."

Sandra brought a collection of books to choose from, and she let the children help her select which ones to read. A teenage boy brought his baby sister and sat on the fringe of the group holding the baby, as she read stories meant for third and fourth graders. Sandra looked up and apologized to the teenager, "I'm sorry; these books are kind of babyish for you."

But he replied, "That's all right. I just like to hear the sound of your voice."

If she had the summer to do with as she pleased, she could take some of these kids to the library with her to get their own books. Of course, if she was back at work, she would probably be too tired to do so. Maybe on Saturdays.

She tunes back in as she becomes aware that Jim is about to make some kind proposal.

"So, if you want to head up the reading clinic this year, I'll have Janet take over the committee on textbook selection. Of course, we'd want you to stay involved with that, give your input, but she could write the final report. What do you say?"

What do I say? Do I say what I'm expected to say, or do I say what I'm feeling? And if I say what I'm feeling, what is that exactly? And what are the consequences? If I leave this job, I might be sorry in a few weeks or months. Sure, it's been great to have these months to explore my options, but what if that gets old? What if I get bored and want to come back in a few months? They're not going to save this job for me.

"Jim, I think I need more than six months to decide what I'm going to do next. I know that is neither reasonable nor professional, but that is all I can say right now."

Jim frowns and looks at his pencil, reading the words engraved on its surface before speaking again. "Sandra, this is the reading clinic we're talking about. It's the most important piece of the pie right now. The governor has made it a priority before the election, and we're going to need to get our team in place and create a stable plan for the district to meet the state mandate to have all children reading at grade level by the end of third grade. I thought that was one of your most important goals. Frankly, I can't understand your hesitation."

"I know it sounds strange, Jim, but reading is just as important to me as ever. The difference is that I seem to have become more interested in working one to one with children again rather than creating policies about it."

"I can't hold this job open any longer, Sandra. It isn't an option to have another six months to think about it. This is one of those cases where if you don't decide, you've made a decision anyway." He looks at her sternly then softens when he sees that she is close to tears.

"Sandra, think about this for another few days. Call me at the end of the week, okay?"

"Okay, Jim. That's more than fair. I'll talk it over with my husband when he gets home, and I'll let you know what I'm going to do by Friday." She extends her hand to shake his, an oddly formal gesture for a colleague and friend that she has worked with for many years. He clasps her hand warmly in both of his and smiles.

"I'm sure you'll make the right decision, Sandra. You're known for that around here. Talk to you on Friday."

Sandra leaves his office and wants to immediately shed her shoes. She wants to run down the stairs, rather than walk. She wants to go buy an ice cream at Dairy Queen and eat it as she walks home from school. That was what she had always done on her last day of school each June as she was growing up.

Is that what this is? My last day of school? She shivers as if she really is eating cold ice cream too fast. My last day of school forever? Sandra can't remember a year that she wasn't in school. After high school there had been college, then teacher education courses, student teaching, and from then on she was teaching in or administering schools. Her time has always been measured by how many days off she has for various school vacations or weeks she has between school years. What would it be like to know that there wouldn't be any new school year for her ever again? What would she really do with the rest of her life?

Reaching her car, Sandra unlocks the door and gets into the driver's seat. She turns the key in the ignition, and the motor turns over smoothly. She puts the car in reverse, preparing to back out of the parking space, but stops when she realizes that she doesn't know where she is going. Home? Dan is away. The cat doesn't need her again until dinnertime. Shopping? For what? She doesn't need groceries. The library? Yes, of course.

Relieved to know her destination, Sandra pulls out of the parking lot and drives past the administration building. It seems dingy and forbidding to her today. She recalls how excited she was to come to this same building to interview for her first teaching position many years ago. She also recalls the good feelings she had when she was called to interview for the administrative opening, and how proud she had been when she was hired.

"For everything, turn, turn, turn…," she hears herself humming. Is that the answer? Is it simply a matter of different seasons in her life? How does that song go? A time for war, a time for peace, a time for beginnings, a time for endings? No those words aren't familiar, but the idea is. Very familiar.

Sandra knows then that she has made her decision.

"A time for change…," she sings out loud. And what better place to begin than at the library. She will look for books about career changes, biographies of women doing important new things in midlife. The library has always been her refuge, and she drives happily now, with a sense of hope and excitement.

Having no books with her to return, she is able to stop and look at the notices on the bulletin board just inside the front door of the library. A woman is pinning a new notice up. Sandra looks at it with curiosity. "Spanish Children's Books Needed," she reads. Sandra looks over at the woman who has just pinned up the flyer. Yes, she appears to be Hispanic, although her hair is red. Sandra continues to read, observing at the same time that the other woman has gone past the front desk and into the adult stacks.

Spanish Children's Books Needed
Tecolote Medical Clinic/Community Center in Tijuana
We provide tutoring & other after-school activities

There is a telephone number and the name "Dra. Bruni Mendez."

Sandra wonders what the "Dra." means. Is that the woman who just pinned up the notice? Bruni Mendez? Sandra walks toward the adult fiction shelves by habit. Then she stops. No, today she is going to get books about career changes. That would be in the six hundreds? No, maybe the five hundreds?

Better look it up, she thinks, and heads toward the computer terminals with the online catalogues. Standing at one of the terminals is the woman Sandra has just seen at the bulletin board.

"Excuse me," she hears herself saying, without really planning what else she wants to say. "My name is Sandra Seaquist. I just saw you put up that notice on the bulletin board."

"Yes," says the woman, and smiles. "Sandra? I am Bruni. It is nice to meet you."

Her English is very good, Sandra thinks, but there is definitely an accent. "Do you have time to tell me about the project you are doing, the after-school project?"

"Of course. I'd be happy to tell you." Bruni looks around her. "Should we talk here?"

"Well, maybe not. How about if we go outside after you are finished?" suggests Sandra.

"Fine, I won't be very long. I just need to find some information on ESL for one of the volunteers at our clinic. Shall we meet outside in five or ten minutes?"

"Great, I'll see you there," agrees Sandra.

She types in the subject "career changes" at the terminal nearby and sees several titles that look interesting. She goes into the stacks, locates the section, and chooses several books to take home. After checking them out, she walks out the front door and waits a few moments until Bruni joins her. They sit on a bench at the side of the building.

"What does the d-r-a mean in front of your name?" asks Sandra.

"'Doctora,'" answers Bruni. "I am a medical doctor, trained in Mexico City, a family practitioner."

"Oh." Sandra is surprised by this answer, although she can't say why. Bruni is about her age, dressed in a skirt and sweater with a matching pattern of black and white. She colors her hair also, thinks Sandra. Aloud, she asks about the project, and finds out that Bruni lives in San Diego but goes to Tijuana twice a week to run a medical clinic for families in a very poor neighborhood called Tecolote.

With money provided by San Diego churches and labor supplied by Tecolote residents, they have just completed building a small community center next door to the clinic, and they plan to operate a before- and after-school program there in the fall. Four full-time volunteers are scheduled to arrive in August, three from Germany and one young man who has just graduated from the University of Michigan. They will tutor children in reading, writing, and math, and organize some sports and craft activities as well.

Bruni is excited about the project as she describes it, and Sandra begins to see the small building in her mind, ready for September, ready to begin when school starts in the fall. She asks Bruni many questions about the number of children (80), the grade levels (K–8) and the types of materials they already have for the program (a few workbooks in Spanish, paper, pencils, chalk, and a blackboard).

"I want to help," Sandra says. "What can I do?"

"Well, how is your Spanish?" asks Bruni.

"I took it in high school. I don't remember it very well, but I learned quickly then. I think I can learn it again."

"You will be doing better than some of our new volunteers, then," laughs Bruni. "Three of our volunteers are from Germany. They all learn English in school, but they will be learning Spanish—how do you say it?—on the job training. They are coming in August for a crash course in Spanish. Then we begin with the children in September."

"Where is the center located?" asks Sandra. She tries to remember from her trip to Tijuana as Bruni describes going up and over a high hill behind the downtown area well known to tourists. The center is tucked into a canyon, almost a ravine, on the south side of Tijuana, where many new colonias have sprung up around the US- and Korean- and Japanese-owned factories called maquiladoras, which make household products and ship them to the United Sates.

Sandra feels that cold shiver again, ice cream—no, this time it is ice cubes going down her windpipe. She coughs. Images come into her mind of the small, ragged shacks she saw from the roadway in Tijuana. She is sure that they are visible to Bruni too, as if a cartoon balloon containing her mind's images is floating above her head. No, really, this would be too much for her to handle, she thinks. She wonders how can she get out of this gracefully. She coughs again to give herself time to think.

"Are you all right?" asks Bruni.

"Yes, fine, it's probably just an allergy," answers Sandra. Allergies, yes—that is what she can say. "Listen, I would like to do something—donate some books at least. May I have your telephone number?" Sandra finds herself standing up, looking for a pen to write with, planning a hasty exit.

"Here, you can have one of these notices. It has my number on it. Call me, and we can talk about the project again. And, Sandra, I...well, I understand how you might feel about coming to visit. It is very different from what you are used to. But, you know what? The children—they are living there. So I decide I can go too. But I am always happy to come back across the border to San Diego, and I was born in Mexico."

Sandra takes the notice. She looks at Bruni. She feels certain that this is a woman who feels some of the same things she feels, some of the same conflicts. She definitely wants to know her better. She thinks she can learn something important from her, something about the world beyond administration buildings and her comfortable neighborhood.

"I will call you, Bruni, and I'm very glad that I decided to come to the library today at the same time you came. It seems like it was meant to be." She reaches out and gives Bruni a quick hug, then laughs. "That's the first time I ever hugged a doctor."

"But not the last time, I hope. I'll wait to hear from you. In Spanish, the word 'espero' means both 'I wait' and 'I hope.' Espero para tu llamada. Adios."

Chapter Fifteen

CROSSING THE LINE

Friday, Sandra was faced with the need to call Jim Goodenow and the desire to call Bruni Mendez. Instead, she called her friend, Hanna, who had recently returned from Albuquerque. Sandra needed a sympathetic ear. She hoped that by talking about her decision of whether to return to work she would be able to clarify her choices.

"Hanna, how are you?" Sandra began, ready to leap into a full-blown description of her meeting at the administration building and the deadline she faced today.

"Tired," responded Hanna guardedly, as if Sandra were calling to find out why she hadn't reported for work on time. "I've been weeding the garden and planting new tomato and cucumber plants."

"Well, that never stops you. Usually, you are ready to hike up Cowles Mountain after that."

"You know, I'm tired from the gardening. It was hot, and I didn't have much to eat or drink beforehand. Why do you always expect me to act like Superwoman?"

"I don't expect that, Hanna. If you are tired, you deserve a rest just like anyone else. Want me to bring you a sandwich and some iced tea?"

"That would be nice."

"Okay, then I'll be there in a few minutes."

Sandra made tuna fish sandwiches with extra mayonnaise and mixed some cran-apple juice with the leftover tea from breakfast. She drove over to her friend's house in Hillcrest, still rehearsing what she would tell Hanna about her job decision and the brief encounter with Bruni at the library. When she arrived at Hanna's craftsman-style house, she found her friend on the front porch, with a Scrabble game on the table.

"Want to play?" Hanna made room for Sandra and the lunch. As they ate their sandwiches, Sandra tried to bring up her dilemma.

"Hanna, I've got a difficult choice to make about my career."

"Listen, Sandra, you may think you have a difficult choice, but from my perspective, you are not hurting any way you go. You can work or not work; you're still well-off by any standard." There was a bitter tone in Hanna's voice, a tone that Sandra could not remember hearing before.

"It isn't a question of money, Hanna. But leaving a career that I have—"

"Well, for most of us, it is a question of money. I have to rent rooms to pay all my bills." Hanna pushed away the remains of her sandwich. There was a silence that neither woman wanted or knew how to break. Finally, Hanna spoke. "Sorry, I didn't mean all that. I guess I'm just worried about my own welfare. What do you say we just play Scrabble? Would that be all right with you?"

"Hanna, I understand your concern. I've felt worried about your future also. I know it's not easy being a single woman living on your own resources."

"You know nothing about it, Sandra. Who are you kidding? You are protected for the rest of your life." Hanna spoke without facing Sandra. Instead, she sorted Scrabble tiles and picked one, the letter *a*. "Well, looks like I come out ahead on this game, at least. You can hardly beat my *a*."

"I'm not competing with you, Hanna. You're my friend. You mean a great deal to me. I...I really don't know what to say."

"I don't either." Hanna paused. Then she began to speak as if she had rehearsed the words. "Listen, for me, friendship is a lot of work right now. You know me. I've always been more solitary than you, and lately, I like it that way. For me, being with people is a drain on my energy. I have to have time alone to regain it. I don't have the same level of energy, social or physical, that I used to. I wish you could accept that."

"What does that mean? Hanna, what you're describing sounds like depression to me. Have you considered seeing a doctor about it, maybe taking something to raise your energy?"

"Sandra, you don't get it, do you? You always want to fix everything and everybody. Didn't you hear me? I said that for me, I like it this way. I'm paring down my life. I'd rather spend my energy on my gardening right now."

Sandra stood up and cleaned up the paper napkins and wrappings from the sandwiches. She didn't have any answer at all. For once, she could think of a thing to say. She watched Hanna pick out seven letter tiles and rearrange them on the wooden rack.

"Listen, I've got to go," Sandra announced. "I think I may have left my teakettle on my stove. I'll call you." She made a hasty retreat to her car and drove home feeling numb. What had she done or said to cause Hanna to reject their friendship? Then, a new thought occurred to her. Maybe it isn't her fault. Maybe she didn't do or say anything. Hanna seems to have explained this situation to herself in a way that satisfies her own needs right now. Maybe Sandra can't change her friend's situation or who she is or what she does with the rest of her life.

It was a startling thought and so disturbing that Sandra was relieved to think of an errand or two that needed doing, some shirts to pick up at the cleaners, a box of blueberries she needed from the grocery store.

When she got home, there was a phone message from Dan, who had called from an airport somewhere. He asked her to make an appointment to have his car serviced. She was glad to have even this small task before calling Jim Goodenow.

When she dialed the administration building and asked for his extension, his secretary answered.

"Hi, Margie. It's Sandra Seaquist. Is Jim available?"

"Sandra, I'm afraid I have very bad news. Jim is in the hospital. He had a seizure of some sort this morning. We don't know how serious it is. Would you like to talk to Dr. Janus?"

"A seizure? What does that mean? Was it a heart attack?"

"I don't know. He just collapsed as he was walking down the hallway. Paramedics worked on him for an hour or more, and then they finally took him to UCSD hospital by ambulance. You might try calling there, but they didn't tell us anything except that he is in the ICU. Here, Sandra, let me connect you to Dr. Janus."

Sandra waited for the connection with Dr. Janus, the assistant superintendent for curriculum; she was not anxious to tell him that she had decided not to take the reading clinic job. It would have been easier to tell Jim.

The deep, authoritative voice came on the line. "Sandra, I'm very glad to hear from you. With Jim sick, we're going to need you more than ever. I hope you are calling to tell me that you'll be back at your desk next Monday."

"Dr. Janus, I'm not prepared to do that."

"What's to prepare? You know this office and the curriculum. We need you now to prepare for the new school year and lead the literacy task force in Jim's place."

"But, I had decided... That is, I think that I need..."

"Sandra, you know that normally I don't lose my temper, but your hesitation makes me see red. You have been one of the most reliable persons on our staff. We understood your need for a refresher, and we bent over backward to allow you that time. But now we need you to repay the district for the investment we've made in you."

"I'd like to support Jim, Dr. Janus. I can offer to come in for a few weeks and help do his work while he's out sick. When he gets well though..."

"Who are you kidding, Sandra? From what I could see, Jim is not going to be back in a few weeks. He's probably had a major stroke. In any case, it's his turn for some R & R, and it's time for you to return to work."

"I'm sorry, Dr. Janus. I've made other plans."

"Oh, is that how it is? You've been interviewing elsewhere? Okay, how much were you offered? If it isn't outlandish, we'll match it."

"No, sir, it isn't that way at all. You don't understand."

"No, Ms. Seaquist, I'm afraid I don't. And I don't have time to play these games right now. Come out with it. What do you want?"

What does she want? That is the question isn't it, thought Sandra. Money, security, a career versus freedom, new challenges, and being able to spend time with children again. The image of a child sitting next to her as they both read aloud from the same picture book came into her mind. It was the clarifying image she had been seeking.

"Dr. Janus, I am going to submit my resignation. I don't expect you to understand, but I have other goals now." As she said these words aloud, they felt exactly right. She was being true to herself. As she hung up the telephone, she felt relieved and exhilarated.

Ten minutes later, as she sat in front of her word processor and tried to compose a letter of resignation, she felt sad, confused, and afraid. What had she done? A twenty-year career terminated? Who was she if not the capable wife, mother, and school employee? Well, at least she was still a wife.

Thoughts of Dan sprang into her mind. What would he think when she told him she had quit? She wished she knew where Dan was at that moment. His calendar notes said Portland. That wasn't so far away. Maybe she could go to the airport and fly up there for the night. She pictured herself meeting his plane at the airport. He'd be very surprised to see her. See, that was the type of freedom she had now. She could do whatever she wanted to do. But a check of airline schedules told her she had just missed the last good connection through San Francisco to Portland for the day. She'd have to be content to stay home with Amigo.

****

Landing in Portland that evening, Dan Seaquist was not thinking about Sandra. If she had been standing there in the airport terminal when he deplaned, he might not have noticed her. As he opened the door into the terminal, Leslie, his copilot again on this trip, was telling him about the way she had dived underneath the sailboat she was on last weekend. Something had become entangled in the propeller of the engine, and she had volunteered to investigate because she could hold her breath underwater for almost two minutes at a time.

"My dad agreed that I was the man for the job," she laughed. "Because I have the smallest hands and was able to work this thing out after four or five dives."

"What was it? A rope?" Dan asked, as they wheeled their suitcases and flight bags out the front door and waited for the hotel van to pick them up.

"No, it was a plastic tarp, or what was left of one. Luckily it didn't ruin our trip. We hadn't needed the engine all day and were just using it when we got back into the harbor to steer into our slip."

"So you had a good sail."

"The best one this summer. You would have loved it. Say, I've got an idea. Next month, if you want to bid for Chicago layovers and they match my schedule, you can come for a sail on Lake Michigan with my dad and me."

"Okay, I'll look at my lines tonight and show you what I'm bidding tomorrow morning. Are there still anymore of those twenty-three-hour layovers at O'Hare?"

"Yes, I think they're still in our schedule."

"Great, I'll work on it. Sounds like fun."

****

It takes courage to cross lines, thought Miguel, as he and his mother gathered together the boxes and bags she had brought with her from Honduras. The crowded bus terminal in Tijuana was filled with other travelers from all parts of Central America.

"Stay with me, Miguel," whispered Salina in Spanish, as she clutched her son's arm, digging her fingernails in just a little bit to remind him that she was there.

"I'm not going anywhere, Mami," said Miguel. He looked around at the other passengers getting off the bus. Some of them were meeting relatives at the station, while others were searching the crowd for familiar faces. No one was meeting Miguel and Salina. Well, no one they knew. But Miguel was aware that even as they stood there, eyes were watching them, sizing them up, looking for signals that they needed the assistance of a guide to the Promised Land.

Within minutes, a man approached them. "Quieren ayuda? Necesitan un taxi?"

Miguel said simply, "Al otro lado?" To the other side?

The man smiled broadly. "Claro que si, señor. Para los dos? Of course, sir. For the two of you?"

"No, for my mother only." Miguel took out his wallet and showed the man his own green card, his resident alien card for the United States of America. The man's respect seemed to grow. He took off his hat. They discussed their options.

For three hundred dollars, the man would escort Miguel's mother across the border and meet up with Miguel in a little-used industrial park on the other side. Miguel would take all the luggage and walk through the immigration checkpoint, showing his green card. He would say that he had been visiting his mother at her home in San Pedro Sula, that she had died while he was there, and he was bringing her things into the US to give to his wife.

"When can you do this?" asked Miguel.

"Stay with me, m'ijo," insisted his mother at his side. He tried to reassure her, but soon enough he was going to have to break the news to her that it was not possible for him to stay with her. She would have to walk alone, trusting this man or another just like him to get her safely across a border that is watched twenty-four hours a day by the US Border Patrol, armed with guns and dogs to prevent the intrusion of undocumented and therefore undesirable aliens into the Land of the Free.

Miguel wasn't even sure he wanted to know the details of the passage. The border had gotten harder to cross every day. Since his own attempts many years ago, the border fence of corrugated metal had been erected for several miles from the ocean to the mountains east of San Diego. A sewer pipe that had been used by many immigrants over the years was now closed up with cement. Some younger and more hopeful crossers still waited patiently for hours and hours at the few holes that had been dug beneath the fence. They watched over the fence for the green-and-white border patrol trucks to drive away, and then they ran down into the gullies, hoping to make it to safety before they were noticed, arrested, and returned to Tijuana to try their luck again the next day.

For people like Salina, the options had become more limited. The first man offered to guide her across the mountains with a group of other immigrants. Miguel refused, saying his mother couldn't walk that far. Another guide approached. He could offer to take her in a car or van that would drive east on the Mexican border to the Sonora desert beyond the mountains. One car and driver were needed to take her across the border; another would meet them on the other side and follow dirt roads to a highway that may or may not be blockaded by border patrol. It would be more expensive, five hundred dollars per person.

Miguel had read frequently about deadly crashes involving vans crammed full of adults, children, and babies that were driven at high speeds to elude border patrol agents and careened into gullies or head-on collisions with other automobiles.

Miguel continued to negotiate for another option. He asked if there were any Honduran guides. Someone knew of a Honduran man from San Pedro Sula. After a lengthy wait at the bus station, the Honduran man arrived. Miguel decided to trust this man. He arranged for his mother to be transported in the car of a Mexican family who all had border crosser cards and were just going to the Target on a Saturday afternoon. She might have to be hidden in a compartment under the seat. It would be crowded, dark, and frightening, but it beat walking across the mountains or being stranded in the desert. He would pay two hundred dollars to the guide for arranging the passage and another two hundred dollars to the driver of the car. They would drop her off at the McDonald's on the other side of the border.

Miguel stayed with his mother in a small hotel until Saturday. He called Rosa to ask her to meet him at the McDonald's restaurant on Saturday afternoon. She was still very angry at him, but there was relief in her voice to hear from him. He knew that she would forgive him once again. She knew that he knew that. She washed her hair that night and put on a special rinse that smelled like rose petals. She had saved it from Christmas, not using it once while Miguel was gone.

On Saturday morning, the Honduran man came to meet them at the hotel. Miguel walked with his mother to see the car she would be traveling in and meet the people who would transport her. They were a somber, unsmiling family who needed the dollars they could earn in this transaction to pay their rent. Landlords in Tijuana expect their rent in dollars. When the peso is devalued, the rent soars.

Miguel watched as his mother climbed into the backseat of the car, an aging black Chrysler with gold-and-black Mexican license plates. The backdoor on the left side had been dented, and the handle had disappeared. Miguel wondered if it had been a real accident, or if the dent was there so that the backseat was difficult to open and inspect. His mother fitted herself into a compartment under the backseat. There were air holes in the front of it, near the legs of the backseat passengers, similar to those in a box used for carrying live chickens or dogs. Another old woman and two children sat down on the seat. In the front seat were three other adults.

As they drove away, getting into the lane for the US border, he gathered up his belongings and walked ahead to the immigration checkpoint, where he entered the United States legally and uneventfully. Again, he gave thanks for his status as a registered alien, the status he had gained in the amnesty during the late 1980s. Someday, he must begin to think about looking into the process of becoming a US citizen. But for today, he was proud and well content to have the immigration official wave him across without comment.

On the other side, he walked to the McDonald's restaurant just a few feet from the Mexican border. Rosa and his daughter, Maria, were waiting for him. Maria had had her hair cut and looked more like a US kid every day. He kissed them both and sat down in the booth to wait for his mother to arrive. He told his wife why he had to go get his mother and how he had persuaded her to uproot herself and return with him to the United States. They decided that Salina would have to sleep in Maria's bed for the time being and that Maria would sleep on blankets on the floor.

"It will be just like camping, Maria."

"Sure, Dad, if it makes you feel better to believe that, go ahead."

All the time, Miguel kept a careful watch on every car that pulled into the parking lot of the restaurant. Several times he thought he saw the old, black Chrysler, but there were many cars like that in this part of the world, and none discharged his mother. At two o'clock, he began to imagine the worst. They had been stopped, and his mother had been discovered. That's why they didn't arrive. If so, his mother would be detained right now at the immigration check-point office he had just walked through.

At three thirty, he could wait no longer. Telling Rosa to keep watching for his mother, he walked back across the border into Mexico, crossed the busy street, and went to the US immigration office. He asked for information about an old woman from Honduras being detained there. One official knew nothing about any Honduran women. Another insisted that there had been no old women detained that afternoon. Miguel didn't know whether to believe them, but if they were telling the truth, where could she be? He retraced his steps from the morning and located the Honduran guide who had arranged the crossing. The guide apologized profusely. He knew nothing. The family had gone to Target and returned. Their passenger had been let out across the border, just as they had arranged.

"At the McDonald's restaurant?" asked Miguel, feeling relief to hear that his mother was now safely on the other side.

"I'm not sure about that, señor. They might have gone straight to the shopping mall. Perhaps they did not understand about going to the McDonald's."

Miguel hurriedly recrossed the border, this time being detained for a short time because he was carrying nothing, and there was some suspicion by US customs agents that he might be carrying something contraband on his person. When he was released, he hurried to the McDonald's and had Rosa drive him to the shopping mall. They did not see any sign of his mother in the parking lots, and Miguel knew that she would never enter such a huge store by herself. At the end of the day, they drove dispiritedly up Highway 5 to their small house near the freeway just east of downtown San Diego.

In his home again for the first time in many weeks, Miguel wept. He had gone to rescue his mother and had promised to stay with her in this strange new world. He had let her go and let her down. He could not protect her if he could not find her.

Not knowing another course of action, Miguel picked up the telephone and dialed his customer, Sandra Seaquist, to ask for her advice. When she answered the phone, he poured out his story, not knowing why he was telling her or what she could do about it. He only knew that she was a woman who had been kind to him in the past, and perhaps she would know what he could do to locate his mother.

Sandra did not have any answers. She asked some questions that he didn't really want to think about at all, such as why he hadn't just sponsored his mother for a legal immigration and whether he had paid the guides before delivering his mother. He realized that he should have withheld half the money until they delivered her safely to the destination they had agreed upon. More guilt and feelings of being a stupid fool heaped themselves on his shoulders.

Sandra looked at her watch. It was seven o'clock. It would be dark soon, even on this late summer evening. Something had to be done. She told Miguel to come to her house to pick her up, and she would go with him back to the border. She didn't know what, if anything, she could do to help, but she would be willing to drive with him and help him think through his plan.

By seven thirty they were driving together down Highway 5 to the border town of San Ysidro. Not knowing where to begin, they went back to the McDonald's restaurant. Sandra ordered Miguel a Big Mac and coffee while he described his mother to every Spanish-speaking person in the restaurant and asked if they had seen her.

Sandra asked the counter attendant, a middle-aged woman who spoke good English, if she had seen or heard of an old woman looking for her son.

"I don't want to alarm you or your friend," the counter attendant said, "but there are some white people who look for border crossers. They take them away."

Sandra called Miguel over to hear the counterwoman's story. "Where do they take them?" asked Sandra.

"Who knows?" shrugged the woman, and indicated that there was a customer behind them who needed her attention. Miguel and Sandra backed away. He ate his hamburger and drank his coffee while they waited for the woman to have a free moment again.

"I really can't tell you anything more than that. I'm sorry. I just hear that some people who cross and don't know where to go are picked up by white people and driven away."

"Have you seen this take place?" asked Miguel.

"No, not with my own eyes. I just hear talk about it."

"Are they taking them back across the border?" asked Miguel. "Maybe they are trying to make them pay again."

There was nothing more to be learned at the McDonald's. Sandra and Miguel walked outside. It was almost dark. They looked again at the parking lots of nearby stores and restaurants. They looked at the trolley station. They did not find Miguel's mother that night. They returned to San Diego, and Miguel dropped Sandra off at her house.

"Please call me, Miguel, if you find her or if you want to talk any more about it. I know how important it is to have a friend to talk with about things like this."

"Thank you, Mrs. Sandra. I will let you know."

Sandra walked inside her safe and comfortable home. She felt a strong sense of gratitude for her life and her family. She also felt a fierce sadness for Miguel and wished that they had been successful in finding his mother. She had not really contributed much to the search. She didn't know the right people who could find an illegal immigrant, or even if she did, they would have been duty bound to deport her as soon as she was located. Then, as Sandra brewed a pot of her favorite herbal tea, she allowed herself the luxurious thought that even though she hadn't been able to solve this problem for Miguel, he seemed truly grateful to have her company tonight. Maybe that is what I can do, she thought to herself. I can listen; I can go along for the ride. I can sit next to children who can't read and listen to them. I can ask questions. I can share their lives and maybe even learn how to share my own with them. It's not the whole answer, she thought, as she turned on her television to watch a travel show on PBS, but maybe it's a part of the answer.

Chapter Sixteen

HOMEWORK

Sandra was making a meatloaf in the kitchen on the first day of September, but her attention was drawn to the familiar, roughhousing noises of her two sons as they argued over who was taking which CD with them when they left for school. Soon, too soon, the house would be quiet again.

"I know we bought this Pearl Jam together." Peter was trying his best to be patient with his younger brother. "But I was the one who wanted it the most. I found it in the store and showed it to you."

"Yeah, and you had six bucks, and I put in ten," said Alex, taking the CD and putting it in his own portable CD carrier without hesitation. "Here, you can have this one." He handed his brother another album that had, frankly, been a big disappointment to both of them.

"Whatever you say, bro," said Peter, giving in. "But I need those headphones with the volume control. "They really work for me when I'm studying something technical. When I have to memorize something."

"Okay, they're yours. They hurt my ears anyway." Alex paused. "Hey, Bro, I am really happy for you that you get to go to med school this fall. Way to go."

Peter recalled the letter he had just received from the University of Washington saying that his waiting-list bid had paid off. He had worked all summer to strengthen a program for wheelchair athletes at his alma mater, and spent evenings working with a paraplegic woman in the swimming pool. Someone was watching, and he was selected to be one of the few candidates accepted from the waiting list that year. The dean had told him last spring that the waiting list was not ordered by rank. The faculty got to select any candidate from the list that met their subjective standards.

At this point, when Dan talked with Peter about the whole process, they both agreed that it was as much an honor to be selected in this way as it would have been to have received an early admission. Sandra felt relieved and sad, in a way. Leaving home for college was one thing, but leaving for medical school was another giant step toward complete independence from the family. His life would be so busy over the next few years that she and Dan would have to be squeezed into a tiny corner of their son's life.

Alex, on the other hand, would only be going as far as Berkeley again this year. A sophomore, he was going to take several courses in the Geography Department this semester. Sandra could see him someday being a guide for an outdoor adventure travel group. If he were the guide, maybe she'd be brave enough to go into the wilderness. It seemed possible, these days. Many things seemed possible.

Putting the meatloaf into the oven, Sandra gathered up her library books and checked one to see the due date. As she did, the flyer about the needed Spanish books fell out, fluttered to the floor, and went under the kitchen table. Amigo pounced on it but found it boring and leaped up to the windowsill to see if there were any birds on the lemon tree outside.

Sandra stooped down and retrieved the paper. Yes, she had been wanting to call Dr. Mendez ever since they met at the library a couple of weeks ago. She picked up the phone, but Dan was on the line upstairs.

"I got ID twenty-four next month," she heard him say.

"Oh, I bid it, but I didn't get it. I'm doing Newark turns," replied a woman's voice.

There was a brief pause while Dan seemed to be sorting through the papers on his desk. Sandra knew that she should hang up. She had never purposely eavesdropped on someone's telephone conversation. But something made her hold on to the phone.

"Well, in my line there's a good layover in Chicago next month," he said.

"Great, we should be able to find a time to go sailing. I'll get the boat ready. We just got a new jib for it. We'll be able to try it out."

"Okay, see you in dispatch. I've got to go now."

"Okay, bye."

The phone clicked, and Sandra replaced her receiver as silently as she could. Her heart was pounding. Who was Dan talking to? Well, she would soon know, as she heard him coming downstairs.

Dan stopped in the family room and got involved in the debate over the CDs. He tried to convince Alex that the Neil Young CD belonged at home. He had been listening to it a lot lately. But he didn't succeed.

"C'mon, Dad. If you want that disk, go online and get another one," suggested Alex, as Sandra came into the family room.

"Yeah! I know what that will lead to," said Dan. "You'll get me online, and suddenly I'll be paying for a dozen new downloads."

"You know us too well," agreed Alex.

"Well, remember, Dad, they say that music builds brain cells, and I'm going to need all the brain cells I can get in medical school." Saying these last two words, Peter threw a handful of pistachio nuts up in the air. He saw Sandra watching and reached out to give her a hug. "Tell him, Mom. Tell him how Mozart affects your brain."

"Mozart? Is that what you want?" asked Sandra, taking her son seriously. "You can take that violin concerto with you if you want to."

"No, Mom, I don't think so. I was talking about Mo's Art. It's a new group from Seattle." Sandra didn't get it, but that didn't stop her from enjoying the easy bantering among all four family members. She felt her cheeks get warm as a sense of happiness washed over her. She looked at Dan. He was feeling it too. They had done very well raising these two young men. She caught Dan's eye and smiled at him. He saw her looking at him and grinned widely.

She was relieved. There was nothing amiss with Dan. He was obviously happy with his life and with his family. Sandra went over to him and put her arm around his waist. He put his arm down on her shoulder. They watched the boys finish up their packing, and everyone went into the dining room for dinner. Meatloaf was Peter's favorite meal, and he ate several helpings. Sandra was glad she had decided to make it tonight.

After dinner, the boys disappeared upstairs, and Dan helped Sandra clear the table and rinse off the dishes.

"What is your schedule for this month?" Sandra asked casually, as she handed the ketchup bottle to Dan to put on a high shelf.

"Three day trips with Chicago layovers," Dan answered. "I'm glad it's not winter, or I'd get stuck there in the snow."

Sandra didn't reply. She wanted Dan to volunteer information about his plans. If she asked him, it would be awkward for both of them. Dan busied himself putting away the butter and rewrapping the bread before putting it into the breadbox.

"Say," he began, "if you'd like to come with me for one of my layovers, we could go sailing on Lake Michigan."

"Oh?" Sandra responded, brightening up and trying to look interested. "How can you arrange that?"

"I'm flying with a copilot who has a boat on Lake Michigan. You're welcome to come along. I get into O'Hare at nine o'clock next Friday night, and I don't have to leave until the next evening. We'll probably sail most of Saturday."

"That sounds interesting." Sandra looked at the calendar in the breakfast room. Her instinct told her to say yes immediately, but once she hesitated she was flooded with worries. What if the weather on the lake was stormy? What would Dan think of her if she came along and then was sick or afraid in front of his friend? What would she wear? She could hardly fit into those khaki slacks right now, and they made her stomach look so round. How would she look next to the young woman Sandra remembered from the trip she had taken with Dan to Denver. That was probably who he was sailing with. What was her name?

"It should be a lot of fun. I guess the boat is very fast."

Sandra let the word "fast" hang there without reacting to it. It was a good sign that he was inviting her to come along, but didn't he understand that the fact that the boat was fast would probably scare her off? Maybe he did understand. He had carefully avoided mentioning that this copilot was a woman.

Then, Sandra talked herself down from these suspicions. Obviously, there was nothing to worry about, nothing between them. They both liked sailing—that's all. She reminded herself that she had men who were friends at work. No, there was no need to go along and embarrass Dan and herself. She could trust him. After twenty-six years, of course she could trust him.

"Oh, I'm sorry, Dan," she said, looking at the calendar. "I have a hair appointment this Saturday." Holding a strand of hair, she added, "And it looks like I need to keep it, don't you think? Miss Frizzle Dizzle here." She laughed.

Dan wiped his hands on the dish towel and hung it over the oven door. "Okay, suit yourself. You can come another time." He walked off toward the living room and turned on the cable news.

Sandra decided that it wasn't worth thinking about anymore. The bigger a deal she made of this, the bigger it would become. She searched for the flyer from the library again. It gave her something new to think about, something for her future. That is the strategy to adopt when so much is changing around me, she thought to herself. What is it that all the psychologists are always telling people? Look out for yourself.

Yes, and look where that had led, she responded as if she were debating herself. That's why there are so many divorces, because everyone is always looking out for himself. Or herself, she added, as an afterthought. She picked up the telephone and dialed the number on the flyer. Four rings, and then an answering machine picked up on the other end of the line. Sandra left a message, saying that she had called about donating some books in Spanish for the program in Tijuana. She added that she would buy some books tomorrow and would give them to Bruni whenever they could arrange to meet again.

The next morning, Sandra drove to a large bookstore and asked for children's books written in Spanish. The section containing these books was not large, but there were several dozen titles, some of them very familiar to Sandra. Here was *Alejandro y La Dia Terrible, Horrible, Espantoso, Horroroso*. Sandra thumbed through it and noticed that the illustrations were identical to the copy she owned in English. The young boy in the book still reminded her of Alex, even though in this case he was saying, "Me voy a Australia," instead of "I'm going to…" She tried to say a few of the words out loud and was pleasantly surprised at how easy it was to read again in Spanish. Of course her accent was probably awful, but she did remember the basic rules of grammar from her high school Spanish classes, and the nice thing was that every letter always made the same sound, not like English, where the pronunciation of letters varied so greatly from word to word.

Next, she spied *Jorge el Curioso*. What fun! She sat down on the carpet in the children's book department and sounded out the words to herself. "Este es Jorge. Jorge vivia con su amigo, el hombre del sombrero amarillo." This was easy, and a very interesting new challenge. She felt her excitement grow. Her original idea was to buy a few books and give them to the Mexican doctor to take to Tijuana. A new idea was now forming. She saw herself sitting on the floor, reading aloud with some dark-haired children—in Spanish!

It was a scary thought, but not as scary as being tossed about on a stormy ocean in a small, unstable boat. Not as scary as telling Dr. Janus that she was not going to return to work. Not even as scary as saying good-bye to Peter tomorrow afternoon and wondering how frequently he would call home.

But then her thoughts turned bleak. She remembered her excursion with Walk and Talk to Tijuana. The reality was that if she wanted to do this and to get to know Bruni and her program, she was going to have to go across the border to do so.

She could see Bruni's face in her mind, especially her warm smile and gleaming brown eyes. She definitely wanted to make some new friends. She had been feeling the need for some new horizons, new options—wasn't that the word people were using to describe opportunities these days? Her old options were not as appealing as they used to be. She could see clearly that she had a choice here. New options would lead to new ways of seeing the world, new friends, new…what? Sandra realized that she was basically talking about a new self-image.

Scary. What would Alex say about this? "Go for it, Mom!" She could hear his voice as clearly as if he were standing right in front of her. She thought how odd it was: it was as if she wanted permission from her children to move on. The peculiar thought struck her as absolutely true. For twenty-some years she had given them permission (or not, as the case might be). Now that they had grown up, it was becoming important to her what they thought. What would Peter think of this idea? She knew that he'd be a little more cautious. He would want to know that she was driving down there—across the border—in a safe car, and he would want her to go with someone else, someone who knew the way around. Someone like Bruni. Sandra realized it was all fitting together, as she gathered up her books and headed toward the cashier's desk to pay for the eight books she had selected.

After ringing up Sandra's purchases, the clerk politely asked her for nearly one hundred seventy dollars. Why, that was more than she had spent on books for herself or Dan for quite a long time. They went to the library for most of their reading materials. She wondered if they had Spanish books for children at the library, as she handed the clerk her debit card. As she found her car in the parking lot, she continued to ponder the wonderful resource that libraries were. She could never live very far away from one. She laughed to herself as she remembered telling the real estate agent that one of her major considerations in buying a house was that it be within walking distance to a library. She wondered whether there were libraries in Tijuana, and decided that she would have to ask Bruni.

At home, she found Dan in the garage, putting a new air filter in her car. "I've changed the oil for you," he announced from under the hood of the car.

"Thank you," she said automatically. What would Dan think of this project? She hadn't thought about his reaction in the bookstore.

"Dan," she said, coming around to stand next to him. "What would you think about me going to Tijuana to look at this after-school program they have down there?"

"What?" he said. "Hand me that rag, will you? Here, hold this cap for me, so I don't drop it again." He busied himself under the hood. "I want to get this done for you before I have to leave on my trip. I don't want you driving around in a car with a dirty engine."

"Yes, I appreciate that, Dan. I guess I'll go in and make some sandwiches. Do you want tuna or ham?"

"Tuna, please, and hold the mayo. I need to lose a few pounds."

Sandra went inside and put her new books on a shelf in the family room where she kept all of the children's old books. She made tuna sandwiches and really tried to "hold the mayo," but in the end, she slathered extra on her bread. Tuna would be tasteless without mayonnaise. She looked down at her belly. What if Dan lost a few pounds and she didn't? Where would that leave her?

The phone rang just as she put the sandwiches on the table. She picked up the receiver, hoping that it would be Bruni calling back. It was Miguel.

"Mrs. Sandra," said Miguel breathlessly, "my mother is found. She is okay. I wanted you to know."

"Tell me about it, Miguel," said Sandra.

"She did get picked up in the parking lot, just like the woman at McDonald's said. But she wasn't taken back across the border."

"No? Where was she taken then?"

"This woman—she take her to her house and want her to work," Miguel explained. "She want her to work for nothing! She wouldn't let her leave the house."

"An American woman?" asked Sandra.

"Yes, she's kind of crazy, I think so. She sees my mother in the parking lot, and she asks her if she want a ride. My mother tell her she is waiting for her son. The lady tell my mother she will take her to her son. My mother believe her. She gets in the car. The next thing, she is in National City in this woman's house. She didn't know where she was or nothing."

"Miguel, it's been four days since we went looking for your mother. Are you telling me that she was in this house for four days?"

"Yes, she don't know how to call me. I don't know where she was. I been looking at the border every day. I been asking questions. Finally, I hear about this woman who tries to get people to work for her, people who don't know where else to go. Someone tells me to go to this house in National City. I go, and I find my mother there."

"You went to the house?"

"Yes, I went this morning. I look around, and I call out my mother's name. I hear her inside, I think. So I knock on the door. I tell the woman I want to see my mother. Then she come home with me."

"So she's all right then?"

"Yes, but she is very mad. She say, that woman—she make her work every day; don't give her much to eat."

"What kind of work?" asked Sandra.

"Just house work. I guess that woman—she want a maid, and she can't afford it, so she just goes to the border and finds someone to work for her like this."

"This is a very strange story, Miguel. I guess you can't tell the police about it."

"Oh no! Never. I am just happy to have my mother with me. And I want to tell you again, thank you for coming with me to look for her. I think I wouldn't find her if you don't come with me and help me think of the right questions to ask."

"Well, Miguel. I'm glad I could help. I'd like to meet your mother someday, okay?"

"Okay, Mrs. Sandra. I see you next week. And I'm going to bring you a new plant, a very nice plant for your backyard. You'll see. It's very nice plant. I grew it myself."

"Miguel, you don't have to do that. You don't have to bring me a plant from your own garden."

"But I want to, Mrs. Sandra. I want to do this thing for you. Good-bye."

"Well, that's good news," Sandra said aloud. She decided to call Hanna to tell her about it. Hanna was at home and listened to the whole story with interest. Then, she read Sandra a notice from the newspaper inviting people to attend a lecture at UCSD by the Mexican author Carlos Fuentes.

"When is it?" asked Sandra.

"Tonight; what do you think? Do you know his work?"

"Well, not really. But, I have heard his name. Let's go."

"I'll pick you up at six-thirty," said Hanna.

Later that evening, the two women walked into the university auditorium.

"I always feel like such a...a gringa at events such as these," Hanna said.

Sandra opened her eyes wide and looked around again with interest at the rest of the audience. The auditorium was filling up rapidly. Many of the voices they could hear around them were speaking Spanish. Three young people in front had a tape recorder and were adjusting its volume control. Perhaps they were students at the university and were going to write reports about Fuentes and his philosophy for a class. In addition to the students, there were also many gray-bearded men in casual clothing, dark-haired Latinos in business suits, and Latinas wearing swinging skirts and high-heeled shoes.

"I guess there is no mistaking what you said a while ago," I whispered to Hanna. "We are definitely a couple of gringas." At that moment another gringa stepped up to the podium on the stage and called for quiet. She was about Sandra's age, late forties or early fifties, with a face and clothes no more distinguished than Sandra's. But she was a department chair at this university and was now introducing Señor Fuentes.

"Ladies and Gentlemen, I have the honor to present one of the most prolific and talented writers of our time, Mr. Carlos Fuentes. Mr. Fuentes will be speaking here tonight in English as part of our bicultural series. Tomorrow night he will speak at the Cultural Center in Tijuana in Spanish. He will be reading from works old and new, including his latest book, *La Silla de Aguilla* (The Eagle's Throne). Please let us welcome Carlos Fuentes."

There was enthusiastic applause as the author strode onto the stage with a spring in his step that belied his years. His warm smile and straight posture put the audience at ease immediately. He began to speak, and within a few moments, his words literally carried Sandra away from the stuffy auditorium to the banks of the Rio Grande. In stories and images, he recounted the history of humanity's migration from Asia across the Bering Strait and down through the northern mountains, forests, and plains to the warm, moist, and fertile soils on both the north and south banks of the Rio Grande, or Rio Bravo, as it was known by the Mexicanos.

Although he spoke in fluent, unaccented English, with only a peppering of Spanish words, the way he wove words together and the quality of his voice created a sense in Sandra that she was hearing him speak in Spanish and that she could understand him perfectly. His language was rich with metaphors and legends that illustrated the historical events he recalled. His version of the movement of peoples from one place to another and the mixing of cultures from Asia, North and Central America, and Europe made more sense to Sandra than any explanations she had read or heard during her American history courses.

After a short time, Sandra no longer felt like a gringa listening to him. When he asked the audience to guess the second-largest Spanish-speaking city in the world, after Mexico City, Sandra was not surprised to hear that it was Los Angeles. San Diego could not be far down the list, she thought, and knowing that, she realized with something approaching certainty that in the next few generations, her own genes were very likely to be combined with Latino genes to produce children who would live in the San Diego-Tijuana metropolitan area.

So she decided there was little reason she should feel like a gringa, as the potential grandparent of a mestizo offspring. She sat up a little bit straighter and listened harder for each nuance of the quickly moving stories and images he read from his books.

"Everything he said matters to me," she said to Hanna, after the lecture ended.

"Let's go see if we can get his autograph," suggested Hanna. "They'll be selling his books in a room nearby."

Sandra was grateful to have a new goal. Her thoughts had turned to the growing differences between her and Dan. Dan would not have chosen to come to this lecture. He wouldn't have much interest in any of the concepts that seem so exciting to me. Like a bicycle with a playing card clothespinned to the rim, these ideas kept flapping and clacking in Sandra's mind as they walked out of the auditorium. She stood up and followed closely behind her friend.

I've come to hear Carlos Fuentes to get a new perspective, a new understanding of what is happening today on both sides of the border, she thought, as they walked slowly toward the book-signing area. Many other audience members were going there also. Some of them had well-worn copies of Fuentes' books in their hands. Sandra thought that she would like to introduce herself to the woman in the next row, the attractive Latina woman speaking Spanish to her companion.

But there is no way I will meet any of these other interesting-looking people tonight, thought Sandra. They will buy their books, get them autographed, and go out to the parking lot to retrieve their cars. I will do the same.

Still, she looked at the faces nearby and nodded her head in the direction of the elegant man with the dark mustache. She smiled to the three women in high heels and let them pass in front of her in line. She brushed sleeves with a burly, white-bearded gringo who was holding five of Fuentes' books to be autographed. She imagined that he was an expert on Latin American literature who was on the faculty here. And me, thought Sandra. What am I doing with my life?

But there I go again. Can't I ever stop replaying that tired record? Sandra came to the table where Señor Fuentes was signing books. She chose *The Eagle's Throne* in English and then put it down again. Instead, she picked up and paid for a copy of the same book in Spanish, *La Silla de Aguilla*. She decided to try to read it, and if she couldn't understand it, she could always take it to the center as another of her book donations. She saw other books written by the author. One, *The Crystal Frontier*, caught her eye. What an interesting metaphor.

The smile Carlos Fuentes bestowed on Sandra was the real gift. Unhurriedly, he asked her name and signed the book, "To Sandra Seaquist, con respeto, Carlos Fuentes."

Con respeto—with respect. Sandra looked at these words and smiled with new respect for herself.

"Gracias," she said, smiling at the author. "Gracias para todos," she said, and she literally skipped as they walked toward Hanna's car in the parking lot. The night sky was filled with promise. She was part of something important—here on the crystal frontier. Maybe he sensed that.

Chapter Seventeen

SEASONINGS

Watching the local news one evening in September, Sandra heard stories of schools and principals she knew; they were having to accommodate the new laws regulating the bilingual programs in the state of California. The principal of an inner-city school told reporters that she was forced to retrain teachers who had been hired to teach Spanish language classes on emergency credentials. Their major asset had been their excellent command of Spanish, and now they were forbidden by law to use it. They had to teach in English.

Sandra felt relief that she was not in the midst of that dilemma, but she felt a great sense of loss as well. Feelings of panic arose as she saw a colleague being interviewed about the new reading tests that would be given to every child in English only. She knew that many Spanish-speaking children would fail these tests and make the district appear to be doing a poor job of teaching reading. In reality, many of these children could read quite well, but not yet in English.

Dan watched the same program and couldn't help saying aloud, "Finally!" He used the remote control to lower the volume on the television. "At last someone is making some sense in Sacramento," he said. "Why should we have to pay someone to speak Spanish to students here in this country?"

Sandra considered her reply to this question but chose, instead, to go into the kitchen to look at the chicken roasting in the oven. The stinging sensation in her eyes was not from the onions roasting alongside the chicken. It was from a burning question that she kept asking and asking herself. "Did I make the right choice to leave my job?"

Every September since I was five years old, I have always gone back to school, starting fresh each year. New clothes, new pencils, new books, new ideas. Every year…except this year. Reaching deep inside herself, she looked for some thought that would comfort her, reassure her, revive her. Way down deep, she found one.

She went upstairs and opened the bag of Spanish books. She spread them out on the bed to look at again. Then, she found the flyer with Bruni Mendez's name on it. She had left a message a few days before, and had not received a reply. Should she call again? Yes. She dialed the phone number and waited.

"Hello," a soft voice answered.

"Hello," said Sandra. "May I speak to Bruni Mendez?"

"This is," answered Bruni.

"You may not remember me," Sandra began hesitantly, "but I met you at the library a couple of weeks ago when you were…"

"Of course I remember you," Bruni responded warmly. "Sandra, right?"

"Yes, Sandra Seaquist. How are you?"

"Very busy, but I am happy to hear from you. I'm sorry that I didn't return your call, but I have been going to Tijuana every morning very early. It is the beginning of the school year, and we are trying to get the families to bring their children to the clinic for inoculations."

"I understand," said Sandra. "Until this year, September has always been my busiest month too." There was a pause, as each woman waited for the other to speak.

"The reason I called," Sandra said, running her fingers over the glossy cover of the *Jorge el Curioso* book in front of her, "is to…that is…I was wondering if I could possibly go with you one day. I bought some books for the children at your center, and I was going to give them to you to take with you, and then I was thinking that maybe…"

"I am very happy to have you come with me. I am going tomorrow in fact."

"Tomorrow?" Sandra tried to think ahead to the next day. Did she have any plans? What was Dan doing? Did that matter?

"Tomorrow," Sandra repeated. Then, without analyzing further, she said firmly, "Great. I'd love to go. Where and when?"

"Where do you live? I can pick you up," suggested Bruni. Sandra gave directions to her house and told Bruni that she would be ready by eight thirty.

"What time do you think we'll be back?" she asked.

"About five o'clock, if we don't get stuck at the border," answered Bruni.

Oh yes, thought Sandra. The border. What will I need? Just my driver's license, I think.

She and Bruni said good-bye.

Let's see, what shall I wear? Jeans? No, too informal. Slacks, then, and walking shoes. Shall I take a purse? No, I think I'll just put a few dollars and my driver's license into my pocket. Maybe, I'll take water. Will that be an insult if I take my own water? No, I don't think so. People carry water with them everywhere these days. I'll take that tote bag Dan brought me from the Pike Street Market in Seattle. I'll put the books and the water in it. What if the water leaks on the books? It shouldn't. I'll put the water in its own plastic bag inside the tote bag. It should be fine.

Sandra walked down the stairs and looked for the tote bag in the cupboard near the backdoor. The oven was dinging. The chicken was ready, and it smelled delicious. She felt happy again. Ready for dinner. Ready for tomorrow. Ready for a new school year, with a big difference.

"Dinner ready yet?" Dan had turned off the television news and come into the kitchen.

"Yes, it's ready. Do you want iced tea or cranberry juice? Or do you want a beer?"

"What are we having? Chicken—looks good. I'll have the juice, and mix it with a little sparking water, okay?"

"Why don't you do that and make me one too. I'll put the dinner on the table."

Together, they set the table and put the food on their plates. Together, they sat down and passed one another the potatoes and green beans and chicken. Together, they shared news of mail they had each received that day and wondered what the boys were doing that evening.

Inside their minds, however, each was thinking about the days ahead.

"Did you pick up my uniform shirts today?" he asked.

"Yes, they're in your closet. Do you have a trip tomorrow?" Sandra turned her head to look at the calendar behind her. Tomorrow was a Wednesday, the middle of September already.

"Yes, I need you to take me to the airport first thing tomorrow."

"Okay, I can do that. Guess where I am going after that?"

"Out to lunch with Hanna?"

"No."

"Back to work?"

"Well, not really. I'm going to Tijuana to take some books I bought to a children's center."

"What?" Dan's forkful of chicken paused in midair. "I thought you were just going to give those books to someone to take down there."

"Well, I was. But then I talked to the woman who works there, and she invited me to come along."

"And you said yes?" Dan's voice registered a puzzled disbelief.

"I said yes; what of it?" Sandra said sharply.

"Okay, don't get uptight. If you want to go, go. Here, I've got some stuff in my bag you can take with you." Dan got up from the table and went to the closet to take out his flight bag. Sandra waited expectantly. What could he have for her to take? Was he really okay with this? She would be going on the first day of his trip. He wouldn't be home for three more days. If something happened to her in Mexico, no one would even know how to reach him. Who would they call? How would Dan…

Dan returned and held out a small clear bottle. She took it and read the label. Waterless Hand Cleaner.

"This way, you can wash your hands, and you don't even have to use the water down there," Dan said with assurance. "I use it whenever I go on a trip to Mexico City."

"Oh," said Sandra. She put the bottle down on the table. But Dan picked it up again.

"Put it in your purse right now, so you don't forget," he insisted.

Sandra got up and put the bottle into her tote bag. Doing the dishes, she watched the water from her faucet splash out on the dishes and glassware. We take everything for granted here, she thought. I can wash my hands or the dishes or take a long, cool drink of this water without ever thinking about it. I guess it's not that easy in Tijuana.

The next morning, Sandra drove Dan to the airport. He said, "Be careful down there," and kissed her good-bye.

"Call me," said Sandra, as he put on his hat and started to wheel his bags into the terminal.

She drove home and got ready to go. She had to use the toilet several times before eight thirty. Nervousness or just her body trying to take care of itself while she was still home and didn't have to worry about finding a clean toilet? Sandra found herself putting a few more things into her tote: tissues, paper towels to dry off the waterless hand cleaner, an energy bar left over from one of Alex's backpacking trips. She was looking in a cupboard, trying to decide whether to bring a can of tuna and a fork, when the doorbell rang.

Sandra went to the door and invited Bruni inside. Bruni stepped in and looked around.

"What a beautiful house," she said.

"Thank you," Sandra answered shyly. "I'm all ready to go."

They walked outside. It was a glorious sunny day. Sandra got into the passenger side of Bruni's brown van. She put on her seatbelt as Bruni started the car and drove away.

"Ready?" smiled Bruni.

"Ready," responded Sandra. They discussed the weather, the traffic, and the views for a few miles. Then she asked, "Do you have children?"

"Yes," answered Bruni. "A boy and a girl. And you?"

"Two boys, well, young men, really," answered Sandra.

"In school?" asked Bruni.

"Alex is at Berkeley, a sophomore. And Peter has just started medical school."

"Oh yes?"

Bruni seemed interested, so Sandra told her the story about Peter getting on the waiting list at the University of Washington and being admitted at the last moment.

"It is a very good medical school," said Bruni. "Especially for family practice. Is that his interest?"

"Oh, I don't know. I don't think he knows yet. Was that what you studied? Family practice."

"Yes," answered Bruni. "I did my training at the university in Mexico City."

Sandra recalled seeing the university on a trip to Mexico City with Dan several years ago. She remembered the huge stadium nearby, where there had been a summer Olympics one time.

"Do you have a practice in San Diego?" Sandra asked.

"No, I have no certificates for the US. I cannot practice medicine here."

That must be difficult, thought Sandra. She imagined what it would be like to have a degree and not be allowed to use it.

"So, you drive to Tijuana every day?" she asked.

"Not every day, no. I go about three times a week."

They were approaching the section of Highway 5 with signs that said, "Last US Exit 1 mile." Sandra hoped that her nervousness didn't show. She decided to just imagine that she was going on a tourist trip to buy a bottle of Kahlua and

walk up and down the main street of town. They approached the border crossing. Sandra watched the cars in front as they crossed the strip of steel spikes in
the road. Each car got a green light that said pase. But when the van went over
the spikes, the light turned red, and a buzzer went off. Sandra looked with alarm
at Bruni.

"Don't worry. It's a heavy car. I always get a red light."

She steered the car to the right, into an area where inspectors were talking
to drivers and looking inside the cars and trucks ahead of them.

An officer approached on the right side and opened the side door of the van,
looking inside. He spoke to Bruni in Spanish, and she answered him in Spanish.
Sandra looked straight ahead, not understanding a word. I might not understand
very much of anything for the rest of the day, she thought, as the inspector
slammed the door shut and waved them ahead.

Bruni drove back out into traffic and made her way through the maze of
waiting taxis and traffic funneling into a few lanes. They drove up on an overpass
that crossed a wide concrete waterway. It looked like the aqueducts Sandra had
seen in Los Angeles but was many times wider than those. At the very center was
a deeper inset, and here there was a narrow stream of liquid moving sluggishly
downhill. Cardboard boxes, bricks, a rusty bicycle, and other detritus littered
the wide expanse.

Sandra recognized the signs overhead for El Centro, the center of town, but
Bruni got into a different lane and drove east. A wide boulevard with restaurants and office buildings stretched ahead of them. Soon, they came to a traffic
circle with a tall statue in the center. Bruni ignored the young, lame man who
approached at the red light and tried to wash the windshield of the van. She
waved him away. He took his bucket of dirty water and went to the car behind
them. After the traffic circle, Bruni got into the right lane and turned onto a road
that said Ensenada Libre.

"This is the free road to Ensenada," she explained. "The other route is a
tollway."

"We're not going to Ensenada, are we?" asked Sandra. She had visited this
town one time many years ago. It was pretty far away as she remembered.

"No," answered Bruni. "We just take that road to get through the city. The
area we are going to is on the southern part of Tijuana."

"I see," said Sandra. She looked at the modern tile stores and large shopping
centers. I didn't even know these stores existed in Tijuana, she said to herself. A
few blocks away, they didn't. Small, crowded stores lined the three-lane street

that turned south and went uphill. Crumbling hillsides began appearing near the edge of the road. She saw small restaurants advertising menudo and birria. What type of food was that? Before she had a chance to ask, she saw a furniture store with a hodgepodge of used furniture spread out in the narrow strip of land between the store and the road. How would people even stop on this busy road to load furniture on and off a truck? Then, she saw the answer to that question. Up ahead, a truck was stopped in their lane. A man was taking a large steel cylinder off the truck to deliver to the restaurant at the side of the road.

"Look down here." Bruni nodded to the left. A narrow road led away and steeply downhill from the highway. It went into a gully that was lined with small shacks built on the sides of the hill. A sign said, "Casa de Esperanza Orfanato." House, Sandra understood.

"There is an orphanage there run by nuns. I go there on Fridays. But not today."

"And today, we are going...," prompted Sandra.

"Today we are going to Tecolote. It is a neighborhood something like that one." Bruni again nodded toward the gully on their left with tiny dwellings perched on every knoll of land. Below many knolls, there was only crumbly sand and gravel in steep grades. Some homes were built on dirt roads. Others were accessible only by paths from a road far below. Sandra wondered how the inhabitants got their groceries up the paths each day.

The road they were traveling went beneath another highway with signs to Las Playas and Tecate. "That is the main east-west road," said Bruni. "We don't have far to go now. We turn left up ahead."

Sandra looked ahead. There was a military encampment of some sort on her right. Large trucks were passing them as they crested the hill and started down the other side. Bruni got into the left lane and waited for a break in the oncoming traffic before turning onto a blacktop road. A graveyard for old cars lay on the right. Cars of all types were stacked end to end for hundreds of yards. A mountain of car tires lay just beyond the cars.

An old man was walking on the side of the road pushing a cart. It seemed to contain a variety of fruits and juices in large jars. He pushed slowly, not looking up as they passed by. Bruni slowed for another intersection with a stop sign. It looked like a stop sign, but said alto, which Sandra decided must be the word for "stop." I wonder how many new words I can learn today, she thought.

"We turn left here at the police station," said Bruni. Sandra looked at the police station. It was a long, low building with a large area in front filled with parked cars, many of them marked with lights and signs as police cars. That's comforting, I think, Sandra mused to herself. Then she reconsidered. Weren't there always stories about how the police in Mexico were involved with criminal activities themselves? There was that story she had seen on the news a few months ago about stolen sports utility vehicles. Investigators from the United States had gone to the police station in Tijuana and found that many of the stolen vehicles had been repainted with police decals and colors. Sandra looked back over her shoulder at the line of cars in front of the police station. Were some of those cars stolen?

Oh well, she thought, as she turned to look ahead again. I can't do anything about that, and it is not why I came. I'll just think about what I can do. Besides, maybe I won't like it here at all. I should look at everything, because maybe I won't be coming back here again. This is my chance to see what this world is like. "What does that mean?" she asked, indicating a sign on a small store that said, "Papeleria, Copias."

"It is a store that sells paper and makes copies," answered Bruni. "And here is a bakery. Do you like sweets? Dulces?"

"Me, no; I mean, yes. I like sweets, but not today."

"Okay, sometimes on my way home I stop at a bakery to buy bread rolls and sweet rolls for my family."

"Oh, that's fine. We can stop. I didn't mean…"

Why am I sounding so awkward? thought Sandra. She could feel more tension as they drove down a narrow, rutted street. Two dogs loped into the traffic without looking. No one called to them. They didn't seem to belong to anyone. At a street corner, women and children waited by the side of the road. For what? A bus? A school bus maybe.

"Do children take the school bus to school here?" she asked.

"No," answered Bruni. "Parents have to drive or walk their children to school. Sometimes they have to go very great distances. When we lived in Tijuana, we had to drive our daughter, Raquel, across the city to the preparatoria."

"Preparatoria?" Sandra said.

"High school," responded Bruni. "That is one reason we moved to San Diego. She went one year to the preparatoria, and we had to leave the house at about six thirty to get her there. So, in her sophomore year, we put her in a Catholic school in San Diego. It wasn't that much more difficult to drive, and she got a better education."

"Is she still at that school?" asked Sandra.

"Yes, she is a senior this year."

"And your son?"

"He's at UCSD."

"Oh, that's wonderful."

Sandra thought about this. Bruni's son and Alex must be about the same age. They were both at the university. We do have a lot in common.

"Oh, darn." Bruni stopped the car. The road ahead was blocked by a large dump truck and men shoveling its contents onto the road. Bruni opened her window and spoke to one of the men. Sandra saw a sign saying TECO and an arrow pointing toward the dump trucks.

"Cerrado—the road is closed. We have to go another way. She backed the van downhill. Sandra held on to a handle in the dashboard as the car came close to a drop off on the right side of the road. At the bottom of the hill, Bruni turned onto a dirt road going in the opposite direction. The direction she was heading alarmed Sandra, who cringed on the dirt roads Hanna sometimes chose to drive on their hiking trips. Ahead of them, a deeply rutted dirt track went straight up the side of a hill. No road in the United States had ever been built at such a steep angle. The van shuddered as Bruni put it into second and then first gear. It crept uphill. Sandra sat forward, looking out the front window, wondering what the scene would be at the top. She hoped that the angle going down the other side was not this steep. Could she ask to get out and walk? Would that be impolite?

At the top of the hill, the road curved in a mild descent. Sandra's panic ebbed. She was able to look at her surroundings again, with interest rather than terror. The streets were dirt, the color of sandstone, and small houses were built on yard-less lots. Three small children were playing at the side of the road, squatting down, poking at something. Two women labored uphill, carrying plastic bags full of food and bottles. Bruni drove slowly so as not to hit or alarm the residents, who seemed to consider the streets their rights-of-way. Every few hundred yards, another old dog walked or lay down in their path, causing Bruni to veer sharply to avoid them. Why so many dogs? wondered Sandra. Then, she answered her own question—no birth control. No animal control trucks to cart away and euthanize unwanted dogs; so they lived, procreated, and died in the streets.

"We're almost there," said Bruni. She turned right at an intersection. On Sandra's right was a fence surrounding a school yard. Boys and girls dressed in blue pants and skirts and white shirts filled the yard. A street vendor with a pushcart advertising frozen treats was pushing something through the holes in the fence and collecting his money from a child on the inside.

"Are we going to the school?" asked Sandra.

"No," responded Bruni. "Our center is right across the street." She swung the van around in a U-turn and parked in front of a concrete block building. "Here we are."

There was no sign to mark the center. An old man and several women waited outside on a plank bench. "They are waiting for a taxi," said Bruni. "The taxis stop here to pick up people who want to go to el centro."

Bruni got out and so did Sandra, slinging her tote bag of books and water over her shoulder. She stretched her legs after the long ride. It had taken them at least forty-five minutes, maybe longer. The people waiting for a taxi watched her with mild curiosity. She tried to appear at ease, as if she came here every week. Imagine that—coming that long trip, over those hills every week. Bruni had to be a saint to do so. No, maybe not a saint. After all, Bruni was used to this. She had grown up in Mexico, lived here until a few years ago. Sandra wondered whether Bruni ever felt ill at ease. She appeared so confident, so comfortable with herself.

Sandra watched as Bruni opened the backdoors of her van and began to take things out of a set of built-in cabinets at the rear of the van. She walked back to help and took a load of clothes and a teapot from Bruni.

"This is where I put things I don't want to show at the border," said Bruni. "They rarely look here."

"Why would they care?" asked Sandra. Who would care if Bruni brought these old clothes and kitchen items across the border?

"Oh, there are rules. The Mexican government doesn't want you to bring clothes and blankets across without paying duty."

"Really," said Sandra. "I always hear about collections of clothes and blankets, especially in the winter. To take across the border, I mean."

"Yes, and the government officially forbids that. To protect the manufacturers of blankets here in Mexico."

So, there are as many rules and laws here as in the United States, thought Sandra, as she followed Bruni down some steep concrete steps built at the side of the building and going down to another floor not visible from the street. There was no handrail, and each step was so steep that Sandra had to turn sideways to go down safely. At the bottom of the steps, a wrought iron gate opened onto an enclosed concrete patio, where some girls were playing jump rope. They stopped as the women passed by them, greeting Bruni and examining Sandra, or so she felt.

Bruni pushed open a door, and they went into a long, narrow room with long, gray wooden tables and benches pushed up against the walls on both sides. At the other end of the room, another doorway led into a small kitchen. A woman was cooking something on the stove. She stopped and greeted Bruni.

"Buenos dias," she said. She reached for the clothes, and another young woman took the teapot from Sandra. "Buenos dias," they both said, and smiled at Sandra.

"Buenos dias," Sandra answered; this much she understood. Bruni introduced her to Elvira, the director of the center, and Petra, a full-time volunteer who had come from Germany to spend a year here. From that point, however, she understood little as Bruni and Elvira shared news and discussed things that had occurred at the center since Bruni's last visit.

Petra invited Sandra to come to her classroom to meet some of the children at the center. She spoke English as well as Spanish and filled Sandra in on the details of the center's mission.

"The children come here before and after school," she began.

"You mean the school across the street?" asked Sandra.

"Yes, they are on half session at the school. The children you saw on the school ground are in the morning session. They will come here at one o'clock. The children we have here now attend school in the afternoon."

Petra pushed open a door to a small classroom with one high window, which let in very little of the sunshine. It was chilly in the room, even on such a warm day. Ten or twelve children sat at desks or around an oblong table with wobbly legs. They were writing in notebooks or on paper worksheets. When Petra came in, many had questions, which they asked in Spanish. Petra answered them and became busy helping with their problems.

"They do their homework here," she explained. "After they finish, we have time for games, then lunch."

Sandra felt awkward, carrying her tote bag. She set it down on a table and looked at the work a young girl was doing. She was copying arithmetic problems from a workbook onto her paper, then doing the calculations. Uno, dos, tres…, thought Sandra. I think I can remember the numbers. Veinte uno plus…?

"What is fifty?" she asked Petra. "Como se dice fifty in español?"

"Cinquenta. Sit down here," she invited. "You can see what we do."

Sandra watched Petra work with one child at a time, helping, prodding, encouraging—always in Spanish. Most of the work involved copying problems or words and sentences onto notebook paper. There were no books, except workbooks, in evidence. As Sandra observed, she noticed that one small boy had completed all his work. He sat fidgeting with a pencil on the empty desk, waiting for the others to finish.

Sandra reached into her tote bag. She brought out *Jorge El Curioso* and showed it to the boy. He took it and opened it. Sandra couldn't tell if he was familiar with Curious George books or if this was the first time he had seen one. But it did seem that he liked what he saw. He opened it carefully, not bending the page back all the way, as if he knew that he was just borrowing it and must return it to its owner unchanged. Sandra moved her chair over closer to him. She took the book and opened it all the way, smoothing the pages back with her hand.

Petra looked up from helping another child. "Antonio, quieres a leer?"

The boy nodded.

"He wants to read to you, Sandra. Is that all right?"

"Certainly," answered Sandra. "That's what I brought it for."

Antonio started to read. He read slowly and carefully, sounding out each syllable of each word. He read with little expression, though. It was as if he had learned to read only words, not stories. The pictures helped, of course. Soon, he was turning pages eagerly and looking carefully at each picture before reading the words on the page. A little girl walked over and pressed her small body up close to Sandra's arm as she looked at the pictures and listened to Antonio read.

Sandra stopped Antonio from turning a page and asked the girl softly, "Quiere a leer?"

"Si," she answered even more softly.

"Un momento," Sandra said. Looking up, she asked Petra, "How do I tell them to each read one page?"

"Lees una pagina solo," Petra told the two children.

"Como se llama?" Antonio asked Sandra.

"Me lla...mo Mrs....Señora Sandra."

"Señora Sandra," the child repeated. "Aqui, tu lees." He thrust the book back into Sandra's hand.

"Me?" asked Sandra.

"Si." Both children nodded.

"Okay, I'll read…I mean…Yo leo una pagina and tu lees una pagina." She looked at Antonio who nodded his assent. "Y tu lees una pagina," Sandra said to the young girl. "Como te llama?" she asked her.

"Lupe," responded the young girl shyly.

"Buenos dias, Lupe, Antonio."

"Buenos dias," they responded.

Sandra began to read her page, "Te va a doler, Jorge—le dijo la ultima enfer…enfermer…"

"En-fer-mer-a," Antonio corrected her pronunciation carefully.

"Don't worry," said Petra. "That's how I learned too. They help all of us volunteers with the words. They know we only speak Spanish un poco."

"Un poquito," laughed Lupe. "Muchisimo poquito."

"Me, too," laughed Sandra. "Yo hablo muchisimo poquito."

The children laughed with her. This is not difficult, Sandra thought. I have the best possible teachers here. She began to read her page again, hesitating even now on the word "enfermera," and having to be reminded again by Lupe and Antonio. But she finished her page, and they read their pages, and then it was time for outdoor games.

As they filed out the door, the children looked to see what Sandra was going to do with the book. What should she do with it? Put it back into her tote bag? No, she brought it for the center.

"Do you want to keep this here?" she asked Petra.

Petra's eyes lit up. "Yes, it would be great. Thank you. Put it on the desk."

"I have some others," began Sandra, but Petra and the children were out the door. She followed slowly. At the front door, she saw Bruni and Elvira again.

"So, how did it go?" asked Bruni.

"Very well, muy bien," answered Sandra. "I had a great time. What happens next?"

"The children go out to play on the field, and then they come back here for lunch," said Bruni. "After lunch, they go to school, and then we have our lunch. At one, the morning session children come here, and we start all over again."

"And you stay here all day?" asked Sandra.

"No, I go to the clinic until three thirty."

"Where is the clinic?"

"Come with me. I'll show you." Bruni told Elvira that they would return soon. She then led the way up the concrete stairs to the street level of the building. Upstairs there were several more rooms to the center. A group of women were sitting in a circle in one room, having a discussion led by two women with Bibles in their hands. In another room, a woman was sweeping up hair that had just been cut. Bruni explained that each day the center taught some class for the people who lived in the neighborhood. They had haircutting classes on Wednesday, cake decorating classes on Thursday, and English classes on Friday. Monday and Tuesday were scheduled for sewing lessons and computer classes, but unfortunately all the computers were down and none of the volunteers seemed to know how to fix them. So until they were fixed, the computer classes were suspended.

The last area of the center they visited was Bruni's clinic. Sandra entered a small waiting room with several folding chairs. A desk and a filing cabinet were in the corner of the room. A door led to a small examining room with a cot and a table.

"That is where I keep the medicines for the inoculations," Bruni said, indicating a small refrigerator that might have been used in a camper prior to its present use. She looked inside and took out a small vial. "This is almost out of date. I must try to get more before Friday. But the Mexican government controls the sale of all inoculations, and they are out of this one. I may have to smuggle some in from the United States."

"Smuggle?" questioned Sandra.

"Well, what do you call it?" asked Bruni. "It is illegal to bring in medicines to Mexico, but they do not have any to sell or give to me. I prefer to think of it as a simple transaction from one country with a big supply to another with a big demand, but the governments do not look at it that way."

"So, how do you do it then?" asked Sandra.

"I put the medicine in a cooler with soda and sandwiches and bring it over. So far, no one has questioned me that closely or looked in my cooler."

Wow! thought Sandra. I am going to drive back and forth with her. What would Dan think? He wouldn't like it. So, why even tell him? He wouldn't understand. Why bother him with such stories?

Bruni closed up the clinic and led the way back downstairs. The children came back inside from their games and sat down on the benches at the tables in the long room. Lunch consisted of a soup made with rice and some chicken backs that Elvira had gotten from a restaurant in Tijuana. One of the volunteers ran down the street to buy a couple of kilos of freshly made corn tortillas for a few pesos, and each child had at least one of those. They rolled them up like cigars before eating them. There was no milk today. Elvira got six gallons of milk from a dairy on Thursdays, and it had to last all week. Sometimes it didn't. The children didn't complain.

After lunch, each child had a job to do, sweeping, washing dishes, cleaning tables. Then they were off to school, and the volunteers had an hour to them-selves before the next group arrived. They sat down and discussed their day. Sandra met three other volunteers who had been teaching in other classrooms that day. Andy, a young man who had just graduated from the University of Michigan, taught the older boys. Uli and Michaela were two other German girls who had each pledged to spend a year of service in this program. They laughed and talked in German until the whole group had a problem to solve, and then they all tried to speak in Spanish. Sandra ate her soup and her tortilla and lis-tened. She picked up a word here and there.

They looked at her as if to say, "Do you have anything to say?" She got out the other books she had brought from her tote bag and asked where they wanted to keep the books. It was decided to keep them in a storeroom until the volunteers figured out when and how they wanted to use them.

"Our main idea is to help with the homework," Michaela explained. Sandra was agreeable, although inside she thought that it was a shame to keep them in a storeroom. But for now, that would have to do.

After lunch, she met forty more children and sat in Uli's room during the work period. She brought her other books and listened as children read them to her. Uli had the youngest children. They needed books with fewer words than she had brought this time. She would look for some tomorrow.

On the way home, Sandra was exhausted but very happy. It had been a day like no other in her life, and yet a very familiar day at the same time. The wait at the border was annoying, all the lines, the car exhaust, and the vendors trying to sell something every time they came to a stop. The afternoon sun was hot and glaring, making the wait seem even longer. But Bruni and Sandra found a lot to talk about: their sons, Bruni's daughter, their college years, what it was like to grow up in Mexico City and Reno, Nevada. The time went by quickly. When Bruni dropped her off at home, Sandra said, "Next Wednesday? May I come with you again?"

"Of course, we are happy to have you," answered Bruni. "I thought you'd like it. I can tell. I see a lot of volunteers come and go, but I could tell you would be good for us when I met you."

"And for me," said Sandra. "You and the program, especially the children, are all very good for me."

Chapter Eighteen

STORM WATCH

On the final approach into Chicago, Dan looked out the window and saw that every tree below was ablaze with color. Forest preserves near O'Hare field were burnished with golden light reflecting from the oak trees. Splashes of brilliant orange sugar maples and the occasional magenta burning bush caught his eye. Light from the setting sun deepened the effect, making the leaves of each tree appear to be lit from within, in contrast to the stark black trunks and limbs.

Dan was happy that it was the copilot's landing so that he could enjoy this view, so different from what he was used to in San Diego.

They landed on twenty-two right with a cross wind of eleven knots—strong for October. The temperature was warm and felt more like a late-summer day when they came out of the terminal and took a van to a downtown hotel for the first of two nights in Chicago. It was an unusual sequence. Landing this Tuesday evening, they were not scheduled to fly again until Thursday morning very early. After checking in at the hotel, Dan called home to talk with Sandra. She wasn't home, so he left a message on their answering machine with the name of the hotel and the phone number in case she needed to reach him. He ate dinner in a coffee shop with Jerry, the copilot on this trip. Jerry was several years older than Dan but lower in seniority because he had worked for another airline that had gone out of business.

"So, you married?" Jerry asked Dan, after they had ordered from the slightly greasy menu.

"Yes, twenty-six years this May," answered Dan, with some pride.

"Great! Me too, but that's eighteen years with wife number one and eight with wife number two. I'm now out of that one, so it's back to the single life for me again."

"Tough," answered Dan. He never knew how to talk about this subject. It made him very uncomfortable to pry into people's private lives, but he found that over the years many of his flying partners wanted to talk. They considered cockpit and layover conversations an opportunity to reflect on or release their concerns. Dan had heard many stories about failed marriages and children acting out. While he listened to these tales, he rarely said much about his own family. There wasn't much to say, anyway. He and Sandra had it good compared to most of the stories he heard.

"Yeah," Jerry continued. "I'm going to be on the phone tomorrow with my attorney and tax man. I've got to figure out some way to protect what little I've got left. My first wife got half of my navy pension, and my second wife is going to get a big chunk of my A fund unless I give her the house."

"Not an easy situation," responded Dan.

"Nope."

The waitress brought their dinners, and they ate in silence for a while.

"Anyway," Jerry ventured, "if you're not doing anything tomorrow, we could go to that museum that has all the great gadgets in the afternoon."

"Well, don't count on me," answered Dan. "I've made plans for tomorrow. "

"Oh?" Jerry raised an eyebrow in a suggestive way. "What's her name? Was she on our flight?"

"No, it's nothing like that," said Dan. "I have a friend who lives here, and we're going sailing."

"Sailing? On Lake Michigan?"

"Yes, if the weather cooperates."

"Good luck, man. That's one fickle lake, I can tell you."

"You've sailed here before?"

"Well, no sailboats for me, but my ex-father-in-law had a great cabin cruiser up in Milwaukee. We used to go fishing and drink beer. I've had some of my sickest moments out there on that lake."

"You get seasick easy?" asked Dan.

"No, not easy, but the way that lake pitches and rolls, I don't know anyone who could hold his beer, except my father-in-law—ex, I mean."

Dan ate his corned beef sandwich and pushed the coleslaw around on his plate like he had pushed his string beans around as a little boy. How could a lake have stronger waves than the ocean? He was used to the swell off Point Loma. It was usually gentle, with waves of three or four feet at the most. Sometimes these conditions lulled him into a very deep relaxation. It was one of the reasons he enjoyed sailing so much.

The men ate dinner and walked around a few blocks of the city before going back to their hotel. When he got back into his room, Dan looked up the telephone number that Leslie had given him and called her to make arrangements for tomorrow.

"Hello," he said to the man who answered the phone. "May I speak to Leslie, please."

"Just a minute. Leslie, telephone." There was a substantial clunk as the phone was put down on a hard surface.

"Hello." Leslie's voice sounded slightly out of breath.

"Hello, this is Dan. Are we still on for tomorrow?"

"Yes, I think so. Just a minute. Let me check with my dad. I was just out running, and I haven't had time to talk with him about this."

Dan waited, wondering what Sandra was doing now. Eight o'clock here, only six o'clock at home. She was probably having dinner and watching the news. Tomorrow, though, she would be going back down to Tijuana. For the past several weeks, she had been going every Wednesday. He had tried to show some interest in her stories about reading to the kids, and he had been careful not to say anything about all those books she was buying to take with her. Whatever makes her happy, he thought. I'd rather have her happy than complaining to me about how her life is over because her kids are gone or something. Only, couldn't she once be happy doing some of the things he liked to do?

"Dan, my dad is not going to be able to come tomorrow," Sandra reported. "He's tied up with something else. If we go, we're a crew of two."

"Well, what do you think?" Dan stalled for time. "How big is the boat?"

"Forty-three feet," she answered. "It's not a hard boat to sail. There shouldn't be any problem."

"Well, I would still like to go, if you would."

"Oh, yes. I'm definitely looking forward to it."

"What about this weather? A little hot for October. We had a mean crosswind from the south when we landed."

"Well, I'll check with the coast guard on the weather, but let's say we plan to go unless I call you back to cancel, okay?"

"Okay, I'm in. Where is it docked?"

"Out here in Wilmette. I'll pick you up tomorrow at eight thirty and drive you up here."

"Hey, that's really out of your way. I can get a cab or something."

"No, don't think about it. I'm an early bird. I'll get up, pack us some lunch, and pick you up in front of the hotel. You're staying at the regular crew hotel, right?"

"Right. Well, if you really don't mind…I'll be down there on time. Shall I bring anything?"

"A jacket, gloves if you have them. We have rain gear aboard in case we get wet."

The next morning, Leslie was right on time, outside the hotel at eight thirty. They drove north to Wilmette harbor, and he followed her to the pier. The boat was a beauty—teak decks, brass fittings, and a wooden mast. Very rare to find a boat fitted out like this these days, thought Dan.

Leslie tied the dinghy to the buoy and told Dan to climb aboard. She handed up the gear bags and then climbed aboard herself. Opening the hatch with the combination lock, she pulled the hatch panels away.

"The salon needs airing out. It's an old wooden boat, and it can really get musty down there," she said.

"She's a beauty," Dan said. "I bet you've enjoyed owning this boat."

"Well, officially she belongs to my dad now. I'm sorry he couldn't come with us, because this is the last sail of the season for her. Dad is putting her into storage next week. I'm really glad we're getting to take her out one more time."

Leslie went below, and Dan passed the hatch panels down to her. The boat was not so different from the sloop-rigged Catalinas he sailed in San Diego. But the hull, masts, and deck were all made of wood rather than Plexiglas. When he looked into the hatchway, he was surprised at the appointments. All the appliances and instruments were new.

"We decided to refurbish it two years ago," Leslie said, as she saw him looking at the instruments. "We also redid the galley and the lighting. The chart table is the only thing we kept. And, as you can see, we redid the navigation station."

Dan turned knobs and flipped switches for a few minutes until Leslie said she was ready to go.

"I'll check the engine while you strip the sail covers and stow them below," Leslie called up to Dan.

A few minutes later, he heard the engine spring to life.

"What is the engine?" he asked, poking his head back into the salon.

"It's a Volvo diesel," Leslie answered. It was an engine he admired. More and more he was looking forward to this trip.

Leslie came back up to the cockpit and showed him the way the boat was tied to the buoy.

"We're ready to get underway. You go forward, and I'll give you the signal to cast off."

Dan went to the bow and un-cleated the buoy lines when Leslie gave him the signal and put the engine into reverse. The boat backed away from the buoy, and Leslie put the engine in forward position. They headed out of the harbor. Dan stood watch on the bow, watching for buoys that Leslie couldn't see from her position in the cockpit. There were very few boats left in the harbor. Most of the buoys were empty.

"We've got a southwest wind; let's take advantage of it. We'll tack a couple of miles out into the lake and then head due south. That way, we will have a good run home this afternoon."

Dan sorted out the lines for the mainsail halyard and stood ready to raise it. Leslie turned the boat into the wind, and he took in the halyard that raised the sail halfway. He wrapped the halyard around a winch and cranked it up the rest of the way. He stowed and secured the halyard and felt the boat shift. Leslie had turned the boat east to catch the wind. Just as she did, the sail filled, and the boat began to pick up speed.

"The ship is under sail!" Leslie exclaimed happily. She shut down the engine. "God, I love this," she said, as the silent boat accelerated through the water.

Dan returned to the cockpit, holding on to the lifeline as it began to heel in the wind. He was impressed with how quickly this big, old boat could move.

"Stand by to set the jib," she commanded.

"Aye, aye, sir." Dan smiled at Leslie, who grinned broadly.

Now that the sails were set, they enjoyed the view and the feeling of being one with the water and the wind. With two sails on a broad reach, the speed indicator read five-and-a-half knots. They were alone on the lake. On this week-day morning, there were no other boats in their view.

"You handle this boat like you were born on it," Dan observed out loud.

"Well, I practically was. My grandfather brought this boat over from Europe just after World War II."

"He sailed it across the Atlantic?" asked Dan.

"Yes, with one other man. They had both been prisoners of war in Germany. The only thing that kept him sane was thinking about sailing this boat."

"So he owned it before the war?" asked Dan.

"Yes, he bought it just before he was captured."

"Captured?"

"By the Nazis," she said. "He was a member of the underground in Sweden. They patrolled the fjords in this boat, trying to rescue airmen downed by the Germans."

"What a history," Dan said, looking once again at the boat, with appreciation for both the past and the present moment.

"So, are you hungry?" asked Leslie. "I brought some sandwiches and beer. They're down below. Can you get them?"

Dan got his first chance to take the helm while Leslie ate her sandwich. It was the fulfillment of a dream to be standing here sailing this beautiful craft with a person who loved sailing as much as he did. Leslie gave him some pointers on setting the mainsail for each point of sail and kidded him when he oversteered while coming about. She was definitely the captain in this conveyance. But he didn't resent her mastery at all. He was completely at ease with her, trusted her judgments, and enjoyed learning her techniques.

After lunch, Dan noticed that there were some scattered dark clouds to the north. He recalled the weather report, which included a small craft advisory for the afternoon. He wasn't familiar with Great Lake sailing and wondered what that advisory signified.

"Towering cu's," he pointed out to Leslie.

"Yes, I've noticed them too. Maybe we should head back toward shore. I don't want to get caught too far out if we have to sail in the rain."

Dan looked back toward shore. He could barely make out the tall buildings of Chicago. They had traveled several miles off shore.

"Good thing you brought rain gear," he said lightly, looking back at the dark clouds. He had flown into clouds like that in the Midwest and gotten knocked around pretty thoroughly. They usually contained strong winds and a lot of rain.

"Stand by to come about," said Leslie, without a trace of concern on her face or in her voice.

Dan positioned himself by the jib winch and announced, "Ready about." He suddenly imagined Sandra standing at the helm of this boat. She would be terrified to the point of panic by this situation. Being miles from shore and seeing the storm heading toward them from the direction of the shoreline was somewhat disturbing to Dan also. He tried to recall where he had seen the life jackets stored when he came aboard.

"Helms alee," Leslie said smoothly.

A moment later the bow began to swing into the wind. Dan waited until the bow was through the wind and then released the port jib sheet and reached across to take in the starboard jib sheet. He took in the sheet until the sail was taut, winched it down, and cleated it off. Their new heading was west toward Chicago. The distant skyscrapers appeared fuzzy and blurred by the rain now visible on the horizon.

The boat moved along nicely on its new heading. They could still feel the sun on their backs as they sat on the high side of the heeling boat. Dan checked the sky again and noticed that in just a few moments the clouds had joined up, thickened, and darkened.

"Those things are really building fast," said Dan.

"Yes, they do that around here," answered Leslie. "It looks like its developing into a dandy squall line. Hope you brought your sea legs."

Dan watched as rain shafts dropped out of the clouds, and he asked Leslie where the rain gear was stowed. He realized that the weather system was moving fast from north to south. They had planned an easy run home, but now they faced a difficult series of tacking maneuvers to return to the harbor north of the city.

"How about if we stow the jib?" asked Dan, thinking that the big sail would be difficult to lower in a storm.

"Yes, let's do that. Then, we'll reef the main," said Leslie.

Dan slacked the jib sheet and took in the furling line. The jib flapped in the wind as if protesting this insult. As the jib rolled up around the furling gear, he watched the horizon to the north.

"Here it comes," he yelled. He could see the squall line moving across the water. The wind whipped up the surface with rain right behind. He cleated off the lines and went to the mast to lower the mainsail enough to reef the sail. They needed very little sail in a storm, just enough to steer the boat with. Too much sail would cause the small craft to be completely overpowered and at the mercy of the wind.

As he got the sail lowered a few feet, he felt the boat turn into the squall line. Leslie was leaning on the wheel to set the bow into the wind. A good move, he thought. This way the boat would present the least amount of itself to the wind. Her timing was perfect. He cleated off the main halyard.

Fortunately, he still had the remainder of the slack end of the halyard in his right hand when the squall struck. The wind force was much stronger than he had ever experienced at sea. The bow rose up over the squall wave, and the rain drenched him. Every surface on the boat immediately became slippery from the wetness. Dan felt his foot slip out from under him, and he fell with a crack to the deck. Just at that moment, the bow dropped into a trough, causing Dan to roll over and slide across the deck. With his left hand, he grabbed the life line stanchion, but it wasn't taut, and the lower half of his body pivoted over the deck edge. He was waist deep in water—half on, half off the boat. Pain shot up his arm as his body twisted but his arm did not. He let go of the stanchion and sank into the cold, pounding water.

For a moment, he felt the cold water grabbing at his body, numbing him. Then there was the soft, peaceful sense of weightlessness as he slowly sank below the surface. He was aware of the boat next to him. Time seemed to stop.

Dan realized that he still had the mainsail halyard in his right hand. It was still connected to the boat, and now, as the boat moved away from him, the slack in the line pulled him to the surface. He felt himself being dragged along the side of the boat, abeam the forward end of the cockpit. Leslie was standing next to the wheel, looking over the side for him.

She locked the wheel and came forward to help get him back into the boat. With his good hand on a stanchion and Leslie pulling on his shirt, he was able to roll up onto the deck. They were both soaked: her from the rain, and him from his dunking.

When he was able to stand, he moved toward her, and without a word, they hugged each other. For Dan, the embrace was…electric. Magnified by the wet clothes, he could feel the warmth of her body. Her breasts pressed against his chest. After a long moment, with great reluctance, he released her. For a moment they just looked at each other. Then, Dan turned and finished securing the reefing lines on the mainsail. When he looked aft, she was back at the wheel.

"There are some dry clothes below. Go change," Leslie said.

Dan went below and found some clothes and four rain slickers. He passed a rain slicker up to Leslie. She was completely soaked, but the slicker would help until she could change. As he dried off and changed, he became aware of a strong pain in his right arm. Counteracting that was the memory of Leslie's warm, strong body when he had held her in his arms.

Dan went on deck and aft to relieve Leslie. The lake was less violent now, but the wind was still strong. "Go below and change. I'll take the wheel."

"Okay," Leslie said gratefully. "I've got her headed for the harbor. Hold this course."

Dan watched her disappear below decks. He wished he could follow her and take her into his arms again. He imagined them disrobing and standing together naked. The pitching of the boat would make undressing awkward, but they would laugh about it, he was sure. Lying together on the forward bunk, they would use the movement of the boat to cue their bodies as to how to come together and how to give each other the maximum pleasure. It would be a once-in-a-lifetime experience, thought Dan.

But for today the wind was still too strong, the route back to shore too uncertain. When Leslie returned topside, they worked together as a team to tack back and forth across the wind, finally arriving back at the harbor in Wilmette well after dark.

Chapter Nineteen

BIBLIOTECA

"Hanna, I'm glad I got you at home," said Sandra, when Hanna picked up on the fourth ring.

"Oh, sorry. I know I've been busy lately. I'm taking a course at City College. It's been keeping me very busy.

"A course? That's great. What is it?"

"It's a technical writing course. Basically, it's about using technology to get the information you need to create interesting documents."

"Sounds very interesting. I'm glad to hear you've started something new."

"Well, I decided I wasn't quite ready to be a hermit after all."

"I didn't think so." Sandra tried to keep her voice light, but she was very relieved to hear that Hanna had developed a new interest. "Are you using your old computer for it, or are you going to have to buy a new one?"

"I can use the computers in the learning center for the course. I'll wait and see whether I really get into it before I buy a new one."

A beep on Sandra's phone interrupted their conversation.

"Just a minute, Hanna. I've got another call. It's probably just Dan, checking in. I'll be right back."

Hanna waited a few moments, but when Sandra didn't come back on the line, she hung up. Ten minutes later, her phone rang again.

"Hanna, I just got the strangest call from Dan," Sandra said. "He's on a layover in Chicago, and he called from an emergency room. He had some kind of accident on a boat."

"On a boat? In Chicago? Somehow, those two things don't seem to go together."

"He was on Lake Michigan, and a storm came up. He was..."

"Is he going to be able to fly home?"

"I don't know. He might have to come home as a passenger. That was what seemed to upset him the most. That they'd have to call in a reserve to fly for him."

"But he's all right? Physically?"

"Yes, basically. It sounds like he was lucky that..."

"Well, he has a good story to tell. Who was he sailing with?"

"A copilot." Sandra was reluctant to say who the copilot was. She and Dan had managed to sustain their marriage for twenty-six years. This situation was scary. That's what it was. And it wouldn't help to broadcast it, even to Hanna. "Listen, I've got to go. He might try to call back after the doctor examines him. I'd better leave the line free."

The next morning, Sandra considered staying home to be there when Dan got in, but she was really looking forward to going to Tecolote with Bruni. She had a new idea she wanted to discuss with the volunteers at the center. Bruni knocked on her door at eight thirty, and Sandra prepared to load a whole box of books into the van.

Miguel was just unloading tools from his truck when he saw her struggling with the box. He came at once and took it from her.

"Good morning, Miguel," Sandra said with a smile. "Como esta?"

"Bien, Mrs. Sandra. Muy bien, y usted?"

"Bien, bien," Sandra said. "How is your family?"

"Todos bien," Miguel said. "My mother is very happy. The only problem is that we cannot take her back into Mexico again, or she will be deported."

"Well, is that such a problem?" asked Sandra. "Why would you want to?"

"Rosa and I—we put some money down on a small lot in Rosarito. We're thinking of building a house there."

"That's...wonderful, I guess. But I didn't know that you wanted to move out of San Diego."

"We don't, but we'll never be able to afford a house of our own here." He looked around and gestured toward the houses in Sandra's neighborhood.

"So you are thinking of moving back to Mexico?" Sandra's voice showed her surprise. After their struggle to come into the United States, why would they give it all up again?

"Not soon. Someday, maybe. Maria is doing okay at her new school. But when she is grown up, we have to think of what we will do. I cannot work as a gardener for my whole life, and we have no pension, hardly any savings. In Mexico, we can build a house on our lot and live a lot cheaper than here."

Sandra couldn't think of a reply. She felt some immediate guilt. She paid Miguel by the month and Rosa by the week, for the work they did at her house. All of this money was cash, and there was no additional amount for social security or a pension.

"Do you have health insurance?" she asked.

"No, but lucky that we are very healthy…so far."

Bruni had been standing nearby, not taking part in the conversation, not wanting to interfere. But even she had similar concerns. Born in Mexico and living in the United States, she could not legally work and had no health insurance or retirement plan. She usually put off thinking about the ramifications of her decision to live in San Diego. A small inheritance from her physician father had allowed her to make the move and also allowed her to pay the tuition for her daughter's Catholic high school and her son's first year at UCSD. As an international, non-US citizen, her son paid a tuition that was much higher than that paid by US, and especially California, citizens.

The issue that was fast developing in her family was that her children had adapted too well to the United States. She could not picture them ever wanting to return to Mexico to live or work; yet, they would not be able to work in the United States either.

Sandra's mind was filled with self-recriminations. How could she have taken part in this system of paying for work without thinking about the workers? They had seemed so happy, so grateful for the work, that she had felt good about their agreements, their unwritten contracts. She had never once thought of herself as a real employer, with responsibility for their lives beyond the work-for-hire transaction.

Sandra looked up the street. There were several other gardeners' trucks parked on the street. All of the workers were dark-skinned Mexican or Asian men. Battered cars with Tijuana license plates were also in evidence. Women had driven them across the border this morning to clean houses and take care of children. They would drive them back across the border this evening to take care of their own families.

Sandra remembered hearing Jan Froelich brag about the low wages she paid her housekeeper. Grant Prescott had stopped by the other day to tell Dan that he had switched gardeners because he was able to get a new one for half the amount he had paid the old one. He had told this news to Dan as a neighborly tip and offered to send the new gardener over to talk to Dan the next time he came. Thank goodness Dan hadn't shown much interest.

"Mrs. Sandra, where would you like me to put this box?" Miguel said, interrupting her thoughts.

Gratefully, Sandra told Miguel to put the box in Bruni's van.

"Good-bye," she called, as she climbed into the passenger seat. "I'm going to Tijuana, to Tecolote, to take some books. I'll see you next week."

"Good-bye. Hasta luego." Miguel picked up a rake and headed for the backyard as Bruni pulled away from the curb.

"You have a lot of books, Sandra," Bruni said. "Are these all for the center?"

"Yes, Bruni, I have an idea for the center. What if we convert the storeroom to a library?"

"A library?" echoed Bruni. "For the children?"

"Well, yes, mostly for the children," said Sandra, with excitement in her voice. "But look…I got a Carlos Fuentes book at his lecture a few weeks ago, and when I finished it, I got this one by Isabel Allende."

"All in Spanish?" Bruni was trying to merge onto the highway and couldn't look at the books Sandra was pulling out of the box to show her. When she got into a clear lane, she glanced to the right.

"*Paula*—that's a good book. Very sad, though." Bruni looked back at the road. "Have you read it?"

"Si. I mean, yes," answered Sandra. "In fact, I read it in Spanish. Well, I understood most of it anyway. It is very sad. I thought she would live. I was really surprised that she died."

"And you know that was a true story. Not fiction."

"Yes, I know it. She was able to write so well; all her real feelings came through. I don't think I could do that."

Bruni passed an ancient truck piled high with used building materials. Sheets of wood, used steel reinforcers, rolls of insulation filled the bed of the truck. It was obviously headed across the border.

"Will they have to pay duty on that load?" asked Sandra.

"I don't know. Probably," answered Bruni. "I have a friend who recently had his van confiscated because he was trying to bring in a few old computers."

"Really? Confiscated? By the Mexican border agents?"

"Yes. He was detained for five hours while they tried to decide what to do, and they finally let him call his wife at about ten thirty at night. She had to come pick him up. They kept the truck. He doesn't know if he'll ever see it again." Bruni drove into the Nothing to Declare lane at the border. They were relieved to see the green light blink as they went by.

"Was he trying to sell them?" asked Sandra.

"No, he was bringing them down to an orphanage. They weren't worth much. But the Mexican government has long lists of things that are not supposed to be imported. The trouble is nobody publishes the list."

They were silent for a few moments as Bruni drove and Sandra looked out the window, trying to commit the route to memory. What if Bruni couldn't go someday? Would she have the courage to drive down by herself?

"I want to stop at a restaurant this morning, if you don't mind. They give us some meat and chicken that they can't use."

"No, I don't mind," answered Sandra.

"Sometimes we get eggs, too," Bruni said.

"What do you do with them?"

"'We cook lunches with some of it, and we give the children some of it to take home, when we can," Bruni answered. She drove into the parking lot of a restaurant and went inside. Sandra waited in the car. A young man came out carrying a plastic dishpan full of chicken parts, mostly backs, as far as Sandra could see. On his second trip, he had a plastic pan full of beef bones and trimmings. The smell of the meat filled the van as soon as he put it inside and closed the door. When Bruni turned on the engine to drive away, Sandra rolled down her window.

At the center, they unloaded the box of books and the pans of meat. Some of the older children came up to help them carry the load down the steep stairs that led into the center. Elvira was cooking lunch that day and was happy to have the meat trimmings to add to her soup. Children were already studying with their teachers in the small classrooms. Sandra chose a few of the books from the box and went to one room to read aloud. Everyone was glad to see her. Petra gave her a big hug and told her that the children had been asking when she was coming again.

After the first group had eaten lunch and gone to school, the staff had time to sit down together to eat and discuss the week's events. Elvira wanted to get a newsletter out to publicize the work done by the center. She hoped that people reading it would want to contribute Christmas presents for the children. Uli said she would write it in Spanish, and Bruni promised to translate it into English and get some copies made.

When there was a break in the conversation, Sandra offered her suggestion.

"I am thinking about the idea of bringing enough books so that each child can take one home to read. What do you think?"

"That would be so wonderful," said Petra. "They don't have much to do after school except watch television."

"That's a lot of books," cautioned Elvira. "We have an enrollment of eighty children now. And new kids come in every week."

"I know that," said Sandra. "I think I can get a discount from some of the publishers I used to work with at the school district. They used to bring me sample books. I plan to talk with them about it if you like the idea."

"It's a very good idea," said Bruni. "You're talking about a real library. You mentioned something about it on the drive down here, but I don't think I understood you correctly. It's a big commitment on your part."

"Well, yes. But I guess that's what I like about it. I feel like you people are giving a whole year of your lives to this place, the least I can do is find a few books for you, for the children."

"Where will we put them?" asked Andy, the only young man on the staff.

"I was thinking about that storeroom." Sandra pointed toward a large closet containing shelves of paper, markers, crayons, and paste. "We could put them on some shelves and have it open for a few hours a day."

"No, not the storeroom," said Elvira. "I would worry about losing some of the other stuff we keep there. But I do like the idea. Maybe we could put up some partitions in Andy's classroom. It's the biggest room in the center. If we could build some walls and put in a door, we could lock it up."

"Locking it isn't so important," began Sandra. But Elvira and Petra quickly disagreed.

"If it isn't locked up, it will walk away. These kids don't have much, and some of them will take anything we leave lying around." Elvira passed around a plate of stale cookies that had been donated to the center. Sandra shook her head no.

"Yes," Petra continued, "it's better not to put too much temptation in front of them. I agree with Elvira. We need a room with a lock."

The discussion continued in a problem-solving manner, and the enthusiasm for the idea grew as the staff convinced themselves it could work. Some volunteers were coming for a weekend from a church in San Diego. They would be willing to do anything Elvira asked them to do. Why not ask them to build a couple of walls and put in a door? They might even paint the walls if they had time.

"Maybe my husband…," Sandra started to say, then thought better of it. She didn't want to promise something that she couldn't deliver. But it would be wonderful if Dan would offer to come down and build shelves or help with the partitions. Then, he could see why she was so excited about coming here.

"Can you get books for all ages?" asked Petra.

"I think so," said Sandra. She opened the carton of books she had brought with her today. "I even have a few adult books here. Do you think the parents would want to take books out?"

"Some of them would, for sure," said Bruni. "Some of the young parents who come to my clinic would probably come look at them. Especially if you can get some books about crafts or childcare."

"Here," said Sandra, handing a few books to Bruni. "Take these to your clinic, and we'll make a sign about the new lib—la biblioteca nueva—so they know about it."

The volunteer staff ended their lunch that day with new enthusiasm and energy. Next to working with the children, the biggest reward they experienced was in working with each other and watching the center grow and serve the community in new ways. Often, a new volunteer would come from the United States and stay for part of a day. Sometimes, they even promised to return or offered to bring or send items badly needed by the community. But most times, they were never seen again, and the supplies never materialized. Petra had expected the same thing of Sandra when she came for the first time.

What made it possible for one person to work here and another to feel overwhelmed by the dirty streets and shabby dwellings? Petra wasn't sure, and she could empathize with their discomfort. The first time she saw Tecolote, she had been shocked too. She had come from Munich to work for a year of service. For her it was a chance to see something different from Europe, to learn a new language. But the poverty and the lack of governmental services and infrastructure she had always taken for granted was hard to believe. Now, well into her second year here, she was more used to it, but each time new would-be volunteers walked in the door, she saw it again with their eyes.

Sandra and Bruni had a spirited discussion on their way home that afternoon. Bruni told Sandra about the hopes she had to get more members of the community involved in the center. More adults, that is. The children were hooked.

"If we are really going to succeed with this center, we have to get more people to come and take an active part in it," said Bruni, braking the van to wait for a bus that had stopped in the middle of the road to let out some passengers.

"I agree," said Sandra. "Are any of the volunteers from the community?"

"Elvira lives here. She has lived here for many years. I think she was one of the first people to settle here in this area. But she is not a volunteer. We pay her."

"Who pays her?" asked Sandra.

"The organization that built the center is called Baja Outreach. We get a few donations, and we're able to pay Elvira for being the director."

"How much does she earn?" asked Sandra. "Do you mind my asking?"

"No, I don't mind. We pay her one hundred twenty dollars a month."

"That is her total salary?"

"Yes, that's it."

"Can she live on that?"

"Well, she does live on that. And she has three grown children who still live at home."

"Forty—no, thirty dollars a week. You're talking US dollars, right?"

"Yes, in pesos, it's nine times that. About eleven hundred pesos."

"What is her rent?"

"She doesn't have any rent. She built her own house just like everyone else did who lives here. You should go see it sometime. It's only a few blocks from the center."

"Does she have a husband? Does he work?"

"No, she's been on her own for many years. She has raised her children by herself, essentially. Many women do."

"Well, that's true on both sides of the border," said Sandra. She suddenly thought of Dan. He might be home now. Home from that trip to Chicago. Home from what? He was vague on the phone. A sailing trip. Sandra remembered the phone call she had overheard last month. He had gone sailing with a woman copilot—that much she knew, or at least suspected.

"Do you mind if I stop for bread at the panaderia?" Bruni asked.

"No, of course not. I'll go in too. Maybe I can get something for dinner tonight. My husband is coming home today."

"He's been away?"

"Yes, he's a pilot. He flies three or four days a week."

"I know. My sister is a flight attendant for Aeromexico. She has a similar schedule."

The stop at the panaderia yielded warm, crusty bolillos that Sandra planned to serve with some broccoli cheese soup she had made the day before. Bruni bought the same type of roll but planned to split them and fill them with ham, cheese, avocado, and tomato for her two hungry teenagers.

At her front door, putting her key into the lock, Sandra looked for a suitcase in the hallway to tell her that Dan was home. It was there along with his flight bag.

"Dan," she called, "are you home?"

"Up here," he said, from their bedroom on the second floor. Sandra put down her rolls and went upstairs. Dan was lying down on the bed, one arm flung over his eyes.

"So, what happened, Dan?" Sandra asked, not sure she was ready to hear the story, but realizing that there was really no way to put it off any longer.

"I did a stupid thing," Dan answered.

"What do you mean?"

"I almost fell off the damn boat. This storm came up, and I lost my footing and…"

"So you went sailing on a layover? Was it a harbor excursion?"

"No, it wasn't." Dan lapsed into silence again.

Sandra wanted to throw something at him. He wasn't going to tell her anything. And she wasn't supposed to be aware of anything unusual. The telephone call she had eavesdropped on last month preyed on her mind, but she had too much pride—or was it fear?—to confront him about it. Who was he sailing with? Why wouldn't he tell her about it? Was he acting tired and out of it because of his injury or to forestall any more discussion with her about where he had been and who he had been with?

Sandra pushed the whole matter out of her mind. Taking its place was the memory of her day in Tecolote, reading with Lupe and Antonio, serving the soup at lunchtime, showing the books she had brought to the staff at lunch, and hearing their enthusiastic approval for her idea of creating a biblioteca for the whole neighborhood.

"Dan, where I'm working in Tijuana, we've decided to build a small library." She couldn't help asking, "Do you think you might want to come with me someday and maybe help build some bookshelves for it?"

"What?" Dan turned away from her. "Sandra, I don't know where you get these ideas, but I've got all I can handle right now. You can buy any bookshelves you ever needed at Home Depot. Now, can I please rest here until dinner is ready?"

Sandra walked downstairs, her happy memories of the day crumpled like the pages of a book that has fallen facedown on the floor. She picked up the paper sack of still warm bolillos and took them to the kitchen.

"I'll be damned if I share these with him," she said aloud to Amigo, who was rubbing her legs in anticipation of getting his dinner, too. She stuffed the bag of warm rolls in the breadbox behind a plastic bag of store-bought stale bread, which she opened to make Dan some toast to go with their soup.

Chapter Twenty

THE BOTTOM LINE

There had never been a time in their marriage when Sandra could recall such a period of silence. Dan had recovered from his injuries quickly and went back to flying within a week. When he was home, he seemed more intent than ever to work on his Porsche in the garage or go out for coffee with other pilots who lived in the area.

Sandra, who usually tried to get to the bottom of things with Dan and work through their disagreements, was less willing to do so for the weeks following the mysterious boating accident. She wanted time to think, and she hoped that Dan would initiate a discussion or at least invite her to go on a trip with him—a sure sign that he wanted to be close to her. But no invitation was issued. The silence lengthened.

Thanksgiving was approaching. Sandra was relieved to have this family event to think about and plan. She called Alex and told him to invite a few of his friends down to San Diego for Thanksgiving. It would fill the house with action and energy. Peter would come home if he could. He was studying anatomy and told Sandra that he could use the quiet days in the library if she didn't mind. Sandra almost wanted to tell him that she needed him home, but she didn't want to press him. Instead, she sent him a plane ticket that couldn't be refunded. She hoped he would use it and come home for just a couple of days.

Hanna was going to be away for Thanksgiving. She was going back to Albuquerque to see her aunt and her sister. Her aunt's health was very fragile; the Alzheimer's was destroying organs as well as brain cells.

There wasn't much to be thankful for this year. But Sandra struggled to overcome this mood. Her natural buoyancy returned when she thought of her recent visits to the center. That was where she felt at home these days. The volunteers who worked there always welcomed her when she came. Her one day a week had now turned into two. She was going with Bruni on Mondays and Wednesdays, and considering going on Fridays as well.

Why not invite the volunteers from the center for her family's Thanksgiving dinner? Sandra's mood brightened even more as she imagined the scene. The dining room would be very crowded, but that just seemed to be a plus. She could picture Alex and his friends talking with the young German volunteers, and Andy and Alex—they would have a lot in common. Peter would probably enjoy meeting Petra, who had worked in hospitals in Germany before coming to Mexico. Sandra could visualize the happy discussion, the full plates of turkey and homemade stuffing. It was a wonderful vision.

Then, she saw Dan sitting at the head of the table, carving the turkey. He would be polite, certainly. But she couldn't see him really engaged in the conversations around him. What would he have to talk about with the volunteers? Did Sandra convey this fear to Dan when she told him of her idea?

"Dan," she began, one evening after the news was over. "What do you think about having the volunteers from Tecolote join us for Thanksgiving?"

"I thought you said they were from Germany?" he responded.

"Three of them are. Andy is from Michigan."

"Well, Germans don't celebrate Thanksgiving, do they?" he asked.

"No, but I think they would enjoy seeing how we celebrate it," she said. Her voice had that wheedling sound. Try again, she thought.

"It would be fun for the boys to have a chance to meet young people from different cultures, don't you think?" she said, as assertively as she could muster.

"Sandra, I thought you told me that Alex was bringing friends home with him. Let's just leave it at that, okay?"

"Dan, that's not fair."

"Not fair to whom?"

Sandra could see that this argument was not going to be resolved during this discussion. She chose to end it rather than cause a prolonged struggle. The vision of the multicultural Thanksgiving meal in their home had evaporated. Walking away from Dan, she turned the bath water on very hot and poured in the rest of her citrus bath crystals. Amigo came into the bathroom while she was sitting in the tub. She focused on his handsome fur and inquisitive face. It helped.

The next time she went to Tecolote, she was greeted by children who seemed to be watching for her car. As she parked on the steep hillside next to the center, children came and opened her car door.

"Ven, Doña Sandra," they shouted. "La biblioteca!"

Small hands pulled at her clothes and arms, guiding her in the wrought iron gate, across the cracked cement patio, and into the large classroom that Andy used. In one corner of the room there were two newly constructed walls, forming a small room. A white door had been installed. The walls did not extend to the ceiling, so that light from the large room also illuminated the new room.

Above the door was a hand-lettered sign that read, "Biblioteca Sandra."

"Mira!" Children prodded and pulled her into the room. All of the books she had brought to the center were carefully placed on tables and shelves made from boards and concrete blocks. A chair and small table sat in the corner. The children led Sandra to the chair and made her sit down.

Tears sprang to her eyes as she took in the scene. She had spawned the idea with a few books and a few discussions. Others had turned the idea into a reality and given her credit. She had hoped that Dan might come down and help build it. But did it really matter who built it? The wonderful thing was that it had been accomplished.

Petra was watching from the doorway.

"How did this happen?" Sandra asked her.

"Those volunteers from the church came this weekend. We told them the idea, and they did it. Andy helped them. Uli painted the sign on the outside. Isn't it great? Aren't you surprised?"

"I'm very surprised. And it's wonderful." Sandra looked around the room. She saw some of the familiar books she had read aloud to the children. She would buy some of those cardboard pockets they used to use in library books before everything was computerized. She would paste them into the books and put cards in, so she could keep track of which child had what book. The little table next to the chair would be the checkout desk.

Maybe some of the older children could learn how to check out books. Maybe some of the parents would come in and learn how to do it. Then, the library—the biblioteca—could be open when she wasn't here. So many ideas. So many wonderful things to think about. Sandra's heart was filled with gratitude and happiness to be part of something so simple and yet so…well, maybe "profound" was overstating it, but important. Very important for these children and their families. And very important for me, thought Sandra. A perfect way to celebrate Thanksgiving.

Later that morning, Sandra asked Elvira whether they celebrated Thanksgiving at the center.

"Some of the volunteers, especially Andy, have also been asking about that," said Elvira. "What do you think? Is it something we should do for him?"

"I think it would be nice," said Sandra. "I could bring you a turkey, and we could cook it on Wednesday."

"I won't turn down that offer," laughed Elvira. "Let's talk about it at lunch with the rest of the volunteers."

At lunch, everyone was enthusiastic.

"I can make an apple strudel," offered Michaela. "Will that fit in?"

"It would be perfect," said Sandra.

"My mom taught me how to make that sweet potato stuff," offered Andy.

"Guacamole, of course," Elvira put in.

"But, who will do that stuff with the bread?" asked Petra.

"I will," Sandra said. "I'll bring all that stuffing stuff with me next Wednesday."

"Along with the turkey?"

"Yes, along with the turkey. Do you have a pan this big?" Sandra held out her arms to measure the length of a very good-sized turkey.

"I think so," said Elvira, getting up and searching on the lower shelf where they stored pots, pans, and baking sheets. "Will this work?" She held up a round cast iron pot.

"No, not quite," answered Sandra. "But don't worry. I can bring one of those aluminum pans they sell in the supermarkets."

"When will we have the dinner?" asked Petra. "Are you coming here on Thursday, Sandra?"

"No, I'm sorry, but I can't come on Thursday. I have other…obligations."

"Well, then, why don't we have it after the children leave on Wednesday afternoon?" suggested Uli.

"I'm afraid that I will not be able to attend," said Bruni sadly. "In fact, I cannot come at all that week. I am going to Mexico City to visit my mother. She has some type of bronchitis, and the pollution down there has made it much worse. I promised her I would bring my kids to visit when they are off for the Thanksgiving vacation."

Sandra hesitated. That meant that if she came, she would have to drive herself. Did she remember the route? Yes, probably so. And by this time, she understood that the same traffic rules applied to driving on this side of the border as the other. Well, more or less.

"I'll come," she heard herself say with a voice more confident than she felt. Everyone else agreed to this idea. They would cook the turkey during the day, while they were teaching, and it would be ready about dinnertime. The other items could be made the night before. Andy told them all that the best part of Thanksgiving wasn't the main meal at all. It was the leftovers the next day.

Sandra bought two fresh turkeys that week. She looked at the Granny Smith apples on the grocery shelf but passed them up. She bought green chiles instead to put in the stuffing for something different. She would make extra stuffing to take down to Tecolote on Wednesday morning.

She got up early the Wednesday before Thanksgiving to get down to the center before the first children arrived. She wanted to have time to help plan their meal and decide with the volunteers when they would put the turkey in the oven. She left Dan a note saying that she would not be home for dinner that evening, and suggesting that he could pick up the boys at the airport and take them for pizza.

The old gas oven in the kitchen had to be lit by a match. Sandra watched as Uli lit it with some difficulty. Then, they took out shelves so that the large pan could fit inside. When the afternoon group arrived, they all wanted to know what the good smell was coming from the oven. Sandra felt badly that they all couldn't stay for the meal, but she also understood that the volunteers needed time for themselves, time to celebrate and renew themselves so that they could meet the children's needs eight to ten hours per day.

When the last child left reluctantly, with his library book tucked safely inside his backpack, the adults gathered in the kitchen. Andy took the turkey out of the oven, sloshing some of the juices onto his trousers and shoes in the process. Uli got him some ice to put on his shins, and he sat down on the couch to watch the rest of the preparations. He told Petra how he remembered his mother making the sweet potatoes, and she followed his instructions while he watched. Elvira mashed avocados and diced up chiles to make her guacamole. There were refried beans left over from lunch, and no one objected to putting them on the table, too. Uli ran to get fresh tortillas from the tortillaria. They were still warm when she returned with the paper-wrapped bundle. Michaela put her apple strudel in the oven when they sat down to eat. It would be ready later for dessert.

They ate the meal on the same wooden benches the children used for lunch, sitting at the plain gray-painted tables. The plastic plates were heaped with food, and Sandra had her first taste of turkey with jalapeños, as she dribbled some of the spicy chiles over her meat and stuffing. It was delicious. She imitated the others as they wrapped up turkey, guacamole, and beans in a tortilla and ate it with her fingers. Had anything ever tasted this good in her life? She couldn't recall it.

Afterward, Elvira made strong coffee by boiling ground coffee and a cinnamon stick with the water in a pot. Michaela's apple strudel was a little burned on the bottom but had a wonderful aroma and taste. They laughed and talked in three different languages while they ate and ate and ate.

"So this is Thanksgiving," said Uli. "I like it. When I get back to Germany, and if I ever get married and have a family, I'm going to do this every year."

"I hope you'll invite me," said Petra.

"Of course I will," responded Uli. "I invite all of you. Isn't that the main idea of it? Wasn't it about the Indians and the pilgrims sitting together?"

They all looked at Sandra, the expert on Thanksgiving. She nodded vigorously while she ate another forkful of apple strudel. Well, that's the way it was supposed to be, she thought to herself. Somehow, it has become something else in my family. She felt that her happiness was diluted by this train of thought. She noticed for the first time how dark it was outside. She had better get going. She hadn't driven home in the dark before.

Driving back through Tijuana in the dark was a new challenge for Sandra. The familiar landmarks were difficult to spot, and the ruts and potholes even more difficult than usual to avoid, but at least the road was dry. She had heard stories from the other volunteers about the way these roads turned to creeks in a rainstorm. And this year, the news was full of warnings and reports on the El Niño weather patterns in the Pacific Ocean. But so far, there had been no rain. People were beginning to doubt the existence of El Niño—especially here in Tecolote.

Sandra pictured rain sluicing through the gully she was driving into and shuddered to think about what it would be like if she were driving alone in that type of condition. Maybe she would not even come down here during a storm. Elvira had told her last week that when it rained in Tecolote, many of the children didn't come to the center. Usually, the school across the street closed, too. Sandra decided to pay closer attention to the weather reports for the next few months, during the rainy season. No sense taking unnecessary chances.

When she arrived home, Peter and Alex were sitting in the living room, watching television. Dan was out in the garage.

"Where have you been, Mom?" asked Peter. "You missed a great pizza."

"Hey, Mom." Alex got up from his chair to give her a big hug. It felt wonderful to be wrapped up in his arms, cushioned by the fleece sweatshirt he was wearing. She walked over to Peter and kissed the top of his head. He reached up and gave her arm a squeeze.

"So, where were you?" he asked, flipping the pages of the television guide.

"I was in Tijuana at a community center."

"Doing good works, huh?" Peter smiled up at her. "That's great, Mom."

"Well, I don't think of it like that," Sandra began. "It's almost the other way around. I think I get more from the children than I give to them."

"I know what you mean, Mom." Alex turned around to join the conversation. "I signed up to do this tutoring thing in Oakland. I had my first session the other day with this kid in middle school. It worked out great. He says he hates math, but I showed him this math trick—you know; you used to do it with us—and he really got into it."

"Yes, I remember using that math trick on you when you were in middle school." Sandra laughed. "Still works, I see." Turning to Peter, she said, "And you probably got some of that feeling last summer when you were working on that project for the handicapped kids."

"Yeah, I guess so," Peter said. "Anyway, what's the plan for tomorrow? Do we have time to go surfing before dinner?

"I'm sure you do. Especially since I haven't even started cooking yet. I'm kind of behind schedule. Alex, I thought some of your friends were coming home with you for Thanksgiving."

"Well, Scott and Brian came down with me, but they are staying with some other friends tonight. They'll probably be over tomorrow for dinner."

"Probably?"

"Well, I'm pretty sure. We're all going surfing at Tourmaline first. Then, I'll call you and find out what time you're serving dinner, and I'll let them know. They'll decide then, if that's okay with you."

"I guess it's okay. Listen, I better go make a pie at least." Sandra went into the kitchen and cleaned up the pizza remnants before starting to put together a pumpkin pie. Stirring the ingredients together, she thought of the group-cooking event she had participated in earlier that day. It was a lot more fun making the dinner together rather than being here alone in her kitchen to plan and execute this holiday meal by herself.

Centro de comunidad, she thought to herself. Community center—that is just what that place feels like to me. Only, what is the definition of community in this case? I know that they created the place as the center for people in Tecolote, but when I'm there, it feels like my community center also. Not to mention that there is no such thing as a community center here in Point Loma. And, with the volunteers from Germany, that makes the community even larger. It's their center too. In some ways, I am actually jealous of the small upstart community in Tijuana. They seem to have something there that we've lost with all of our prosperity.

Dan came in from the garage and gave Sandra a kiss as he passed through the kitchen. "Smells good," he said. "Hey, Peter, Alex, come out here. I want to show you how I rebuilt the brake system. I put in a new master cylinder. You might have to do this someday."

Thanksgiving Day dawned sunny and warm. Sandra was dismayed by this weather. It meant that her sons would be tempted to stay at the beach all morning and well into the afternoon. She had hoped to put the turkey in the oven and go for a walk at the end of the point or up to Torrey Pines. Well, she and Dan could go. There was nothing stopping them.

Dan agreed, and when she had set the dining room table for dinner and done as much precooking as she could, they drove south to the end of the peninsula that separated San Diego from the sea. It was a bright, windy day. There were many other people looking out from the high bluff to the Pacific Ocean to the west and the city of San Diego to the east. They heard many different languages being spoken, as people from all over the world came to see this view.

Dan pointed out the submarines docked below them at the navy's Point Loma base. Sandra looked south and saw the hills of Tijuana in the distance. She wondered what the children were doing now. Were some of them visiting the new library, selecting books to take home tonight?

Dan used his binoculars to watch a couple of jets take off from the naval air base on North Island. "Wonder who has the duty on Thanksgiving?" he asked. He remembered his own tours of duty in the navy. He had eaten many holiday meals aboard the aircraft carrier his squadron was attached to. He hadn't minded so much. There was always so much happening aboard ship.

Several sailboats were leaving the harbor, going out to sea for Thanksgiving. What a concept. "Why don't we go rent a boat from the sailing club and have our Thanksgiving dinner onboard?" he asked kiddingly.

"Well, why not?" Sandra answered, surprising him. "Do you really want to?"

Her easy agreement caught Dan off guard. Did he really want to? Was she serious about agreeing to the idea? No, they couldn't do it. Better not test this any further, he cautioned himself. Better just let it go. Thanksgiving dinners didn't happen on small sailboats. He just couldn't picture it.

"And, Dan, I'm warning you that I am cooking the turkey very differently. So you better get used to it."

"What kind of different?" Dan said, scanning the horizon to watch other boats out at sea.

"Well, I put some jalapeños in the dressing," Sandra giggled.

"You're kidding, right?" Dan asked, but he wasn't sure if she was kidding. It was probably some Mexican concoction. "Oh, c'mon," he said. "The kids might be waiting for us. Let's go home."

Dinner was enjoyable. It was good to hear about the boy's new lives. They were happy and satisfied with their schools and friends and sports. Dan announced that he was thinking of bidding for the 777 as soon as he could hold it. He was ready for a new challenge, new destinations. Sandra was the one to bring up the idea of Thanksgiving itself.

"What are each of you most thankful for this year?" she asked. A few plates were passed before anyone reacted. Then Scott made a polite response that he was most thankful for all the good friends he had.

"Thank you, thank you," joked Alex. "Always happy to oblige."

"What about you?" Scott returned to Alex. "It can't be your surfing ability, not after that wipeout we all witnessed today."

"Okay, Mom, here is Scott's plate. He's finished eating."

"Give that back."

Sandra looked around the table. They each had so much. It wasn't easy to take the question seriously. With so much stuff and so many resources, it was sometimes difficult to see the value of anything. She looked over at Dan.

"With two college tuitions," Dan put in quickly, "I'm just happy to have a bottom line that isn't in the red...yet!" He glared meaningfully at the boys as if to warn them that they shouldn't stretch their luck by asking for another thing.

"I'm just happy to be in medical school," Peter said with sincerity. "I thought for a while there last summer that I'd have to find something else to do with my life, and I really don't want to do anything but this."

"I understand," said Sandra, looking back at Peter. "That is exactly the way I feel about my life right now. I read this saying the other day that the bottom line of happiness is gratitude—or was it that the bottom line of gratitude is happiness? Anyway, I am very happy and grateful to have people to love and people who love me and something useful and important to do to show people how much I care about them."

"Yeah, Mom," cheered Alex. "And you really did it with this great dinner."

"Okay, what's for dessert?" said Peter.

Chapter Twenty-One

EVERYTHING NICE

The week after Thanksgiving, Dan and Sandra flew to Pennsylvania to visit his parents. The older couple had accommodated themselves to life in their new retirement community and appeared to be very comfortable in their apartment. Having many friends in the area, their move from the family home had turned out to be much less traumatic than Dan and his brother, Bradley, had envisioned.

Josephine Seaquist showed Sandra the menu published and distributed to all residents of the community. They could choose to eat in the dining room, or they could cook something in their own kitchen. The only restriction was to let the staff know by noon whether they would be eating in the community dining room that evening. This plan held a distinct advantage for Josephine, who had never enjoyed cooking very much. Dan and Sandra would be their guests tonight in the dining room, she told them with pride.

Simon showed Dan his new collection of old watches. Formerly, he had worked on clocks of all sizes, including the tall grandfather clocks that had been built by craftsmen in Pennsylvania for hundreds of years. Now, with no workshop of his own, he had adapted by collecting pocket watches with etched brass and gold cases. He also had a thriving business within the retirement community of repairing clocks and watches owned by other residents.

In bed, the first night of their visit, Dan and Sandra talked quietly about the relief they felt to see his parents so well established in their new home. Sandra couldn't help but feel that Dan's parents were somewhat better adapted to their new life than she and Dan had adjusted to having their children leave home.

The next morning, they drove from Lancaster out to see the family farm, now owned by a younger couple, an attorney and a teacher. The black walnut trees still towered over the house. The fallen walnut shells still littered the ground beneath them, although squirrels had confiscated most of the nuts themselves. Simon shook his head to see this litter. Under his stewardship, the leaves and shells had been swept up on an almost daily basis. He would never have left the grounds looking like this.

Josephine was dismayed to see that the shutters had been repainted salmon pink. They had always been dark green before. The whole effect was very disturbing to the elder Seaquists, although Sandra believed that the shutters made the house more welcoming than it had been before. No one was home, so the question of whether to knock on the door and try to see inside the house was resolved without dispute. Simon would have counseled against it, had it been possible. "Better to leave well enough alone," he said, as they rolled up the windows of the car and drove into town again.

Dan asked his father about other relatives and neighbors in the area. Simon reported bare essential information about births, illnesses, deaths. Sandra asked Josephine about the types of activities sponsored by their retirement center. The older woman described craft classes and trips to local museums. "I made the wreath on our front door at a class last week," she said.

After admiring the wreath, Sandra could not think of much else to say to her parents-in-law. She always ran out of things to talk about with them long before the visit had come to an end. One reason, she realized, was that they never asked about her and Dan's life. We come to visit, and ask about family events, news of their friends, occupations, and interests. They never ask about ours.

Sandra wondered what they would say if they knew about her visits to Tijuana, her newly discovered ability to speak and read Spanish to small children. Josephine would probably worry about the diseases the children might carry. She was a very fastidious person. Better not to bring up the subject at all.

"What are your plans for Christmas?" Sandra asked, as they drove past an Amish horse and buggy near a bare field ready for planting next spring.

"We'll have dinner in the dining room. We've already made our reservations," answered Josephine.

"Are you sure you don't want to reconsider and come home with us for a few weeks?" Sandra offered.

"No, I don't think so," answered Simon. "We're better off here. That's a big trip for us. All the way to California."

Sandra thought of the few hours of flying that had brought them from San Diego to Harrisburg with one easy change in Chicago. It wasn't the travel that stopped them. It was something else. She pictured their sunny dining room, filled with Alex and Peter's roughhousing, and added the extra classmates Alex was bringing home with him. Then she pictured Josephine sitting primly and silently throughout the meal, and Simon blending into the wallpaper. No, they were right. They were better off here.

"What were Thanksgiving dinners like when Dan was growing up?" she asked, with real curiosity. If she could get a real answer here, maybe she would learn some clues about Dan's view of the world. Funny, she thought, after this many years of marriage, I still feel that I have much to learn about my husband. I think he may still have much to learn about himself, as well, but is he open to that?

"We always ate at four o'clock," Josephine answered briefly. Sandra waited for more details, but they were not forthcoming.

"Who did you invite?" Sandra asked. "Did you do all the cooking every year, or did other people bring things?"

"I always did the cooking," Josephine answered. "We had turkey, chestnut stuffing, green beans, cranberry relish, and Parker rolls."

"Every year?" Sandra couldn't help it. The question popped out unbidden. But even as she asked it, she recalled that that was the menu for every one of the Thanksgiving dinners she had eaten in Dan's home over the years. Unchanging. And there hadn't been many guests at the table. Simon's sister, before she passed away. An aunt or two occasionally. Thanksgiving dinners had seemed like such an ordeal to Sandra. A brief prayer, the same prayer every year. No real celebration or spontaneous expressions of gratitude. Sandra looked at Dan. What was he thinking right now? Was he even listening to this conversation, or was he mentally thinking of landing patterns or engine overhauls? She moved over to sit closer to him in this backseat of his parents' car. He reached for her hand and held it lightly but maintained his silence.

Dan's thoughts were not as distant as Sandra had suspected. He, too, was thinking about his parents' lives, so different from his own. Yet, he knew that he and his father were very much alike. They were both men who felt most comfortable with machines or clocks to fix. They were both hesitant to speak up and take the risk of raising a subject that was controversial in any way. They were both married to women who...

What if I had married a woman more like my mother? Dan asked himself. Would I have stayed in one place all my life? Would I have concerned myself with how tidy everything is as much as he does? Sandra does shake things up from time to time. And she shakes me up. No cobwebs grow with Sandra around. She's on to the next thing before I have time to get used to the way things are. He held Sandra's hand more firmly, rubbing his thumb on her palm. Her hand felt warm and welcoming. When was the last time he had ever seen his father hold his mother's hand? Dan could not recall any such sign of affection. There had been brief kisses for hello and good-bye, but even these seemed formalized, as much the same as the oatmeal for breakfast every morning.

Am I susceptible to this mindset? Dan continued to probe his own psyche. My parents seem more and more set in their ways as they grow older. Will that happen to me? Is it happening?

A disturbing thought entered his mind: Leslie. Did she represent a fresh new change in his life? Sailing through sun and storms together? Would life be new and challenging with Leslie? Dan took his hand from Sandra's grasp. She holds on a bit too tightly, doesn't she? A bit too long. What does Sandra want from me? What do I want for myself?

Sandra took her hand back into her own lap. She rummaged in her purse for a mint to chew on. She looked out the window at the perfectly groomed farm fields, the manicured lawns, the well-shaped trees, and freshly painted fences. Why wasn't it beautiful to her?

Dan pictured coming to visit his parents to tell them he had left Sandra and was going to move in with Leslie, live on a sailboat perhaps, buy a plane they would fly together, bid their trips to coincide, sharing layovers in Paris, Hong Kong when they were able to hold the 777 bid. Dan felt the stirring of an erection, imagining this life. It was as different from his parents' lives as possible. Wouldn't they be shocked? He shifted in his seat, pulling his jacket onto his lap.

But, of course, he could never tell them about this. He'd have to wait until they died before he could do anything like this at all. Commitment, family, morality—these were strong components of Dan's makeup. Fantasy—that's all this was, this imaginary life with a woman who shared his passion for flying, sailing. Wasn't it?

"Here is the cemetery, Dan," Simon said. "Do you want to stop?"

"What?" Dan shook his head to erase the imagery. "No, not particularly."

"I think we should show them, Simon," insisted Josephine.

Dan's father slowed the car and pulled over to the side of the road. On the left side of the street was a large, plain wooden building, probably a Mennonite meeting place built centuries ago. On the right side of the road was a very old cemetery.

Simon and Josephine got out of the car and walked to the gate without looking back at their son. Sandra and Dan exchanged glances and then followed his parents. At the far left of the cemetery was a new, gray headstone, slightly larger than the ones surrounding it, but made of the same material. Dan and Sandra read the inscription quietly, not trusting their voices to say anything. The names "Simon R. Seaquist" and "Josephine L. Seaquist" were inscribed on the stone, along with their birthdates and a dash pointing to as-yet-unknown dates of their deaths.

"We wanted to take care of this while we were alive, so you wouldn't have to worry about it," Simon explained.

"We talked it over, and we knew what we wanted to do, so we did it," added Dan's mother.

"Well, Dad…" Dan couldn't finish the sentence.

"It's very nice," said Sandra. They wanted to make sure it was done right, she added to herself. It had to be just so, just like all the others. Just like it had been done for centuries. No surprises. She looked around the cemetery, taking in all the other stones. It was very tidy and clean here. No walnut shells allowed. No vandalism. Even all the names are similar: Seaquists and Johnsons, Richters and Livingstons. No Sanchezes or Ortegas here. No Changs or Suzukis. Not even any Menottis or Kowalskis.

"And all the costs are taken care of. It's in a trust. The grounds fees are included," Simon was telling Dan with pride.

"It's very nice, Dad." Dan's face was a mask. What was he thinking? Would he tell her later, when she asked?

They got back into the car and drove into Lancaster, stopping to pick up vanilla ice cream to have for dessert, although Josephine assured Sandra that there would be several desserts to choose from in the dining room.

"Still, it's nice to have our own dessert, in our own place, don't you think?" she asked Sandra, woman to woman.

"It's very nice," Sandra agreed. "Here, would you like to get these mocha pirouette cookies to go with the ice cream?"

"No, dear. I don't think so. I've never tried them."

On the airplane, heading back home, Sandra read a magazine and watched the inflight movie. Dan went up front to chat with the flight attendants and an off-duty pilot he knew. The sun felt especially warm when they walked out of the terminal. Sandra felt its heat on her face and shoulders as a gift, a healing touch from…well, who knew where from? Not from the heaven that Dan's parents envisioned. She shuddered to think of being transported to the all-Caucasian, all-vanilla heaven that they aspired to.

"Let's go buy some mocha cookies on the way home," she said to Dan, who agreed without question. He was already planning the packing he needed to do before he went on his next trip. December, already. He had a good line this month. Christmas off—a rare treat in the airline business. He wouldn't have them if he took a 777 bid. He'd be junior again for several years on that equipment and would probably be in Bangkok next Christmas.

Well, is that so bad? he mused. Who might be with him? Sandra and the kids? Not likely. She would have some excuse or another. Leslie? Better think about something else. No, really, he had better think about this matter. But not now. Dan wished there was someone he could talk to about this, someone who would understand, who had maybe had a decision like this to make himself.

Who? His brother Bradley. No, they talked about cars and skiing, never about their wives or feelings. Other friends? No one came to mind except copilots, like the one he'd had dinner with in Chicago, on his third marriage. Dan shuddered. That isn't what he wanted. Then what do I want? he asked himself, as they drove into the driveway of their house.

"Listen, Sandra, I'm going to drop you off. I need to run down to the hardware store for a minute." Sandra looked puzzled but didn't argue. She took her bag into the house, and he saw her picking up Amigo as he drove back out of the driveway.

Dan drove toward the hardware store, but he couldn't think of anything he really needed to buy today, so he turned away from the business district and drove, instead, down to a parking lot near the beach. He turned off the engine and sat looking out at the ocean. As usual there were a few sailboats off Point Loma. Why such an obsession with the sea these days? he pondered. What is missing in my life that I think I will find out there?

Excitement? No, not really. That sail on Lake Michigan was a little too exciting. That's not it. Is it about sex? Do I think someone new, someone like Leslie, will be more interesting, sexually? Well, she might be or she might not be. I have never felt that I was missing out on much in that vein. Memories of making love with Sandra were reawakened, and he felt happy thinking about them. They were ambitious and loving partners, sexually. The pleasure and joy that Sandra obviously experienced in their lovemaking was important to him. And she was generous and spontaneous with him, anticipating what he wanted from her and giving it willingly. Why mess with success? It would take many years to create that type of sexual relationship with someone else. No, it wasn't about sex. Of that, he was sure.

Then what? He saw a picture in his mind of the boys going off to kindergarten or first grade. He saw himself walking them to school. Sandra was always off at her own first day of school, so he always bid his schedule to be available to take the boys. He saw them approaching the school. Peter was cautious, Alex more eager. One year, Peter had come home for the whole first week of school with his lunch uneaten. Dan had asked him why he didn't eat it. Peter shrugged it off, couldn't or wouldn't say why. So Dan had gone to school at the beginning of the lunch hour the next day. He stood and watched as Peter came to the lunchroom and didn't seem to know which way to go, where to sit. Instead, he went into the boy's bathroom and didn't come out for a long time. Dan followed him. He called his name. Peter came out of one of the stalls, surprised to see his dad there. It turned out that because he was buying milk, Peter didn't know whether to sit with the ones who were buying or the ones who weren't buying their lunch. Dan listened patiently. He walked with Peter to talk with the lunchroom attendant and find out where he belonged.

Dan felt very good about being there for his kid. It felt good to be the one who helped him solve that problem. And there had been many other problems over the years that Dan had worked through with both boys. He also remembered waiting at home some days, looking at his watch, waiting for them to come home. The house felt very empty some of those days when Sandra was working and the boys went back to school. He was always eager to see them coming home, flinging their backpacks down on the couch and emptying the contents all over the place. The house came back to life when they walked in.

Sandra talks about those same feelings, recalled Dan. That's probably why she's so involved down there in Mexico with those kids. And what have I done to fill the void? Worked on my sports car, thought about sailing a lot, and bid the 777. The sailing, especially, seems to replace some of that energy we lost with the kids gone. It's an exhilarating feeling, and there is always a problem to solve and a challenge to overcome, just like parenting. Only, in this case, Sandra isn't interested. So, what's the answer? Do it without her? Do it with someone else?

Or do something else altogether, something with Sandra that we could enjoy doing together.

Dan felt brighter, more optimistic as he drove home. He had no idea what else he and Sandra might find to do together, but he was willing to try to find something if she was. When he walked in the door, he called her name. There was no answer. The house was sunny and spotlessly clean, beautiful and empty. A note on kitchen table told him that Sandra had gone to the bookstore.

She probably went to buy more damn books for those Mexican kids, he thought, with some anger replacing his optimism. She doesn't want me. She doesn't even need me anymore. Why don't I get it? Hell with her. I can take care of myself. He opened the refrigerator and found a cold beer. He made a sandwich and ate it hurriedly. Then, he called the crew desk and asked if he could pick up an extra trip. With December schedules bursting at the seams, they were glad to accommodate him. They assigned him a three-day trip to the East Coast starting the next day.

That meant he'd be working almost every day until December 22. Good. They could use the extra money with Christmas here, and he wouldn't have to think about this rift between him and Sandra. Maybe, when the boys came home, they could all sit down and talk about it. The boys were usually good at problem solving, although he was reluctant to alarm them, make them think he was unhappy or worried about his marriage. That wouldn't be the thing to do. His parents would never have involved him and his brother with their problems.

Dan pictured his parents again as they had looked yesterday at the cemetery. Straight, serious—always so serious. Things had to always appear to be fine with them. They didn't want anyone to worry about them, even when they die. "Is that the way I act?" wondered Dan. "Do I have a streak of that—what would you call it?—running through my blood? Did they hand me a script when I was born? Be polite. Don't push. Never try to impersonate an officer. Work hard. Don't cry. Do what you're told. Be a good provider. Don't show your feelings. Don't even have any feelings, if you really know what's good for you. Above all, don't complain. Is that my script?"

If so, what of it? What's wrong with that for a script? It's a pretty damn good one. It has worked out well for me…and for Sandra. We have a good life. We did a great job as parents—are doing a great job, I mean. We've had good careers. Sandra may be tired of hers, but I still love mine. Isn't that enough for anyone?

Yes…and no. It has been enough, more than enough. We've been lucky, although we've made most of our luck, if you ask me. We've been happy. My parents didn't write the script about our sex lives. Hell, I've never even seen them hug each other, but Sandra and I made our own script there, and we wrote it well. Is that what we have to do again, now, at this time in our lives? Write a new script for the time after our kids are grown and we've fulfilled all the other goals we set for ourselves?

Yes, Dan knew he had come to something very important here. We need a new script, something we write together. I'd like it if she'd go sailing with me, maybe even buy our own boat. She'd like it if I...

The certainty and momentum of his thinking lost power here. Hell, I don't know what she wants of me. But, after Christmas, I will try to make some time to talk with her about it. Maybe we could even take a trip somewhere together and work on this. Maybe there's something besides sailing that would excite her and that I'd enjoy too.

If not, well...That's not productive, he chastised himself, even as the fleeting image of Leslie pulling him out of the cold Lake Michigan water washed over him again. She was so brave, so competent. If I wasn't married...But I am.

When Sandra returned from her errand to the bookstore, she was quiet. She had bought some things for Christmas and took them away to wrap. She asked Dan to get the Christmas decorations out of the garage, and when he told her he had volunteered for an extra trip the next day, she seemed annoyed.

"Then we had better go get the Christmas tree tonight. I don't think I want to do that alone, too," she said.

"What do you mean—'too'?" asked Dan.

"Remember when we all used to go get the tree?" she asked.

"Well, we could wait until the boys get home and get it then," he offered.

"No, they won't be home until a day or so before Christmas. We better do it now," she said.

Buying and decorating the tree was a chore—that's what it was. They both felt it, and neither of them could think of a way to get out of this loop they'd been in lately. Everything they said to each other just seemed to irritate their problems and make them worse. They went to bed that night, quiet, lying side by side but not touching, each very aware of the closeness and yet at the same time the distance between them. Only the cat seemed to benefit from the situation. He climbed into the space between them and lay so his back was against Dan's side and his paws were touching Sandra's arm.

Chapter Twenty-Two

EL NIÑO CONTINUED

Am I to blame? he asked himself. Was I such a lousy husband that she came down here to pay me back? We had a good life, especially when the boys were young. She was such a good mother. I know it's hard on women to have their children leave home. Maybe I should have paid more attention to her. God, I hope she doesn't think that I was fooling around on her. Is that what it is? Did she get herself in this situation to pay me back for being attracted to Leslie? Is that why she insisted on coming down here so close to Christmas, because she thought that something was happening between Leslie and me?

"We're getting there." Miguel's voice interrupted Dan's thoughts. "Here, Petra, squeeze through and see if you can reach someone in there."

Petra got down on her belly and pushed herself on the slippery mud into the hole they had wedged out. She reached in with her arm and felt a small hand grab hold.

"I've got you," Petra exclaimed triumphantly. "Vamanos!" She held on to the small child's hand while the others started digging a space for her to climb through. Dan watched his sons put all their effort into saving this unknown child.

"Sandra," he said, "you've got to be okay. You would be so proud of your sons if you could see them now."

Petra was being pulled into the muck as the ground beneath her was undermined. Alex grabbed on to her legs and held her firmly, while the others cleared a passageway for the child. Petra looked up at the men with a plea to hurry in her eyes. The child's hand was slippery, and she was losing her grip. Miguel saw what was needed and used his rake handle to extend their reach.

The limp and unresisting child was finally freed. Mud caked her eyes and hair. She spit vigorously, and everyone cheered. When she saw Petra, her eyes never left her face.

"Mami," she said to Petra.

"Yo sé," responded Petra. "Vamanos." Petra looked at the others, who had resumed their digging. She took the child in her arms and carried her back to the center, where she could be cleaned up and fed.

Dan called again for Sandra. There was more hope now. The child hadn't been badly hurt, although she was obviously in shock. Dan reviewed what he knew about aiding people in shock: warmth; lower their heads, so the blood could flow more easily. He was ready.

"Peter, get that tarp out of Miguel's truck and put it on the ground, so we can lay your mother on it," he said.

Peter ran to the truck and retrieved the tarp. The unremitting rain and wind made it difficult to hold on to the slippery plastic material. It was a good idea, though, to have it ready. Who knew what condition Mom would be in when she was brought out of the mud. Again, Peter had to remind himself that this was really happening.

When he fought his way back up the slope and spread the tarp out on the slippery ground in the flattest place he could find, he found the activity heightened. A woman, not his mother, was being hauled out of the site. The first thing Peter noticed was that she was very pregnant. Peter watched as his father and another man carried the woman over and laid her down on the tarp as gently as they could.

"Dad, we should call for an ambulance," Peter advised.

Dan looked questioningly at Miguel. "Do you know who to call?" he asked.

"I can drive back to the police station and tell them," suggested Miguel.

"That will leave us without transportation until you get back," said Dan, thinking that as soon as he was able to get Sandra out of here, he just wanted to put her in the nearest conveyance and get her back across the border to the United States. Who knew what the hospitals would be like here.

"No, Dad, it's all right," interrupted Alex. "Mom's car is here, remember?"

"That's right!" Dan relaxed a bit. He gave his attention back to the pregnant woman, who was coughing and gagging from the mud in her windpipe. One of the other men who had been helping dig seemed to recognize her. He called to a teenage boy watching from the hillside and gave him some directions. The boy ran off to do what he was told.

"What did he say, Miguel?" asked Dan.

"He told the boy to go get this woman's sister. She lives nearby. I can help him bring back the sister, or I can go to the police station." Miguel's statement had the tone of a question. "Or I should stay here and help get out Mrs. Sandra?"

For a moment, everyone waited to hear what Dan wanted them to do.

"Go get help," Dan told Miguel. "We'll be all right here." He realized anew that this rescue wasn't the one he had been working for. He put the woman's head down on the tarp, stood up, and began to walk back to the demolished casita. She coughed again, and he felt drawn back to help her. He looked up at his sons and asked them with his eyes to fill in for him.

Peter knelt down by the woman's side. He took off his Gortex jacket and spread it over the woman's chest. Two women came from somewhere and started talking to the pregnant woman in Spanish. Peter heard her respond and understood that he was now free to help his father.

Dan leapt back into the action. Alex handed him a shovel, and they carved another hole in the debris at a different angle from the empty gaping hole where the woman and her child had emerged.

They discovered one of Sandra's shoes. Soon, they saw her gray flannel pants leg. Separating the used plywood from the mud, Dan looked down into the hole. A metal cabinet was lying across Sandra's midsection. Its doors were open, and the entire interior of the cabinet was filled with heavy mud, cooking pans, broken pottery, and a Barbie doll with the head broken off. Dan picked up the doll's body and threw it aside. He didn't like the image it suggested at all.

Alex climbed in and threw out other remnants of a family's homelife. Some things were familiar to him, such as a soup ladle; a heavy, black, iron frying pan; socks; and a sweatshirt with a Miami Dolphins logo. Other things were new to him: a tortilla press, with its mud tortilla encased inside; an open can, half filled with lard, half filled with mud. Finally, the cabinet was empty enough to move.

"Take it away," he yelled to his father. Dan and another man pulled it up to the surface and tossed it farther down the hillside.

Alex saw his mother's face. The cabinet had been a barrier between his mother and the mud. Her face was recognizable. Her mouth was open, and she was breathing rapidly now, as if to make up for missed opportunities. She moaned, tried to raise herself, winced, and lay back down.

"Dad, she's alive!" Alex called over his shoulder. "I can see her breathing."

"Sandra!" called Dan. She moved in response to her name. She smiled. Her lips formed a word, but no sound came out.

"Mom, it's me, Alex. We're all here," her son said softly. He felt a gentle warmth throughout his body. He maneuvered his body down beside her and began to lift her by the head and shoulders. She moaned again.

"Dad, every time I touch her, she cries out. What should I do?"

Dan reviewed again what he had learned in safety courses on the airline. Moving someone was the worst thing to do in most cases. Broken neck, broken back—these were the worst things he could imagine. What should they do?

"Peter, what if her back or neck...?"

"I know, Dad. We should have paramedics here. They'd put her on a body board and strap her to it.

"Well, that's what we'll have to do, then. Get that piece of plywood."

Peter understood. He retrieved a piece of plywood, previously a portion of the roof of this house. He broke it in two pieces and chose the narrowest piece to pass down past his father into Alex's waiting hands.

In this case, the mud was helpful. It cushioned every impact. Alex was able to slide the plywood beneath his mother's body because the mud gave way to the pressure he put on the wood.

"I need something to hold her onto the wood," he called out. It seemed as if she recognized him. "I'm here, Mom. We're all here. We'll get you home soon."

Dan and Peter looked around, seeking a solution to this problem. Dan took off his belt, and Peter did the same. One of the Mexican men saw their action and wordlessly took off his belt and handed it to Dan. It was a larger size and was the one they used to secure Sandra's torso to the splintery wood. Dan's went around her feet; Peter's held her forehead in position. Alex's fingers were numb, and he had difficulty getting the belts underneath the wooden pallet, but he worked diligently to complete this task quickly.

When he was satisfied that his mother was securely bound, he signaled to his father to begin to pull her out of the ragged opening. Peter and Dan pulled while Alex raised the pallet up and guided it out into the open. He followed quickly behind, and the three men confronted their own worst fears and their best hopes. They had succeeded in a task that none of them had ever imagined having to do. Dan wanted to ascertain the extent of Sandra's injuries, but Peter urged him to move her down the slope and into her car, so they could take her home.

Sandra began to talk to them, but they really couldn't understand what she was saying.

"Are you in pain?" asked Dan. "Where does it hurt?"

Sandra nodded and blinked her eyes. She couldn't move her arms to point, so any further diagnosis was unlikely at this time. Trying to fit the makeshift stretcher into the backseat of the car was not easy, but they chipped away at the wood with pocket knives until the newly curved edges were able to clear the back door and lie relatively flat on the seat.

"Good thing you're not any taller, Mom," quipped Alex. Was that a smile? It seemed like it was. The three men fitted themselves into the two front seats of the small sedan, and Dan started the engine with the key on his ring.

"Now what, Dad?" urged Peter. "Get in, let's go."

"I'm trying to think," responded Dan. "Should we wait for Miguel to come back to show us the way back to the border?"

"Where is he?" asked Alex.

"He went to get help at the police station," said Dan.

Sandra moaned in the backseat of the car.

"Dan," she whispered.

"Sandra, we're here. We're all together in your car. We'll have you home soon."

"The baby...the little girl..." Sandra's voice was as quiet as the sound of bubbles surfacing on a still pond.

"The little girl is in the center, Sandra. Someone is taking care of her. The baby wasn't born yet."

"No baby. Good." Sandra seemed to relax somewhat. Or was she fainting, falling into unconsciousness again.

"We've got to go, Dad," said Alex. "Just drive."

"Okay, okay."

Dan backed out of the muddy lot, spinning the wheels of the car several times before he got enough traction to maneuver onto the street. Now they had to get up the hill. It wouldn't be easy to get up this hill on a dry day. It was deeply rutted and pocked with stones. Dan put the car into first gear and moved ahead slowly, avoiding the largest rocks. At the top of the hill, he stopped and looked left and right. A white-and-yellow station wagon was approaching from the left. It had a sign that said, "Teco Taxi."

"Do you remember which way we came?" asked Dan.

"I think we turn right here," answered Peter.

"Follow the taxi, Dad. Maybe it's going to a main road," suggested Alex.

They followed the taxi, and certain landmarks, such as the sign advertising tri-ply and an overturned recreational vehicle they had seen before, convinced them that they were retracing the steps they had taken that morning. They saw the church on the right and looked for Miguel's truck there but didn't see it. At a T in the road, they saw the police station. There was Miguel's pickup. Dan stopped the car and allowed Alex to hurry inside to tell Miguel what was happening.

Miguel followed Alex outside and shrugged his shoulders in answer to their unasked question of what he had learned at the police station. They interpreted this to mean that he was still waiting to tell his story.

"Miguel, we're going home. We have Sandra with us."

"What about the other lady?" asked Miguel.

"I don't know, really," answered Dan. "I think she was okay. Two other women came to take care of her."

"I'll follow you," said Miguel.

"No, we'll follow you," responded Dan. "I'm sure you can get us back to the border faster than we could."

"I'll ride with Miguel, Dad," said Alex, as he climbed into the passenger seat of the truck.

A thick fog was descending. Perhaps it was a good sign, meteorologically. The rain did seem to be lessening somewhat. The mist softened the landscape they were driving through in much the same way that a fresh snow enhanced a bleak mountain landscape. Dan concentrated on driving, keeping the dim taillights of Miguel's truck in view. Peter turned in his seat to keep an eye on his mother.

"Turn the heat up, Dad."

Soon, the warm car allowed them to feel a sense of well-being begin to return. They talked of practical matters on the drive through Tijuana. As they arrived at the border, the frontier between two nations, they jockeyed into position in a middle lane with about thirty cars ahead of them and six or eight columns of cars on either side. The line moved slowly, but it moved.

Hawkers of plaster birdbaths, hand-blown glass Christmas ornaments, and soggy blankets and lace tablecloths tried to get their attention. "Señor? What else you want to buy?" But Dan and Peter looked straight ahead, not making eye contact with any vendor. To do so would be to risk a negotiation that neither of them had the energy to take part in.

An old man with no legs sat in a wheelchair with a paper cup extended list-lessly at the end of his arm. No one put in any coins. A young mother carried a baby wrapped in a blanket and had a two-year-old holding on to her skirts. She had a paper cup as well, which she showed to each driver as she wove through the lanes of traffic, dodging the starting and stopping vehicles and expecting her toddler to do the same.

On the right was a large sign in Spanish and English. "Help Us to Help Them," it read. "By Giving Money, You Are Encouraging Them to Continue Begging."

Peter pointed out the sign to his father, who nodded grimly. It was comfort-ing to have the Mexican government support his own conviction. But some-how he heard himself say aloud, "I wonder what the government does for these people."

In the backseat, Sandra seemed to hear this statement. She made a sound as if she was also thinking that same thing.

Just before they reached the booths housing the US Customs and Immigration officers who would ask them their citizenship and what they were bringing back from Mexico, Dan and Peter noticed a huge wooden horse, shaped something like the Trojan horse they remembered from books of mythology, except for one thing: it had two heads. The figure was made of plywood—tri-ply, the same material Sandra was lying on. It was huge, at least twenty feet tall, and appeared to be hollow like the Trojan horse. But one mighty head was facing back the way they came, and the other was facing toward the United States. It was located in the middle of the traffic lanes going into and out of Mexico.

Peter and Dan both noticed the figure and may have had questions about it in their minds, but these were quickly erased when the light ahead of them turned from red to green, and a customs officer waved them forward. Dan rolled down his window. The woman didn't look at them for a few moments. She typed something (their license number?) into a computer. Then she put her hand on the lowered window of the driver's side of the car and asked, "Citizenship?"

"US," said Dan, who was used to going through customs at airports around the world.

"American," answered Peter.

The officer peered into the back seat. "What about her?" she asked. "She's my wife," answered Dan.

"What happened to her?" asked the customs agent.

"She was in an accident. We need to get her to a hospital."

"She looks like she has been badly hurt. Do you want me to call an ambulance?" asked the agent.

"Well, I think it would just take more time. I'm going to drive straight to UCSD Hospital from here," answered Dan.

"Wait one moment," insisted the agent. Dan and Peter looked at each other and waited impatiently. What was happening? Didn't they believe that she was a US citizen? Did they think that they were trying to smuggle someone across the border? Dan was concerned. He didn't have Sandra's purse or identification. He hadn't even thought of asking for it at the center in Tecolote.

But when the customs agent emerged from her cubicle, she said, "One of our agents will escort you. Good luck, sir." As she spoke, a green-and-white, four-wheel-drive vehicle with "US Border Patrol" painted on the side drove up in front of them. It turned on its flashing lights and began to move forward again.

Dan sat there, watching, waiting.

"Go ahead, Dad!" said Peter. "He's waiting for you to follow him."

Dan put the car into gear and drove forward, following the lighted vehicle.

They wove through a manmade maze of tight left and right turns, constructed of cement road barriers. At the end of this blockade, designed to prevent illegal border crossers from outrunning patrol cars, they saw a large, green sign for Highway 5 north to San Diego. Relief flooded through both men as they drove seventy-five miles per hour behind the US Border Patrol truck. A black-and-white San Diego police car caught up with them at Dairymart Road and got behind Dan's car. They drove for ten minutes without saying another word. Their escorts stayed with them through the exit to Washington Avenue in San Diego and on to the emergency entrance to the hospital.

Miguel and Alex had been leading the way until they arrived at the border crossing with its confusing lanes of traffic. In the last few minutes, they had chosen one line of traffic, while Dan had driven into a parallel line. They had seen the same vendors selling the same products.

They had also seen the old man with no legs, and when they got abreast of him, Alex said, "Wait a minute."

He rolled down his window and emptied his pocket of coins into the paper cup. When he saw the woman holding one baby and pulling another along through the lanes of traffic, he wanted to go yell at her for endangering the children's lives.

"Look at that," he uttered aloud.

"I know," answered Miguel. "It is not a very good life here for the children."

"That child could be killed," said Alex. "And he's breathing in all these exhaust fumes."

"Yes," Miguel said. What else could he say? There were no right answers to this problem. His own mother had lived from peso to peso all her life. She had stooped to begging from time to time. There was no safety net here, not for children or for old people. Only the able bodied, who are willing to work, can hope to escape this future, thought Miguel.

"Citizenship?" Miguel rolled down the window to speak to the border patrol official. He got out his registration card. Alex got out his driver's license. As the customs agent looked at their identification cards, Alex watched his dad's car in the lane next to theirs accelerate and follow a border patrol truck onto Highway 5.

"What are you bringing back from Mexico today?" The customs agent looked curiously at the equipment in the back of Miguel's truck. It was then that Miguel realized that he had not gone back to the center to retrieve all of his belongings. Shovels, a tarp, and other equipment that he would need for his work had been left behind. He knew they would be hastily gathered up by the residents there for their own use. How could he blame them? He would never be able to resist such a windfall either.

"My mother is in that car over there. She's been hurt in a mudslide. We went to find her," said Alex.

The agent looked over to the lane where Sandra's car was waiting. He quickly assessed what he had heard and decided he could believe them. His instinct had been honed to pick up falsified statements and suspicious actions. These two men seemed truthful and trustworthy. He waved them ahead. They pulled out into the barricaded lane and started weaving through it. Ahead of them they saw flashing lights. As they exited the barricades, they could see the border patrol vehicle with flashing lights, followed by the Seaquists' car.

"So, what do you think about today?" asked Alex, when they had settled into one lane and were driving at a discreet distance behind the Seaquists' car.

"I don't know," responded Miguel. "Perhaps there are two Mexicos," he ventured.

"Two Mexicos? What do you mean?"

"The Mexico that has a proud heritage and history and the Mexico that is so poor that its people must escape it to have a good life."

Alex considered this for a moment before responding. "Perhaps," he said. He waved his arm to indicate the complicated landscape outside their windows. "It is impossible to tell where one country ends and the other begins, except for…"

"La linea," said Miguel.

"What?"

"La linea—the line. That's what we call it."

"But a line. That's such an easy thing to walk across. Why would you call it that?"

"Perhaps it is wishful thinking," Miguel suggested mildly. This young man was not well known to him; he didn't want to cross the line with him. But something about their easy back-and-forth discussion led him to think that it would not be too dangerous to do so. This was Sandra's son, after all. And he had always felt comfortable talking with her. Why was it that some Norte-Americanos were so closed and others so ready to open up?

"Right on," agreed Alex. "You know, that reminds me of something one of my professors said in an urban geography course I just took. He said that there really is a new country right now at the border between the United States and Mexico. He said that this new country isn't US, and it isn't Mexican. It has its own unique culture that is a combination of the two countries."

"Yes, I agree with your professor," said Miguel. "You can use the peso or the dollar in these stores we are passing right now." Miguel indicated a 99 Cent Store, a McDonald's, and a Burger King just to the right of the highway. "And you can use both in any store in Tijuana."

"I see what you're saying," said Alex. "It isn't just the culture that has been combined, like burritos at the Burger King and the street names that are almost all Spanish words. Even the name of the city—San Diego. It's also the economies that are being pushed together."

"Yes, in fact, some people who live in Tijuana get so tired of the long waits at the border that they did a protest a few months ago."

"A protest? That sounds interesting."

"Yes, but do you know how they did it? They didn't cross the border for a full day. A Saturday—the busiest shopping day of the week."

"And what happened?"

"The stores didn't have as many customers," said Miguel, signaling with his right turn signal the exit at Washington Street.

"And I don't just mean the stores down near the border. The big stores up here—the Nordstrom's and Macy's. They all noticed the difference that day."

"So then what happened?"

"So then they hired more border agents and kept more lanes open every day."

"The food, the street names, the economy," Alex said, and ticked off the points on the fingers of his left hand. "What else is characteristic of this new country, and what do we call it? United States of Mexamerica?" he suggested lightly.

"I call it 'home,' amigo," said Miguel, as they drove up to the hospital emergency entrance.

"So do I, amigo," said Alex, offering his hand to Miguel when the truck came to a stop.

Miguel took Alex's hand and shook it warmly and solemnly. Was this what it felt like to be welcomed as a real citizen of this country? If so, he promised himself to look into it very soon.

Alex got out of the car and looked back in the window. "Hey, thank you for helping us. Thank you. We couldn't have found her, and we couldn't have brought her back safely without you."

"You're welcome. Please telephone me when you know how she is doing, okay?" Miguel reached into his pocket and pulled out a slightly soiled business card that read, "Ramirez Garden Trimming Planting—Blooming Guaranteed."

Alex put the card in his pocket and smiled at Miguel. "I'll call you as soon as I can," he said, and he turned and followed his family into the hospital.

Chapter Twenty-Three

FREE TRADE

In January, Sandra came home from the hospital. Walking into her home caused her to weep with joy. For a brief instant, she imagined that she never wanted to leave it again, not to go on vacation, not to go to Mexico, not even to go to the eastside neighborhood where she read for Rolling Readers. She might go to the grocery store to stock up on all her favorite foods, and she would definitely go to the library to replenish her stock of unread books. But that's all. No farther.

Dan helped her settle down on the sofa next to the large window in their living room. He hadn't gotten used to his role as caretaker, and he held her arm as if she was breakable, which, in a way, they had both discovered she was. He felt as if he should offer something, but he wasn't sure what. Coffee? Juice?

"No," she declined, "but maybe a nice cup of tea."

Dan rattled teapots and tins of tea for longer than it would have taken Sandra to make dinner and finally emerged with a pot of lukewarm tea made with one teabag. Sandra considered asking him to warm it but decided not to. She accepted the tea gratefully and moved her legs aside, motioning Dan to sit down at the other end of the couch. When he did, she thought she could see sort of a trapped look on his face.

"I'll be fine here," she told him softly, sipping her tea. "Go ahead, if you have something to do."

Dan considered what he had to do. He had the brake pads to do on the Porsche, and he had wanted to vacuum out the back seat of Sandra's car. The mud was dry now. It was time to remove it.

Dan looked at Sandra, and he considered what else he had to do. Apologize? Explain why he hadn't shown an interest in her work down in Mexico? No, this wasn't the time to bring that up. Not yet. Ask Sandra to explain what she was doing down there, and why it seemed so important to her? Ask her why she had put herself at such risk? Ask why she was willing to risk her life—yes, that wasn't too strong, considering what had just transpired—her *life*, damn it? And his life, too—didn't she understand?

Sandra sipped her tea and considered the silence. Which one of them would break it first? It was usually her job to do so. Dan could wait much longer than she could in total silence. What should she say? What did he want to hear? Did he want her to promise that she would stay home and be a good wife and…? Was she waiting for her to say thank you again for rescuing her? She had said that in the hospital. Sandra recalled that when she was pregnant with Peter, Dan had shown signs of what they called in the parenting books "com-pregnancy." He had developed the same hunger for certain foods that Sandra had. He complained of feeling tired and how his legs hurt during that last couple of months. Perhaps, he was experiencing that now. Was he feeling vulnerable, fragile, in need of healing, just as she was?

And if he was, was that unreasonable? Not really, conceded Sandra to herself. They had both been through a very significant ordeal, a time of genuine distress, not something in a movie or on the news, but something that had happened to each of them and to them as a couple. They had almost lost each other. And it wasn't just in the muddy hillside.

Sandra could wait no longer. She broke the strained silence to ask, "What do you think we lost down there?"

"Huh?" Dan wasn't sure he had heard her question. "What do you mean?" he asked, needing clarification and time to consider what she wanted to hear from him.

"Do you think we're the same people as we were before Christmas, Dan?" she asked, looking directly into his eyes. "Or have we lost a part of ourselves?"

Dan looked away. A part of him wished he could turn on the television or pick up a newspaper. This wasn't what he had hoped for when he got up this morning and drove to the hospital to pick up Sandra. Then, what had he hope for? He had hoped that she would walk out of the hospital whole and unhurt. He had wished she would come home and make dinner for the two of them. He wanted their old life back. But it seemed an impossible wish. Was that what she meant? They had lost a whole way of life, a set of patterns carefully established by the two of them over the years. What would she think if he said that out loud?

"Ha...," he heard himself emit. Who was kidding whom? That would not go over at all well, he edited carefully. Careful, here. This is a minefield.

Sandra looked puzzled at his brief exhalation. She knew that he was editing his thoughts and feelings, figuring out what to say that would save his own face and provide her some peace of mind as well. He was looking for the safest possible response before he allowed himself to speak.

"Go ahead," Sandra urged. "You can tell me what you are thinking. I think I can handle a few words after all that mud."

All that mud suddenly dropped with a thud on the sofa between them. All that mud splashed and stained their furniture and their clothing. All that mud came between them with the force of a hit-and-run vehicle, causing Dan to veer backward, pressing his back into the sofa cushion, and his head almost hitting the lamp on the table behind him.

Sandra reached out to him, but her taped ribs would not allow her to bend forward and complete the embrace. Her eyes filled with tears. Dan recovered and moved her legs aside so that he could sit down facing her. He held her gently as she wept. He allowed himself a few tears as well. They held each other for several minutes as the sun set beyond their windows and dusk fell.

Click—a light flooded the room. Dan had set a timer so that lights would come on at sunset for days when no one was home. He was aware that the neighbors could now look into the window and see them in the lighted room. He separated from Sandra and got up to close the shades in the room.

The room seemed clean again. No muddy residue. He sat down again at Sandra's side.

"I'm sorry," they each said at the same time. Dan smiled; Sandra laughed out loud.

"I think there is a rule, one I remember from third grade, that if two people both say 'sorry' at the same time, that both people have to accept it and truly forgive the other person," suggested Sandra, inventing as she went along.

"I remember that exact thing," smiled Dan, recalling only the game played when spying Volkswagen Beetles.

Okay then, I guess we move on from there, thought Sandra. "I'm very happy to be home, especially home with you," she confided aloud.

"I am very happy to have you home with me," agreed Dan.

"What's for dinner?" Sandra asked.

"Dinner? Okay, I guess it's my turn. Let me go see what we've got." Dan began to get up from the sofa, and Sandra pulled him back down for a kiss. "Look in the freezer. I think there is some leftover turkey noodle casserole from our Thanksgiving turkey."

They ate the warmed-up casserole and drank lukewarm tea and considered themselves luckier than if they were dining at Chez Something-or-other. The home-cooked flavors were intoxicating to both of them, and both had several heaping platefuls.

****

January and February passed quickly, but Sandra and Dan would always remember this time in their lives as the days they spent talking on the sofa. Each day that he was not flying, Dan would find himself coming in from the garage or an errand to see Sandra sitting on the sofa with her legs up, and he would come in and lift up her legs and sit looking at her, always grateful to find her there.

They talked. They listened.

They talked. Twenty-six years of married life did not prevent them from exploring each other's minds, hearts, and souls as if they had just met, just fallen in love.

Dan talked about flying. As if she had never heard these stories before, Sandra thought his stories of snow-caked runways were completely enthralling. How brave, she thought, as she heard him describe the last-minute decisions he had to make about whether to land or go around. Why am I enjoying listening to him talk about this so much again? she wondered. It's as if we just met, as if I am hearing these stories for the first time. Are we, in fact, meeting again? Meeting again after a long absence or…It's really more like we're meeting new parts of ourselves—parts we've kept hidden, or never even knew about before.

Sandra talked about watching children's eyes light up at the sight of a new picture book, feeling them snuggle closer as she read the words aloud. It's not as if she is telling me anything new, thought Dan, but I feel more open to listening to her. After almost losing her and my marriage, everything she does and thinks seems more important, more valuable somehow.

Dan ventured into new territory one evening as they shared a bottle of zinfandel and munched on some crackers with artichoke dip. It was a cool evening, and Dan had started a fire in the fireplace, little used except for Christmas Eve over the past few years. Sandra put on a new CD that Hanna had brought her, an Irish band playing O'Carolan tunes with fiddles and flutes. The wet logs in the fireplace crackled and spit. The music soothed their fears and animated their conversation.

"I feel that I need to tell you this, Sandra," he said, looking intently at his wine glass for a moment and then turning to face his wife. "The time I was in that boating accident in Lake Michigan, I was sailing with a woman named Leslie. She's a copilot with the company."

"I know that, Dan," answered Sandra. "I overheard the two of you talking on the phone one evening."

"But you never said anything," said Dan.

"No, because you didn't," she responded quickly.

"I don't want to make light of it, Sandra," said Dan.

"Neither do I," she agreed. Then she waited. The fire sputtered. Dan looked over at it and considered getting up to add another log. But he knew that was just a delaying action, so he chose to stay where he was.

"She is a fantastic sailor. I owe my life to her, in fact."

Sandra nodded, encouraging him to go on.

"I can't exactly say what sailing means to me these days. I've tried to think about it. There is something about being out on a small boat and interacting with the wind that reminds me of…" Dan took a gulp of his wine.

"Youth?" suggested Sandra.

"Well, maybe so. But that's just part of it. You've been out with me a few times."

Sandra felt more trepidation hearing this sentence than she had hearing Leslie's name spoken out loud. She had been out with him a few times, and all the other times he had gone, he'd had to call other friends or club members. She looked down, unable to meet his gaze.

"When I'm in command of the boat, and I anticipate what the wind is going to do and what I need to do in response, there is a wonderful feeling of accomplishment. When I adjust a sail and feel the power of the wind amplified, I feel stronger, more powerful. When I have a crew, and I can tell them what I need them to do, and they do it smoothly and efficiently, it's…I don't know…in some ways it's a lot like a family. Is that a silly thing to say?"

Sandra tried to recall her own feelings about the sailing trips they had done together. She decided to be as honest as Dan was being. "When I'm on the boat, and I feel the boat tilting—"

"Heeling," Dan interrupted.

"Heeling, then," she went on. "I feel like my life is out of control. I feel like I could slip off the boat and be lost at sea."

"Sailboats were meant to heel, Sandra. They're perfectly…" Then Dan remembered that he needed to listen to Sandra, even when he didn't agree, even when he didn't share her experience of something. "It can be scary, Sandra. That's true. I understand that you like to feel in control of your life. We all do. You must feel like I did when I was falling off that boat in the storm."

Sandra felt her shoulders relax. He had heard her. "And for you, it's a powerful feeling to be in control of the boat, of the wind, of other people's lives. You like that feeling. I'm not sure I do." Sandra looked up again. She smiled at Dan and moved her feet toward his legs to feel that power more clearly.

"Maybe it's because I am the one steering the boat. I feel in control. I wonder what would happen if you tried steering, and I handle the sails."

Sandra thought about that. "You know, you may be onto something. When we learned to sail, you learned everything and passed every test, while I really just glanced through the books and other course materials. I still don't really understand the difference between jibing and coming about."

Dan laughed. He was about to explain the difference again, but Sandra cut him off.

"But whose decision was that? You never told me not to study the material, not to learn the terms. I think that for some reason I purposely remained ignorant, maybe because I was trying to compete with you."

"Compete with me? I don't get that at all."

"Well, maybe I was sure that if I did compete, I would lose."

"Lose what?" Dan could sit still no longer. He got up and poked around in the fireplace. Then he turned back to Sandra. "Lose what, Sandra?" His mind was spinning out remembered images of Sandra saying, "No, go ahead. I don't think I'll go today after all." But then he saw her muddy, injured body being dragged out of that shanty in Tijuana. "We did almost lose, I guess. We almost lost everything. We almost lost each other."

"Dan, I hope that I have lost some of my fears as well. I've tried to picture myself going sailing with you again, and I don't seem to feel the same way I used to. After being buried alive in mud, the idea of sailing on a nice clean boat over the water seems pretty appealing to me right now."

"Really?" asked Dan. "Are you just saying that to make me feel better?"

"No, I don't think so. Of course we'll have to test it out, but I think some of my fears of mortality, or whatever it is, have dissipated somewhat. I'll tell you what. When I get this cast off, we'll go test it out together."

"Great!" Dan grinned and came over to hug her. He bent down on the floor next to the couch. "Dr. Jolliffe said he thought that he would be able to take off the cast in a couple of weeks. I'll call the sailing club tomorrow and set it up."

"Okay, Dan, but now I want you to finish telling me about Leslie, and I don't just mean about what a good sailor she is."

"Well, she's a hell of a good pilot, too." Dan tried for lightness.

"Does that mean you want me to learn to fly also?"

"No…well…I mean, yes, if you want to. Do you?"

"Dan, get on with it. What happened between you?"

"Nothing, Sandra. Nothing physical, that is. We started talking on our trips together, and she seemed to be interested in all the things I was."

"And all the things that I wasn't interested in?"

"Yes, I guess so, at least back then."

"Go on," urged Sandra.

"We got to talking about sailing, and she told me that she had this boat. It was her grandfather's boat, and her dad is a sailor too. Then she invited me to go sailing with her, and I told you about that, and I invited you to come with me to Chicago. You do remember that, don't you?"

"Well, I do remember that you invited me, but you didn't mention that your copilot was a woman."

"I know," Dan said.

"So you went sailing?"

"Yes, we went, and I remember that this storm was predicted. There were small craft advisories that day, but she said that just made it more interesting."

"She did? She really said that?"

"Yes, it surprised me, too. Then we got out there, and she was amazing, especially when the storm hit, and she had to rescue me and keep the heading at the same time." Dan pictured himself again, slipping toward the water; he felt her strong arm holding onto him, giving him the support he needed to climb back aboard. How could he explain that to Sandra?

"Well, I have to say I appreciate that myself," said Sandra, with a smile. "Was there anything more between you, Dan? Other than the sailing and the attraction you felt for her knowledge and skills?"

"Not really. Oh, I don't deny that there could have been more. She is a very attractive woman, and I have to admit that I had a few fantasies about her during that time, but I never acted on them."

"Yes, I remember that she is a very attractive woman."

"You've met her? When?"

"Isn't she the woman who was the copilot on the trip to Denver?"

"Oh, yes. She was."

"Really, Dan, I think I understand this situation pretty well. That was right after our anniversary, and you were still disappointed that I wouldn't sail with you to Catalina, weren't you?"

Dan was quiet for a moment, remembering. "Yes, I guess I was. Although we had a very good time there, didn't we?"

Sandra smiled, and they moved together for a kiss.

"You know, I feel better," said Dan. "I feel like you really heard me without blaming or getting uptight. I really appreciate that."

"Mm-hmm. And I appreciate that you told me what you are and were feeling. We are learning how to be honest with each other again."

"Yes." Dan sat looking at the fire, thinking. "So, Sandra, do you remember when we were dating, and we couldn't decide what we wanted to do on a date?"

"Yes?"

"Well, do you remember that sometimes we would trade favorite things? We would do your favorite thing and then mine."

"Yes, and I remember that your favorite thing always involved sex," Sandra laughed.

"Still does." Dan gave her his best dirty old man leer.

"Well, we've agreed on that a long time ago, so I don't think that is what you are talking about today, is it?" she said.

"No."

"Then what?"

"Let's pretend we are starting new again. Is that too silly?"

"No, it's not too silly at all. It feels just right."

"Okay, let's say that I want you to try to take some sailing lessons and go sailing with me. What would you trade?"

"Trade?"

"Yeah. What would you want from me?"

"You mean besides your body?"

"Yes, we've already established that you can have that anytime you want it."

"Okay, let me think." Sandra considered how to say what she wanted to ask for.

"What I want is that you come down to Tijuana with me the first time I go back and build me some more shelves for the biblioteca."

"You do? That library is that important to you?"

"Yes, it's that important to me."

"Why? Can you tell me what it means to you?"

"Dan, you remember how we felt when Peter was born?"

"Yes, of course I do."

"We started a new life together that day, didn't we?"

"Yes."

"Then, remember the last fall when they both left for school?"

"Yes, although I think I left on a trip the next day myself, so maybe I didn't feel it as much as you did."

"I think you felt it as much as I did, Dan, but you purposely bid that trip so you'd have something important to do the next day."

"I didn't think about it like that, but you could be right. But what does this have to do with the library in Tijuana?"

"Everything, Dan. I need something important to do for this next stage of my life."

"Yes, I understand that. In fact, just before Christmas, before your accident, I was thinking along those lines."

"You were?"

"Yes, I was. And I thought that, for me, maybe the sailing replaced some of the feelings of being a father."

"Oh really? That's very interesting. I never would have thought that."

"Yes, but we've talked about me. Go on; tell me about your important thing."

"Thank you. Okay, here goes. When I work at the center in Tecolote and feel the appreciation of those children and the staff, I feel necessary again."

"Yeah, I get it. It's almost as if our lives are too easy right now, isn't it?"

"Exactly. I need a challenge, and I need some small children who can hardly wait to see me come in the door."

"It's funny; I don't hear other people our age talk about this so much, do you?" Dan was thinking of friends on the airline who seemed completely engrossed in golf or travel. He thought about their neighbors who seemed well satisfied with keeping their yards and houses well maintained.

"No, I don't," agreed Sandra. "And frankly, I don't understand it. I used to feel like I fit in to my peer group. As a teenager, I was always trying to dress like my friends and—"

"And drink like my friends," Dan laughed. "But, I knew I wanted more than that. I had a dream to fly."

"And you made it happen. Do you know how proud I am of you for that, Dan?"

"Yes, I know how proud you used to be, at least."

"I still am."

"Thanks, maybe that's another thing I'm looking for." Dan seemed lost in thought. "I want you to be proud of me like that again."

"And I want you to be proud of me." They both laughed. "Aren't we silly?" Sandra said. "We're not teenagers anymore. We…I mean, you are almost over the hill, age-wise."

"What do you mean—me? You're right behind me, kiddo."

"But, in some ways, it is as if we are teenagers again, isn't it?" asked Sandra.

"Yes, it could be," agreed Dan. "It's as if we are starting new lives."

"And most of our friends seem to want to fit in with the crowd again, don't they?" asked Sandra. "They think they're going to find happiness in the next golf game or the next shopping trip to Nordstrom's."

"Well, maybe you're being too hard on them. We can't speak for anyone but ourselves here, Sandra. We don't have all the answers. I have to admit I thought I could find happiness in the next sailing trip."

"Yes, I'm sorry. Really. I understand that it is very difficult to choose how to spend this time in our lives, and there aren't a lot of models out there, showing us the way," said Sandra.

"No, but you know, we're getting off track here. You were telling me what you wanted to trade."

"Oh yes. I was asking you if you would come with me and build some shelves for the library."

"I'll be happy to. And I also noticed that the front steps of that place are a death trap. I'm going to try to figure out a way to add a handrail or something, so people don't fall off into the mud."

"What a great idea. They will really appreciate that, Dan."

"I've got another great idea. I know we can't really make love with your leg in that cast, but how about if we go upstairs and fool around a little. You know, like teenagers?"

"Like teenagers?" Sandra sat up and began unbuttoning her blouse. "What's wrong with right here then?"

The log in the fireplace still had a few sparks left. The music on the CD was programmed to play again. It was perfect.

****

A few weeks later, in late February, Sandra's cast was removed, and Dr. Jolliffe gave her the green light to go back to her regular activities. Sandra laughed and said that she was planning to add a few new activities to her life as well.

Dan reserved the thirty-eight-foot Catalina from the sailing club. It was the boat with the most stability and the most room in the cockpit. He tried to interest Sandra in reviewing the sailing textbook, but she promised to do that on her own, later. "For the present," she told him, "let's just go out there and see how we feel about sailing off into the sunset together."

"Well, I don't know about sunset," Dan looked serious. "I think we should go in the daylight for now."

"I'm just kidding," Sandra said. "Here, take these sandwiches and put them in the cooler."

"Do we have any cookies?"

"Of course we have cookies," Sandra laughed. "You don't think I would put my life on the line without cookies, do you?"

At the marina, they boarded the boat, and Sandra stowed the food down below while Dan got the engine started. Guiding the boat out into the San Diego harbor, he asked, "Where to?"

Sandra looked around her at the beautiful skyline, the sparkling water, and the hills of Point Loma, where she could almost spot their house halfway up the hill.

"Sandra, where shall we go? Catalina?"

"No, not yet. Let's head south, toward Ensenada. That way I can see the shore."

"Aye aye, Captain," Dan laughed. "Get over here and steer, then."

"Me?"

"Yes, you. It's easy. Well, it isn't easy, but it is a wonderful challenge."

Sandra took Dan's place behind the wheel. She felt the boat pull forward as the wind filled the sails. She steered into the wind just to see what would happen.

The sails drooped, and the boat handled more sluggishly. She positioned the boat again to take full advantage of the wind. The feeling was exhilarating. She began to understand what Dan had been saying. It felt so good to be in control.

At the end of Point Loma, she kept the helm and steered past the channel buoys before she turned the boat south. The steady west wind and calm seas gave her courage. They sailed past the Del Coronado Hotel and talked about going there for dinner some night. That reminded them of how hungry they were, so they took turns at the helm to eat their sandwiches.

A few miles south, they were about three-quarters of a mile from the shoreline. They looked at the land and saw the Tijuana River coming out to the sea. They could see the beaches on the US side, the hills of Tijuana on the Mexican side, and the swathes of barren gullies in between, patrolled by the US Border Patrol. The rusty corrugated iron fence that marked the boundary between the two countries was marching out toward the sea. Their boat glided across that border effortlessly.

"You know, Dan, I have to tell you. I love going to Tijuana, and I really enjoy working with the children. Every morning when I start out, I can hardly wait to get there. But in the afternoon, when I get in my car, I can hardly wait to get home."

"I think I get it, Sandra," said Dan as he reached for her and tousled her hair. "Sometimes we will go your direction and sometimes we'll go mine. Either way, it will be a new adventure."

"Yes," responded Sandra, "We've made a great trade, haven't we?"

12887021R00158

Made in the USA
San Bernardino, CA
03 July 2014